# VERMiLLION
## ISLES

BOOK TWO OF *THE HARMION SERIES*

# RICHARD A. SWINGLE

LWP

Cataloguing in Publication Data is available from the British Library.

Cover illustration by Johnny Lindner. Licensed through Pixabay.

ISBN 978-1-916117-04-4 (B-format)
ISBN 978-1-916117-05-1 (Kindle eBook)

www.richardaswingle.com

# ALSO BY RICHARD A. SWINGLE

HARMION SERIES

**The Kill List (Prequel Novella)**

**Harmion**

**The Vermillion Isles**

THE TIME THIEF SERIES

**The Heart Thief**

**The Spirit Thief** *coming soon!*

*To all the adventurers, let nothing sway you from your course, may your cause always be just.*

HARMION

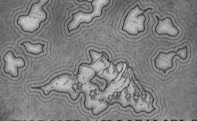

THE VERMILLION ISLES

DROWNED SONS

MALVABAW

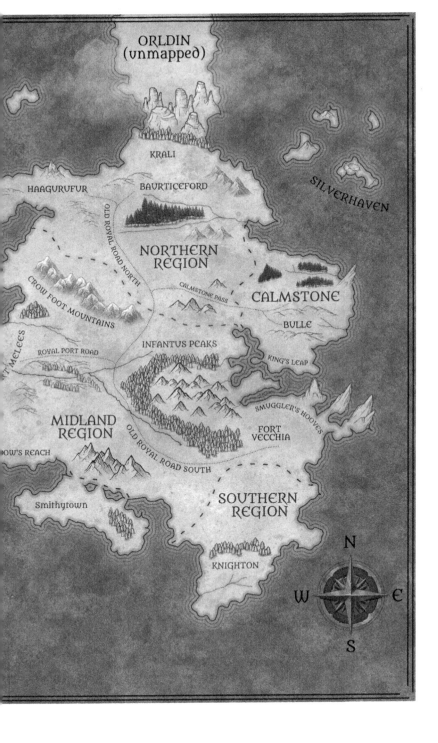

# PROLOGUE

A s two stones cannot be forged together, nor could two lovers merge as a singular entity, though they may be two halves of one whole. To amalgamate would be an unnatural binding of particles, an aberration. Abhorrent.

Adjoining flesh of purity, carves out monstrous beings. Such beings have existed in days now forgotten. Their twisted and deformed bodies, soulless, burned to ashes lest no skeleton tell their tale.

It is the trick of life, when restrained, to mutate thus.

Maldus had been saved through love of his mother. His life sowed a seed that bore fruit. A tree of life to protect the land and the creatures who would excel from its natural gifts.

So too did Vermillion rise, a haven within which the perished could rest.

A mystery long forgotten in the wake of forty brutal years of war.

. . .

THE CLINKING of the rocks echoed throughout the forest. They sparked, igniting a fire that illuminated the pathway in the dark, dry night.

With her scarred hands, the tribe girl clutched a torch that was borne from her camp.

She left the fire burning behind her. A small wall of stones kept the embers from drifting into the thickset treeline.

Her breath rose with each step, cascading like the mist at the base of a waterfall.

She clung to a small slate, its markings barely legible. Her map was part destroyed.

It had been some years since she had become the leader of her people. She had known peace since that time, albeit briefly, for now she was guardian to all natural life on Harmion. A seed of doubt that had existed in her grew with each full moon and as the mother of light in darkness shone through the forest, its blueish beams tickling the contorted shrubbery, the tribe girl found the stone doorway she had searched for.

Markings in the old tongue of her language were written upon the sealed entrance. She knew few of the words.

Speaking those few choice phrases that she had learnt as a child, she began to drag her fingers across the stone. The tips of her nails scraped across the rough slate and she found a split in the rock. A space where her slate map had once been.

She placed the slate in the hole and the roots of the earth stretched upwards to embrace the unified rock formation.

The ground was alive and she stepped backwards to allow the arms of the trees to pull open the cave entrance. The roots and branches shrivelled, revealing an opening.

All movement stopped and the tribe girl stepped inside, her flaming torch flickering in the echoic chamber.

Faded images were sketched on the walls all around her and

she swept her burning torch in an arching movement, revealing the warnings of the Archaists.

Her brow creased and fear flooded her eyes. She wished not to know the meaning of what she saw but it was as though her deepest fears had been carved into the stone before she had ever been born.

**1**

Better to float helplessly in the obscure, salty seas than to be a victim of hers. Relinquishing arms to cold waters. Blinker wet, twitching eyes. An abolition to the obsession for life. Essential breaths passing lips to conjure one final thought before the consumption of the body to the crushing depths.

Better that, than to be a victim of hers…

A BODY CRASHED into the ocean. Weighted armour acted as an anchor, pulling the bleeding corpse down towards the seabed. Forgotten and lost. There were shouts and screams on the flaming decks of the warship above.

A storm rocked the ship side to side and waves extinguished some of the fires that threatened to ignite the sails.

'Where is she?' shouted a sailor who clutched his feeble sword, a final hope for survival.

He twisted and turned. The rain pounded his skull, blurring his vision. The weakness in his knees was evidence enough of his fear. He shivered and held his position, daring not to take a step in case he fell. All he heard was the rain and wind.

Beneath the sound of the squall, the perfect slits that appeared on his thighs and abdomen were a silent series of cuts. He was overcome by a dizzy sensation as blood mixed with the tears of the sky and for a second, a distant spark from the storm illuminated the face of his killer. It was enough for him to see the curved blades in her hands and the hatred in her eyes. Those beautiful green eyes.

'She's there! Get her,' a faceless voice called out across the deck.

The assassin turned her head in a snapping motion to see the dozen crew who were circling around her. The bleeding sailor stumbled to the ground behind where she stood.

She tucked her blades into her jacket as she ran towards the side of the ship and dived over the ornate wooden rail, disappearing into the raging sea.

'Cover your sixes, don't let her out of your sight.'

The order came from a young captain. He was tall and broad and despite the threat, he held no weapon. Instead, there were twelve men behind him carrying swords.

'Man all sides, we can't cope with any more losses,' the captain shouted as he cautiously paced across the deck. His heavy skin boots thudded against the woodwork, making his path through the twenty or so cadavers that were strewn from bow to stern.

It had been one against thirty when the attack began. Now there were only twelve of the captain's crew remaining and the assassin hadn't suffered a scratch.

He looked to the distance, at the rocky coast of the island they had been sailing towards. Its uninviting beaches that seemed so unreachable, dangled the only prospect that would re-balance their odds. To bring the fight to land.

'Hoist the sails,' he commanded. 'We'll crash the bitch into the rocks.'

But of one thing the captain was wrong for the bitch was the sea and their ship was just a new-born pup being dragged by the scruff of its neck.

Three of the men broke ranks and followed the order, the sails went up and caught the tempest by the throat.

The entire ship lurched and nearly capsized, thrusting the guard patrol into the woodwork of the decks and bulwark. Two of the men were lost overboard but the captain pursued his course.

What a foolhardy mission to breach The Vermillion Isles. The losses had been catastrophic but the point of no return was long since past.

The captain took a stubborn breath, drawing the falling water into his lungs as he felt the speed of his vessel accelerating towards the rocks.

'Man the rail,' he cried.

The ten remaining allies regained their footing and held their positions, staring out to sea. They were searching for a needle in a haystack but the needle found them.

The assassin fell from the mast, plunging two blades into the shoulders of a sailor. He fell to his knees, echoing the screams of the lightning above. The blades retracted, slicing the tendons beside his neck and, before the pain reached him, a dozen more wounds appeared across his back.

It was a merciful death. A quick death.

Surrounded again, the assassin stood her ground. Her peaked hood dripping across her frozen expression. This time she didn't run, nor did she attack. The moment lingered and no sailor dared break the statuesque procession.

The sea had other plans.

A large wave smashed the side of the ship thrusting the two parties together.

The assassin had waited for the moment and jumped from the deck seconds before the intrusion, holding her blades forward like a spike wall and whilst she floated mid-air, a sailor lurched into her knives. They pierced his eyes as the duet fell to the ground.

The captain picked up a small fighting axe from the body of his comrade and charged the assassin but once again she was too fast and dived into the sea.

'Captain, we can't keep this up, we'll all be dead before we hit the beach.'

A panicked sailor vomited the words that soiled his pride. But the captain knew he was right. Just eight of them remained and despite their velocity, the cliff face they raced towards seemed a dozen lifetimes away.

'Down to the hull, follow me, and quickly.'

The captain ran to the stairwell and brought his axe down upon the lock he had put in place to protect their compartment. It was against all his instincts to trap his men beneath the decks, leaving the ship to cascade across the waters at the volition of the storm. But he knew no other way to defeat the mermaid demon that ruptured their souls.

He didn't have time to wonder how it was possible for their assassin to survive beneath those tumultuous waters. She was like a deity of the sea and wielded her knives like nothing he had ever seen.

They ran and tumbled down the stairs into the hull. Every last remaining sailor clambered to their feet, grabbing furnishings to barricade the entrance.

The captain looked around the hull for some saving grace or a moment's inspiration. Anything to ensure they would reach the beach beneath the cliffs. He saw a lantern dangling above his hammock. It was still alight.

'We are but breath upon a lion's back. It was an honour to sail with each of you. I desire the chance to wish that whatever comes next brings you safely upon the shores or to peace beyond the wreckage of this ship.'

The address was felt by all the sailors as a bitter truth. Their inner children yearning for a father to make it right. How could he make this right?

The captain took the lantern and opened a hatch that led to the lower level of the ship; he twisted the knob that raised the wick and grew the flame. He looked each and every one of the sailors in the eye and saw the flickering light reflected back at him in all their gazes.

'I do not lead you from this moment forth. We do this together, unanimously. All in favour say aye.'

'Aye,' said the first.

Then came a chorus of *ayes* and the captain took the lantern and thrust it down the hatch into the void beneath them. The lantern smashed beside an oil barrel and a flame grew upon the barrel's side. The captain closed the hatch and toppled a desk across it.

'Let's see if she can climb fire!' he bellowed.

The sailors cheered and their former fearful frowns became snarls of blood lust. A shot of adrenaline for each of them brought a new found courage. The captain led them into the next compartment away from the growing inferno beneath.

They made their way towards the chamber beneath the decks at the bow of the ship. Each of them slid the small defence hatches to the side to reveal small outlooks where they armed themselves with bows and arrows.

Even when the flames grew at the sides of the exterior of the ship, obscuring their view of the ocean, they held their positions, waiting.

The floor beneath grew warmer and the heat inside the hull became intense and sweaty. The falling water that hit their metallic armour plates sizzled. But the flames kept away.

The fire had broken from beneath the ship and now wrapped itself around them. They were trapped in a cocoon of flames. But the assassin had no way in and so they waited. Waited to burn. Waited to crash into the island rocks. Waited for a demon to invite them with an open palm to the final dance of their lives.

In that ecstatic moment, there came a small explosion from beneath. Several of the oak boards on which they stood broke upwards and a waterfall of fire caressed the ceiling.

When the fire died there was a pause and through the new opening, the assassin swung upwards, landing in the room with her prey.

An aroma of burning hair and flesh filled the hull. Her jacket was singed. They could smell her wounds.

The assassin pulled her left glove away from her forearm and a layer of skin came with it. But she clenched her blades, ready to finish what she had started.

Time slowed to a crawl.

A majestic sight she saw then with those fierce green eyes. A final moment of bravery as the sailors charged her as one single unit. Those that still had swords, raised them. Those with arrows in their hands, held them like tiny spears.

The captain with his axe, pulled back his arm behind his head ready to throw it across the hull and through the flames that divided them from their huntress. She was ready; she had been born ready, and more than that, she had been trained every moment of her life and she was now more than just an assassin, but no mere ghost.

Her soul connected with every one of her enemies and right then, they were one being. A single union of matter that all belonged to a greater whole.

It was the shortest meditation of her life. Away from the comfort of the woven blanket her mother had made her as a child that she had practised on. But the lesson was the same as in those teachings she had been raised to hold as verity.

*Acceptance is the greatest quencher of the thirst that is fear.*

The moment ended, as all moments of splendour must. Brought to a halt by the crashing sound of wood colliding with stone. The ship had reached the cliff beach.

With a terrifying crash, the bow raised at such a height and speed that all those who were inside were thrust up to the ceiling.

The hull was crushed against the rocks like a paper castle flattened by a boulder. The fire was snuffed out and all went dark and wet.

Smoke from the extinguished flames filled the remaining crevices.

The captain felt a wooden structure fall onto his chest, taking the air out of his lungs and his vision faded as though a dark curtain had been drawn on his life.

He had time for a final thought before his mind slipped away.

*Better that, than to be a victim of hers.*

## 2

T he night twitched to the sound of wild nocturnal animals stirring. They observed a smouldering camp that sat beneath a clearing in a dense forest that boasted trees as high as mountains. No scraps remained from the evening meal after a hungry group of travellers had lain down for the night.

Hoarfrost settled across the remnants of the burnt out firepit.

A wolf scoured the surrounding area, pattering across the crunchy ferns where its companions slept and if any beast felt the urge to prey upon them, it was poised to come to their defence.

Pietrich had fallen in love with the sound of the wild forest. It was loud and overwhelming at first but he soon found that he slept better to the song of nature than anything else. Perhaps the noise drowned out the inescapable thoughts that occupied his mind. His sensitive mind that was an echo chamber, drowning him in fatigue without warning.

He longed to see the shades of green in the trees and fields. He imagined them instead.

With the help of his father, Pietrich had silenced the heightened sounds in his mind as he had grown older. Tritan had noticed the boy covering his ears on many occasions. One afternoon when he worked in the fields and Pietrich's pain was unbearable, Tritan had resolved to find a solution and so they trained together, dulling the senses through concentration.

The difficulty had been that Pietrich didn't seem to hear the indiscernible distant sounds through his ears like most would, but seemed to sense them through his battered subconscious and so they adopted a form of reverie. Something Tritan had himself tried for his own sanity after being accepted back into the village he was cast out from. It was a mercy most welcome.

Pietrich now lay awake in his skin-lined hessian sack, too much on his mind to sleep. The images that intruded were so vivid it was impossible to clear his thoughts.

Instead, he played his usual game of guessing how many species he could decipher from the wild sounds of the night. He heard monkeys swinging from high branches, snakes slithering along the earth. He felt a cluster of birds breathing. A gentle breeze, which to him was a chorus the rest of the animals built their song upon. But it was guilt that kept him up tonight and guilt is the heaviest chain one wears around one's neck.

A new voice had come to him in the night for several weeks and he hadn't told a single one of those who now travelled with him. But the voice was not directed towards him and in fact it never made sense. It was as though he stood in a cavernous space, surrounded by an army of murmuring idiots whilst one single being shouted across the din, but by the time their voice reached him it was quashed. He wanted the cavalcade of moaners to stop so he could understand that sole voice.

Frustrated, Pietrich tried to focus his thoughts on a single cry of a distant raven, the way his father had taught him. But those little tricks didn't work anymore. He was an open book that all wrote their fears and hatred in. He didn't want it. He never wanted any of this.

Pietrich rose from where he lay and threw his blanket around his shoulders, rubbing his hands across his tired face. He picked up his staff and used it to knock against the path ahead lest he fall against the root of a tree that was unknown to him. He took a short stroll away from the camp where his companions slept, venturing through the wood to a small clearing.

He tilted his head up to the sky that shone brightly.

The stars were fierce and he recalled the last promise Eira had made of him the day he had left Knighton. To raise his head up to the stars and sense the position of the brightest star whenever he couldn't sleep, for she would be awake too, staring at the very same star.

He wasn't sure that he ever got it right. As remarkable as his sense for light had become, he was still blind and his efforts were no more than childish guesses.

How he longed to lie beside Eira and look up to the stars with her as they had once done as younger children. They had found shapes of creatures on the black canvas and invented obscure animals of their own. He longed so dearly to see again. A stupid thought he knew.

It was the funniest thing that his greatest joy could be to simply exist in Eira's presence. Something he didn't know if he would ever do again.

THE MORNING BROUGHT about a milky sky and the curtained sun faintly cast misty beams through the gaps in the trees as the damp rose from the earth.

Pietrich hadn't slept a wink and he slowly prepared himself for the day as the rest of his travelling companions rose and packed up their things to continue with their journey to nowhere.

Lynden, an aged woman, studied Pietrich's shadowed eyes with scrutiny. She was as free as any person could be, an elder of the old political order, who had lived to the west for the latter years of her life.

Now Pietrich was her concern. She had dedicated herself to ensuring his safety.

Every day the unlikely rabble moved from one spot to another, with no particular place in mind. Moving unseen was the only agenda.

Occasionally Grace and Olafur, a couple from the coastal town of Haagurufur, would venture further towards civilisation and go to market to trade the wild animals they hunted in exchange for other produce. Pietrich always stayed away for it was too dangerous for him to risk being caught near civilisation.

He hadn't visited a town or village since the day he had left home with his group of protectors. That year had gone by as fast as a hummingbird's heartbeat.

The unlikely squadron, five strong, rode on horseback through a makeshift pathway, cutting across the dense forest terrain. It was slow progress but they rarely journeyed the main routes.

Fritz, their hired sword, paid for by the leftover profits for as long as they could afford him, rode up front and hacked at the thistle weeds that blocked their path. He picked his teeth and spat out the remains of his breakfast. Though uncouth, he was a great fighter and witty.

As the morning temperature rose, all remnants of the night's damp evaporated and the air was filled with fine drizzle. They rode in silence. The repetitive nature of their situation made it hard to find a reason to talk sometimes. But Pietrich couldn't keep his thoughts to himself any longer.

'How long must we do this? I can't be the only one pained by the daily grind.'

Lynden, who rode slightly ahead of Pietrich, slowed her pace to fall in beside him. 'Must we go over this again? It's not safe to stay in one place. Certainly, we mustn't take you into any of the towns. You know that.'

'Yes, there is danger everywhere. But what danger? We don't even know what it looks like, what it sounds like. How do we know there is any real danger at all?'

'The most dangerous enemy, is the one you don't even know exists. That is why we must be cautious of everyone. Every town could have lookouts and scouts. It wasn't by chance that we were attacked on the outskirts of Rhyne. I knew we had ventured too close to the town walls. Never again can we make such a mistake.'

That mistake had been a trading mission where they had camped outside the town walls. Hired guards who patrolled the circumference had followed Grace back to the hedges that grew by the walls to hide its guests. Fritz hadn't waited for the conversation to start and had killed all the guards before they had time to draw their swords. Pietrich was afraid of the man and for good reason, but the fear was the kind he had held for his father as a younger child.

'But this isn't life,' Pietrich protested. 'Must we ride and camp with vultures at our backs until we drop down and die?'

Lynden sighed. It was a strange prison they existed in and the risk of going mad was severe. But they needed time.

'I can't tell you when or how, but we must be patient. Time will give us knowledge. We will continue to talk to those we know we can trust, as fleetingly as we dare, and when the time is right, our patience will be repaid.'

Pietrich sighed and gave up his efforts of protest. It was just another day on the road after all. And the road was long. It met them with rocky, overgrown pathways and the usual slow grind of having to turn around at dead ends where there was too much vegetation to contend with.

Fritz cut them through a narrow treeline where it had been possible and after scouting ahead for any signs of threat, sheathed his sword and fell beside Lynden to address a matter of pressing concern.

'It is nearly that time, Lynden. We should veer towards the Infantus Peaks where you can take refuge in the caves,' said Fritz.

The sellsword had agreed to accompany them for as long as required or until they ran out of coin. He used his earnings to support his family, which meant on occasion he would ride home for a few days.

'A month is no time at all these days,' Lynden replied. 'It feels like you were home just yesterday.'

It was a statement as much as an accusation.

'Yes, but it can't be helped. I won't stay but a night this time. My girls are getting too used to my absence it seems. Staying home too long does them no favours.'

Lynden nodded.

'And how is Karla? I know it must be a strain on her to have you with us.'

Fritz chuckled to himself. 'Karla can give me a run for my coin; we both knew what we were signing up for and we survived the last ten years of the war under worse circumstances.'

Fritz took a swig from his water bladder. He was a lean and hairy fellow. His eyes piercing and hidden amidst the dark matted mop on his head. Pietrich was grateful to have such a warrior as him in their ranks.

Fritz had fought alongside Tritan for the last years of the war and though he maintained that he hadn't really bonded with the boy's father, Pietrich knew it was a lie and he knew too well the effect Tritan would have had on a younger soldier.

'Very well,' Lynden started. 'We will follow the Arn River to the base of the Infantus hills and take shelter whilst you're gone.'

Fritz agreed their plan and the group carried on for the best part of the day. The spiteful rain didn't let up so they skipped lunch with nowhere to get a fire going.

The Arn valley was a beautiful place, filled with some of the tallest trees amongst the land. It was common in these parts to spend most of a day travelling beneath a dark canopy before entering out into an opening. Pietrich knew when they did as he felt a cloud lifting in front of him. It was as though a dense fog parted and his sense of light made him feel like he was stepping into a warm, white blanket. He loved the clearings in the forest for that.

When they reached the base of the hills they all bid Fritz farewell as he began his solo ride to the family home he loved so dearly.

Fritz would be gone for at least three days and so the others would have to wait at the top of the hills in the shallow caves. It was more like an outcrop and Lynden always felt afraid when they returned here. She never liked staying in the same place twice, not least for three days at a time. But it was their only choice. Fritz was the only fighter they had and he had saved them on more than one occasion. Fritz was several years younger than Tritan, but Pietrich knew that he had learnt how to fight from his father. Anyone as capable as him couldn't have learnt from anyone less.

That night they slept well, the rain abated and the westerly winds crashed against the hills behind them and so the night for them was dry and still. It was a good chance for their horses to rest and the wolf continued to scour his nocturnal perimeter.

Lynden didn't know how Pietrich had bonded so well with the wolf but it was a loyal companion. They never saw the creature during the day and on many occasions Lynden had assumed it was lost to them, but it always returned at night to watch over them. Pietrich had named the wolf Jack. Jack seemed like a good loyal name for a wolf who kept him safe as he slept.

As the sun began to rise, Pietrich stirred and a rushing sensation of heat came across him. He began to sweat profusely but he could not wake. Something latched onto him and tore apart his insides. All his veins were being tugged in opposite directions and his limbs split at the seams. It was painless. He was held together by wooden tentacles that cracked as they grew and spread their reach.

Pietrich was suddenly outside the cave, though he was also still inside it. He was home in his village and he reached out to touch his mother who slept alone. He dared not wake her. His feet became unsteady and he realised he was in a ship, sailing out from port to some unknown land but the tides rocked him and as he lay still he was no longer a boy, but he was part of everything.

The voice came to him again but he didn't wait for the words to drift faintly into nothingness across the crowds that were the souls of the earth. For he was the crowd and he was the voice. He was everything and he heard the words as clearly as he felt the cold stone of the cave beneath him where he slept.

Lynden shook him hard. Pietrich cried out and felt the elder's hands grappling his shoulders.

'Pietrich! Are you alright?' she asked, panicked. 'You're burning up. Say something.'

Pietrich wailed as all his parts were ripped and torn from

him. He wanted so much to open his eyes and to see Lynden's face so that he knew he was awake.

'Where am I? Is this real?' he asked as he shivered with fever.

'You're with me, love, it's Lynden and we are in the cave at the peak of Infantus. You had a terrible dream. You must drink some water.'

Pietrich took the skin of water and glugged it down in one effort. He had never been so thirsty and as he swallowed the last drop, Olafur helped him to his feet to breathe and he leant back and opened out his lungs, coughing up mucus.

His three companions looked at him as though they were looking at a being beyond this world and though he was blind, Pietrich knew the looks he received and he accepted them before he spoke.

'I know where they're keeping him. I know where my father is.'

twirling patch of dust danced around the iron bars, freely moving in and out of the cage like a fool tormenting the enclosure's captive. It was hot and dry and the waves lapped up against the sandy shores a good distance from the high cliffs to the north where the ship had beached. The rocks were shaped like a talon and held the broken vessel hostage in its claws.

The captain lay on a patch of sand and breathed faint breaths. His limbs were sprawled apart by rope and he couldn't move one of his legs without intense pain. It was clamped by some form of brace.

He squinted and saw a jagged wound beneath the dressing at the lower part of his injured leg. It appeared as though a snapped bone had pierced his skin. Someone had reset the bone for him whilst he was unconscious.

He had been here before. A prisoner, treated with empathy. *First they heal you, then the torture begins.*

The sand upon which he lay was blisteringly hot, heated by the sun. It scorched his skin. All his armour had been stripped from him and he lay naked as the day he was born; save for a modesty garment around his waist.

The sound of peaceful waves upon the shores should have been a comfort. But this was suffering in its infancy. To dangle the refreshing ocean just metres from his cage, close enough to hear its inviting flirtation. He hated them for it.

The mission had been a complete failure. How many of his companions had been killed that stormy night? He suspected every last one. Soon he would follow them. But first he needed confirmation, for if any survived he could not rest.

In the distance he saw a well-dressed crew in remarkably dark attire considering the heat. They were withdrawing from the shipwreck with supplies in hand. His supplies. Though there was very little of value remaining for the ship had set sail with a humble selection of food and weaponry.

An old man broke from the group of scavengers and wandered towards the cage that held the captain, followed by two cohorts. He approached and leant his head between two bars and squinted as though his vision was impaired. The captain squinted too.

'What of the others?' asked the captain. 'Am I the last?'

The islander spat rotten phlegm.

'Why have you come to where no one has come for many years?'

A rhetorical question or a statement. The captain didn't know which.

'Why should I tell you anything, after what you've done?'

The islander leant back and raised his brow.

'You are thirsty?'

'Yes.' The captain tasted the hot sand on his lips. 'Will you allow me some water? I speak better without a dry mouth.'

The old islander gestured to his side. A young woman came forwards, unlocked the cage and stepped in. She took a large coconut from the sack that hung around her neck and pulled out a curved knife. The same knife that had taken the lives of so many of the captain's soldiers. She stuck the knife into the hard shell and then inserted a bamboo spout.

Her gaze was an insult. The captain stared up at her emerald eyes as she passed him the drink. He hated himself in that moment, for her beauty made him forgive the things that she had done. If she were a wretch he would hate her still. He damned himself for his forgiveness. Was it because she seemed so young? Maybe she was a tool and the man beside her deserved his hatred more. The captain tried to picture the faces of the fallen soldiers from his ship. He pictured them with their families in their homes. His hatred returned.

The water from the coconut was warm but it didn't matter. He took it all down.

The assassin, who now appeared to be no more than a servant, loosened the ropes enough for him to sit and face his jailers. She left the cage, locked it again and fell into place behind the old man.

'River, you may leave us.' The old man spoke over his shoulder, looking at her scorched arm. 'You should continue with your treatment.'

'Yes, Father,' she said. 'Shall I bring you the manifesto once it is repaired?'

'No, no. No mind. I have no need to rush.'

The assassin, River, left them and as she circled around the cage to head further inland, the captain's eyes followed her with his judgment. She refused to meet them with her own. The ground was her safe place. Her green eyes were wasted on the sand.

The old man's eyes didn't waste their gaze.

'Captain, your manifest was recovered and though severely burned and torn, I am told it will reveal enough. Do you wish to tell me anything or do we wait? I will enjoy the unbearable heat from my shack beyond the dunes. Time passes blissfully in the shade. Do you wish to remain here?'

'I like the sun,' said the captain. 'Where I am from it rains all the time.'

The old man chuckled. 'I wonder, could that be why you were named after a forest. Boscelito. I have never seen it but I hear it is enviably green, more so perhaps than my daughter's eyes. We too name our own after the things of nature. It is just, do you not think? To pay our respects in such a way.'

Boscelito felt a large grin upon his face. He enjoyed the playfulness of this man, in a twisted sort of way.

'You're so full of the shit you're shovelling. But I think I like you for it,' Boscelito replied. 'I work for a man without a sense of humour. The irony that my enemy has one.'

'I would not like to meet this man, he sounds dull. You do interest me, however. But you are not yet my enemy. There is time for that of course, but it is far too soon.'

'Your daughter killed thirty-three of my best men and women. Men and women with families. Mothers, fathers, sons and daughters just following orders. I'm pretty sure that qualifies us as enemies.'

'Yes, River is surprisingly effective at taking the lives of invaders. Enjoy your evening, the scorpions here are quite friendly I believe, once the sand has cooled.'

'And what piece of nature were you named after? Should I call you snake or rat?'

The old man laughed out loud this time. He began to walk away with his remaining cohort, enjoying a slow pace.

'They used to call me Quicksand,' he called behind him. 'I am too old for that title these days. Now all call me June. If you ever want to continue this pithy game, ask for me.'

June continued to walk away, not looking back. Boscelito was left alone again in his cage.

The beach emptied out as the tide rose and began to wash at the base of the cell. Burning hot iron sizzled as the seawater evaporated against the metallic bars.

Boscelito used his new freedom of movement to collect some scattered palm leaves that had blown within arm's reach and made a form of cover. It wasn't perfect, but enough to protect him for now. He crawled under it, wincing as he dragged his injured leg across the sand. All he could think about were scorpions and he dared not sleep. But at least he was safe from the burning rays of the sun.

By the time daylight had escaped the beach, a scythe-like moon had risen, trickling its light against the calm ocean. Boscelito had slept and slept well. He rolled over and gazed up to the sky and saw the moon like it was the assassin's blade pointing towards him. It wasn't far from the truth. He didn't need to turn to know that she was there, watching him.

'Your father lied about the scorpions didn't he?' Boscelito broke the short silence. 'I would have done the exact same thing.'

River knocked her knife against the bars of the cell. The sound reverberated like a wind chime.

'Why are you here?' she asked.

He yawned his response. 'What's the matter? You don't like sleep?'

'Why? Tell me.'

Boscelito was curious about her desire to know how he had been tasked to sail to these islands and to enlist aid for his legion. He wondered how the fight back home was playing out. So much confusion and severance of alliances had made this war impossible to determine. The young King Elik remained protected inside his castle walls. His ongoing survival was the only thing keeping the rural lands united. Would Augustus ever forgive Boscelito for his failure? The captain knew the answer.

'Ask me again someday, when I walk freely in the next life perhaps. Your insecurity has ended me.'

'Insecurity?' River was offended by the word. 'We have always led our defences through offence. It's the only way to remain safe.'

'Yes. If you can handle the moral fragility of attacking those who would seek your aid. It is a coward's form of defence.'

'You disgusting man, to lecture me of morality! You are the right hand to a monster.'

'Yes, I've heard that before,' Boscelito said, sullenly. 'That monster saved my life.'

'Well it is a deal not many of us get to make.' She accused him with her tone. 'To trade your soul with a demon in exchange for mortal life.'

Boscelito felt the cutting truth rupture his ability to speak. A moral man he had once been. He cared for those who served under him and never followed through with a single action that he didn't find to be the right course. But the exception had been Augustus. Every command, wish and request from the warlord were the only paths he trod without thinking. How many lashes to his soul had he suffered now as a result? He dared not count them. He wondered if that was his real cage and he was now safe from it within this false prison made of iron. He wondered from what prison the assassin was trying to escape.

'River, I sense a strange affinity to others who share my predicament,' he said. 'I wonder, is that why you are here? In the depths of the night. You want me to help you understand yourself.'

'You're an arrogant bastard. When they are done with you they will kill you and you will die without a soul and there will be nowhere safe for you to rest peacefully as your own demons will cut you infinitely with blades that cannot be forged by men.'

River turned on her heels and headed back inland. Her anger had risen like a rising storm as she had spoken the words. The truth they shared, assassin and prisoner alike, was that their incarceration to another's authority unified them.

The subtle hint of quivering in her voice was evidence enough that she only half believed what she had said. It was not only her eyes that fascinated Boscelito anymore, but also her mind.

THE NIGHT GREW THICKER and a cold breeze swept the sand clean of the fallen palm leaves. River made her way across the dunes that separated the beach and the tree-lined settlement she was heading towards. It was sparse and contained just a dozen or so wooden huts. The collection of trees that were sheltered by the dunes held enough space for a selection of platforms to have been built, raised above the earth.

River had built her own home when she was still a child. It was the smallest of them but had the largest terrace and a hammock hung from two posts beneath a canopy made of vegetation.

She hated the indoors. Every night she spent inside sheltered from the rain was a burden and the warmth and stillness of this seasonal time was something she cherished for she slept out in the open nightly.

River collected some firewood and threw it on the smouldering embers of a small stove. She took a pan and filled it with herbs and milk from a pulped coconut and made a calming brew. The herbs were local from the farms beneath the mountain at the centre of the island.

She loved dearly to wander amongst the fields alone, picking wild plants that grew there. She would later dry them in her hut and make a range of concoctions to help settle her mind. They caused some hallucinations but she barely slept without them.

Once the brew had come to the boil she filtered out the mash that remained and poured the infused milk into a small clay cup. She strolled across her decking and unrolled a thick woollen mat which she sat upon. She sipped the drink and closed her eyes, allowing her mind to wander. She prayed for the lives she had taken, prayed that they may find peace wherever they now rested.

Her frustration was that the man they had retrieved from the wreckage had so easily angered her. She prided herself on her resilience of mind and body. She had faltered. Were they so alike that it was as though she had stared into a mirror where all of her own failings had been laid bare?

She believed in her duty to her people, and had been born into a world where you did not question authority. She loved her father dearly and never questioned him or his commands. But she doubted at times if she was free. Boscelito had seemed so free to her. In his cage, his mind was at peace.

She closed her mind off to her intrepid thoughts. She latched onto a white mist that rose inside her and she let it fill her completely. The pure white was the source of all life and it freed her from her guilt and fears. It was the safest place she knew.

# 4

Rain has a habit of drowning out the vigour we feel from the caressing sun. Then comes the lightning. Then the thunder. It's a moment we dread at first, before it becomes intoxicating. Like anticipating jumping from a high cliff into a pool of water with unknown dangers beneath it. Once the leap of faith has been taken and your feet hit the cool water, you feel a surge of shock through your body, followed by bliss and you realise that sometimes you have to get wet to feel alive.

Rising slowly to the east, the sun dared to show its face. Dawn was its call to arms. The skies so fierce and beautifully bloodied were a call to prayer that would be obeyed by all.

Boscelito shivered as the early morning cold awoke him and rendered his body stiff. There was no strength or energy left in him to fight off the gelid winds that had swept upon the shores.

He looked out at the front of his cage where a guard had been posted to watch over him. It didn't matter. He had no strength to put up a fight.

Deep down he knew his captors would kill him soon; they

had fed him long enough. They may still try to extract some useful information from him, but death was waiting aboard the next ship he would sail. It would be his last voyage.

There were few men who had served with Augustus and knew the tactics the warlord employed the way Boscelito did.

*Strength and numbers are simple tools,* Augustus had once said. *The manipulation of a man to make him believe his ally has wronged him. That is real power.*

The words were a lesson first and then an instruction.

Boscelito had carried out an early mission for his general; to inspire hatred in the poor landowners of any foreign settler who had become their neighbour.

It was deemed prudent to show how the land and produce that should have been cultivated by locals had fallen into the hands of outsiders. The truth of course, was that those outside settlers had been invited to move their families and work on the land of those who already owned them. Often they had been recruited and brought to these places due to a lack of a willing, local workforce. All they wanted was to improve the lives of their children.

Boscelito sowed his seeds of doubt and sat back and watched as riots broke out amongst the villages.

When enough time had passed and the ongoing disputes had still not been settled, Augustus made his move, slaughtering several fathers, mothers and children of the local families as they slept. He blamed the outsiders and told the lie over and over until he himself believed it was the truth.

A fury rose from the ashes of the cremated loved ones. Augustus had inspired the misguided to fight for what was already theirs and they joined the legions that were under his command. In many instances, forcing out the very workforce they had themselves employed. Many had expected that this would be the final blow to convince Elik to show his face and put his army to task. But the young king remained hidden and his intentions an ongoing mystery.

Boscelito hadn't thought about those murders for some time. One of the more painful days in his life was accepting those orders. The only mercy was that Augustus had carried out the killings himself. But Boscelito had been complicit in whispering poison into the minds of the deceived. Maybe now, it was time to pay the price.

The Vermillion Isles would be the place of his reckoning. He would be tortured, beaten, and cut from head to toe and every last piece of useful information extracted from him and then they would kill him.

A banging sound came from the gate that held him within the cage. The door swung open. June stepped inside and placed a jug of cool water at Boscelito's side. He then presented a bowl filled with nuts and fruit.

'Eat.'

Boscelito was disoriented. His head still pounding from the chill of the night before, but now the sun was raising its stare over the dunes behind them. He drank first. Then he ravished the fruit.

'You will need your strength,' said June.

'The feed before the slaughter?' Boscelito replied, as June smiled back at him.

'We have a journey ahead of us today.'

'It'll take more than water and fruit to get me on my feet. I can still barely move my leg.'

'That's why I put lava in the water.'

Boscelito shuddered.

'Lava is poison.'

June shook his head.

'Hardly. It will give you unnatural strength for an hour or

two and then you will sleep. It will cause you no long-term harm.'

'I knew a man who used lava once. He climbed a tower to rescue his daughter from captivity. But the lava wore off before he made it to the top and he fell to the walkway beneath. He painted his death on the walls of the castle.'

'Then he was not a man of Vermillion and didn't understand its risks. Yes, its effects are short lived, more so for some than others, and that is why we shouldn't wait. Today you will make the climb.'

Boscelito didn't understand June's intentions but it must be some clear trick. Lava was a substance that originated from The Vermillion Isles. It was forged from a weed that grew on the highest volcanic peaks.

After the herb was cultivated a fine powder was made and the value of the substance had once been greater than gold as no outsider traders ever made it to the isles. Instead, those who resided on the mainland of Harmion relied heavily on the islanders making their way across the seas to sell it in minimal quantities.

It was scarcer now due to the years of trading, though not impossible to track down. Fighters used it on occasion before heading into battle. But its effects were unpredictable and many soldiers found themselves losing strength before the fight was done. It was said to shorten the life of any who used it. Boscelito doubted he would live long enough to find out.

He felt the elixir coursing through his veins and so he stood as the pain of his injured leg was numbed.

'Maybe I should fight you now. Before the tiredness comes.'

Boscelito felt the soldier in him rising. June expected it.

'Then you will never see the most beautiful sight in our world.'

Intrigue. The way to dispel the raging heart of a fighter with a conscience was to appeal to him with beauty. Boscelito would play along for now.

'I am at your service,' he said.

June left the enclosure and Boscelito followed him. They walked across the dunes and into the forest dwellings where a heavy set of provisions were waiting to be loaded. Boscelito was made to carry a large sack across his back with food and water. He was told it was for an islander who lived at the top of the highest mountain and Boscelito begrudgingly agreed to carry the supplies.

A small gathering had formed and Boscelito recognised one of them as River. She ignored his bidding of good morning and ordered her companions to keep watch over him as she led the march.

They trekked through the foothills and sandy pathways for around an hour before reaching the base of a steep set of steps.

A rockface that lingered above them had thousands of stones bolted into its side, reaching up into the sky. It was a daunting sight and any healthy person would have begrudged the effort to climb it.

'This is as far as I go,' said June. 'I wouldn't hang about if I were you. The lava will wear off soon enough.'

Boscelito gave June one last look and didn't waste any time questioning his departure. He began climbing the steps and this time he led the group. River kept watch towards the back.

Fever and sweat took hold of Boscelito as he fought against the stony stairwell. Each step was a mountain and there were hundreds still ahead of him. He noticed that his injured leg was shaking and blood spilled from the re-opened wound. The lava wouldn't last much longer and he would be left a ruin. This was a one-way journey, either by the making of his captors or his body which would fail him.

Beneath, the long, steep pathway petered out into a vast

view of palm forests and farmland. It stretched for miles. There was hardly any evidence of a large community. He wondered how The Vermillion Isles had avoided invasion for so long, with so few. Then he remembered that River alone, had been worth more than thirty of his soldiers.

'We're halfway,' said River from the back of the group. 'You three stay here and wait for me.

She spoke to her companions, fellow assassins Boscelito presumed. He couldn't stop himself from imagining the hundreds of dead soldiers that would have died by their hands.

'You,' River spat at Boscelito.' Carry on up. Take the supplies from this one. I'll get the rest.'

The islander below Boscelito passed up another sack that he took unwillingly. He saw River load herself up as well. It was too much for the pair of them to manage. Surely she must know that?

'We'll never make it,' Boscelito said.

River tied off the last sack around her waist and shoved past him to continue the climb.

'We make it or we die.'

'Not the deal I was hoping for.'

River ignored him and carried on with the ascent. She didn't slow her pace or wait for Boscelito. He knew he couldn't turn around now. It was too late to return before his fatigue set in. The three knife-wielding assassins they left behind would also have something to say about any attempt he made to descend the mountain.

'Perhaps a moment to rest?' Boscelito shouted above him.

River carried onward without a moment's hesitation. Boscelito doubled his efforts to catch up to her.

'Are we soon to arrive? I'm awfully tired.'

'Shut up!' River demanded. 'You're like a screeching cat in my ears.'

'You'll be rid of me soon.'

'Not soon enough.'

Her reply was sharper than the knife strapped to her belt. Boscelito should have expected it, he goaded it out of her. But it hurt.

River yelled out in frustration and stopped to turn and face him.

'Every day I hate you more, because every day I learn something new about you that is worthy of my despise.' Boscelito was confused, and for once, lost for words. River continued her onslaught. 'I saw your manifesto, you had a pregnant woman on board. It didn't take much to figure that out, given the specific supplies and limited amounts.'

'One thing I will say for Augustus,' Boscelito replied. 'He's not prejudiced about who can fight. She was a very brave warrior. May she rest in peace.'

Boscelito felt the shame oozing out of River and into his well of guilt. It was already overflowing so he outsourced some of the blame.

'I wasn't the one who killed her. Another flaw in your kill first, ask no questions later approach.'

'Pin nothing on me, captain. Your soldiers, your rules.'

River was done with talking. She turned back to continue the steep climb and quickened her pace. Wishing for the day to be over. Boscelito rushed less so, caring for nothing.

One foot and then the other. Each moment the burning muscles reminded him of his mortality and he knew the lava was fading like the final moments a candle burns before revealing the darkness. He was the ember of a wick. The amber glow was all that remained of him as he made his final push.

The steps doubled in size and the stones were looser and badly maintained at this height. Boscelito thought of the irony of the need to be more careful at the stage where you can barely think for the strain.

They passed a plateau as the steps came to an end, where Boscelito saw a skeleton lying face down in the dirt. It was his mate in death. He had so much in common with the grey remains of the life that had carried those bones to this lofty height. He wanted dearly to lay down next to them and to say goodnight dear life.

*Goodbye to those I have loved and good day to those I have killed. I join you now.*

'Get up!'

A boot struck the side of Boscelito's waist. He opened his eyes and realised he had collapsed at the summit of the volcanic mountain. He heard a hissing sound all around him and the brown dusty arena of heat spat out debris and steam and burning hot water.

'Am I in hell already?' he asked. 'I hoped for a moment's peace before you led me to the lair of the demon.'

'Not dead yet. Lucky for you. Bad for me.'

River held out her hand and those green eyes met Boscelito's for the first time since their journey had begun. He reached out his own hand to accept her offer. Their gaze locked and neither could look away.

Around them the sun was illuminating the islands that surrounded the mountain. The sea was visible on all sides and it truly was the most beautiful vista that could have ever existed. But Boscelito didn't distract himself from the view that enraptured him. To him, River's eyes were more beautiful than all the sunsets and all the oceans and mountains and forests in the world.

He felt a new rush of energy. Not from the effects of lava but of adrenaline. An uncontrollable desire to grab the assassin where she stood was feeding his spirit. River turned and walked away.

The adrenaline dwindled and it was all he could do to follow her into a cavernous enclosure that was cut into the summit of the mountain.

The inside was dark but visible enough as flickering yellow light from the spitting lava illuminated their path. It was hot. Too hot.

'Stay close to me, Boscelito. Don't stray from the path or you'll touch the heat of the sun.'

River walked along a very particular route that cut through the cave. On either side of the path the glowing lava flow lit their way. It led to an opening and inside it was a modest dwelling, filled with paintings upon the rock walls and ornaments lining wooden shelves that lay upon the exterior of the circular space.

At the centre, a man sat upon a mat. He had a long white beard that almost reached to his waist. He was aged, like June. The man was so skinny you could see every one of his bones through his thin posterior.

River dropped her supplies by the side of the entrance and told Boscelito to do the same. He did so and they stepped towards the man at the top of the mountain.

'Volcan. I'm sorry for the delay. We had trouble on the beach. These are this month's supplies.'

Volcan waved them closer and he looked up at the man that River had led to his home.

'Father wanted you to meet this man,' she continued. 'His name is…'

'Boscelito. Yes, I know. Please sit.'

Boscelito was lost in a mirage of wonder. He sat and the two men and assassin formed a triangle on the soft mat.

River spoke to Volcan, updating him on the situation of the shipwreck and the captive. She passed him a piece of parchment that detailed the ledger of the ship. It was a shortened summary of the manifesto that had been recovered. Volcan glanced it over and nodded and then folded the parchment up and placed it to his side.

'We have much to say to one another, you and I,' Volcan said, addressing Boscelito. 'But I can see from the redness in your eyes that the lava has left you. Sleep. It is okay. You can sleep now. Talking comes later.'

'I am ready to talk now,' Boscelito lied.

Volcan placed his finger on Boscelito's forehead and pushed him backwards. He floated down towards the mat and the sounds around him began to echo. A high-pitched tone reverberated around his skull and what little he could see became specks of black, dancing inside his eyes. Little flecks like a swarm of flies at the end of spring. The flecks became a blanket and then all was dark and all was still.

## 5

A fist struck him in the ribs. Black bruises covered his torso like a Rorschach nightmare. So much pain. So freely given. It was almost boring. Tritan spat blood across the dark cell and waited for the next round of beatings to come.

His arms were chained to an iron hoop in the ceiling and he hung there, swinging like the punchbag that he was.

The guards had gotten used to this daily ritual of inflicting as much hurt as they could. It was a dance of iron and flesh.

Broken bones would heal in time and then break again.

Tritan had resisted the interrogations about Augustus and his journey into Orldin. A year of being asked the same question, met with silence.

His captors didn't even bother to speak to him anymore. They just took out their frustration on him. But their orders were to keep him alive.

The pleasure was found in taking Tritan to the brink of death and pulling him back before they went too far. There was something unnatural about the amount they could abuse him. It made it all the more fun for them, but also exhausting.

Tritan felt a final crack when his skull met with an iron bar. It was forged specially for this purpose and the man who wielded it panted and moaned through exertion.

Tritan knew the guards by the way they moved and breathed. How frequently they would strike him and with how much force. With his eyes closed he could tell it was the final blow, for it was the heaviest and an awkward groan came with it as though the putrid guard had climaxed.

The guards left Tritan's cell, leaving him dangling like a beaten dog. Tritan could feel his swollen eyes puffing out and his vision was impeded.

The sound of the pattering drops of blood upon the stone floor were a sermon to the aches that he felt through his entire body.

He wondered how long his body would hold out. In time he would succumb to his wounds, either external or internal. His heart raced as it sent blood flooding to his wounds. It must have been confused. The least part of his body was uninjured.

He forced a look upward to see the blackness that enveloped his arm. It had spread further towards his chest, and his hand had been rendered useless. He was still able to twist his wrist and clench the muscles in his arm but the tentacles of the plague beneath his skin now reached out towards his torso.

Tritan heard footsteps scattering around the tunnels of the subterranean prison. From the echoes he could tell that the corridors were long and high. Rushed and panicked sounds resounded through the space. There was some sort of commotion.

A man passed by Tritan's cell and looked in through the bars. He studied the prisoner with sincerity and then moved along.

'Soldier,' Tritan yelled. 'I need some water.'

The man turned to face him.

'It's a bad time for requests.'

Genuine was the need to quench his thirst. But there was no chance Tritan would see his demand dealt with.

'Wait here, will you?'

The man ran off down the corridor leaving Tritan alone again.

'I'm not going anywhere,' he said under his breath.

After several minutes. A guard came to the cell and unlocked the door. He walked over to Tritan, grabbed the chains holding him from the ceiling and unlocked those too.

Tritan went crashing to the ground. He smashed his knee on the stony floor and curled up in a ball, writhing in pain and screaming out for help.

'Pathetic.'

The guard looked down at Tritan with pity.

Tritan continued to roll around the floor as his mind processed all the hurt in his body.

'You're coming for a breath of fresh air,' said the guard. Tritan shot him a look. A new development. 'It's best we don't keep her waiting.'

The long, cold walk through the stony corridors was exhausting. It was as though a labyrinth had been built beneath a castle. A labyrinth filled with all the hatred of the world.

Tritan passed dozens of the guards who had abused him and he winced as he passed them. He felt a shiver coursing up his spine.

Fear. He felt afraid. The fear of leaving his cell for the first time? Perhaps it was the fear of coming face to face with so many of his attackers.

Tritan hated himself for the fear he felt. Had he fallen so far that he was nothing more than a broken man? He was tormented and his spirit had been destroyed. He cried and fell to his knees, shaking. Who was he now? Not Tritan. Not the man who had led legions at the age of seventeen. No longer.

'Get on yer feet, you bitch.'

The guard feigned a kick. Tritan sprang away instantly against a wall. It was the fastest he'd moved since he could remember.

'I, I can't go on,' Tritan muttered. 'Whatever they want from me. Just tell them I'm done.'

'Bullshit, you think I'm going to fall for your fucking games.'

It wasn't a game. Tritan didn't want to admit it, but pretending to be lost would have seemed shrewd, if only it were no performance.

He railed again against the fear that had consumed him. *Fear is the absence of courage. But the absence of fear is proof that the soul is lost.* He remembered Augustus' words as he had remembered so many these past months. *The desire to be loved, is the love of desire. The hope of the fool is a fool who is hopeless. You are a ruined man, and ruins are indestructible.*

Tritan played the words over and over in his mind. He could hear Augustus saying them as though he were whispering into his ear as he lay helplessly in the stony corridor. The booming voice of the tyrant. *Ruins are indestructible.* It was one of the last things that Tritan had heard from his false father's lips. Augustus said it as he bled Tritan to near death.

Tritan had been so close to dying too often. He had been a ruined man. Augustus was right about that. But he had also been forgiven. He had travelled home and seen his son recover from his ailment. He had spent three whole years with Pietrich, teaching him the ways of the world. He had become a good father and a valid member of his village. He had tasted the sweet life and it had made him afraid. Afraid that what he now had would be lost.

A ruined soul had made the fiercest warrior of him. He had become a loved man and, *a man who knows love is weak.* That could not be the way of the world. Not the way of a just world.

Tritan calmed himself from the episode. He slowly got to his feet and met the gaze of the guard who shook his head and laughed.

'Weak prick,' he said, as he continued walking along the torchlit hallway.

Tritan staggered as convincingly as he could. His heart rate had slowed and his panicked breaths diminished as the fear slipped away. He recognised the attack for what it was as he had comforted many soldiers in his command who had suffered attacks just like it. He'd never expected it to happen to him.

The tunnel led to a set of uneven steps that spiralled around a central column. There were several levels, lined with large oak doorways, but the guard continued upwards and Tritan followed.

Eventually, when they were high enough to feel the draft billowing throughout the corridors, they turned off through an opening that led to a high walkway. Tritan saw the outside for the first time in a year.

They were high above a castle keep that was adjacent to a large town. The whole settlement was enclosed within a perimeter wall, dozens of feet thick and higher than any castle defences Tritan had seen since the old palaces had been destroyed in the war.

There was construction going on beneath them and the whole town was a marriage between the light of a blue moon and nectar torchlight.

A crow was perched on the ledge, cawing at Tritan as he walked past. It tapped its beak on the stone, demanding attention before it flew off towards a partially built bell tower.

'Keep moving,' said the guard. 'We're almost there.'

They entered an interior passageway which led to a tight spiral staircase. Tritan leant on a railing that lined the circular wall to steady his footing.

The stairwell came to an end and they entered through a small awkward doorway.

Smoke and exotic aromas filled the room and candles lined the shelves on all sides. There were books and scrolls stacked from floor to ceiling. At the side of the large space was a four-poster bed, neatly made and covered in a thin transparent veil. Beyond it was a writing desk, facing a window.

There stood Tritan's host, by the window, smoking a sort of long thin pipe.

The woman was elderly, but age had been kind to her. Streaks of white hair intersected with black and fell to the waist of her slender body. She wore a dark red gown.

'Leave us,' she said to the guard.

The man nodded. 'I'll be outside if you require my service, ma'am.'

Tritan watched the man go and, without permission, leant on the chair in front of him.

'Sit, if it pleases you,' said the elderly woman.

Tritan didn't wait for a second invitation. She continued to smoke, and didn't turn to face her guest.

'I never understood men like you, obsessed with your own pride. You would let yourself be destroyed before cooperating.'

She withdrew from the window and began to walk around the room with her head bowed. Tritan tried to follow her movement but it hurt his neck to do so.

'You're of little use to me,' she said, 'but you frustrate me because you cannot die until you lead to me to the boy.'

Pietrich. She was talking about his son. Tritan had been tortured for information on the whereabouts of Pietrich so many times he could not remember.

'I've heard them talking about you. The nameless woman. They think you are a god,' said Tritan.

'Yes, some believe as much.'

'Why?'

She stopped and walked towards Tritan and placed a hand on the top of his head like he were a small child.

'Uncountable men and women have fallen by your sword. On the battle field, fellow soldiers remarked at your godlike ability to end lives. As you were a god to those who kill. I am a god to those who use their minds to harness power.'

'If your mind controls the men who wield the swords that cut me, you are also the sword.'

The nameless woman laughed.

'More of Augustus has rubbed off on you than you know. May he rest in hurt.'

'On that point, we can agree.'

She shook her head.

'I do not resent him for what he did. I resent him for what he did not do.'

Tritan tried to think of the value he held to this woman; he could think of little other than the land he had travelled to beyond the northern borders. Orldin. 'If you're after the Maldus tree, no one is stopping you. If I can make it there, if *Augustus* can make it there, you with your new army have nothing to worry about.'

The nameless woman sighed and walked towards a map on the wall. What it showed wasn't a geographical map, but a spiritual map. The Maldus tree was at its centre. She placed her finger on the tree and ran it upwards to the depiction of the sky.

'The tree is the heart that pumps lifeblood into all things. I am no longer interested in the heart. I want the soul.'

There was a knock at the door. Two guards entered with a

man in chains dragging behind them. He had a hood over his face. It was soaked with blood.

'Bring him to me,' the nameless woman commanded.

The guards pulled their prisoner into the room and dropped him to his knees. The nameless woman took the hood off his head and revealed his battered features.

Even behind all the blood and swollen lips, Tritan could see through his blurry vision, the face of a man he once know.

'Fritz!'

Fritz groaned. He was beaten, but perhaps not as devastatingly as Tritan had been.

Tritan shook his head. No words could summarise his hatred for this woman.

The nameless woman held Fritz's head up by the jaw and forced his eyes to meet with her own.

'A tremendous fighter, but family is your weakness. I hear it didn't take much for your wife to give you up. Shame. I too trusted love once.'

She nodded to one of the guards. He pulled out a knife and held it to Fritz's throat.

'No!' shouted Tritan. 'Are you mad? You'd kill your only leverage?'

The nameless woman smiled.

'So, you agree then. That he is leverage? Very well.'

The nameless woman retracted her knife and gestured to the guards. They replaced the hood over Fritz's head before forcing him to his feet and leading him out of the room.

'What life have you lived, to make you so cruel?' Tritan asked her. He didn't expect a response. But she offered him one.

'You may never know the full extent of the pain your family has caused me. Before you were even born your life was a plague on mine.'

She walked behind Tritan and casually placed a hand upon

his cheek. It was an awkward moment, her actions were not clear but Tritan felt a strange sensation. A throbbing at the back of his mind.

'Useless, you have a hollow mind. If you knew what you had done.'

She appeared truly frustrated and Tritan longed to know the reason why. She wandered to a cabinet and took out a needle; it was attached to a small vial filled with a dark liquid.

'I have lived so many lives in all my years. So much time to suffer. I wouldn't want you to miss out.'

The nameless woman inserted the needle into Tritan's dead arm and injected him with the fluid.

He grabbed his blackened wrist with the one that still worked and screamed out in agony. It was a blistering pain that no iron bar or sword could ever inflict. In all his years, he had never felt anything like it and he wailed. Praying for the moment that the pain would stop.

It didn't stop.

The nameless woman circled him as he lay on the ground, writhing and kicking out.

'If you were to hold your arm into a fire, burning hot as the sun, you would not feel pain like this. But as for the pilgrimage of your suffering, Tritan. Both physical and mental. That journey has just begun.'

## 6

B reaking the cool, damp night. A vague daylight lifted, bringing about a heavy deluge. The grey, misty sky remained ominous and depressed.

It had been over a week since Fritz had left them and Lynden was convinced, now more than ever, that he had either fallen into harm's way or abandoned them.

'He'd never leave us,' said Pietrich. 'Not without fair warning.'

Lynden threw her pot filled with boiling water against the wall.

'I'm sorry,' she said. 'You're right. It just makes me feel so crazy sometimes. You reach my age and you've seen it all, but it makes you mad all the same.'

Grace and Olafur began tidying up the camp. They folded all the bedding and collected the cooking pots. Grace took pause to comfort Lynden.

'We have to keep moving. We've no more food and the game around these parts has become scarce. If Fritz is okay, he'll know where to find us,' she said comfortingly. 'He's a good tracker.'

Lynden shook her head.

'That's what I am afraid of. What if they have gotten to him?'

'Then they'd have found us here already,' Olafur replied. 'Grace is right, we best move on. We're all in danger here now.'

There was a moment's silence. Spoiled only by the orchestral rain that fell beside them to the entrance of the cave. Lynden stepped to admire the torrential downpour.

'It's beautiful, is it not? I don't care much for stepping out into it and soaking myself through to the bone. But there is something peaceful about watching it fall whilst we stay dry. Perhaps we have been hiding from the rain long enough.'

'Lynden, what are you saying?' asked Grace.

'I'm saying it is time to stop running. I'm old. I'm tired and I just wonder, what happens if one year turns into five. Then five into twenty. Do you think I will be around that long? Because I don't. Whoever got to Fritz, will be the same people that captured Tritan and pose a threat to Pietrich and the rest of us. Pietrich is right, we need to stop running in circles. If we can find but one of the other elders.'

Her sudden change in tactics startled the rest of the group. Lynden had been the ringleader since they left. She preached caution and never dared travel to the populated towns to find her brethren. No matter how much aid they might be able to give. It was never worth the risk. So, to hear her speaking so boldly now was difficult to believe.

'What about my father? If we snuck into the town near to where they are keeping him, we could learn something from the local folk.'

'If what you heard was real, then I suspect that is exactly what his captors are hoping for. It is time to be bold but we can't just walk up to the front gates of the enemy and expose ourselves.'

'But—'

'No, I'm sorry. I know you worry for your father, but he isn't worth risking you for.'

Pietrich had been animated by the prospect of finally taking action. But he hated the idea of heading anywhere other than where Tritan was being kept. He swallowed his hope.

'What are you proposing then?' he asked.

Lynden turned on her heels and the rain fell heavier still behind her as though she had conjured up a white veil.

'An army has been growing under our noses since the forty-year war ended. It is time to build our own.'

Lighting struck a tree that protruded the rock above the entrance to the cave. Sparks of wood and fire fell with the squall and landed at the entrance. It should have surprised Lynden as she was close to the landing point of the torrent of splintered, sodden wood and flames. Instead she smiled and looked up to the sky and spoke.

'I'll take that as agreement.'

BRANCHES WERE STREWN across the pathway they rode upon. Thick mud and pools of water blocked their path, forcing them to take detours as they went, but they pressed on. Lynden had decided their first task was to find one of the elders who might understand something about Pietrich's ability to sense things that others couldn't. If he could learn to control the obscure sense somehow, use it for good, he would be a leader worth following.

The secret plan that had been brewing in Lynden's mind since they set out from Knighton the previous year had come to fruition. But she dare not share her dreams for fear of sullying them.

Pietrich was special. She had known it long before they ever met. But she could not rush him, he was still so young.

'We'd best get ourselves to the nearest village,' said Olafur. 'We've still got some coin left; we can buy some supplies to see us through until the weather brightens and the hunting conditions improve.'

The four riders were now trotting side by side as the pathway had opened out to a clearing. Somewhere the wolf lingered ahead of them, though they had not seen Jack for days.

'Where the Arn river breaks off to the north is a fairly small settlement,' Lynden suggested. 'It's a good place to start. They won't have much but we'll only need enough to see us through the day.'

'Where do you intend to set up camp?' asked Grace.

Lynden pointed to a set of hills that were barely visible for the mist that tried to obscure them.

'Over there,' she said. 'We'll head to Port Melees. What's left of it.'

'That's two days' riding at least,' Grace said, confused.

'Yes, that's right. Best prepare yourself for a sleepless night. I don't want us to hang around the Infantus hills any longer than we have to.'

Olafur was unsure of the plan.

'Port Melees has been derelict since Castellar was killed and the village burned,' he said. 'What purpose could there be to venture there?'

'Well, for a start, as you rightly pointed out, it is derelict. So the chances of it having been inhabited are few.'

'Lynden, I just do not see how a derelict town that will require us to ride through the night will be of use.'

'Let an old woman satisfy a hunch. If I am wrong I will let you decide where we head following on from that.'

'Do you think an elder might be there?' asked Pietrich.

'I don't know,' she answered. 'But it is still well located and should allow us to get our bearings.'

Olafur's horse brayed and kicked its hoof. He grabbed the reins and pulled them taut, hushing to calm the steed.

'He's hungry,' Olafur said. 'I hope we find some feed soon or the long ride ahead will be cut short.'

After the horse had been calmed they carried on through the dredge of the low valley forest they had entered. Their pace was slow thanks to the downpour, which had created thick impassable bogs on the track.

Sometime after mid-afternoon they arrived at the outskirts of the tiny village. There were no more than three homes and long flooded fields that sat at the base of a plateau. The Infantus mountain they had descended earlier that morning sat proudly above the village, its peak jutting out from the fog that rested on the plains.

Olafur dismounted his horse and took a pouch of coin from a saddlebag.

'Wait for me here, I will find what I can.'

Grace called out, telling him to be careful. This was usually one of the tasks Fritz carried out. He nodded and headed down a lane to the side of one of the slate-roofed cottages.

'We'd best think about our route,' said Lynden. 'We cannot continue as we have done this morning or we will not make it to Port Melees for another month.'

Pietrich tied his horse to a post beside the fence that circled the village. He fumbled the leather strap into a loop as he had done many times before.

Lynden watched with intrigue.

'I sometimes forget you cannot see, your father taught you admirably to handle such things.'

Pietrich patted his horse and stepped away.

'He used to tell me it was better to learn to do everything for myself, just in case I ended up alone.'

'Wise, but you are not alone, Pietrich. We are with you.'

'Yes,' he replied. 'I wish that Fritz was here as well.'

That was something they all agreed on. They shared a sombre moment. The uncertainty of either having been abandoned or the knowledge that harm had befallen their beloved Fritz was unbearable.

Olafur returned as they waited in silence. A ray of hope to dispel their dark thoughts. He carried with him a large bale of hay and a huge sack full of produce.

'Two days' worth of supplies for us. Hay enough for now and the morning for the horses. There are not many traders travelling these areas with the weather as it is. We fetched a decent price on that account.'

'Well done, my love,' said Grace.

'Here.' Olafur passed Pietrich a cup of hot stew. 'They had it on the boil. There's enough for one cup each.'

What a fine stew it was. They guzzled down the contents of the cup and it warmed their hearts. Pietrich loved fresh garlic and the broth was full of it. The horses tucked into the hay and ravished near half of their feed in the time it took their human counterparts to ready themselves for the road.

'Let us pass through the village and to the western road. It is close by,' Lynden suggested.

'Are we to break all of our rules now?' Grace asked. 'That road is likely patrolled.'

'With the rain such as it is, we will take our chances. I am more concerned Fritz is being used to track us. If that is the case, he would take them through the overgrowth we have traversed all this time.'

Lynden mounted her horse and signalled for the rest of them to follow her.

They passed through the village and waved to the man who had sold them their fresh supplies before venturing to a crossroads where the western route cut in. It was a wide concourse and visibility was good.

A large cage was hanging from a wooden stake lodged in the ground. Pietrich's horse whinnied and nearly threw him off.

'Whoa, boy,' he shouted. 'What's there?'

Lynden took her walking rod from her saddle and smacked the cage, spinning it towards her so she could unravel the thin hessian cloth that was draped over the bars.

Beneath it were two fresh corpses. A man and a woman. They were intertwined as one and held a wooden sign. It read.

*Those who do not pay their taxes to the Winter Queen are traitors and will be executed at her behest.*

'There is something written here,' Lynden explained to Pietrich. 'It talks of a winter queen. I guess that is what they are calling their new leader. It is nothing for us to dwell on, we should move.'

'I can smell rotting flesh, I know it is an execution chamber. You don't need to hide such things from me,' Pietrich rebuked.

'I'm sorry, Pietrich. Either way, this road was a bad idea. I was wrong, we should head back around. We'll find another way to Port Melees.'

As they turned back to face the village a band of seven armed soldiers jumped out of the thickset woods and surrounded them. The four companions backed towards each other and their horses lurched, distressed and helpless.

They had found the executioners. Rather the executioners had found them. It was a killing party. These were no mere soldiers carrying out orders and arrests but paid killers with one single purpose.

Their swords were unsheathed.

Blood stained the jackets of the predators like wild beasts returning from the hunt. They were enthralled by the gift of fresh victims for the kill.

Footsteps shuffled behind them and a horrific howling sound distracted them for a moment. Jack ran at the feet of one of the killers and bit feverishly.

The man swung his sword down, but Jack pranced out of the way and fled into the forest.

Pietrich spun on his horse and didn't know where to turn. He heard the breaths of the seven men and the sound cascaded into his head and he fell to his side, landing in the dirt.

'Pietrich,' Lynden cried, as one of the swordsmen swung his blade at the chest of her horse. He cut a deep gash sending the horse reeling and Lynden joined Pietrich in the mud.

Pietrich felt the taste of blood in his mouth. Had he landed so poorly? He wondered. But the blood did not taste like his own. He felt a chunk of flesh between his gums and fangs. He tried to pull it out with his fingers but there was nothing there.

He heard the cries of the swordsmen as they readied their attack and suddenly he saw himself through their eyes. Not clearly, the way he had seen in his former life, but the blur of a vision, like a memory. Distorted and twisted.

He saw his helpless teenage body lying in the dirt about to be struck down. Though it was more knowledge than sight. Behind him a large wave rushed through the deluge. It was a dozen horseback riders, an old legion, yielding their swords and the cry for battle stunned the group of killers where they stood.

The leader of the seven signalled for them to run and they sprinted with all their worth into the thick, tree-lined canopy.

The battle cry continued and the legionaries circled the

crossroads, forming a partition between Pietrich and the forest. Lynden got to her feet and looked up at the riders. It was mayhem and she wondered how her own horse had not been disturbed by the cavalry.

In a flinching moment, one of the riders turned and rode towards her. He hadn't seen her. She closed her eyes, cursing herself for having been so stupid. Readying herself to be crushed into the ground.

She could not survive that.

The impact never came. The battle cry lifted. A moment of trepidation and then she opened her eyes. The riders were gone and Grace and Olafur had run to Pietrich who was convulsing. Lynden ran to them.

'What's wrong? Is he alright?' she questioned.

Grace shook her head. 'I don't know.'

'Let's get him on his horse, quickly,' Lynden urged.

They picked Pietrich off the floor and laid him across his horse before mounting their own and without delay they rode off down the western road, for fear of the killers that still hid within the village.

Once they had reached a safe distance, they turned into an outcrop for shelter. The thick woods would make a good hiding spot for a time. Olafur dismounted his horse and ran to Pietrich. He dragged him down into the weeds and checked for a sign of breath.

He was breathing faintly. His eyes flickered. He spoke feebly.

'Did it work? Did they come?' he asked.

His three companions shot looks to each other. Confused and afraid. It was Grace who answered him.

'Pietrich, tell us what you mean. Tell us what you did,'

'I asked for my father to save me. I wished that he was young again. That his legion would ride by his side and kill those men who sprang on us. I listened to the footsteps of the horses. I saw the fearful speed at which they rode and I dreaded the steal they wielded. But I wasn't seeing or hearing those things as myself. I was inside the mind of one of the attackers. But only one at first and through his eyes I saw that the others were about to slaughter all of us so I split myself into fragments and then I was inside all of them and I made them see what I wanted and I felt their fear. They believed me. I lied to their minds and they believed me.'

## 7

A crimson shaft broke the darkness of the hut, casting itself upon a narrow bed. It wound around the window pane as the sun dipped, tickling the face of a young woman. She stirred from her sleep and smiled. Pulling the arm draped over her breasts ever tighter.

The girl was sweet and she wriggled seductively, grinding her behind against River's body. They intertwined their legs and arms, clutching each other's hands as they kissed, dappled in the fading light of day.

The girl was a daughter of The Vermillion Isles, like River. She had begun her training but was not yet ready to be put to use in the field. She longed for the day that she could go out and fight alongside River. Though River had always maintained that she would always work alone.

The girl had been named Summer by her mother. She didn't know who her father was. She could take her pick given her mother's past.

Summer would walk around the isles as a child, playing in

the fields and wondering if each man she passed had any physical similarity to her. But none ever did.

Summer moaned. It wasn't a moan of pleasure but one of a spoilt lover. River had a mission to carry out and was due to leave at sundown. They stole the final moments the dwindling light gifted them without remorse.

'I have to go,'

River nibbled Summer's ear playfully.

'Can't they die another night? Whoever it is you're going to kill.'

'Who says I'm going to kill anyone? I'm not just some mindless executioner. Everything we do is investigated and considered and then...'

'And then June tells you exactly what to do and you get no say in the matter,' Summer said, butting in.

She'd heard it all before. They had this conversation each time River went on a mission.

'Sounds like the work of a mindless executioner to me. It must be sweaty work. Wouldn't it be nice, to be in control of one's own fate?'

'I wish it could work that way. But I don't get to choose where or when.'

'Of course not,' Summer replied. 'I'm playing with you, silly girl.' She rolled over to face River and licked her face like a child.

River repelled, but too late.

'Thank you, for that, my love,' she said, wiping away the saliva from her cheek, smiling.

'Everyone always says that you're the fastest, River. I think they are wrong.'

'One way to find out.'

The final rays of the sun dipped beneath the windowsill and

plunged the room into darkness as River took her hand and caressed Summer gently.

Summer groaned and screamed out and clasped her mouth with her hand as she thrust her hips upwards. It was over in less than a minute. *Pretty quick,* River thought.

River rolled out of bed and threw the blanket over Summer who drifted into a contented sleep. She went to her cabinet and unlocked it with a key she kept in a tiny side pocket.

The cabinet was filled with her dried herbs for making tea. She brushed them aside and released a false back panel that contained a series of tiny jars. Each of the jars had fine powder in them, like an assortment of spices.

She took a few of the jars and loaded them into a pouch that tucked into the thin jerkin she had thrown on.

River then moved to the corner of the room where there was a case. Summer had thrown her nightdress over it earlier that afternoon when they had first made love and River picked it up carefully and held it to her nose, breathing in deeply. It filled her with warmth. She placed it to the side and opened the chest and took out a tiny case that held two small blades; they filled her with cold.

The blades were almost knifelike in size. She tucked those into her jerkin around her midriff and collected all the other supplies she would need for her journey.

She hated travelling to the mainland. It took weeks to make the voyage, even with the superior ships that The Vermillion Isles armada boasted claim to. This mission required her to have no convoy and so she would sail one of the smallest vessels on the island and one of the fastest.

The beach was deserted as River walked past the iron cage that now sat empty. She threw a glance to where Boscelito had been captive and wondered how his time on the mountain would play out. *Would he still be alive when she returned?*

River carried on towards the shore and walked along a small jetty towards the Jaghtschip, a small pirate boat that she had prepared earlier that morning. It was fast and small enough for her to sail alone. But it was hard work. She didn't mind. The labour kept her sane.

River loaded her things onto the ship and loosened the large rope from the dock. She threw the rope onto the deck and jumped aboard, making ready for the voyage. Once she was out to sea she hoisted the main sail and caught a westerly wind that would carry her to the Harmion mainland.

Night had set in and the moon shied away from view. It was pitch black in all directions. River took out a small compass from beneath the helm and set a course for Port Melees. She sat back on her chair and cracked open a flask that was filled with a strong spirit made from fruit. It was her own recipe and she loved to drink it at sea. It warmed her as the cool sea air brushed against her.

River rested her head back against a rolled-up blanket and allowed herself to disappear into her thoughts. She meditated for a time. But it was not a peaceful meditation. Flashes of distress bubbled inside her and she saw Summer, angry at her for her betrayal. *What betrayal?* There had been none. But she didn't have to wonder long as her mind drifted to the mountain where Volcan and Boscelito sat in discussion.

Why did he bother her so much? He was just a prisoner. Not a person of any special value to her and soon his value would be spent. Volcan would divulge anything of use from the man before River was done with her mission and he'd be food for the crows before her Jaghtschip beached the islands again.

River thought next about June, her loving father who had supported her when she had revealed her relationship with Summer. He had intended for her to be married to one of the armada generals but in the end, he had said that her happiness was all that mattered. He required her to be focused in order to carry out her work protecting the islands.

So many times, she had sailed to the mainland to assassinate the brewing threats that conspired to invade The Vermillion Isles. She was one of several assassins who had been trained since birth in the arts of killing stealthily.

On occasion the islands had been attacked by naval fleets and so she and her comrades had met them on the seas.

Never had a ship reached their shores.

That was before Boscelito had sailed under their noses until it was almost too late. She thought about that night and all the killing and she grazed her fingers across the bubbling skin on her forearm that flaked away. A good a scar as any to honour the dead.

Something vexed her about what Boscelito had said. How attacking those seeking an alliance was cowardly. They had never asked questions about the intentions of any ship that was not of their own fleet. For hundreds of years The Vermillion Isles had remained elusive.

*It was a lie.* Boscelito may have been terrible at fighting, as were the rest of his men who now resided at the bottom of the ocean, but he had known exactly how to rile her and she wouldn't let him continue to do so. Especially in his absence.

FORTUNE FAVOURED HER VOYAGE. The wind was strong and it blew the appropriate direction for her course. So much time to think at sea with nothing but the black of night or endless horizon of day was not good for someone with a killer's conscience. She thought about the pregnant woman who had been aboard the ship that approached their island and it made her feel sick to the stomach. Despite convincing herself that

Boscelito was to blame she couldn't shift the guilt that engulfed her.

River may have been the most efficient assassin from her islands but she was her own greatest danger on these long thoughtful nights.

After five days of sailing, a morning sun revealed a distant set of hills, caressed by a rolling mist as the previous night's rain evaporated. It had been a gratefully swift journey.

Finally River felt relief from her own mind.

She adjusted her course to run parallel to the western shores and headed north towards the harbour town. She was no more than an hour from Port Melees. Her contact would meet her there as usual to register her ship as a drink merchant's.

She had a dozen barrels of the strong liquor she made beneath the decks that would satisfy any harbour inspection.

The port was busier than usual. It had thrived since Castellar Dell'Anima had settled there and implemented fair tariffs for all the traders. He was a new beacon of hope and had formed his own serene alliance to attempt to end the war through a peace treaty. Those who stood to earn more than just a sack of coin from the war were fearful of his influence.

War was profitable and he threatened the economy of the rich and violent. Somehow, River would seek out an audience with the man and learn just how far his influence had spread and, in turn, she hoped to learn how much danger he was in.

June hadn't yet decided if Castellar was someone they needed to save or someone they needed to kill. Time, as always, would tell all.

River disembarked and signed the ledger under one of her many false names. She headed through the centre of the town and traded a few bronze coins for a leg of chicken that she gnawed on as she walked brazenly through the streets.

It was crowded and she disappeared easily into the rabble.

Port Melees was a vibrant town and full of life. The local residents had settled above the high street, up a steep pathway a short walk from the outskirts. There was a series of quiet cottages with views of the harbour and she knew that Castellar resided in one of those.

It would be too bold to simply walk up to each house and knock on the door however, so she started her investigation at the first obvious place. The central tavern.

River walked confidently through the door and the sound of drunken voices, sailors singing, and prostitutes laughing bounced around the low ceilings and wood panelled walls.

She ducked under a low timber support beam, headed for the bar, and asked for a jug of ale. The barman poured her beer and accepted her coin graciously before turning back to the group of men who were leaning against the counter.

They were familiar with one another and River turned around and leant on the bar herself, listening keenly.

She sipped her ale and overheard parts of the conversation but it was too loud to know exactly what each of them was saying without getting involved herself. A move too bold for one who wished to remain discreet.

From what she understood, the group were discussing the shipping channels and how heavily guarded they were.

The cost of wood had suffered on account of the rising cost of security for the trader's vessels. But wine was still being fetched for a decent price as demand had shot upwards due to the families who drowned their sorrows in wine. River was familiar with the type. It was most people these days.

River finished her jug and walked through the tavern, listening for any useful discussions. She heard mention of Castellar on several occasions. But only for the praise they all bestowed upon him. Life had improved in the port since he had settled here and his value to the traders, sailors and local inhabitants seemed to be the only reason that violence had moved on to bloodier pastures.

There was a noticeboard on the wall beside the entrance to the tavern and River went over to observe the various clippings.

'There's a folk night here this eve' if you'd fancy it,' said a large man at her side. 'We could do with filling out our numbers.'

He was a musician for certain. River didn't fail to notice the size of his belly that had clearly been fed daily by the tavern's beer. *Lucky for some*. The best way not to have to fight seemed to be by learning how to sing songs about others fighting.

'I'll consider it, thank you, sir,' she said.

'I'll look forward to seeing you then.'

River nodded and the man eyed her curiously before turning back to his band. She returned her gaze to the noticeboard where there was information about a social discussion that was happening the following morning. It didn't explicitly state that Castellar would be there but the odds were better than imagining he might attend a tavern jam session with the drunk traders.

Back in the street, River wandered past a band of buskers playing an instrumental tune. They had their hats laid out on the ground and were mostly ignored by the passing crowds as they passionately struck their instruments. The tune was exotic and reminded River of her time off the southern shores, far from home.

Sieekah on the island of Maluabaw had been the most colourful place she had ever travelled to and she wished one day to return to walk amongst the market streets, looking at all the finely woven shawls. Yellows like the setting sun. Red like blood, and greens that were second only to her own eyes. It was somewhere she had promised to take Summer one day.

Of an evening, you could board a disused fishing boat and

eat upon the river as row boats passed, selling you barbecued food from their coal grills. Other sailors would sell vats of wine for a small fee. Lanterns lined the promenades that ran along the river's edge and glowed a fierce orange as the flames flickered through dyed paper.

'Watch your step, young lady,' said a beggar, wiping fresh boot dirt from his knee.

River had let her mind wander. It happened from time to time and she hated it for it was her at her weakest and most vulnerable.

'I apologise, sir. Do forgive me.'

River took a coin and threw it on the ground in front of the beggar.

'Thanks, miss. Reckon you'd be wise to look down from time to time, instead of just towards the horizon. Kind of you all the same.'

River carried on past the man but his presence in this place tugged a cord of curiosity. She turned back to him.

'I heard those without a home had been taken care of in Port Melees. Some kind of camp or common shelter. Did you get left behind?'

The beggar shook his head.

'I won't throw in with that business. I'm poorer now than I was when we had all the rivalries carrying on in town. Here I get to mind my own business. In those camps and shelters they make you register and ask you to look for work.'

'You mean that there was more generosity and freedom when the rivalling factions ran things?'

The beggar frowned at River.

'No, of course not, but I used to have a purpose. Minding the horses. Not many need that service now, there's too much trust.'

River considered the freely given trust that the beggar spoke of.

'Strikes me as though you could just steal the horses yourself and change the way people see things.'

'Not on your life,' he replied. 'Think I'd last five seconds here if I did? That Castellar might be peaceful as a goose but you think he doesn't outsource violence to keep the peace?'

'Sounds like any dictator I ever heard of.'

'Dictator,' said the beggar. 'Good choice of word.'

River threw another coin down.

'I gather you must be the eyes of the port,' she said. 'You must see a lot, hidden down there, minding your own business. Any recollection on his whereabouts? Does he ever wander the streets himself or is he one of those that hides behind his principles?'

'Sounds as though you have a thing for him.'

Another coin went down. River waited for her answer.

'Return to the well at the centre of the plaza in town tomorrow morning. I'll take you to him then.'

'Very well,' said River. 'Sleep warm, sir. Until tomorrow.'

'Until tomorrow, miss.'

The beggar turned his head away and rocked back and forth on the spot where he sat. He crossed his arms and folded over the hood of the full-length cloak he wore.

River walked on and found a small inn offering cheap, private quarters. She paid the lady on the front porch and went up the rickety stairs to her room.

The room offered a view of the port and central plaza beneath it. It was noisy, especially for one who slept so often in solitude at sea.

River pulled the curtains closed to block out the view from the street and took a small chair from the dressing table at the foot of the bed and wedged it underneath the bolt of the door that led into her room.

Once she was satisfied that her room was secure enough she threw a rolled-up blanket under the bed linen, creating the false shape of one who is asleep and laid another sheet onto the stone floor in the corner then leant up against the wall, facing the door. Her eyes drifted closed as the sound of the buskers in the street faded into night and the voices of the town became a hazy drone that was her lullaby.

River thought about Castellar. What kind of a man he might be and how his crusade had been so compelling. No one had ever driven out violence from a town without violence. She suspected foul play and before judging the value of his life, she would seek out the truth from his own lips.

## 8

*Where now foregone the steely vines as the window to your heart is closed and prone to judgement. Sip the cool water lest the heat of day rises and carries you beyond conscious-ness to be led astray by some unwieldy predator. Do not sleep for fear of the dreams you may have. But do not wake for fear of the things you will do when dreams are distant memories, shyly washed upon the shores of history.*

Pietrich ran his fingers across the rough page of the journal his father had given him. A collection of thoughts and confes-sions. There were thousands of entries in the form of poems, stories and simple musings. He longed to read the words. He had memorised only a handful of what his father had written when Eira had read to him. Not all of it made sense but Pietrich understood that Tritan had suffered a split between the life he lived and the one he longed for. Pietrich prayed that his father had at least found comfort in the few years they had shared together in the village before he was taken prisoner.

It was likely that Tritan had expected his departure one day. Either by choice or by force. He was no stranger to being uplifted from one place to the next. The days spent together had gone by so fast in hindsight. Pietrich had always been sad that his parents' love for each other remained unrequited in those years they had stayed as a true family. But there had been too many differences and too much hurt to put the pieces back together.

Marilia and Tritan had remained friends but Pietrich could never tell if it was for his benefit or not. Now they were all split apart as far as the eye could see. Much further than that in fact. As he thought about his parents, their love for him and the increasing desire to see them both again, the rising tide in front of him threatened to wet his boots and wash away his daydream.

Avoiding the lapping waves of the abandoned port beach, Pietrich gently moved along the shoreline, closing his father's journal and placing it within his shirt pocket beneath the cloak that billowed in the ocean breeze. His toes nudged against driftwood and soft infant dunes crumbled beneath the soles of his boots. The waves extended their whitewashed cries to bury the signs of his passage.

He tuned his ears to the rhythm of the rushing waves. The tender sound of water flowing across sand entranced him and he stepped away when they came close. Ahead was an alcove that had been carved by storms over centuries. It was an old cavernous dwelling where smugglers and pirates had once hidden the overflow of goods that had been procured unlawfully upon the high seas. They would send their youngest comrades upon rafts to hide within the cave as the ships were docked and, as night fell, they would be relieved by their masters and the goods hauled up the rock face and into horse-drawn carts.

Above the rock was where the old cottages had been built to overlook the port, the remains of which were now no more than weed infested piles of stone. It had grown wild and derelict. The home of Castellar had been deemed plagued and haunted. Tales of his tortured soul standing guard over the killing grounds of his family kept away all would-be settlers, superstitious or otherwise.

It was another sleepless night for Pietrich who wandered alone, further from the camp than he usually dared. Jack was close by and that gave him some comfort, but he missed Fritz. It was like the distance between him and his father had increased since Fritz had left them. The sellsword was similar to Tritan in many ways and he gave Pietrich comfort when he had occasionally spoken of the missions he had carried out with his father.

The journal and the words it contained were the only thing Pietrich had left. He wanted to learn them all with borrowed eyes.

Marching agilely up the bank to the side of the alcove, Pietrich reached the old cottages and re-joined his fellow travellers. They had awoken in his absence and started a fire to boil a broth. It was the last of their supplies and the horses were tired from the long journey they had endured.

'Morning,' Pietrich offered.

'Good day, lad,' Olafur replied, as Grace stirred the pot and tasted its contents.

'It could do with a touch of salt but we used that up last night,' she said, disheartened. 'Well, it can't be helped.'

Lynden grabbed a cup for each of them and sat at her side.

'We've had worse I don't doubt, Grace.' It was reassuring and true. They rarely ate well.

'How is he doing, Lynden?' Pietrich asked, referring to her horse who had been injured.

She tilted her head and pondered the horse's condition.

'Aye, good,' she replied. 'I washed his wound at sunrise and it's healing nicely. Couple more nights, he should be good as new.'

Lynden's horse had been lucky to avoid infection from the cut of the assassin's blade. It had made the journey slower as they had to double up on Pietrich's horse to give her own the chance to recover. It was a longer ride than anticipated and Pietrich had slept most of the way, trying to regain his own strength.

As expected they had arrived at a derelict Port Melees and the town itself, though still standing, had been abandoned. They had chosen not to settle in the old tavern or market square in case it drew any attention and Lynden had deemed it wise to camp in the old cottages instead, in the face of the old myths and fabrication.

After breakfast, they wandered down into the town, leaving behind their possessions, giving the horses a break for the day. It was eerie to walk the cobbled streets that now overflowed with knotted weeds. Stray cats scurried into the shadowy corners of the stables, afraid of the uninvited guests who made their way through.

Many of the doors and windows had been smashed and kicked in, anything of value taken, and big red X's had been painted on the bricked walls of the buildings. It was desolate, like a vision of a ruined world, presented now as a warning to all who may set foot here.

'Not much here to speak of, let's get to the docks. See if we can't find an old vessel,' Lynden suggested.

They all agreed, lost for alternatives and made their way down to the jetties.

Like the town, the years had not been kind to the port. Old crates were smashed along the concourse and several ships lay wasted in the docks. They each looked around for any sign of life, and there was. Rats darted along the drainage at the side of the promenade that housed the piers. There were three jetties in total that seemed like they may still be of value. Olafur walked along one of them and tested the timber plank that reached up towards the ship it housed.

Pietrich stumbled upon a small barrel to sit on whilst the others carried out their investigation. He smelt the air and listened to the sea. It was a putrid smell but not rotten as he expected. Instead there was a smoky feel about it, like burning corpses.

Pietrich began to feel unwell and afraid of their decision to come to Port Melees. Lynden had made very few mistakes since she had taken charge of his safety. But these last few days she had become strangely reckless and Pietrich wondered if her mind was not as it used to be. He felt unkind as he thought the words, knowing full well her position amongst the Harmion council during the early days of the forty-year war. She was only sixteen at the time but had boasted claim to the greatest mind for politics of all her consorts.

Suspicion of betrayal amongst the council had led to its dispersion and those remaining members still loyal to the idea of royal rule were now known as the elders. Lynden had once been the top adviser to the last king before the royal lines fell to ruin. She knew the time for kings would one day come to pass but having served the young King Elik, who held such potential, made her question whether they would be better off fighting for a world where kings could rule once more.

By Lynden's last count, there were still five living elders, including herself and her brother. Like her, they had all gone into hiding throughout the war as their affiliation with the council made them prime targets for anyone opposed to them who might crave information. Pietrich wished he understood her plan better but he could only assume she wanted to put the elder's back together somehow. Maybe if they worked in unison one last time, they would know what to do about the Winter Queen who had risen to power. The nameless woman was a shadow, cast over all their lives, suffocating them as though her very existence was a chokehold.

That tenebrosity haunted Pietrich and as he thought of all the ways in which his guilt devoured him, he still could not bear to reveal his secret… that the Winter Queen had spoken directly to him.

Pietrich had always been able to listen to the voices in his dreams, like an unknown entity, browsing and infiltrating their thoughts, too many to discern. It was done without him reaching out and searching the way he had once done to communicate with Boscelito, his grandfather. Somehow, the Winter Queen had instigated the conversation. She called to him, telling him his father longed to see him. That all would be well if they were together again. But he knew trickery well like an old friend and it is a fiend who wears the brightest clothes and offers you ripe fruit. But inside the fruit are maggots and beneath the rich garb is a liar's dagger.

'I've found something!' Grace called to the group.

Lynden ran to the trade office that Grace had stepped out of. It was the old building where contracts were agreed and stored. The archives had been ruined over time though some files remained. But it was not the documents that had caught Grace's attention. She had found a small campfire, smouldering inside the room, with old furniture used as firewood.

'It's fresh. From this morning, I don't doubt,' said Lynden.

They rushed back out into the open and joined Pietrich who had stood from his barrel to move towards the office. Leaning on his staff, he inhaled a deep breath. It was the smoky aroma he had smelt earlier.

'It's more than just wood burning on that pile,' he said. 'I don't think we should be here.'

Grace looked around the port, concerned and afraid. 'Where's Olafur?'

She darted her eyes around the port. Searching desperately amongst the ships.

'Olafur!' Grace cried out, fearing the worst. The last any of them had seen he was boarding the derelict ship from the middle pier.

A whistling sound echoed across the dockyard, piercing the panicked silence that had befallen them. Pietrich flinched at the sound and he heard a scraping of metal against skin. His heart sank.

Grace and Lynden looked towards the forward side of the ship where Olafur stood with a cloaked figure behind him. The figure was holding a knife to his throat. Before they had a chance to determine the nature of the threat, a dozen more cloaks rose around them. They piled out of the buildings and ships from all directions. It was a stealthy band but of what making Pietrich and his group could not tell. They weren't soldiers or thieves of the normal sort. In fact, for a collection of people apparently living in such squalor, they were remarkably well dressed.

'Don't move another inch or I'll slit his throat. I swear it,' shouted the cloaked figure from the ship. Olafur remained calm and Grace looked at him pleadingly. But she dared not speak.

They were surrounded and, as hard as he tried, Pietrich could not call the cavalry this time. He closed his eyes and focused his mind but it did no good. No horses came charging to scare away the danger. He was as helpless as the rest of them.

An old man walked towards Lynden where she stood beside Pietrich and Grace. He pulled his hood back to reveal his bristly white beard and short thick hair. He gave them all a good looking over and snatched the walking stick out of Pietrich's hand.

'Please don't, he's blind,' Grace pleaded.

'Yes, I can see that,' said the man. 'It's still quite a weapon, a stick such as this. I can see it was carved out of the old wood of the northern borders. You're not going to swing it at me, are you, lad?'

The man asked the question as he held the stick out to Pietrich who humbly shook his head. Pietrich reached out to take back the stick but the man lifted it a few inches out of the path of his reach. Pietrich heard the air move around the man's arm like a tiny flutter of a bird's wing. It was enough of a sound for Pietrich to answer his jest by grabbing the stick perfectly from his grasp. The man smiled wryly from the corner of his mouth.

'Fairly capable lad, aren't you,' he said, raising his hand towards the other who yielded the knife against Olafur's throat behind him, gesturing for him to release it. 'You'd better come aboard my ship.'

'Can we talk, in private?' Lynden asked.

'You have secrets you wish to keep from your friends?'

Lynden shook her head. 'No, it is your friends I don't want listening.'

The man raised an eyebrow at Lynden, amused by her tenacity. 'We believe in openness and honesty here I'm afraid. Seeing as talking is the only thing keeping you alive, you're better off entertaining us all with your story. Let us remove ourselves from prying eyes and wicked ears.'

The man led them to the ship and Grace wrapped her arms around Olafur, the relief of looking each other in the eye was a glimmering light. The next moment they were taken below deck, into darkness.

The inside of the ship had been organised impressively well. Many of the town's archives seemed to have been restored upon the shelves of the vessel. Lynden watched as their host wandered over to a chair behind a commander's desk. The table was littered with maps and trade routes.

'Somehow, I knew all along. From the moment I heard about

your murder to this day. I knew you lived.' It was Lynden who had spoken first, much to the surprise of the man who sat before them and all others who stood in audience to the bold statement.

Curiosity filled the air like burning incense. They breathed it in and waited for the haze to clear.

'I read all your papers when I was in hiding,' she continued. '*Fighting fire with fire lets the whole world burn.* I wish something as compelling and obvious as that mattered more than greed. But people are greedy and we dig ourselves holes daily, before complaining that they are full when we bury our dead in them.'

The sermon had begun. It was the old Lynden Pietrich admired that spoke and a knowing caress of his arm let him know all that he needed to. This chance encounter was no chance at all.

'I've brought with me the only hope I now know of,' she continued. 'I will seek the elders who remain and we will turn the tide of the dark night that settles upon our land. Forty years of war. All the death and suffering just to resurface in a world of poverty and dictatorship. We're cruel to the ones we love and so those who we hate never stood a chance. But we can set aside our differences. You proved it can be done, if only for a short time.'

The man squinted from behind his desk as though something was caught in his eye. He looked as though he wanted to respond. But the silence followed by his sigh made it seem to Pietrich as if the man had been waiting for this speech for some time. A revealing of truth that would rouse a proud creature from hibernation. The man dared not interrupt her flow with any words he could dream up. Lynden had plenty more to offer.

'I believed in my king. Despite the flaws that any leader suffers, he cared for his people. He understood that one day the monarchy would be rendered useless and, in fact, he longed for a life as a draughtsman. His spare time would be used drawing sketches of beautiful homes amidst the luscious landscapes of his land. Not exorbitant castles or villas, but humble homes that even the poor could strive to build, nestled proudly in the green hills of nature's embrace. His vision of the future was to distribute power across the separate regions of Harmion. Our council was formed as an alliance and only when the central weakness was exploited by one of our key generals did the war become inevitable. The weakness was generosity. Elik was a kind young soul and his dream was to provide for all people and most of all protect the natural world. He was the true enemy to gluttony and that made him the enemy of too many powerful traders and business folk who stood to lose the most. The impoverished landscape and dwindling crops needed a leader of his kind, they should have been so lucky. Peasants voted in favour of austerity. Such mind games the powerful play upon the poor.'

Stunned and silent, Pietrich felt a growing pain in the back of his head. It was the judgement of all who stood before him flooding his mind. Suspicion rose amongst the ship's gathering and he felt a responsibility rising that he cared nothing for. Lynden was pitching her sale to market and he was her cattle. She stepped closer to the desk to give the man her best gaze laced in scrutiny.

'The day this boy's father slaughtered you and your family. The peace you built fell into instant ruin. So many years of negotiation and building of alliances, fallen by the swing of a sword. But I knew, despite your philosophy, despite the way you lived by example, that you could not have died that day and let everything you had built crumble around you. I found a document that traced back to your mother's time at a humble infirmary. I was sorry to hear she had died in childbirth. I wonder if that didn't cause you to feel an affinity to the boy, Tritan, that he had no hope of understanding at the time. But the curious thing about the medical report was that it didn't just speak of an orphaned boy being given into care, but two.'

Castellar stood and a tear formed in his eye. He leant his head back and a dark frown formed on his brow, the lines made ever more prominent in the candlelight that shone upward from his desk and onto his face. He finally found the words that had floated on the edge of his lips.

'You have carried a secret that none who have known me ever knew,' Castellar paused, as grief came flowing back to his heart. His voice was trembling but he persevered. 'I lost my whole family that day. When Augustus raided the town and his legion rode up to our village, I knew it then. I knew my family would be slaughtered. My wife, my son, and so, selflessly my twin brother who decided himself that I would live, for no other reason than he had been born first. And now you bring me the son of the man who took them all from me and ask what of me? To be his protector? To see in him some glimmer of hope. No. The man who would have done that died that day as much as all those he loved. The man you admired once isn't who stands before you now.'

Without realising it, Pietrich had stumbled forwards onto his staff and slowly made his way towards Castellar. He was in a trancelike state, filled with sadness and compelled to give Castellar some peace. He sensed a fermented suffering inside him. If pain could be multiplied by time then Castellar mourned his family by infinity. Moans and concern broke out amongst Castellar's companions and Pietrich raised his hand to touch their leader's head. Lynden gestured for them to remain calm, unsure herself what events were unfolding.

The boy's palm touched the hot, sweaty skin of the older man. They were thrown into a gale that took them away from Port Melees and they flew across the seas, enraptured in a mysterious veil of emotions that belonged to neither one. Suddenly they sat upon a ship that rose and dipped with the tumultuous waves of a storm. There were screams in a cabin below. Castellar reached out to grab the hand of the woman who made them. She smiled at him and said, 'He's coming. Our boy is coming as sure as did the storm.' Castellar cried. He told the woman he loved her and that he missed her. She was confused, as though it was not a memory that he was reliving but as if he had gone back to that day to share the moment of their son's birth with her. He felt the tentacles of time around his arms and legs and he was being pulled away again.

The wooden surface met them with a crash as both Castellar and Pietrich fell to the floor of the ship. They were back inside the docked vessel at Port Melees and the gathering crowd around them rushed to help them to their knees. Pietrich was breathing wildly and held his palm to his pounding head. Castellar could barely talk but desperation forced his mouth to move.

'Forgive me,' he began, 'I spoke out of turn. I never thought such things were possible. Dreams and visions yes. Predictions of what may come to pass, maybe. But to reach through time… I…' Castellar threw his look to Pietrich first and then to Lynden. 'You, who have shown such wisdom, can hardly know the uniqueness of this child. It is not me who should protect him, but he that would protect us.'

## 9

V enom dripped along the edge of two small fangs within the serpent's mouth. The dense, scaly creature appeared like a tree trunk made of rubber. It stretched out its slithering long body and stood high as a human and hissed derision at the man who sat before it. With a sharp snapping motion, it plunged its teeth into the inner thigh of its prey and spat blood upon the rocky cavernous floor. There was no time to be afraid as the venom worked its way into Boscelito's bloodstream. How many times he had endured this ritual he knew not. He ran his fingers across his wounds and counted a dozen puncture marks before giving up the count.

The serpent stood again and hissed, like a cornered cat, as though it was not finished with its target. But Volcan grabbed it by the neck and threw it into a wooden crate, closing the lid tight.

Boscelito leant his head backwards and waited for the hallucinatory rush to take hold of him. His brow furrowed and beads of sweat formed on his hairline, flattening his dark matted mop to his face.

'The venom becomes more effective with each dose,' Volcan claimed. 'I don't get any pleasure from forcing this serpent upon you anymore than you do from receiving its bite.'

'Do you always accompany the truth with a lie?'

'On to the subject of lies and truth again so soon? I thought you had a diverse mind, Boscelito.'

Another bite, this time of words but he felt it more than the serpent's fangs.

'For someone who seems so compelled to know the truth that they harbour a snake with venom to dispel all inhibitions, I rather thought you were fond of the subject.'

Volcan sat himself beside Boscelito and prodded a fire that was burning in the centre of the cave dwelling.

'Fondness, now there is an interesting concept.' Volcan snorted as he spoke. 'Should I do the things that please me more frequently? Or should I do the things that provide for my brothers and sisters, sons and daughters? I show you these things because information is inevitable. I simply wish for you to speed up the process so we can change the course of the war. Before half the lives of the world are lost.'

The warm-up act. The tease of information before the poison was flowing fully through his veins. Boscelito tried to focus, he was losing control of his thoughts. Time for one last rebuke.

'You always did strike me as a do as I say, not as I do kind of man,' he said.

Volcan nodded in agreement. 'Just as well, I suppose. It is somewhat unsustainable to live at the top of a mountain. It requires patience, servitude of others to bring you food and water, and worst of all, solitude. I would not recommend it.'

'And you do it because you enjoy exhausting all those who must climb the thousand steps to visit you?'

Volcan grinned at Boscelito, amused by the diminishing state of the man before him who was now rocking back and forth as though he were a babe in a cot.

'I am too old to descend the mountain,' said Volcan. 'That chance has gone. If I could though, I would not. I would hear less and deafness serves no man who wishes to serve his people.'

There was a murmuring sound outside, coming from a procession of people that had made their way up the mountain. A pilgrimage to seek advice from Volcan. He interrupted his conversation with Boscelito and got up from where he sat, walked outside to greet them, and invited them in. Volcan suggested they form a circle at the edges of the round cave. He bid them remain quiet and still, to listen to all that was to be said.

The procession was made up of twenty or so young men and women. They were students of the farming society at the base of the mountain. Oftentimes these pupils would learn first about agriculture and the importance of a close relationship to nature. Spending their days working the land and sowing seeds for harvest. It was tough work; at times, they were compelled to work eighteen hours a day for weeks on end. Only when they had become proficient in their tasks of harvesting and producing food for the community would they make the climb to speak to Volcan and learn of the world outside of The Vermillion Isles.

It usually took several years for a student to be approved for the pilgrimage as each harvest brought about different lessons. But for the war enduring on the mainland, they were sent up after just twelve months.

Boscelito would be their lesson today. Volcan hoped he would give some insight into the tyrant, Augustus, who was wrecking all the systems that had been in place on the mainland for centuries. What better way to repay the service of those who grew the food that they ate upon this mountain.

'Remind me, you said you sailed to these isles in search of aid? That is what you claim, though your true reasons are disguised beneath those lies, is it not so?' Volcan dived into the interrogation; his audience had lent him arrogance.

Boscelito looked at Volcan through weary eyes. The truth, when not believed, is no ally to a prisoner. He shook his head and shot a look at the proud islander who sat above all of them on his perch.

'I really have no desire to sing the same song each night, but as you insist that I must, I can tell you simply that I was ordered to go in search of allies where no allegiances had yet been made. Seeing as Harmion was thrust into a confused sort of disbursement of treaties and, what you might call betrayals, it seemed shrewd to come to The Vermillion Isles as no others had.'

Volcan studied the man, the story had not changed.

'I know what you're thinking,' Boscelito continued. 'The venom is still not working. But if you are so convinced of its effectiveness at what stage must you doubt your own incertitude.'

'I would suggest simply that you continue for now,' Volcan stated. It sounded more like an instruction than anything else.

'Very well. We knew the risks in coming here of course. Though a vague mystery, the isles are not without their reputation and rumours in the face of unknowingness are useful.'

Boscelito tilted his head back, he felt a heavy flush come over him. 'May I have some water?'

'Of course.' Volcan stood and grabbed a jug from a shelf by a mat that he used for meditation. He placed it down by Boscelito's knees. Poison continued to work its way through the captain's veins.

Boscelito felt a dreary sensation. He glanced about the space and eyed all the students curiously.

'Maybe you should take a vote after class has adjourned, see how many of them believe what they have heard.'

Volcan said nothing. He simply stroked his chin, waiting for the confession to continue. Boscelito spoke again.

'The simple fact is, we have taken so much land and fought so many battles that there are few legions remaining in our army. The array of victories has left many dead in their wake. If the peace alliance knew this as I do, and now you. If they were willing to pick up steel and cut down those in their path who opposed them, they would wipe Augustus from the face of this earth for good. King Elik is sitting upon a hill of certain victory and he doesn't even realise it. Every day that passes, the advantage dwindles. You say you want to save lives. Perhaps you should send word to the young king and tell him to cut down the armies of Augustus.'

Volcan deliberated the information. It was not the first night he'd heard something similar to this. But never had Boscelito delivered the facts so plainly as to carve the birth of a task in his mind. The impression burned away at him like a hot coal. The task was obvious. But was it really true that Augustus had so few forces? Volcan had struggled to reach his ear to the warlord's camp. Should Elik and Castellar join together on either side of the mainland, they could pinch Augustus in the centre. Volcan had heard of the stubbornness of Castellar Dell'Anima many times and knew it was impossible to dissuade him from his peaceful path. Turning such a man to violence in order to carry out the bidding of his brother June, who wanted nothing more than to rid the world of Augustus. Suddenly the solution seemed so simple and yet so impossible to achieve.

'We are aware that King Elik is holed up in his castle to the east of the mainland, trying desperately to find a way to return the world to peace; being tugged in twelve different directions by the elders who make up his council.' Volcan sat himself back down in front of Boscelito, the students listening eagerly to their conversation. 'The king's advisors have warned Elik of an inevitable attack if he does not act. But the young king has held strong to the principle that he will not use his army to attack first, not yet. He dares to find a peaceful resolution to the war over land and power.'

Boscelito laughed at that. 'The war is so much simpler than anyone realises, land and power may be at the heart of it but greed and control are the things all sides are fighting for.'

'Yes, you are right. Yet land is greed, and power is control. They are one and the same. The drought around the eastern river by Elik's stronghold has angered the royal army generals as the cost to secure water for their people has risen beyond any price they have paid before. Their allies are dwindling and no moneylenders will aid them. Still, the young king holds a defensive stance as the royal gold reserves are further depleted. And yet, we are to believe Augustus has fought himself into such a precarious position as to need assistance from us? He truly believed to make allies of Vermillion and yet we could not see it.'

Boscelito nodded, it sounded absurd to hear it spoken aloud. Could it be that Augustus had been so naive?

Volcan studied the man in front of him. He felt no need for further questioning. Maybe the time had come to put an end to the life of the captain. His purpose was spent but that decision would be made by those who lived beneath the mountain.

'Before you are done with me, may I ask a boon of you?'

Boscelito had seen the cogs whirring inside Volcan's head. Their tells were equally apparent to both men after so many weeks alone on the mountain together. If they had played tavern games and gambled with their coin, it might have been high entertainment to watch for an outsider. Volcan nodded to Boscelito, signalling his approval of the request.

'You have your spies, assassins and informants. No doubt spread throughout regions I could not even predict. But most of what you learn comes from a place darker than knowledge handed down by papers or informants and accounts of interrogated travellers. This mountain is no home, not even for a shaman. You said you must remain up here, lest you become deaf to the things you hear. What magic is there in this world that exists up here with you?'

'My dear Boscelito,' Volcan replied. 'It is the oldest magic of them all.'

## 10

Clattering metallic chimes rang throughout an enclosed and damp basement infirmary. Grimy drips fell from an arched brick ceiling and reverberated through the chamber as they splattered against the floor. There was no distinguishing between the moans of the multiple patients that lined the halls. Here squirmed victims of severe illnesses, unmanageable for the most skilled physicians. Those who were brutally wounded and riddled with infection were left unattended. It was a bloody mess.

In the darkest corner, with a drape hung around the palliasse that kept him from the bug infested floor, Tritan lay in a dreamlike state. Bodies came and went, fussing over the black magic that had ravished his arm.

The pestilence he had received in the enchanted forest beyond the borders of Orldin had plagued him for too long. He had anticipated the spreading disease would consume him within two years at the most, though he had outlived that expectation.

The Winter Queen, who remained nameless, had now

administered several doses of her mysterious elixir into his arm. Each with the inexplicable pain that must be endured as it burned through flesh to the bone. Each episode lasted for hours and it was worse than she had warned it would be.

Tritan would rather lose the arm. He had known soldiers to survive the severing of a limb at the point where it met the shoulder. Surely the risk would be worth it? He didn't care anymore. He wasn't a soldier any longer and without that arm he could live a good life. Now, he was just a shadow that was afraid of its own penumbra.

The familiar sound of a razor-sharp scalpel being dropped onto a welded dish echoed through his skull. The bloodstained healer walked around Tritan's immobile body without any sign of concern for his pain. A sterile liquid was used to douse the blade before the healer made his incision across Tritan's useless forearm. A dark pus spilled out. Not blood, but an ominous oily purple viscous liquid. The healer opened out the wound and used a syringe to extract the mucus. He coughed as the smell finally became too much for him to bear.

'Gahh, filthy shit!' said the physician. 'I do not see any progress whatsoever.' He shook his head. He looked through his thick eye glasses at Tritan who stared up at him helplessly.

'If it is all the same to you, you can lose it to the bottom of the river. I don't need it anymore.' Tritan referred to his arm. But the look on the healer's face made him realise that was not an option. He wished he knew the reason why.

'We shall have to endure another afternoon of the elixir. I will make the request for its deliverance.'

'No!' Tritan screamed. 'You mustn't! I… I can't take it any longer. What do you endure as I writhe like a squealing pig? There must be another way.'

'To answer first your question on endurance, I cannot cope with more of your screaming and fussing any more than you can endure the tonic. But I fear there is no alternative to remove this affliction. We both have expectations of us.'

Tritan shook his head at his administrator of pain and pleaded with his watery scarlet eyes. 'Why does she force this? There is no need for it. Tell her I will accept the dismemberment. You have tried and failed. You must accept it.'

The healer dropped his tools and removed the layers of clothing that were caked in the bodily fluids of his patient. Tritan couldn't tell if he had considered his plea or if he was going out for air. But he dreaded his return. Dreaded the elixir that burned through to his bones and tore the rotting flesh from them.

Hours passed by and the choir of the sick sang their song. Out of tune and out of time. It was a sound that would insult any composer. But these were composers of their own death and the tune was a lullaby to send any who could no longer take the pain to an eternal slumber.

Tritan had slept and imagined he would awaken to another round of the dreaded tonic. But he was still alone. The wound on his blackened arm had been cleaned and taped shut. A peculiarity dawned on him then as he rolled his eyes towards his bruised body and saw the unfamiliar pink pigment that was usually a canvas of blue and purple. He couldn't tell if it was pain he felt or a phantom sensation of his past beatings.

Tritan wanted to get up from his stuffed mattress and to walk away from it all. He longed to be reunited with his son in their village and to play amongst the dirt of their farmland. The conversations he had enjoyed with Marilia were faint whispers, dancing in a breeze. Her voice was a comfort. She had always been there to bring him out of his depression; even when he hated her for it, she had stood by him. Now he was truly alone. His mind shook inside the cage that had been forged to shut away his hopes and desires.

The next moment was a voyage into the abyss of hurt that the elixir they used to relinquish the death from his arm caused with each treatment. Several healers crowded around his body and placed their palms calmly on his extremities as the head physician once again injected the fluid into the open incision just below the wrist.

Tritan shook and kicked out his limbs in all directions. He was not so strong or powerful as he had once been; a year in confinement had wasted away his muscular form. But it was nonetheless a struggle to hold him down as the fire burnt through him. The healers rotated in shifts as the hours it took for the tonic to do its work were exhausting. Tritan never let up. He never went still. At one stage he managed to pull his good arm free and launched the back of his fist in the face of one of the healers. The healer staggered backwards, holding their cheek and then, overcome with a fit of rage, lashed out at Tritan where he lay. It made Tritan laugh a sadistic laugh, for what pain could there be beyond the burning that encompassed his entire being. Perhaps it brought some comfort to the man who had thrown the blow. Worth it for spite if nothing else.

Minutes dragged on like years and Tritan imagined himself lying at the base of an execution platform. A stage he had performed on many times in his subconscious. On this occasion he was tied to a stake and surrounded by dried logs. A flame was lit and the stake along with everything around him became an inferno and the fire reached up and kissed him.

Anger flooded through him. It was the first time he had felt the emotion of such hatred since he had been brought to the castle fortress.

He was alone again.

Sleep had taken its turn to hold him prisoner and once again the fading agony slipped away.

But the anger didn't leave him. His plague-filled arm

remained as it had these past weeks of suffering but he felt the rest of his body healing at an unusual rate. He rolled to his side and placed his bare feet on the cold, damp stone. He stood up straight, staggering at first but finding his footing shortly thereafter.

Tritan pulled the drape of his private enclosure aside and stepped into the hallway of rotting passengers, awaiting their voyage to the afterlife. His physician appeared, surprised at the encounter.

'Your ears must be burning, Tritan,' said the man. 'You are going on a journey. But given your destination, you'll want warmer clothes.' Tritan's heart sank. The inference was clear. But why were they moving him? The physician responded as though he could read his mind. 'You'll be going far to the north, our infirmary isn't equipped to deal with you, no matter what potions and ointments are placed in our hands.'

It was settled then. They would be taking him north and in the birth of spring it would be a bitter ride.

'I suppose I will be given a full account of where and why before we leave?' Tritan asked rhetorically.

The healer signalled to the two guards he had brought back to the infirmary with him. They grabbed Tritan and led him up a cobbled stairwell and towards a dark chamber. Here he was dressed in thick woollen clothing, given sturdy boots, forged with a sealant that would see off any residue from the morning dew or flooded pathways they were likely to tread. His headgear was comfort in its immaculate form. He had never known such luxurious versions of base items existed. Certainly, none had been afforded him throughout his war campaigns.

After he was ready, the guards took him down to a courtyard that was lined with flaming torches and beautifully scented by rose bushes that had been shaped to form a centrepiece within the otherwise derelict opening. It was the forecourt to the fortress that had been his home for the long year that had passed.

As the man to his side bellowed orders to a shadowy figure on a distant tier above them, the large wooden gate that had kept him from the outside world began to rise. Tritan felt the fear enter his soul again. He had been institutionalised and within a matter of minutes, forced from his place of healing to the outside world. He did his best to hide the nerves that had grown inside him since his torture had begun.

He was shoved forwards through the wooden gate and a horse-drawn cart arrived to greet him. It was leading a charge of half a dozen horseback riders and a large wooden cart that was pulled by two riderless steeds at the rear.

The door of the cart swung open and Tritan was pushed towards it and, as he approached the candlelit opening, he saw a luxurious interior, lined with soft cushions and a red fabric formed the seating arrangement of the passengers' chamber.

That was the moment he saw his companion for the ride as the Winter Queen bent her head around to peek out and wave him forwards.

'I do hope you will enjoy your new home for the coming weeks. We have a long way to travel and I am too old to ride a horse these days. The cart is slow but it is comfortable I can assure you.'

The Winter Queen welcomed him into the tight abode that they would learn to share. Tritan was in a state of bewilderment. Only one word could he think of and as it tinkered across the bottom of his mouth he allowed it to slip out.

'Why?'

'Ah, yes,' said the Winter Queen. 'A poignant question with so much depth that I feel compelled to respond in kind, naturally.'

She paused and leant forwards to face Tritan, who had been

pushed into the seat opposite her before a guard shut the door, closing them in together. The horses whinnied and the rein master, who rode above the carriage, whipped them into a canter. The procession of hoofs clomping the sodden pathway began and, as they pulled away from the fort entrance, the nameless woman spoke the final words that either of them would utter that night.

'Because I can, Tritan. Because I know where he is. The healer who once saved your life, and will do so once again.'

**11**

---

Restlessness was a kind word for the enduring night that never ended. So much heaviness and confusion had surfaced in River's mind as she tossed and turned in her dingy inn quarters. It was tormenting to dream-feel the comfort of her lover, pressed against her skin, only to awaken and discover the loneliness that was the reality of her present situation. Summer was her comfort in a life of death. She longed to be back by her side.

River sat up and pressed her back gently against the uneven surface of the wall. She tilted her head and took deep breaths to clear her thoughts. But June was always there. Her father always worked his way into her dreams and though she carried out her orders without resentment or judgement of his intentions, she always judged herself for the lives she took and plotted to take. An assassin with a conscience ought not to be so efficient, she thought. She wondered if she'd invented her conscience to avoid living with an evil spirit inside her.

If it wasn't real, she would know it. This was not some trick she played to entice a victim or to convince Summer that she had no regrets for the work she carried out. It was a secret just for her and there need not be lies. Summer had chosen to follow the same path as River. At one time, it had made her proud but now she simply felt concern for how the sweet girl would be irrevocably changed when she would first draw blood.

Trade carts began to bound down the high street and stall workers who had risen early unloaded their produce ready for the morning's market.

River opened her eyes and pulled herself from within her thoughtfulness opening the window to peek out at the town below. The main square was filling up and already quite a crowd had gathered.

She readied herself and packed up all her possessions that tucked neatly into her clothes. She wore a set of loose trousers that billowed around her hips, adequate for hiding her blades. Small incisions had been made in her jerkin and re-stitched to create hidden pockets where she kept her powders and coin.

River always mixed her own powders, all for separate purposes. Some would send their victims to sleep almost instantly, others took their time. A selection of her most lethal powders ended the lives of her victims within minutes though sometimes she would administer more tactful recipes to those who inhaled or digested them and weeks would pass before the effects transported them to the next life.

Leaving hastily, River left a generous tip with the host who waited at the doorway. She scoured the streets for some sign of the beggar but his spot by the street was empty and all his possessions removed.

River asked around for information about the gathering that was due to meet and a trader at the market pointed her in the direction of a talking stage.

It was a small wooden platform that was situated just down from the central square. It could house perhaps three to four people comfortably and there was a pit beneath it where others could gather to listen. Clearly this had been an execution block previously. The posts and nooses had been removed but this was a hangman's galley if River had ever seen one.

Banter carried on throughout the pit where a gathering had congregated. They stood beneath the stage which remained empty. River slid herself seamlessly into the crowd, to observe what would unfold.

There were all sorts of characters in the crowd; port workers, traders, mothers carrying their young on their chests with tied shawls. All ages had come to hear the words of Castellar Dell'Anima. Old and young. Even those who were physically incapable had made the journey from faraway towns. They sat in chairs that had accompanied them on their travels, placed now to the side of the procession.

Standing a few rows in front of River was the beggar she had run into the previous evening. He was stood with a straightened back and was watching the front platform eagerly. He didn't interact with anyone else around him but simply waited there. River suspected him instantly. She moved to within a few feet of where he stood and made sure that he remained in her peripheral vision.

The crowd quietened at last as three people walked onto the platform. There were cries and cheers from the crowd and the three sat themselves upon the platform. They appeared to be officials of the port, no sign of their philosophical leader.

'A warm and pleasant morning to you all,' the host began, a charming smile on her face. 'I have no doubt you are eager to hear from our key speaker so I'll start by covering just one short topic beforehand.'

The crowd listened intently, they were indeed trained well.

'As some of you know, we have the Auctumnus festival taking place towards the end of this week. You'll be welcome to

share your new produce and, of course, the whole purpose is for
us to celebrate and taste the delicious new oils, cultivated in the
hills just outside of the town. I believe some of the olive
pressing will be taking place over the next few days and I
encourage those with children to take them along to see how
the process works. The pressing only comes about once per year
and it is a valuable education.'

The other hosts who she gestured towards nodded their
heads in agreement. There was no reaction from the impatient
crowd.

River slipped away to the side of the gathering, dipped her
finger into her jerkin and watched eagerly. The beggar made his
way forwards as the introduction was concluded and he made
his way up the stairs to the platform. He pulled down his hood
to reveal his face and then the crowd applauded.

'Welcome, Castellar, please, the audience is yours,' said the
host who graciously backed away and let him walk forwards to
address the crowd.

None of them had noticed him standing there amongst
them. Did they ever notice him? River wondered. As he sat
upon the cobbled stone streets, pretending to beg, did his identity remain so easily concealed? He was the eyes of the town
indeed. Keeping watch from within. Castellar had gone up in
her estimation before speaking a word.

'Good day, thank you for your patience, I had some pressing
matters to attend to and so, here we are. I have just a short
consideration to share with you today. It is a kind of story. We
will call it the *King and the Sword.*'

The crowd murmured. Eagerly waiting and fidgeting. River
slid her hand back from the interior of her jerkin. A small
amount of yellow powder rested on her fingertip. Her head
began to hurt and a nauseous feeling entered her stomach. For a
moment, she wondered if she had foolishly eaten something

bad the previous evening. Maybe the water provided at the inn was unclean? She tried to regain her focus.

'As you all well know, we gather here to speak, at the place where lives were once expunged.' Castellar gestured to the stage upon which he stood. 'Rarely would the accused see trial or be considered for fair punishment. The executioner's guilt is not unlike that of an assassin. A king's ignorance to guilt is the arrogance of the gods. There once lived a king, before any of our lifetimes. He was young and born into power before he had come of age. All those who were positioned around him praised him daily and told him he was a divine ruler by birthright.'

The headache crushed River harder, a vicelike grip clutched her brain.

'Impressionable, the king grew up to believe he was more than human,' Castellar continued. 'One day, one of the king's closest advisors, overwhelmed by the audacious exploitation that he suffered each day on the king's account, plotted to reveal the truth of his king's brutal insanity and have power taken from him. The advisor was arrested of course and brought to a stockade, where the king awaited him and offered him the chance to admit his sins.'

*Remove yourself from here at once.*

The voice caused River to spin where she stood. She looked all around her, all eyes faced Castellar. No one had spoken.

'The adviser did admit his plot, but he was an honourable man and truthful, loved by all, and the king was begged to show mercy. The king abruptly silenced the pleas of the crowd and signalled to his executioner to bring his sword down swiftly, decapitating the adviser in an instant.'

Castellar took a pause and walked up and down the stage, keeping his eyes on his feet. He picked up a small sack containing a large fruit and thrust it into the crowd. They staggered back and cried out, as though they imagined the severed head were inside the sack.

*You mustn't do it. It is not the time.*

River panicked. Someone knew her intentions, or at least guessed at them.

'Many years later,' Castellar continued. 'The mourning of the adviser had still not abated and the executioner approached his king and asked him if he felt regret for having taken the life of someone so loved. The king disputed the fact that he had taken any life. For it was of course the executioner who had swung the sword, but the man who now stood before the king shook his head and disputed his own part in the proceedings. Eventually their argument became so fierce that the executioner was killed by the king. The entire castle was thrown into despair. The king went mad, just as the adviser had predicted he would and he eventually became an outcast and was never seen again.'

River had heard enough. She was dizzied by the voice in her head. She had to act fast. She brushed past several of the members of the crowd, picking her target at random.

The voice in her head screamed but the words were indiscernible. She fell forwards and her hand brushed across the lapel of a man who stood transfixed by the sermon.

Too much. Far too much of the powder had come off as she tripped. The man pushed River back to her feet and she humbly dropped her head in shame, making her excuses and slipping past.

Castellar sat on his stage and slowly glanced across the entire crowd. His students were speechless, as they always were.

'Our institutions are designed to create lines in the sand and apply blame at the feet of those who do our bidding. It cannot be that the lies we tell others seem as though truths to ourselves. As love is not a choice, neither is regret or guilt. Why then do we separate ourselves from the responsibilities with which we are bestowed in order to avoid confrontation with guilt? Because that confrontation will come, my friends, and it is the pathway to madness.'

A cry came from within the crowd.

A woman dropped to the floor where her husband had collapsed. Blood poured from his nose and a white foam bubbled in his mouth.

Castellar was ushered off the stage by the hosts who tried to take him away from the commotion, but he pulled himself free, refusing to go. He went to the man and woman on the floor.

'Give me some space, please,' he said.

Castellar rolled the man over and without realising, some of the blood brushed onto his hand and he wiped it on his gown. He tilted back the man's head, trying to open up the airways, but there was too much mucus. He stuck his fingers in the man's mouth and scooped out the frothy bile. The man coughed and his yellow saliva sprayed across Castellar's face.

River had rushed to the edge of the crowd and looked on in horror, a lethal dose. The powder was designed to appear to kill its victim but they would resurface after a long dead sleep. But not with the amount the man had inhaled. And now Castellar was in danger. He had been covered in the poison without knowing it was there. River wasn't sure whether to run now and let the consequences play out as they may. But she hadn't meant to kill. The man was done for, but Castellar may not have been as heavily affected. Could she not leave that to fate? The conscience that complemented the assassin in her forced her into action.

She had to think quickly.

'Murderer, poison!' River screamed, pointing into the crowd.

Within seconds the whole congregation had gone wild,

running in all directions, scattered like autumn leaves in the wind.

River met the look of Castellar and she knew somehow, she had to save him. She grabbed him under the armpit and dragged him away from the crowd, his advisers struggling to cross through the wild townsfolk to his aid.

Castellar's face had gone pale and his breaths were blood fuelled wheezes.

The man behind him was dead, his wife lay by his body crying.

A disaster.

River cursed herself as she pulled Castellar across the main square, all eyes on them, suspicious eyes that caused the market sellers to halt their sales and set their attention on the stumbling duo. They passed the innkeeper, to whom River handed a generous sum, and headed into the corridor. Castellar staggered as River pulled him up the steps and kicked open the door to her room and laid him down on the floor.

He writhed, the white foam at his own mouth now choking him. River guessed she had seconds. Even though it was a second-hand application, the whole pinch of powder was strong enough to attack every part of the lungs and eventually he would drown in his own blood.

She mixed a concoction with a series of crushed seeds and poured the milky substance into a wooden bowl. River dropped to her knees, took a long breath of the substance to protect herself and then held out the bowl in front of Castellar.

'Do not drink this, you must inhale it. It will not be pleasant but you must.'

Castellar was not one to wait for a second instruction under such circumstances. He inhaled the fluid and coughed for dear life as it filled his lungs. He was lathered with sweat.

River threw the bowl to her side out of frustration. Damn

her for being so clumsy and damn the wicked voice in her mind that had caused her to stumble.

A droning sound began to grow outside. She cracked open the window and saw a large crowd had gathered in the streets. This was not a peaceful mob any longer. The innkeeper stood in front of the entrance and prevented the seething group from spilling into her accommodation. She was the only one that separated them from River, unsure if they would turn violent; they were certainly angry for answers.

River did the only thing she knew she could and locked the door to the room and closed the window. An amateur's tactics. But what else was there for her to do? The innkeeper became overwhelmed by the crowd who shoved themselves past her and she was forced to stand aside as they ran into the inn and up the stairs.

River stood staring at the door as the banging intensified and the shouts for answers increased. Her father would see her as a failure. How could they hope to convince Castellar to form an alliance with King Elik now?

Guilt and anger filled her entire being and River wondered if, like the king in the story, madness waited for her, buried and laced with fury in the accusations of the mob who stood just inches from her. She wondered how strong the old wooden door would be should it have to withstand a battering. Insanity was calling for her head and if it broke through to her room it would claim her.

'What have you done? You will kill the boy!'

Darkness. Pain.

'If we do not press him, we will never know what he is truly capable of.'

Blinding light. Too much light.

'If he dies then his ability means nothing. You've endangered his life and ours in the process.'

Thunder. Shouting loud as thunder.

'You who are so bold must know that now is not the time to sleepwalk our way into whatever future the boy allows us to have.'

Peace, a moment's peace. Never long enough.

'You overthink his position. He is not a god.'

Water. Give water… 'Please give me water,' Pietrich finally mustered the strength to speak through dry and cracked lips. Everything around him was moving. He was surrounded by the sound of boots clomping on timber. They were aboard Castellar's ship, but the sound of gulls cawing overhead suggested they were still docked at the port.

'Pietrich,' Lynden cried out, relieved. 'Here drink this.'

She passed him a canteen filled to the brim. A few seconds later it was empty. Pietrich lay his head back and rested it on the pillow they had placed under him when he had collapsed.

'I'm so sorry, we will not force you to do anything like that again.'

Lynden took a damp cloth and ran it across Pietrich's brow. Despite the fact he was blind, his eyes were rolling around in his head. As if he didn't have the strength to keep them still. He tried to move his arms but they wouldn't respond.

'Am I paralysed?' he asked.

'No, I should not think so, lad. Just rest for a while,' Castellar said. He was offered a look of derision in return. Lynden held her gaze on him. He calmed his response.

'I am sorry it was hard on him, but you must understand, if he can transcend communication across the landscape of time, it is something we cannot simply wait to discover by accident. The magic that runs through his veins is of the Primavemani, the first humans who walked the land, descended from creatures of the sea.'

'I know who the Primavemani were,' Lynden retorted, 'and I know full well the magic you speak of. Even now as it dwindles into extinction, it was never credited to the transcendence of time. Pietrich suffers dreams, and yes, sometimes they are as if a prophesy, but until we know for sure we must treat him kindly and tread with soft shoes. If you know as much as you think you do, you ought to realise that it is a magic that passes memories from ancestors to its bearer. I understand your pain from suffering a loss, and I do not doubt that the memory of your wife invoked a dormant ambition, but we can't exploit the boy.'

Castellar pondered for a moment. He knew he must choose his words wisely.

'It was no memory; memories do not react to our external gaze. I believe Pietrich is a descendant of The Vermillion Isles. Perhaps when this fussing is over, you will agree at least that we should set a course for the islands and see what we can learn. The Audacia, where we now stand, is a working ship and it was built for war; she was in fact a vessel of the Vermillion armada for a time. We can ready her for departure almost instantly.'

'The isles have never been beached. The last effort to try and do so was led by a battalion of Augustus' army and none returned alive. I don't see how venturing to such a place will do us any favours.'

'If you once saw value in my words, as you claim, you must trust me, Lynden. I understand you have cared for the boy for so long that he means more to you perhaps than the things he represents, but without the daring that you have yourself shown in these last days, we cannot progress.'

Lynden knew he was right, but it was the wrong time to have this debate. Her concern was for Pietrich and she resented turning her attention away from him to indulge in this discussion.

'I want everyone to leave this cabin at once. If you will respect an elderly lady's request, you may in fact find her more open to fanciful ideas, risky or otherwise, later tonight.'

'We have much to learn of one another, you and I,' Castellar responded. 'You are among the very best of people, Lynden. I have full respect for you and what you have achieved this past year. Eventually you will see, as I do, that we will not be the ones making the decisions. Again, I wish not to have caused you anguish. For that I apologise a final time before I leave you. We will all leave you in peace now.'

Castellar gestured to all those who stood as audience. Grace and Olafur led by example, having said not a word, but digesting many. Eventually the whole room was empty, aside from Castellar who nodded at Pietrich out of respect, although the boy was unaware. Castellar threw a mild salute towards Lynden. The look on her face suggested she was finally calming and appreciated his departure and so Castellar turned and climbed the cabin stairwell to the upper deck, leaving the companions alone.

'Rest, Pietrich. It is just you and me here now,' said Lynden. 'We will give you your space. Are you comfortable?'

'Yes, I mean, I think so.'

Lynden threw the damp cloth into a metal dish.

'At least your temperature has dropped. Do you remember what happened?'

'There was a crowd, a large gathering. I heard them all shuffling around. I could smell the air. But something was wrong, the port was cleaner, filled with people. Someone was there, trying to undermine Castellar's peace. She heard me. Castellar was so much younger and the townsfolk spoke about the war as though it had only just begun.'

Lynden offered him more water. It was sometimes hard to know what to say to Pietrich after he suffered one of his dreams.

'Castellar had no right to ask you to dive into a dream. I don't know what happened to him when you touched him, but... Whatever he believes, you cannot let him bully you to believe it too. Do you promise me?'

'Yes, although, you wanted to find him, didn't you? You believed he was alive. You were right, and now we've found him you do not want to listen to his advice?'

'I do not want you to suffer, Pietrich. I, of course, agree that there is something special about you. But I care more for the boy than the power he possesses.'

'And if you could trade my life, to save a thousand others, what then?' he asked.

Lynden fell into sad reflection; she didn't know if she felt ashamed or afraid of the question.

'Pietrich, my boy. That is not a question I will ever justify with an answer and I hope you will never burden me by asking it again. Would you pose such a query at the hands of your mother, knowing the poisonous well that you would be plunging her into?'

Pietrich fell silent, deep in thought. Ashamed and confused.

'Forgive me, it is hard sometimes, not to think such foolish things.'

'We all have these wicked thoughts that plague us, it is what makes us human. As does the protection we offer each other from them.'

Lynden ruffled his hair reassuringly, hoping the lesson had been well taught.

Pietrich felt the fading warmth through the porthole where the sun was setting. He imagined a purple crest cast on the horizon. All he wanted to do was sleep but the pressure of his life was growing with each passing hour and suddenly he didn't have time to sleep. It was now an inconvenience that would prevent him from his higher purpose. He sat up, determined not to drift into a slumber.

'Lynden, if there is any chance that the voices I hear are from another time, that they can hear me too, does that mean I could change the course of things?'

Lynden leant back. Castellar had certainly set him off on a path that he would not turn back from now. She hated him for it. Though she hated herself too, for deep down she knew that if there were any chance it were true, they had to find out somehow.

'I believe you will change the course of things. This world needs you, and you need your rest.'

Lynden passed him a blanket and wrapped it over him. He

was lying on a soft palliasse in the corner of Castellar's cabin but Lynden promised him he would not be disturbed for a while. She left him as his rolled onto his side and fell into a rare, peaceful sleep.

Pietrich dreamed an autumn dream. He was back in his village chasing Eira around the farmland. The local villagers were cursing them for trampling on the sown fields. But they were carefree and they laughed so hard it hurt them in the pits of their stomachs. It was another time. The joy was so unfamiliar it didn't feel like it could have ever happened. The dream was short-lived. Pietrich had not slept long. When he awoke, he was still alone but he could sense that the light of day had dwindled.

Pietrich wanted to go back to his dream. Always the dreams that bring such joy are over faster than a heartbeat. He wondered how Eira was coping in Knighton. He knew she would be well and probably had met a boy she liked by now. She was his oldest friend. The idea of her finding comfort in the company of another boy troubled him greatly.

Pietrich had asked Lynden several times if they could call back at the village to visit Eira and his mother. But they never did for it was too dangerous.

Marilia had agreed to keep an eye on Eira and though it brought Pietrich much happiness to hear the pledge, he believed that it was his mother who needed looking after. He had left her alone, the way his father had throughout the war. She didn't deserve that.

Before he could think more of his mother, the world shook as though there were an earthquake.

A loud explosion sounded outside.

The entire ship shuddered to its core and Pietrich was thrust towards a cabinet. The glass doors swung open and a dozen books fell onto him.

The crew above screamed.

Pietrich worried first for Lynden, but Grace and Olafur were also above. He tried to focus his hearing but another explosion came. This time it was further away and whatever caused it had missed the ship.

Pietrich regained his strength and stumbled to the porthole, knocking his staff against the wall to find the opening. He sensed flickering burning light coming from the dockyard. Footsteps and the sound of swords clattering rang out above a series of aggressive shouts and cries.

How many were there? He knew from their arrival that Castellar oversaw sixteen, perhaps seventeen followers. That made twenty aboard the ship. But the sound tormenting him was of no less than one hundred pairs of boots kicking up the dirt.

Pietrich staggered backwards and swung his staff around in a wide circle, trying to find the steep wooden stairwell that led to the Audacia's deck.

He smacked his shoulder against the side of the staircase.

Another set of screams came from the docks. This time it was the sound of horses. Was Luna safe? He feared for his white steed. They had left the stallions tied on land.

A third explosion.

This one burst through the cabin. A flaming ball of metal, wrapped in straw, doused in oil. It missed Pietrich by a matter of inches and he fell back to the floor as the hatch above him burst open and three men came running down with buckets of water to extinguish the flames.

Pietrich grabbed the ladder; he could feel the heat of the flames on his face. Clutching his staff, he barged open with his shoulder the hatch that had fallen shut.

Falling to the deck, he heard panicked voices all around him.

They were preparing the ship to sail. He could not discern any of the voices of his companions.

The sound of a sword entering the body of a human was wet and harsh. He had never paid attention to it before. It was like dragging ripe fruit across a coarse stone. Pietrich shuddered as he heard the dreaded resonance.

Clutching at the main rail overlooking the port as the ship rocked, Pietrich faced the ensuing battle, praying for some sound to guide him. He had to find them. He calmed his nerves. An arrow flew beside him and struck the deck behind but still he held true.

*Release the horses, quickly. We must get them aboard.*

It was Lynden. The voice had come from within the stable to the farthest point of the port where they had left the steeds.

*We have to get back to Pietrich. The ship is alight!*

Olafur had spoken next.

*The ship is our only chance to flee.*

Now it was Grace who spoke. They were all alive. He had to keep it that way. Pietrich reached out to them. All at once he spoke to his friends.

*I am alive. Come quickly, bring the horses!*

The three shared a moment of shock. He had never spoken to any of them this way before. But they understood it immediately and Lynden left Grace and Olafur to lead the horses to the jetty as she ran back to the ship, heavy footed and slow. She ran across the docks as metal met metal. She was an easy target.

All time slowed to nothing.

The bowstring tightened. A twang sent the arrow flying across the battlefield. Blood ran through the cracks of the cobbled landscape as if streams of an estuary.

*Get down!*

But Lynden was too slow and she only had time to turn her gaze to the shaft that was propelling towards her head.

She felt a shove on her shoulders. An invisible giant pressed her into the ground. It hurt, but the arrow sung its song above her, whispering its contempt for having missed its target.

Turning around to face the one who had saved her, Lynden was met with shock for she was alone. She didn't understand it but she didn't have time to waste on contemplation. She carried on towards the ship.

Pietrich felt the tentacles of his life force growing from within. They reached out and touched all of those who were fighting. All those who were running. The archers on the hills. Castellar's men who were fleeing to the ship.

He sensed his wolf hiding in an abandoned building on land, he willed Jack to come to him but the wolf remained cold to the instruction, a wise and cautious creature. Castellar was leading those who retreated to safety upon the vessel but as more fighters fled the onslaught, their attackers made ground and approached the pier, ready to bring down their steel on their victims aboard the Audacia.

A crack in the sky opened and lightning struck the sea beyond the horizon. Thunderous catastrophe echoed across the port as the sea became a mountain. A fluid mountain that grew and tormented the peasant lifeforms that existed beneath its stare.

The rising wave approached the port, twice the height of the ship. All who fought staggered in the shadow of the sweeping monsoon of the sky that fell towards them. Some fell still, others ran. A feeble effort for what was to come.

The wave crashed across the top of the ship, extinguishing all that burned. But the ship remained unmoved and its crew untouched. Those who were with Castellar continued to board and braced themselves to be swept away, but they too remained untouched.

For those who were against the humble crew, Castellar's

sixteen and Pietrich's few, the same could not be said, as the wave crashed down upon them like rocks and crushed them into the earth. The archers were swept off the cliff edge where they stood and fell to their demise on the hard, cobbled streets below.

The tidal force passed and of the hundred lives that had threatened them, Pietrich could now sense only a clutch of confused, bitter, dwindling swordsmen.

'Get on board now!'

It was Castellar who broke the stunned silence. The confusion was hard for all to bear but the threat was not completely removed.

Olafur and Grace clambered aboard and led the horses to the lower deck's stable.

Castellar's crew pulled the panel shut that locked the entrance to the ship and the anchor was fully retracted. By the time those who had survived the arcuatus surge realised what was happening, the ship was pulling away from port. The dumbfounded group of sword bearers watched from the jetty, as the Audacia disappeared further into the distance.

'Pietrich!' Lynden shouted, panic-stricken for he was nowhere to be seen. 'We must find him, is he aboard?'

'I saw him standing on the deck, facing out to the docks.'

It was one of Castellar's crew who offered the insight.

'Where is he? What happened?' Lynden asked sternly.

The man shook his head. 'I do not know. The wave came and it was as though he was guiding it with his hands. I'm sorry. I looked away for I thought it was real. I mean, I don't understand why we aren't all dead. But then the wave was gone and when I looked back he was no longer there.'

Lynden ran to the spot where the man had seen Pietrich. Castellar, Grace and Olafur joined her and they looked for any sign of him.

'We have to go back; if he's not aboard then he'll be all alone on land,' Grace demanded of Castellar.

'If he is still alive, sailing back into port won't help us. We have lost half of our crew already thanks to whoever tracked you to us.' A foolish apportionment of blame, Castellar regretted it immediately before he continued. 'If they have but one archer remaining they would pick us off individually before we even reach the pier. Then how could we help Pietrich if we are all dead?'

Lynden stepped forwards and slapped Castellar so hard it hurt her hand. But her pride was wounded more. Never before had she lashed out at someone. Her face grew scarlet, as though she herself had received the blow.

'I'm sorry, but that wasn't for me, that was for Pietrich.'

Castellar held his cheek; it stung immensely, but he didn't begrudge her for it. Lynden addressed all who stood aboard the ship. 'What just happened, you must realise, all of you, is that Pietrich saved us from that onslaught. I am sorry for the losses you have suffered and I will help you to grieve for those who died ashore. But we cannot abandon the boy.'

'You're right,' Castellar replied. 'But we cannot help him by leading ourselves directly into the path of arrows. We will sail a few leagues upland and double back to find him. We must be subtle and sly.'

Lynden looked around her and saw the dejected looks of those who had lost their friends, in some cases their loved ones.

'If you think it the best course, I will not disagree.' She would trust this man on tactics for she was no fighter or scout. He nodded and Lynden continued. 'Very well, whatever aid you need from us, Castellar, we are at your service, but we must be swift.'

Castellar signalled for those of his crew who remained to return to their posts.

'There is a shallow river, about an hour's sailing inland once we reach the estuary,' said Castellar. 'We should be able to bring the Audacia towards the road that loops behind Port Melees if the tides favour us. But we'll have to send a search party out after Pietrich on horseback whilst the rest of us make the journey on foot. It will take too long for us to make the trek together. But be warned, when the tide changes the ship will get stuck upon the sand.'

'The smaller the crew the better, and we'll worry about freeing the ship from sand another time,' Lynden replied, encouraged at the idea of as small a party as possible, still uncomfortable with the new company they kept. 'We are not efficient at fighting and we would be best served to remain hidden if we can. We must pray that Pietrich has taken himself somewhere discreet and that we find him first.'

'Oh no, wait. Look here,' Grace signalled to the wooden railing of the ship. 'It looks as though he has scrawled a note into the wood.'

They gathered around to read the roughly etched message. It read;

~Do not come for me, I endanger you all. Grant me solitude. P~

There were no words for them in that moment. None to be spoken nor either to be thought.

When a loved one passes away or is taken from those who are not ready to be left, anger and sorrow become prevalent. But a conscious decision to leave them, for fear of endangerment, is a cruel pain and there is no relief from the hurt of the magnitude of abandonment.

They all felt responsible for the boy, but he had chosen to leave them. For what purpose, other than to protect them perhaps?

They had failed him. All felt as though they had failed him.

None of their eyes met but Lynden caught a glimpse of a small knife that had been discarded on the floor. She knelt down and saw it was the hilt blade of Pietrich's staff that he had used to carve the note. The staff itself lay by its side. He had abandoned that too.

## 13

I t had been a long and hurtful journey to Baurticeford. Too much time to think about the past. For several weeks they had ridden from Fort Vecchia, the old castle buried to the far east of Harmion. Tritan had recognised the fort as a new renovation of the old royal castle which hadn't been occupied for most of the war. He never bore witness to his own arrival on the day he had been captured. Or at least, the day he had allowed himself to be caught, but some of the hallways he had seen were at least a thousand years old. King Elik had occupied the castle during the final years of his reign. He had made it a haven for the populace and the outer walls were near impossible to breach.

It was the toughest decision Tritan had ever made, to give himself up, but deep down he knew the only way he could protect his family and the village where they lived was to stage his own capture. His family had all wondered who had eventually revealed his whereabouts. But he couldn't sit back and wait for the soldiers of this new army to claim him in Knighton, putting Pietrich at risk. Especially after word began to spread about how the boy had survived such a terrible condition. Rumours spread like plagues and truth no longer withstands the battering of false accusation. There is no worse frustration than watching lies become common knowledge whilst you cling to a singular reality as it evaporates into the air. The only way Tritan could fight it was to spread his own mistruths. None of it mattered now, for Tritan had made his decision and he stood by it.

He'd never been the most intellectual member of his legion but this plan had come together perfectly. He amused himself that a ruse to get captured without anyone knowing he was the instigator of his own fate went smoother than many of the campaigns he had led throughout the war when it had been others who were due to suffer. A simple irony.

Fritz had been in on it from the beginning and played down his old friendship to the captain in order that it would seem as though Lynden had handpicked him herself. Lynden had been sought out by her brother, Jonah; her old connection to the last king gave her a drive to set things to rights, though it had been curious to Tritan how willing she was and how much she seemed to already know about his son. Fritz had made himself known to her in other ways so it would be her idea that he would be brought into their small crew.

It was a tricky web constructed through a series of lies and loyalty lent to him from his mercenary alliances. He had staged an event that was intended to be a launch of a new business venture under a false alias as a shipping recruiter. Tritan had learnt enough about ships as a deckhand on various missions and though his title as captain had never extended to the high seas, he knew enough to be a credible agent.

He thought back to the time he had conceived the idea and put it in motion. The complexity overwhelmed him even now. Fooling one such as Lynden was no mean feat. Regardless, when all was said and done, the result would be suffering and he had suffered. But if his boy was safe, and Marilia was safe too, then it was worth it.

Tritan had waited until he was sure he only had months left to live before firing the arrow of his demise. The region he had travelled to, Verdant, was dominated by merchants and shipping channels, due to the wide and deep estuaries that ran into the south-eastern seas. He relied on gossip to spread news of his new venture, and, as any who worked the shipping lanes knew, gossip carried with the tides and the coastal winds as though it were whitewash and pollen.

Those final months had passed by and somehow his body had clung on. Fully intent on succumbing to his ailments as a captive, Tritan had been disappointed by his own strength. For a full year, he had tolerated the beatings of his captors, learning nothing of who they were. Now, as he was dragged north, he sat affront the leader of the army that had hunted him. She had been revealed to him at a time of her suiting, after much speculation that she were in fact a young boy descendent of the lost royal lines. But those rumours were quashed. No royal descendent lived after Augustus had ordered the massacre of the family's remnants. The royals and their heirs, down to every bastard who may hold a claim to the throne, and even the councillors who worked for them. In that regicide, Tritan had played his part. Another irony that Lynden, one of the surviving few who had escaped, now protected the son of the man who had been sent to kill her.

Winter had emerged as neither young nor a royal prince. It was still a mystery how she had taken charge over so much land and so many soldiers. How had she come to occupy the old castle and instruct an entire settlement to her will?

Tritan lost himself in a deep well of wonderment, he no longer knew whether he had judged the situation well at all.

Such a spiral of confusion and doubt. *Stick to the sword that saves you*, he thought. But his sword was lost to him, as was the arm that wielded it. The spirits in the land of Orldin had taken it from him. He deserved it, he knew, but the dead flesh that now spread from his fingertips to his shoulder was a constant reminder of all those wives he had widowed.

As the cart rolled over a cluster of hills and rose above the frosty mist, Baurticeford came into view. The town sat proudly at the base of the river that ran beneath where adjoining sides of the valley met.

Tritan noticed that its inhabitants had done well to renovate Baurticeford since the flooding several years earlier when he'd last set foot in the town. They had built high flood defences along the river and at the top of the town, there was a new drainage system in place to combat even the heaviest deluge. He hadn't wanted to come here all those years ago, to conspire to ruin the farming trade, and he certainly didn't want to be here now.

A horseback rider came up the valley through the mist towards the carriage and pulled alongside the open window where Winter sat, admiring the view.

'Ma'am, we have word that the treatment is working, there is more to be done for he has a strong mind, but the healer believes that with a couple more weeks you'll have what you need.'

Winter raised her brow and contemplated her response. Two weeks was too long.

'Are you saying he is not ready to be trialled? I think a show of progress would do wonders to determine if we can upscale the process imminently. I wouldn't want to disappoint our new guest.'

The rider gulped, he had expected such a reply.

'Well, it is not advised, dare I say. But should you wish, I am sure we can perhaps arrange a small demonstration tomorrow?'

Winter waved her arm at the man, disputing his pessimism.

'Nonsense, what is your name, sir?'

'Troy, ma'am,' he responded, discomforted by the title of *sir* she had bestowed upon him.

'Well, Troy, we will do the test immediately.' She scowled at the rider, the instruction was clear. 'Ride back to the healer's abode and bring him forth with his creation. Meet us by the walking fields along the riverbank, and bring two of your bluntest swords. Do not delay, young man, our caravan is not so slow as you might think.'

The rider nodded and with no need for further instruction, he rode back down the lane towards the town. Winter knocked her fist against the inside of the carriage wall and the driver above yelled out to the horses, whipping his reins and they sped along, causing the carriage to bump uncomfortably.

'How is your arm?' she asked Tritan.

He looked at it, black as night, useless as mud. 'If lack of spreading is progress then it has progressed.'

She shook her head, agitated.

'Dammit. It should be receding by now, and the movement? Try to grip my hand.'

Tritan flinched. Was this a kind of trick? It had occurred to him that not only had she risked riding alongside him all this time, but she now held out her hand as if he were a servant boy who would be pleasured at the opportunity. But he knew he had no violence in him. Winter knew it too.

Tritan reached out to take her gloved hand and attempted to squeeze his own blackened one around it, but he was barely able to create a claw.

She sighed, disappointed. 'Very well.'

That was all Winter offered as she pulled away her hand and turned back to the view from her window.

The cart drew closer to the town and as the travelling party approached the main street, it diverted along the river pathway that led to the walking fields. Her man was there, awaiting their arrival eagerly; he had been swift indeed. But the healer was nowhere to be seen.

Cool air blew from the rushing river that bellowed its loud charge from the cascading waters beside them. Winter withdrew from the cart and directed that the supplies and her consort were to head to her hired quarters at the top of town. She had rented out a large estate that overlooked the entire valley. It had once been home to one of the richest landowners of Baurticeford of the Qualchaid family but after the father of three had died in the war, along with his two sons, his only daughter, Resonance, had taken charge of it as a retreat for guests. Resonance Qualchaid was as shrewd as any businesswoman or man in the northern region, or indeed all of Harmion. Her business was accommodation and she made a point of befriending all her clients. Winter was no exception and preparation for a fine evening's meal would be underway, awaiting her arrival.

'Food will come after work,' she had told her companions as they left her alone with Tritan and Troy.

Chilled winds and rushing water were the only sounds that dispelled the awkwardness of the silence. Troy was a nervous man and in the presence of a famous warrior such as Tritan and his cold and mysterious mistress, he was completely at a loss.

Troy fumbled with the blunted blades that had been requested and let one slip, sending it clattering to the floor. He picked it up instantly as heat grew inside him and flooded his face. He bowed his head in shame as Winter cast a disturbed look at the fool. Tritan was once again a passenger on someone else's journey, a blunt a tool as the swords that had pricked his interest.

'How long will he keep me waiting?' Winter demanded of Troy.

'I… I don't know, ma'am. I explained that it was urgent. But he was flustered. He said he is ill prepared.'

'Pathetic.' She spat the word into the air. 'Time for preparation is never a luxury in war.' Winter looked Tritan up and down. 'Perhaps that is something you can teach your old friend.'

The moment Tritan had dreaded came next, as Thomas came plodding down the hill. The man who had saved his life, and in return Tritan had stolen his betrothed. Both men acted as though the other were not there. Let the past be buried deeper than spite or knowledge. But it was impossible for either of them to forget; they would have to dig with the shovels of ignorance yet.

Tritan felt a loathing sensation come over him, but was it for himself or for the healer? He could not tell. They were both Winter's captives, that much was clear. Time had not been kind to Thomas. Tritan recognised the look in his bloodshot eyes. He was a drunk, maybe not today, but the man had spent the years since he left Knighton at the bottom of a bottle.

Thomas bowed his head as he spoke. 'Winter, please accept my apologies, I was—'

'Unprepared,' she interrupted. 'Yes I am aware.'

Standing behind Thomas was a hooded man, with three guards holding him still. He stood tall and strong as Winter walked over to inspect the specimen.

She whipped off the hood and the sullen face hammered a seasoned fear into Tritan's heart as his dear Fritz stood as though a theatre-piece. Fritz looked directly ahead as if oblivious to everything that was happening around him.

'He seems, dim-witted,' Winter said, somewhat accusingly.

'It is possible that the dose was too high. When he woke after the last administration he couldn't recall his name.' Thomas walked around Fritz as he explained the new characteristics of his subject as though it were a patient on his autopsy table. 'What I have observed is that the level of impressionability comes at the price of long-term memory. It is there somewhere, buried deep but I think in the case of Fritz, we have burned out the things that made him who he was.'

Fritz continued to glare forwards, offering an unknowing look at Tritan. There was no recognition in his eyes and as drool slipped down the side of his mouth, Tritan felt a tear forming in the base of his eye. He was attending a funeral for the man he once knew, who had died in the operating theatre here in Baurticeford. He didn't know what creature now resided in the body of his old mercenary friend.

'You have made him dumb, look at him drooling!' Winter shouted in an accusatory tone at Thomas.

'We still have work to be done, he can still speak and understand everything we say perfectly well. He just needs pulling out of his mind.'

Winter turned to face Troy. She held out her hand as if he would know what she wanted.

'The swords, Troy, hand me the swords.' Her frustration was growing. She was surrounded by idiots.

Troy ran to her and passed her the blades. She passed one to Thomas and then glided over to Tritan with an air of curiosity. She had been waiting for this test for some time and finally the spectacle was about to begin. She offered him the hilt. He simply shook his head and stepped backwards.

'Thomas,' she called out behind her, not removing her stare from Tritan for a moment. 'Give Fritz his sword, tell him to kill this man.'

Winter stepped to the side and threw the spare sword to the

floor. She had asked for the bluntest swords, but there was sharpness enough in them to take a life.

Thomas did as he was instructed and whispered in Fritz's ear. Fritz snatched the sword out of Thomas's hand and took a soldier's stance. Some things he had not forgotten.

Tritan remained dumbfounded, the blade at his feet calling to him, but he did not want it, nor could he yield it the way he once had.

Fritz ran towards him screaming, holding he sword high above his head, readying to strike a killing blow.

'Fritz, no!'

Tritan screamed with all the power of his lungs but to Fritz it was as if the man had screamed a war cry and he met it with his own, bringing the sword down fast and hard.

Tritan lunged low and forwards at the last second, forcing the blade over his head but taking the hilt on the top of his skull. It broke the skin above his crown and blood spewed out across the once green grass as it turned a scarlet shade.

Fritz twisted his hips to bring about the blade in a swift motion and it caught Tritan in the back. He yelled a cry of pain, blinded by the blood that had oozed into his eye. The large winter coat he had been gifted for the cold journey was the only thing that had stopped the dull blade from breaking the skin on his back. But the weight of the blade bruised the lower part of Tritan's spine and he rolled in agony to the floor.

Relentless were the attacks of Fritz, the monster, who brought his boot into Tritan's face before swinging his blade once more. Tritan managed to catch the sword between the thick material of his jacket, beneath his armpit. Fritz pulled out the sword, slicing through some of the leather layer. A sharper blade would have taken an arm off.

Tritan dived onto the elbow of his ruined arm and reached out for the spare blade before him.

Winter allowed herself a wry smile. Thomas himself was impressed at the performance of his patient. But Tritan was a wasted version of his former self. Thomas had not seen him for some years and the hulking form that used to intimidate him was now diminished. He was slower, skinnier and one arm was useless. Thomas considered the weight of the task that Winter had set him. She had warned him that he had months of hard work ahead but as he now watched the muted performance of the once legendary soldier, Thomas dreaded the impossible mission set before him, more so perhaps than replacing the man's insides during the war.

A loud clang rang out as the two swords met and nearly deafened the group. Tritan was back on his feet and, yielding the heavy sword with the arm that still worked, he swung furiously, deflecting the blows that Fritz threw at him.

A loud cracking sound accompanied the metallic clanging. An upward thrust into Fritz's head from out of nowhere had turned the tides. Fritz staggered backwards and checked his nose which had slid from one side of his face to the other. Blood streamed down his mouth and chin and his eyes were wild as fire.

Tritan wiped his forehead, soaked with Fritz's blood, and he fell sideways.

He threw the sword down in front of Fritz and looked up at the unwavering fury in his stare.

Tritan coughed, dizzy and afraid. He shivered where he knelt.

'Fritz, this is not us. It is not us. What have they done to you, lad?'

Winter leant in to whisper in Thomas's ear. 'Why has he stopped?'

Thomas had no answer, other than the one he dared not speak. It was obvious to him he still needed time to work.

Fritz stepped towards Tritan where he crouched before him. He dropped his sword down to his side and held out his hand, the fury in his eyes turning to love. Tritan took his arm and stood. The two men stared hard into each other's gaze and Tritan did his best to find the soul of the man beneath those confused brown eyes. It was there somewhere, hidden beneath the madness.

With a swift interruption, the hood was replaced over Fritz's bloodied head and three guards led him away. Thomas made a brief apology to Winter and left with his guards and Fritz to return to his clinic.

'Right, well. That was exhausting. It must be time to eat.'

Winter said the words as if everything she had seen had gone exactly to plan. Tritan had given up trying to understand her and instead focused his mind on the fresh hurt he had been dealt.

'You'd better wash-up before dinner,' she continued. 'I don't think Resonance would appreciate you attending the table in that state.' Winter mocked Tritan with her words. It was her way to rise above the failure of her test he was sure. 'Troy, please show our man to his quarters and make sure the servants are ready with his bath.

'Baths and fancy dining, what is this? Are you falling into madness? Or is it I who imagines these things?' Tritan asked. 'Did I die and now I am mocked with comfort in death?'

'Tritan, my boy, I need you strong and clean. Tonight, we will pour lava into your veins.'

## 14

River wanted to flee the room as the incessant banging continued. First she had to make sure Castellar was no longer in danger. When they had made it back to the room he was barely breathing but her milky elixir was doing its job. The very fact that he was coughing and his brow furrowed incredulously was evidence that perhaps, he was departing from mortal danger.

She had to be certain, this mess could get no worse for if Castellar died then all his work would be undone and the port would descend once more into violence and despair. It was bad enough that she had faltered and left an innocent man dead in the street with his wife crying over his cold body.

At times, River despised her work, but her victims were usually corrupt leaders or plotters. Where needed, she would rock the boat and stir up a mess, but in this instance, she was only meant to test the resolve of Castellar and his followers. Her usual prey, their deaths, she told herself, always brought about a peaceful resolution. Though there was no excuse for

what she had done by the market square today. She would have
to bear that for as long as she lived.

Shouting continued to pass through the wooden door and
her fear for the safety of those who stood outside in the hallway
rose with each second that passed. They were just a mob of
tradesfolk and angry disciples. If they attacked her she would
have to retaliate and Port Melees would be home to a massacre.

Castellar rolled onto his knees and retched up a pint of
phlegm, blood and yellow viscous fluid. The smell was putrid.
But he was out of harm's way.

'Can you breathe?' River asked.

'Yes, just about.'

River helped him onto the bed that lay untouched in the
centre of the room. Castellar couldn't help but notice she had
put her sheets on the floor in the corner of the room before he
perched on the bare mattress.

'The man you killed,' he spluttered. 'He was the eldest son
of one of the longest standing merchant families in Port Melees.
He was a good teacher and one of those I relied upon to keep us
from reverting to a place of anarchy. I fear I do not know what
they will do when they decide to break down that door.'

The banging seemed louder after he had spoken. River
wasn't sure if she imagined it but the hinges seemed now to
vibrate as though a great force were pushing against them.

'Can you calm them? Maybe if you spoke to them from in
here.' River knew it was a bad idea before she had even
suggested it.

'And what would I say? Some inspirational sermon to
appease their anger? No. Many do not realise that this peace has
been built by an arrangement of fair trade legislation that we
extend also to our neighbours and foreign merchants. You
would call it more of a treaty than a peace settlement.'

'But you led a march, where those who walked by your side

were stoned from the streets by the former occupants of the port before they abandoned it.'

Castellar raised his head and nodded. 'Ah yes, we were lucky that no one died that afternoon. Many were severely injured of course. But the real reason they left is we priced them out of the market. Coin is the best negotiator of peace, not the words of some rambling man.'

River took a chair from a small desk across the room and wedged it under the door to enforce the barricade. She began to tie her long, dark hair into a top knot that fitted beneath a small cap.

'There is more to it than that,' she insisted. 'The way you spoke to them in the square. You made them think about their own humanity and I only wonder if you leave yourselves open to invasion by insisting you will not respond with violence. That man wasn't meant to die. I only wanted to create a show to see how you would react. He would have been fine if it were not for...'

Castellar awaited the end of her sentence. It didn't come.

'For what?'

'Nothing, never mind. I am confused by your approach is all. I want to understand it.'

'If you tasted the finest wine you'd ever tasted. Put bread in your mouth, infused with olive oil and natural salts of such delicacy that you felt a surge of pleasure like no other. If you ate fresh roasted vegetables that gave you strength and melted in your mouth like butter. Would you kill those who made such delicacies, only to steal the land where they grow them, knowing full well that you would never learn the secret of their process?'

River was a shrewd woman; she knew a hidden meaning when she heard one. Her frown told Castellar as much.

'Of course,' he continued, 'if you yourself are a producer of such goods, jealousy and diminishing profits can cause an uprising. So, we must appease those concerns.'

'You mean you pay those who would otherwise attack you? You're funding the war campaigns of others to keep your little haven secure.'

The penny dropped. River didn't know if she was satisfied or disgusted with the resolution.

Time was slipping away. She took off her dark jacket and turned it inside out. The inside was sewn with a light tan colour and it appeared baggier than it once had. Castellar turned his head as she removed her trousers and turned those inside out too. The same light tan colour and baggy material hung by her ankles as she replaced it.

'Eventually a network of trade agreements and taxation will spread,' Castellar continued his explanation. 'If we create such an economy where everyone benefits from it then there is no longer a need for war.'

River took his meaning. Something about this man fascinated her and she wished she could listen to more but as she went to ask her next question the door buckled open and wood splintered across the floor.

She ran to the window and opened it, the crowd of protestors were spread across the square below. River threw one last glance at Castellar before hopping onto the window frame and leaping up to grab hold of a small indent in the pebble wall above. The wall was weak and crumbled in her fingers but she managed to swing her ankle above her head and hook it onto the iron guttering above. Wherever she stayed, she always arranged a top floor room, just in case she needed a swift escape. Finally, those preparations had paid off.

With a forceful tug of her arm and leg she swung up and onto the roof, if any had seen her swift and elegant movement they would have thought she floated. But all eyes remained on the ground level of the inn.

A crashing sound came from below as she tiptoed across the roof. The crowd had broken into the room. She heard the cries dispel as they would now have found Castellar sitting on the bed, alive and well and in need of peace.

River did not outstay her welcome any longer than necessary, not even to discover what outcome would present itself for the man, re-united with his followers. She fled across the rooftops and cleared the large gaps that separated them, flying almost, like a weighted bird. Despite her abnormal speed, she barely made a sound and before any could catch a glimpse of the assassin, she dropped down to a service alley behind an eatery and rubbed the muck from the floor across the front of her clothing and all over her face. Two sacks of rubbish lay to the end of the alley and she took them both with her as she strolled casually out into the market square, having barely wasted a breath.

She blended into the crowd with ease and kept her eyes low to the floor. Despite the events of the day, traders continued about their work and a parade of white adorned sailors made their way up from the docks. The new arrivals were on a stopover and River recognised them as part of the south-western armada that was growing in numbers to combat Augustus directly.

June had told her about the resistance that had been developing in the south amongst landowners. They were simple folk but loyal to their cause.

As she passed them by, River stumbled and knocked into one of the sailors, covering his white uniform in muck and rotting food waste that seeped out of the sack she held.

'Oh, my. I… I'm so sorry, sir!' River pleaded. 'Please forgive me. I'm just so unsettled I can barely walk straight.'

The sailor frowned at her and wiped as much of the mess off his jacket as he could, but his comrades laughed at him all the same.

'This'll cost a night's keep to clean up, you bloody fool,' he said.

'There's a wonderful wash house up the street, sir, but please, do be careful. Someone was killed here today, just off the main square. I've been told that Augustus sent an assassin from his army to infiltrate the port but something went wrong and an innocent man was killed.' The sailor looked at River as though she were mad but her tirade continued. 'Begging your pardon, sir, but he was the eldest of one of our most valuable families at the port here, sir. I do hope you'll take care and please accept this offering for the mess, sir.'

River placed a coin in the man's hand and rushed off down the path to the docks. His face was a painting of confusion and wonder. He shook it off as his party continued up through the square and, looking at his coin, he saw it was a piece of silver. Valuable enough to buy an entire wash house let alone a single service. With that in mind, River knew she had bought her alibi. Before the day was done the sailors would have spent the afternoon drinking in the tavern and rumours of Augustus's assassin would have spread throughout the entire town.

The docks were quiet, as most of the workers had now congregated in the upper part of the port town. A few smaller craft stalls had popped up since the day before and they offered a wide array of jewellery, hand-made and carved delicately by the most skilled artisans. These were foreign traders and looked to River as though they may be from the Maluabaw islands. A small cluster of these artisan tribes, who were settled to the south of the southern shores, traded in such fine ware to provide for their kin who often suffered drought.

The islands were unique on account of their hot temperatures and fertile soil, despite the lack of rain. Even at such a time that most of the land in Harmion was being fought over and ravished, the value of these islands had increased and, without the means to defend against foreign imperialism, they had gullibly sold most of the agricultural businesses. The natives to the islands had fallen into poverty and had worked the land they used to own. The goods they had sold produced just a fraction of the required income for their families, the rest being divvied up by those who had taken ownership. But the lands had been ravished through mass production and the new owners abandoned the Maluabian people. The tribes now grew crops only for themselves to consume and traded with their artistry. It was the single remaining currency they had ownership over.

River had been to Maluabaw once before and though she had promised to return with a gift for Summer, she had not found anything suitable, except for a bracelet that had not been for sale.

That was when she saw it, sparkling in the sunlight that beamed across the market stall. River dropped the sacks of rubbish by a disposal area by the entrance to the piers and doubled back to admire the fine craftsmanship of the jewellery. She cast her eyes across the small clay pots, painted with vivid colours, and eventually fell upon the bracelet that was made up of multiple white gold hoops, all interwoven with a yellow silk thread. It was the very one she had seen worn by the Maluabian leader years ago. It looked delicate but was made of some of the toughest materials that the island had to boast.

'Is this enough?' River asked, holding a small fortune in her hands.

The woman looked over the coin and smiled up at her customer.

'It means something to you, this bracelet?'

'Consider my offer a donation to your people.'

River made her offer and the lady accepted her price, graciously bowing in respect of the exchange.

'Mamasufie will be pleased that it found its way to you at last.'

Mamasufie; the one who had denied her the bracelet the first time. It had been the tribe leader's own bracelet once. Now it would feed her tribe.

River knew that Summer would love it. She hated going home empty handed and as she tucked the bracelet into her filthy jerkin, River bounded off towards her ship and paid the dockhand who scribbled her off the ledger then she set sail for home.

The seas were calm and although no winds favoured her, as they rarely did when sailing west, she made good time in her hasty ship. She had the opportunity to meditate once the main-sail and course were set. She thought about the man who had died and the screams of his wife still resonated in her ears. *There must be a better way to control the war than this.*

She was riddled with guilt and confusion.

Castellar would have suffered a major setback, but River didn't doubt that whatever the man's true talent was, he would no doubt spin the events of the day to favour his cause. In present circumstances, any incident that could strengthen the resistance to Augustus was a good thing.

Time slipped by calmly on the clear-skied nights that followed. The stars shone down brightly and the moon was fierce enough that River could see whales swimming in the sea to the south. It was her time, no mission to pursue, no killing. No expectations of her or nagging from her father. The whole ocean appeared to have been made just for her and she breathed in sea air admiring this aspect of her life. The private moments that washed away all sins and anxiety were a remedy for the shadows that haunted her.

Moments before her vessel beached the shores of the islands, River allowed herself to gaze admiringly at the beauty of Vermillion. It appeared to her a paradise and the calmness made her think of a simple life without complications. She remained blissfully unaware of the difficulties that awaited her ashore.

River arrived at the beach and stepped upon the warm sands, allowing herself a moment to fall upon the white beach and let the waves lap up against her. She smiled as she looked up to the red evening sky that encompassed the mountain and the sun began to dip below the horizon, but not before Summer could dive into her hands and kiss her passionately.

The two lovers rolled in the sand, giggling and splashing like frivolous girls. It was a moment of requited love and such happiness and they wished it could last forever.

'Here, I got you something,' River said to Summer as she revealed the Maluabian bracelet.

Summer took the exquisite piece, caressing it in her fingers, and placed it on her wrist.

'It's beautiful. I will never take it off.'

A short moment, just for the two of them. The intrusion came next.

'I trust the voyage was fruitful?' The voice that spoke was neither River nor Summer, but June. He stood towering above them, a silhouette against the fading light in the sky.

'Hello, Father, must I make the report so soon?' she asked, somewhat perturbed by his presence.

He kicked the sand with his boot heel and looked for a way to break the news to her.

'No, that can wait, but we have trouble on the mountain. I need you to head up there immediately.'

Summer stood to face June then and she glared at him as she spoke. 'She's only just pulled up on the shores? How can you send her up there without rest or, the skies forbid, time for herself?' It was said with anger, but her quivering tone suggested she knew it was out of place.

'If I wanted the opinion of a mere pupil, I would ask one of the other students who are far more advanced than you.' June shot his look at River as he continued. 'This cannot wait, Volcan is dying.'

## 15

Volcan lay there helplessly, delusional and weaker than Boscelito had seen him throughout his stay upon the mountain. Had Volcan learnt all the things he wished to learn, only to succumb to his aged body? No doubt by now the students who had visited and first discovered Volcan, curled in a foetus-like shape beside a fire, would have gotten word to June on the beaches below.

The two men had conversed in earnest as Boscelito took it upon himself to care for his captor. An old man, whose dignity was struck with the axe of time, still deserved the saving graces he could be afforded. It was unpleasant work but Boscelito had cared for dying men before and aiding them when they soiled themselves was just something you got on with.

Volcan had explained late one night, after falling sick, how the quickening had changed his life. It was the moment he had been trained for, as the eldest born son, to use the ears of the mountain.

Boscelito brought a pail of water to Volcan as he attempted to sit up straight enough to sip it.

'I'm afraid it is warm,' Boscelito said with sympathy.

'It is always warm, my boy, everything up here is always warm.'

Volcan sipped the water slowly and placed the pail by his side. He threw a resigned glance to Boscelito, his prisoner. His carer.

'It would not have been hard for you to descend the mountain, and leave me to die alone. Instead you aim to prolong my life. Why?'

Boscelito considered this for a moment. He wasn't sure he knew himself but he attempted to answer with verity.

'I have nowhere to go, I am no stranger to The Vermillion Isles by now. I would have been caught quickly and my leg is still not healed.' Boscelito paused, he had told half the truth. He decided to tell the rest. 'I have learnt more from you than at any stage of my entire life. I was never given a real education. Just thrust into a household to be a servant boy to a child who was destined for greater things than I. No one ever spoke to me the way you do. I never knew of the Primavemani or the magic of which you have spoken.'

Volcan reached forwards and grabbed Boscelito by the neck. 'Listen to me, Boscelito. Listen to all I have to say. For someone must know these things. We are one people, the same as those who we fight and those who we ally ourselves with. In the end, we are all part of the heart and soul of the world. When we are born, we are born alone. When we die, that is when our purpose is fulfilled and we come together again. You recall I told you of the quickening?' Boscelito nodded his head. 'Well, I was born before June and so it was burdened to me to inherit the mountain one day. All of us carry the soul of the earth within us. But I was born at such a favoured time as to heed its call. There is speculation that the position of the moons and stars affect our agility of body and mind, as much if not more so, than any hereditary transference.

I heard such bizarre things as a child. I experienced agony and I began to endanger the lives of my friends until I was trained to manage this strange soul-magic that I was privy to. It was my great grandmother before me who was the last to reside within this cave. She lived until she was over one hundred years old. It has always been that every third generation in our family were favoured with the gift. But I bore no children for myself and June lost his first and only son. When River was born, June decided she would be trained and one day join me to prepare for the quickening. Though we saw no signs of the soul-magic in her, the choice was limited, lest she produce a child of her own, though even then we would have to wait for yet another generation.'

Volcan sighed heavily, he was exhausted. Boscelito was entranced and he wondered whether he should convince the man to rest, but he wanted… no, he needed to hear more.

'Vermillion volcano was said to be a central source of nature, where the souls of the dead would travel to lay to rest. Its connection to the Maldus tree was unmistakable and some of the earliest Vermillion islanders travelled to the northern world beyond the borders of Orldin in order that it should be protected. These were the first men and women who walked the earth, before the mainland of what is now called Harmion had even become inhabited. So you see, we have the heart of the world at its very tip and the soul resides here, in this mountain. I listen to the soul each day and it sends me scattered voices. Sometimes I learn things of value, other times I cannot make out the words that are being spoken and the effort is too great to bear.'

Boscelito helped Volcan take another sip of water. He scruti-nised the man with his stare. 'These are not things I would tell an enemy. Indeed, it would be more prudent to keep such teachings for only my most trusted allies and those would be few.'

Volcan shook his head.

'This is not about allies and enemies, right or wrong. It is about the survival of our world. If we do not retain balance the heart will die and the soul will be lost. Humans fester upon the world like locusts and we do more damage than we know. I fear this war over land is in its infancy. Elik remains dormant but one day he will be forced to play his part, as will all Harmion's people. Sometimes the information I pass to June determines that we must sacrifice the most well-meaning of leaders, simply because their desire for growth is too severe or resistance to violence so dangerous. That is the burden of The Vermillion Isles. An impartial settlement of assassins that act neutrally, even when it means taking the most abhorrent of actions. But we are becoming extinct; an heir to the mountain is needed. River must bear a child. You love her, I know you do.' Boscelito felt ill at ease as he heard the truth out loud. He had never considered the nature of his feelings for her and now, as Volcan spoke them, they hit him like a hammer to the chest. 'There is no use denying it, Boscelito. Do you think it is only the words that have passed from your lips that I have been aware of all this time? The mountain has spoken. But the girl loves Summer. I know that to be true, but they could never have a child together. That much is certain.'

'You imply I could easily persuade her to lay down with me and that she would forget the one who truly claims her heart? If it is so that she should provide a child to continue the lineage, surely there are thousands upon this island who would be better suited than I?'

'No, none would dare get in the way of the love between River and Summer. It must be an outsider, with no alliances to lose. Anything else would shock our community into a state beyond repair.'

Boscelito had been given multiple missions as a soldier over the years. Ordered by the most vehement warlord whose campaigns had brought about more suffering than the rest of the armies put together. But now his enemy was instructing him to court with a woman whose heart belonged to another and he was sure she held nothing for Boscelito other than contempt.

'Is it possible, that the lineage you speak of should be lost? Maybe it is an imbalance that one creed alone harnesses the power to listen to the thoughts of others. You cannot be right all the time, nor from where I am standing, would you truly be able to say that every decision is impartial. Half the time the words you hear, as you have admitted, are scrambled and indiscernible.'

Volcan formed a wry smile. 'I will admit that is something that crossed my mind on many occasions. But the idea of the ability being lost for good. I don't see how we could survive in such a world. After all, it is not our decision. The soul-magic chooses who it will. End the line of those who possess it and it will find a new host. Gatekeepers are employed to hold the keys; they should not be the ones to decide who may pass through the door.'

'It sounds to me like that is exactly what you're doing.' Boscelito offended Volcan with the retort. Their conversing was causing the dying old man much discomfort. The two men paused for a while before Boscelito spoke again. 'I would make a mortal enemy of Summer, but you already know that.'

'You cannot build a home without first breaking rocks.'

Footsteps echoed throughout the chamber in the next moment, drawing nearer as River hurried towards them. Summer was with her, just a few paces behind.

'Volcan!' River shouted as she approached. She shot a disgusted look at Boscelito. 'You, get away from him, you're smothering him.'

Boscelito moved out of the way, this was no time to stand proudly. River and Summer knelt beside Volcan, concerned and overly energised from the sprint up the mountain they had just undertaken.

'We have brought you a mild dose of lava, it will not endanger you but you must take it so we can get you off the mountain.'

Volcan shook his head. 'I cannot leave this place. Lava or no, I will not survive the journey. This is where it ends for me, River.'

'No,' she said, vindicated. 'I won't let that happen.'

River took out a small vial from her shirt and filled it halfway with water. She then gave it a good shake and passed the vial to Volcan. He sighed and gave her a pleading look but nothing would dissuade her so he took the vial and swallowed the contents.

After a few moments of waiting for the effects to kick in, River led Volcan outside with the help of Summer and Boscelito and they lay him on the stretcher that the newly arrived pair had left by the cave entrance. It was a tightly fitted hammock attached to several solid strands of bamboo tied together with fresh vines.

'Grab the front end,' River instructed Boscelito and Summer. 'I will take the back.'

'My leg won't survive the walk in this state, not if I am to aid you carrying this man,' Boscelito said, not objecting, but pointing out a simple truth. River knew he was right. Men of the mainland were so much slower to heal than those of The Vermillion Isles.

'Very well, lava for you also. Just don't get cocky and try anything stupid.'

'A mistake I have already made once in your presence. I recall losing my entire ship and crew on that occasion. I think you can consider me yours to do with as you wish.'

Summer shot Boscelito a sly glance, she didn't like his flirtatious tone.

When the lava had taken its effect on Boscelito, the three of them carried Volcan to the top of the treacherously steep stairwell and made ready to make their descent. It was a tremendous effort and worse even than having made the climb up here the first time with the supplies.

On more than one occasion they had to stop and rest, placing Volcan onto a platform as carefully as they could, relying on the lava to keep him from suffering shock.

'Is this one of what you might consider your brightest ideas?' Boscelito mocked.

'Shut up, stupid bastard. We'll gut you and leave you where you stand.' It was Summer who replied and were it not for River, more reasonable and sound of mind, Summer would have happily carried out her threat there and then.

'Summer, ignore him. We need his strength but this one carries with him a poisonous tongue and it is better for his unpleasantness to fall on deaf ears.'

'If only I could close my ears the way I close my eyes,' Summer responded.

They continued their descent and the darkness of night that enveloped them made for hard work. It was slow and the lava had certainly worn off from Volcan by the time they were approaching the footpath beneath. He began to fall into a slumber and Boscelito knew that tiredness was waiting for him too.

'We must be quick. Volcan will be weaker now and he will need sustenance,' suggested River.

'You had better carry on without me, I'll never make it to the beaches with you in time. You don't need me to help you walk the footpath, the stairs were the troublesome part.'

'Boscelito, nothing would please me more,' River replied. 'But if we leave you here in the dead of night you will be ravished by the wild beasts of the forest.'

'Sounds like a plan I can get behind,' Summer said. The derision in her tone had not abated.

'No! He must come with us.'

It was Volcan who shouted, roused suddenly from his sleep. But he was unable to remain conscious for long and his next words slipped out like soil from a tipped pot. 'We need, we need him...'

'Let's move,' River suggested, and so they hurried through the forest as fast as they could manage.

It was the best part of an hour's march through the shrubs and with the densely lined trees the light from the moonlit sky was sparse. River knew the path like the back of her hand and led with the stretcher held out behind her. Summer took the rear and Boscelito was allowed to handle his own struggle. The pain of his leg gaining as the lava began to leave his system.

He felt his mind wander and on many occasions he called out, shouting indiscernible noises to try and keep himself awake. He excused himself as his two companions wondered what nonsense was going on behind them. But with each grunt and groan came reassurance that he had not dropped dead behind.

Somewhere between a clearing in the woods and the dunes of the small settlement by the beach, Boscelito finally collapsed to the floor. Exhaustion was something he would have been keen to suffer in exchange for how he felt now, having pushed himself beyond the limit of what he thought was possible. The lava took away the pain of his leg and lent him strength but when it was gone it took everything from him.

River and Summer had gone far beyond where he fell, unaware that he had stumbled. They were nowhere to be seen. Boscelito closed his eyes and listened to the sounds of forest life as morning threatened to awaken.

Out past the borders of the sandy woods, River and Summer emerged with Volcan, out cold on the stretcher. June had prepared a medical tent; the curtains that had been hung for Volcan's modesty, billowed in the cool dawn air.

'Get him in here at once,' June instructed them. They raced into the tent and placed Volcan onto the table that had been prepared with all sorts of equipment. Various devices to aid with breathing. A clamp to hold his tongue to prevent him from swallowing it should his muscles truly give up, and a thin tube that was fitted with a needle to pump a concoction into his veins. It was as likely as walking across the ocean that they would save him, but they had to try.

'Where is Boscelito?' June asked, suddenly aware that the man was missing.

River looked around and raised an eyebrow at Summer. 'I told you to keep an eye on him!'

'What? I was more concerned with getting your uncle back alive. So what if that bastard dropped dead.'

It was a petulant rebuke and Summer knew it, but she didn't care. Nothing could make her hate the mainland idiot any more than she did already.

'Wait for me here,' River exclaimed as she rushed out of the tent, leaving Summer and June to oversee Volcan's treatment.

River ran back through the forest, quick as a wild animal and though the dawn light rose to help guide her, she hardly needed it. She had no idea how far back they had lost him but she prayed it wasn't too deep, where the wild nocturnal animals dwelled.

She ran and ran for what seemed like an age and eventually stumbled upon a mark on the sandy path that suggested a large creature may have dragged a body off into the shrubbery. Her heart sank as she thought of the condition she would find Boscelito in, but she cautiously moved into the brushwood. A rustling sound startled her and she pulled her blades from her belt, slowing her pace as she tiptoed cautiously towards the noise. The rustling stopped and River held firm in her spot, listening intently as she breathed in slowly through her nose, slowing her heart and attuning her senses.

Suddenly out of a dense fern bush, a large roaring mouth shot its dagger teeth at her and launched its entire four-hundred-pound body at hers. She spun swiftly to the side to avoid the prancing mammal but she didn't have time to get a clean swing of her blade.

It doubled around and roared at her. There were few beasts of its kind in the Vermillion forests. In fact, not one casualty had been noted for over two years at the hands of these deformed creatures and the islanders had assumed that perhaps they were now extinct. And yet, here it was. The beast that was rarely seen had been thrust in her face on account of a mainland captain. She hated him more for it. The beast was strong as a horse and fierce as a lion. Its jaw was lined with fangs as long as knives and blood red eyes were inset within its scaly head.

It charged her again and this time River managed to leap up above its ravaging jaw and plunged back down with her blade, catching its hind leg before it scurried into a densely packed bush. River stalked the area, her eyes keen and ears pricked. She knew the beast was close but she had lost its scent.

Before her, lying like a pile of rags, was Boscelito. He was barely conscious and aside from fresh teeth marks around the calf of his injured leg, he was unharmed. The beast had clearly meant to drag him off for a private meal.

Another roar sounded and River spun just in time to see the claw swipe across her waist. Her reactions were better than any human she knew, but that wasn't enough. The claw ripped her jerkin and pulled her to the side, grazing her stomach. She only had time to realise she had nearly been killed before the next attack came. She met the second claw with her blade and severed the forefingers off. The beast roared and swung its body around. The full weight of the animal sent her flying into a tree trunk.

River clambered around for her blades but she had lost one in the mayhem. The other she still clung to for dear life and as the beast charged her, pinning her with its large jaw against the tree, she brought down her blade into its neck, slicing and swiping over and over, taking out chunks of flesh and covering herself in the burning hot blood of her attacker.

She felt the front teeth of the animal pierce her midriff and shoulder. Aside from the severe agony, she remarked to herself how large the animal's head must be to puncture her flesh at two such extreme points.

She was clueless how to stop such power. Twenty cuts and it still continued to crush her against the trunk. She heard her back cracking against the pressure.

Thirty cuts. The pressure waned but it was not enough. She'd have ordinarily killed a whole squadron by now.

Her eyes began to stream as she felt the fangs deepen their reach inside her.

*Was it time to submit? To admit defeat and wander from this violent life to whatever peace awaits?* She allowed herself a moment to wonder at the simplicity of passing from this life at the hands of such a creature. It would be a good death.

Boscelito answered the question for her, diving from the

spot where he had lain. He screamed an inhuman scream, yielding the blade that River had lost. He plunged it straight into the skull of the beast and felt the tip make contact with the iron skull. But his rage forced the blade through and he plunged it down, again and again.

River met his efforts with her own and continued to slash at the throat, the only part of the beast she could reach. They worked together as sculptors of death, bringing the magnificent animal to its knees and, with a series of savage cuts, the grip of its jaw relaxed, giving space to River to remove herself from its clasp. The beast fell backwards, Boscelito still clutching its back like an ape. By the time it hit the ground it was dead.

Boscelito raised himself to his feet. No lava ran through him now but he was fuelled by an adrenaline like he had never felt before. It had awoken him. Hatred for the beast and love for the woman who had come back to save him.

River looked into his meaningful eyes and before the flow of blood that she was losing spilled out of her body, causing her to see stars that were not of night, she drifted into an unconscious state and she allowed herself one final thought. *Not bad, captain, not bad at all.*

## 16

'Are we that which others determine us to be? Or is there something greater that each of us possesses, unknown to even our closest relations. Can a warrior, feared by many, be as though a timid child, afraid of speech with strangers? Could a weak child not entertain a palladium crowd with the gift of wit, wittering words the way a swordsman swings his blade? Was kindness only something indeterminable and infinite, and not reserved for those we judge to deserve it. None are truly equal in our own eyes so we should expect not to be treated equally by others.'

The passage resonated with Pietrich the more he repeated it out loud. Sitting uncomfortably on a rock he swayed back and forth in a trancelike state. His only audience was Jack. His wolf skulked around the stone upon which he was sat.

The tide was coming in again. That would wash away the bodies, Pietrich thought. He stood and wandered across the shingle of Port Melees beach, beside the outcrop where he had taken shelter from a passing deluge. He had hoped the rain would wash away the stench of blood from the corpses that scattered the port. It hadn't.

Jack pattered towards the six dead who lined the beach. They were the surviving search party that had watched Pietrich's allies sail away. It was merely a teenage boy they had to deal with at that point so they tracked his footprints in the beach to the overhanging cliff beneath the docks. When they had found him Pietrich had simply stood there before them. He had heard the sounds of their heartbeats racing as though they were a marching band beating their drums. From that alone he could tell that there were six sword bearers.

Pietrich had pleaded with them to turn around and leave. He just wanted peace. But they wouldn't let him have it. They couldn't return empty handed they had said and by this point dead or alive would do.

It had turned out that the man who was left in charge of the remaining mercenaries was content to take Pietrich's lifeless head back to his queen. Six blades formed a multi-pointed spear and pursued the blind boy where he stood.

His wolf howled.

The pleading child within Pietrich had just seconds to make his choice. But in the end, he only needed one.

Pietrich, still riding the ecstasy of the tsunami he had created, synchronised his mind with the six beating hearts and, faster than he could click his fingers, they ceased to pump life through their bodies.

Before the first aggressor had taken a step towards the boy, the six had all dropped to the floor, the life extinguished from them.

Pietrich didn't know how he had done it. He wasn't sure he wanted to know, for in return he had felt a part of his own heart die. What was he becoming? Not Pietrich, the boy his mother loved so much. Nor the cheeky child who chased chickens around his farm. The things he had done were the acts of a monster.

'Stop it, Jack,' he shouted to the wolf, who licked the bloodied wounds of the corpses, gnawing at them where they lay. It was as though the actions of the wolf were a reflection and Pietrich saw himself, stained by the blood that he had spilled, and he hated what he saw. Then he remembered he couldn't see and it was his imagination taunting him.

*What I would give to turn back time,* he thought.

'We have done enough to these men, Jack, let us leave them in peace now.'

Pietrich began to walk away and Jack reluctantly followed, still blood hungry.

Walking without his staff troubled Pietrich at first but he could hear the way the sound of his boot changed as it neared the surface in front of him. With even a light breeze he had discovered that he could listen to the changes in pitch that the wind made as it drifted across the landscape where he trod. It was almost like seeing again. Every tuft of grass and stone before him were as clear as a freshwater pool.

It took great concentration at first and his head hurt the further he went. Pietrich had to stop to rest and recite his father's words to shut out the white noise. But when he recovered, he stood and carried on his journey.

After several hours walking, Pietrich had put a fair distance between himself and Port Melees. The further he went, the less he needed to stop and rest his mind. Before long, walking would become second nature to him again, as it once was when he could see.

Judging by the milky light that he sensed through his eyelids he reckoned that he was heading south. At least he hoped he was, for south was where home was, and that was where he was going.

The next few days were gruelling. Pietrich relied on Jack to kill wild hare and keep him on track but they still lost hours each day making wrong turns here and there.

Pietrich learnt how to get a fire going by listening to the sound of the wood he scoured from the forests. Many times the kindling he put together was too damp but it didn't take long for Pietrich to learn how to distinguish the difference. Sometimes it was almost as if the fire started because he had willed it to do so.

As he had hoped, walking was an effortless task by the end of the first week. Sleeping had been a kind of torture for he did not travel with any of the comforts of his formative travels with Lynden, Olafur, Grace and Fritz. He longed to know if they were okay. Fritz may not even be alive but Pietrich dared not reach out to any of them, he wanted his plan to be his alone. He had bought himself a lot of time to contemplate it. So many unanswered questions could not be left to restlessly swim the seas of his subconscious.

Castellar had told him he was a blood descendent of the first men. He didn't know what that meant, so that was a starting point. It was a strange experiment they had carried out that had caused Pietrich so much pain. The peaceful leader had told him of a day whereby his newly-formed port haven was put to the test by an assassin and Pietrich had imagined the events unfolding until he eventually found himself listening to the thoughts of the assassin as though he was there with her.

She was full of fear at the intrusion, but it was not strange to her to have him roaming inside her mind the way it had been to others. She recognised the infiltration of her mind as though it were a natural part of life.

Lynden had made her protests. 'Of course the boy will see what you want him to see, he has the most powerful imagination I have ever known,' she had said, knowing full well some of the voices Pietrich conjured were real and that when he spoke back to the voices, they heard him.

Her biggest accusation of the test was that if Castellar wanted to somehow change an aspect of the past, there was no way for them to know if they had been successful, for the event he wished to change would have never taken place and they would be none the wiser to the impact of their meddling.

It was a complex web and Pietrich had determined that he was perhaps able to sense the past through a stream of rushing thoughts and at the time it had felt as though he watched a million souls flying past him in the sky and he had to pick out just one, somehow listening to them with clarity. No wonder it hurt so much.

The day had become cold and damp and Pietrich feared for another restless night, sleeping in wet clothing with nothing spare to dress comfortably in. He wished his mother could take the dirty shirt from his back and wrap him in a cosy blanket by the fireplace in their home as she once had. Maybe if he found her he would be lucky to know her love again, even for a short while.

There were many travellers on the roads. Traders, mercenaries and farmers, each with their own path in life. Pietrich heard the desires of each man and woman as they drew close, all their hopes and fears. It didn't sit well with him to pry into the lives of others but he had to keep his ears pricked lest he be spotted by any who would recognise a blind boy of certain age and turn him in.

Pietrich would duck away from sight and take refuge until the path was once again clear.

Everything was simpler now he was alone. In charge of his own destiny for the first time and after the worst night's sleep he'd had in months, Pietrich stretched out and yawned. With no breakfast to energise him, he stumbled on but cared not for his hunger, for, as he meandered along a pathway that led to the top of a set of lowland hills, he heard the distant sounds of wood burning in a half dozen cottages and children were laughing by the well at the centre of a village. It was Knighton and he was close to home.

The valley below where he now trod was calling to him. Everything he had learnt pointed him to a distant world he had never known and although Pietrich knew where he had to go and what he had to do, and though Knighton played no part in that, first he had to say goodbye.

The town was much the same as he remembered, cattle-drawn ploughs were preparing the fields for new seed to be sown. The earth was warm, and families had congregated on the stony steps of their homes to pass the time away, basking in the late summer sun. He heard the work taking place in the fields and listened to the idle chatter of the villagers. It filled him with sadness.

Pietrich had entered through a new fence that had been built around the perimeter of the village that joined the watchtower facing the forest where he had once run off with Eira. He could hear two watchmen at the top of the tower chatting away about the taxes that were due each quarter annum. They were debating how it left the village in such a state financially and the local traders were forced to sell more of their produce and cancel the harvest festival two years running. But after a time the trade roads out of the village had been renovated and the new fence erected. Paid for by the Winter Queen.

Pietrich diverted his mind from the towers, suddenly realising the watchmen were not villagers at all, but guards posted by the new army who had enforced the taxation. He knew now why home was a dangerous place to him and why Lynden never wanted to return here. He began to regret the decision to come and he hurried through the central street that divided the small village in two and he headed straight to where his mother's home would be, praying that none would recognise him.

Pietrich opened the familiar door and went into the cottage that he had spent most of his life living in. It was warm and the smell of garlic and rosemary was delightfully intoxicating. It smelt like home and his mother's lavender perfume lingered in the air.

'Mother?'

A crashing sound came as a large wooden crate hit the stone tiled floor.

'Pietrich!' Marilia called out as she ran to her son, oblivious to the mess she had just made at the shock of seeing his face.

'What on earth, where is Lynden? Where are the others? Are you hurt?' The barrage of questions was to be expected, as was the way she squeezed him tight and suffocated the life out of him. It felt so good. Worth the pain, he thought as he formed a wry smile.

'Mother, please. Slow down and I will explain all to you. At least as far as I am able to do so.'

She looked her son in the eyes, they never looked back at her anymore. Not since he had gone blind. But she could see the truth in them all the same.

'What is it, my love, what has happened?'

Pietrich recounted his journey to her since they had left. Eighteen long months had now gone by and there was much to tell, despite the fact so many of their days had been spent wandering aimlessly, waiting for the world to change. Pietrich came very close to telling her the terrible things he had done, but he didn't want the way she looked at him to change. He knew her smile by the sound of her eyelids blinking and her deep breaths told him that his visit had brought her such joy. Nothing should change that, not even the truth.

They sat and talked for hours and the heat of the day dwindled, leaving them with a refreshing evening to enjoy in each other's company. The stew had been on the boil all afternoon and the evening's meal was local tender meat in a broth of fresh vegetables, herbs and spices. Marilia, as ever, had made a life-giving elixir. Pietrich had forgotten what it was like to eat so well.

'You should know, Pietrich, that the new army has stationed guards around the village. Not just ours in fact but many others too. We have, it pains me to say, been treated kindly, but only because there is no choice but to comply with the wishes of this new leader. I dread to think what would happen if they find you here. You shouldn't have come, as much as it brings me such joy. You are the birds that sing in the morning and the warmth of a summer's night to me, you know that. I only fear for you. The truth is I fear for us all.'

'You will be a poet yet, mother,' Pietrich said. 'I know it was foolish of me to come here, but I have to go away somewhere and I don't know if I will return.'

'Not yet sixteen and you speak like a general who goes off to fulfil a war campaign. Why did you have to grow up so fast, my love?'

Pietrich smiled at Marilia. 'In the end, we are all just passengers on the White River. Eventually it will drop us on the restful banks of Silverhaven where we will stay together in peace. When it is time.'

Marilia raised her eyebrows, impressed. 'Lynden has been educating you well I see. Better than I ever could.' The sadness in those words was not hidden well.

'Mother, you have given me all the things that no one else ever could. There is no replacing you nor is there a comparison to any of it. You are the answer to ninety-nine questions out of a hundred after all.'

Marilia chuckled. 'I am not sure that is how the saying goes, my love, but it is sweet of you to reimagine it on my account.'

Pietrich had been delaying the question that had first entered his mind, hoping that Marilia would offer him the information he sought. He could delay no longer. 'How is Eira? I had hoped to speak to her briefly before I go.'

'She...' Marilia stuttered awkwardly, searching for the right words. '...Eira has gone away for a time, with her betrothed. She will be a married woman soon. Her mother made a good match for her. I am truly sorry she is not here for you to hear these things from.'

Pietrich took the blow to his heart and rocked his head back and forth. Somehow he had anticipated the news, but he had never been able to sense Eira the way he could others. His greatest pain was listening to all the voices of the world at night and not once was she there, drifting amongst them.

'I do not think it was wise of you to leave your companions the way you did. I'm sorry to scorn you but you must know you need them.'

She meant well, but Pietrich knew there was so much she no longer understood. How could she? For to understand the dynamics of his position meant to understand the ethics of Castellar. The torture that Tritan must endure. Lynden's political mind and the world that was forming beneath them. A unified world; formed by blood and taxes. He prayed she remain ignorant to these things, as he no longer could.

'Mother, there are things that will never become clear, but I can't stop wondering about my heritage. It seems to be at the centre of why father was taken and why I have been hunted too since that day.'

'If only we knew everything that you were,' she replied despondently. 'You are the sky, Pietrich, made up of many bright stars and ones that have existed long ago but no longer burn brightly, except to us, as they linger on in memory. You are the history of our family and its future. Multiple worlds exist beyond our reach and they all have a history that goes back before recorded time. But you are also the stars that shoot across the dark curtain of night with ferocity and an energy that no person could ever understand. Multiply that complexity by the mystery that is time and I think we will still have not a salt grain of understanding as to what makes you so special.'

'I love you, Mother,' he responded. 'You always have the best answers.'

She burst out laughing and ruffled his hair. 'That is the best way of telling me that I talk nonsense.'

Pietrich shook his head. 'No, I mean it, you always describe yourself as an imposter but it is your words that led father to a brighter path. If you would read his journal, you would know how much credit you are due.'

Marilia wiped a tear from her eye and huffed as she stood, clearing the bowls of stew they had devoured from the table. 'Oh my, I must go easy on the garlic, the blasted stuff always goes in my eye.'

Later that night, when the dishes were done and the embers of the fire in the kitchen had all but burnt away. Marilia fell into a quiet slumber upon her old rocking chair and Pietrich sat with her for a time, imagining her beautiful face resting peacefully in the candlelight. He drew the contours of her face as a picture in his mind and he wanted to linger here forever. But the morning would bring with it new surprises and he dared not outstay his welcome.

Pietrich wandered to his old bed and sat upon it, thinking of all the nights he had been sick, when Eira had comforted him in spite of her mother's protests. He longed to be back in that time, to suffer the nightly fevers that ate away at him, just to have her at his side.

As he strolled carefully and quietly towards the cottage entrance, he felt Jack pulling him away, as if to say it was not safe to remain any longer. The wolf always sensed danger, as though he too could listen to the voices of the world.

Pietrich lay his father's journal upon the kitchen table and unbolted the door and left.

As he walked across the village in the striking moonlight, Jack drew his attention to the tower upon which two other guards were now stationed. They worked shifts throughout the night. There was a sense that the peacefulness of Knighton had been lost, despite the safety of all who dwelled here. But worst of all was the lack of the joy of Eira who had brightened the whole village like a carnival lantern with her kindness and her smile.

Pietrich snuck out through the gate. The air was still and so Jack led the way, his pattering footsteps a guide for his master who hung back just for a second as if his aching heart would bring Eira running towards him from the track below. But she didn't appear, nor would she. Pietrich turned and walked away from the only home he had known, though an abyss now existed at its core and he grasped the realisation at each passing step, drawing further away, that it was the last time he would ever step foot in Knighton.

## 17

'Somewhere between the beginning of time and now there is a moment, un-recorded, that changed the course of all life. Where balance was thrown into a perpetual state of flux. It was the day consciousness came into existence. When the first humans debated their purpose and the pendulum began to swing. Since then it has never stopped. If we veer too far towards a course that would bring about destitution, all efforts require that we lean against it with our combined weight and effort to tip the scales the other way until we find the balance again. But it lasts just a fleeting moment for we then push too far against that new harmony. If we look across the course of time, how many instances have there been that were shrouded in bliss as nature might call it. Perhaps every hundred years we may recall just one instance where things were put to rights. Maybe two? If it is not a mistaken judgement, could the boy not be one half of the pendulum, to lean his weight against the scourge of the world. Does that not mean we must help to give him a push?'

Castellar allowed his wandering mind to form words in dulcet tones. Words for all to hear, and to regard with scrutiny as he would insist on nothing less than for his sermon to be put to task.

Lynden wanted to respond in some way. But she could not find anything to say. She simply stared towards the hundred or so bodies that were scattered across the beach. The mauled faces a blend of wounds that were filled with debris as though the coastal offerings pledged to hide the true horror of what had befallen those who rested on the shore.

'The wolf did this,' Lynden finally offered; nothing else came to her mind.

'Yes, I do not doubt it was responsible for the mauling, but a wolf alone did not kill these men and women.' Castellar shook his head, pondering the lives that had been lost. Desperately trying to feel something. 'I never thought I would feel so numb at the sight of this many dead. So far have I fallen from the path I once trod. Is this truly the only way? Should such power be harnessed?'

'I am afraid for Pietrich, he is still young and cannot comprehend what impact he has made. We must guide him, Castellar, the way you once guided this haven. *If you can reach one person with light, the world is a brighter place for it.* Those were your words once, and now I feel as though they hold more meaning than ever. We must reach *him*, Castellar. He is the only one who matters now.' Lynden reached to put a comforting hand on Castellar's shoulder. But she too could not comprehend a mind so capable of things she could only imagine. To reach Pietrich was to climb the highest mountain.

The rest of the party stayed unmoving, incapable of speech as they watched the sea wash its salty kiss across the dead. Olafur wrapped his arm around Grace and held her close, kissing the top of her head and smelling her sweet hair.

'What more can we do, my love?' she asked him. 'We have walked the earth, neglected our children, and used the skills we have to arrive at this point. But all of this death. It is truly beyond us. Olafur, we are not built for such things.'

Olafur looked beyond his beloved wife and met eyes with Lynden. She had known their small union would eventually come to an end, and she knew that time was now. But a sadness crept over her. They had become a family these past eighteen months and now she would be alone.

She walked over to the couple who had accompanied her on the road since she had left Knighton. They had acted as though wandering traders, building their connections through their reputation and it was they who had kept the group fed and clothed. Lynden held out her hands to Grace who took them and smiled a loving smile. They shook earnestly and then embraced one another as friends. They did not need to say anything, for all was spoken in the closeness of their embrace. Lynden took Olafur in her arms next and gave the tall man a kiss on his red-bearded face.

'Go to them, your family awaits you. It is time,' she told them.

'Will you be safe, Lynden? Do you know what you will do?' Grace replied, her concern abundant.

'Are any of us ever safe? I do not know. But I feel a comfort in the company of Castellar. His rashness might make me ill at ease but mortal fear grows with age and I must resist it. I sense that it is his very rashness that will guide me at this uncertain time. I am at a crossroads, for I must seek the elders but I cannot let Pietrich linger alone too long; he will need guidance or I fear he will put himself and others in grave danger.'

'He has grown into a rare kind of man through your guidance, do not underestimate the impact you have already made on him, Lynden,' Olafur offered. 'We will miss you. Your kindness and your wisdom will be a hole in our lives from this moment forth.'

Lynden formed a knowing smile. 'We make holes wherever we go. To have known such good folk determines that it must be so. Grief is the burden of love. But we can keep the crevices filled with the memories that our minds permit us to recall.'

They embraced again as three and when they broke apart Lynden gave them a knowing wink, reserved only for those closest to her heart, and then she returned to stand beside Castellar. Seven of his crew had survived the attack at the port docks and they worked at retrieving the dead, laying them onto flat hay carts.

'They will recover the bodies of those who were against us too?' she asked him.

'They were against us only because they were led to do so. Death does not discriminate against race or creed so they will be returned to the earth as our brothers and sisters.'

'Ah yes, the King and the Sword.' Lynden knew the story well. 'Let us bury the sword. But as for the King, well. Perhaps that is trouble for another day.'

It was a long afternoon, taking the bodies up the hill to the old settlement and then beyond to where the single home stood in ruin where Castellar had once lived. They found an unmarked grave from when he had returned from hiding after his family had been slaughtered to bury their remains together. Castellar told Lynden that his brother now kept watch over his wife and child, in death as he had also done in life. He was a watchman of Port Melees and now he would extend his protection in the afterlife to the hundred or so who had died by the port.

The graves were dug deep enough to ensure none of the wild creatures that lived nearby would disturb their rest.

As night fell, a pyre was built in their honour and it burned brightly as the eleven who attended said their prayers. It was a peaceful, sombre moment amidst a haze of confusion. They would soon return to the uncertainty that lay ahead but tonight they would dance and sing and wash away their fears with liquor and love.

As the morning sun rose, Grace and Olafur said their final goodbyes and rode off on horseback to Haagurufur to return to their former lives.

The remaining band of Castellar's followers were all granted leave should they wish it, but none of them had any intention of departing and Lynden prepared herself, along with all of them, for the long ride to the river jetty beyond the high hills of the Melees valley where the Audacia awaited their return.

Decisions had to be made and there was much to discuss but as Lynden rode beside Castellar, they would not speak a word to one another for the entire journey as they let the tangled knots of the previous night unravel in their minds.

PLACID WAS the river that lapped the jetty where the Audacia tickled silted banks. There was a carnival of masts breaking the skyline of the lowlands on the other side of the tributary. All abandoned schooners. The watercourse was not typically built for such a vessel as the Audacia but the high tide had allowed them to make their way several leagues inland, which had aided the rush to determine the events that had unfolded on the port beach.

'Unseaworthy,' the first mate had said as they had done their rounds of the Audacia to determine the extent of the damage. It had been hard to truly grasp just how much work would have to be done, as the intention had been to depart without delay.

The central mast was intact but the rear mast had been

splintered and its sail was peppered with holes. The crew had begun work with immediate effect, tirelessly rummaging through the supplies below deck.

Without greater numbers, they barely had time to rest. The worst of the damage had been to the hull where the main cabin had been penetrated just beneath the stern of the ship. It was not close to the waterline but any storm would flood the area below decks.

The ship graveyard across the river had been generous to the crew who now planed timber from the first light of day until the moment the sun set. It was trying work and Castellar worried over the difficult progress.

'Tell me the worst of it. The masts are much improved I see.' Castellar addressed the first mate, Diccon. He was a knowledgeable fellow and blunt as a spoon when it came to the truth. He shook his head. Clearly he was unhappy.

'I could probably piss on her and she'd sink. What we need is a shipping yard and a real construction crew to service her. Could take a few weeks that o'course, then there'd be the issue of gettin' 'er to one.'

'And what is the bad news?'

'The bad news is I ain't had a drink for coming up on forty-eight hours and I can't see nought but slaves' work ahead.'

Castellar noted how Diccon scratched at a torn piece of shirt that he had tied around his upper arm. It was stained with blood.

'How are you faring, Diccon?' Castellar asked. 'Maybe you should rest a while. Let the others do the heavy lifting.'

Diccon had been caught by the tip of a blade in the fight. As luck would have it that sword was freshly sharpened and clean and he had staved off infection by dousing his arm in liquor.

'Beggin' your pardon, sir, but we all need rest. This ship's a heavy bitch and we can't sail no long voyage with a seven-man crew.'

'Can't or won't?' Castellar asked simply and openly.

'Well, we need our carpenter to fix whatever surprises the sea throws up once we're on the ocean proper. Sure as a fire burns we'll find holes we missed once the water chugs up against us. Then there's the cook to consider. Obviously as we're nine including you and the lady, it won't be full time but whoever that would be, seeing as the last one was buried in your brother's grave just two days past, is beyond me.'

'I can take care of that; save those of you who know about the sea to get on with the real work,' Lynden offered, much to the surprise of Diccon. He screwed his face up in approval like a badly bred dog.

'Fair do, ma'am. I look forward to tasting your grub 'n' all. Course there's the shift pattern to consider too. Unless you're planning on needing no sleep en route to wherever we're going?'

'A lookout and a man at the helm at all times, others will be permitted rest and their duties on hold until sun up. If anything out of the ordinary should happen, all will be roused with immediate effect.'

Diccon popped a damp rolled-up paper filled with leaf in his mouth and smiled at Castellar and Lynden.

'Very well, it'll be a laugh. I always said a calm sea was boring.'

'I rather hope you find yourself disappointed at the journey ahead in that case, Diccon.' Castellar didn't quite meet his enthusiasm for adventure on the seas. The first mate gave the man a heavy pat on his shoulder before turning to cross the decks towards his crew. He used a wood burning stovetop to light his smoking paper and as he inhaled a deep lungful of the old leaf, he looked over the ship one last time. The final few pieces of welding were to be done but under the circumstances, they had knocked her up into good shape.

The rest of the day passed them by like a shooting star. The ship looked like a patchwork quilt with the varying materials that had been recycled to fix the holes in the sails and the hull bulged at the side where the welding had been done effectively and quickly. The Audacia was no longer a pretty vessel but she would earn her name if nothing else.

'This audacious cretin of the seas is ready to sail to whichever port suits your fancy, sir,' said the ever enthused second mate. 'What heading should we set a course to?'

Castellar stood upon the deck and considered the options. He was worried about taking the Audacia out into the ocean as, despite the rate of repair, the ship was not one hundred per cent and that made them an easy target for pirates. Add to that the fact, pointed out kindly by Diccon, that they didn't have the numbers to sail the Audacia properly let alone defend themselves. It was true that most pirates had previously been hired by the various factions to join in the fighting when the forty-year war was still in full flow, so fewer of them roamed the seas now, but it was still a risk.

Castellar turned his head to Lynden, to offer her the choice of responding. She bit her bottom lip and took to thinking whilst staring at the deck.

'The question we have to ask ourselves is, where would Pietrich be heading? I don't suppose there is any value in trying to track his movements so we should anticipate them instead. That is unless we trust to fate his well-being and seek out one of the elders to the north.'

Lynden was truly at a loss. She had a hunch about where Pietrich would have gone of course, but would he have been so daring as to head to Knighton? It was not far from Port Melees after all, and although the boy had no horse, he could have easily made his way there in the time they had spent repairing the ship.

'If I may?' Castellar interrupted her train of thought. 'If he wanted to return home, as he may well have done, it is unlikely he would stay long as he knows the dangers. Every village has been laden with guards at the command of the Winter Queen. So, if I were the boy, I would have snuck in quietly and left in the middle of the night, which means by now he is headed to his true destination.'

'He will want to trace his heritage to find answers,' Lynden offered.

'Yes. Exactly. Whatever he may learn will only help him to understand his gift. It is not likely he would have concluded to simply disappear into hiding.'

'But, he spoke of a fortress where Tritan is being held. He already voiced his passion to infiltrate it. If he has grown stronger, and I think we can agree that appears as if it is so, and confidence has gotten the better of him, then…' She shook her head like a spinning top. It felt like one. 'I just don't know.'

'Do you trust him, to consider your advice unrelentingly prudent? And if so, would he have turned his mind against your advice for a fool's chance at saving his father?'

'You are asking me to second guess the most complex mind throughout the world entire,' Lynden rebuked him. Castellar accepted it.

'Yes, I am. Because that is exactly what we must do. He has probably learnt more about his nature these past two weeks, as have we all, than ever before.'

'You're right, and he would be as eager to continue his education I am certain, as we are. The time for the elders to reform as council may be close but perhaps now is not it.'

Lynden leant her elbows on the wooden railing of the ship and looked across the wide river mouth where they contemplated the course that they would take. She looked out at a flock of birds that flew downstream, low flying gulls, that squawked as they passed the Audacia and became a cluster of silhouettes against the fearsome brightness of the sun to the west.

'Yes, I think so too,' she said as she watched them fly. 'We sail for The Vermillion Isles.'

## 18

Seventeen days. It was a lifetime. The course of humanity could be changed in a fraction of the time that Summer waited for River to rise from her comatose state. She cared very little for the mainlander who lay beside her. For him, seventeen days, clinging on to life, had been seventeen days too long. The infirmary amongst the sand dunes that contained the three patients was tended to by dozens of healers, each with varying treatments and ideas. June made his daily rounds in the mornings and evenings to hear of any progress, though frequently there was none.

Thousands had emerged from the varying settlements and the smaller islands around Vermillion. Word had spread quickly to Shadow Cove of Volcan's condition. The big island school and town existed by a bay that was hidden from the light of the sun in the volcano's shadow all but seven days of the year. That week was usually a time for celebration where the light of the high sun shone upon the town and bay and lit up all the coral that lived in the waters. It was a colourful time and it ought to have been the first night of the festival but no one would be celebrating this year.

The student pilgrimages to the summit had been put on hold and instead young pupils walked the now heavily guarded forest path to pay respects to the teacher and protector.

Summer had been perturbed at their prying and fuss. Her peaceful beach haven had been turned into a carnival. The unsettled feeling grew inside her and she pleaded with June to restrict them, but it was hard to convince the students not to make the trek. Instead, they had determined that none could enter the infirmary and so a series of large gazebos had been set up on the sand for them to pray together. Summer scorned any appreciation of their sentiments, she just wanted to be left in peace to worry about her lover.

June had begun to converse with her about the nature of the quickening almost from the moment that Boscelito had emerged from the woodland path with River limply laid over his shoulder. The mainlander had found some impossible hidden strength but the moment he had spotted the white infirmary tent he had collapsed and had not risen since.

The conversations bothered Summer for she knew from her training that these were the conversations that River had feared one day. If Summer was being prepared to see her sick lover sent for a life of solitude atop the mountain to listen to the voices from the volcano, then to hell with all of The Vermillion Isles. She would wait for River to rise from her slumber and they would slip away in the night and settle down for a simple life together, away from all the islanders of Vermillion and mainlanders of Harmion. Indeed, anyone who was fighting this stupid war. She wanted no part of it. She only wanted to be with River.

Summer had gone herself to Shadow Cove to visit her mother during these past weeks to seek solace. She had not expected to be rebuked and called selfish for wanting to ignore her responsibilities. Their relationship had been tumultuous over the years and Summer had argued countless times against responsibilities being imposed on her against her will. Training as a mature pupil in the ways of the soul-magic, to one day be an assassin or informer as River had been. It was her best means of escaping the work that had been set out for her at the time. Never could she have imagined that June would now be seasoning her for the worst job of all.

'You chose to have me and so I am your responsibility, but I did not choose this life,' Summer shouted at her mother.

'I had no such choice in having you, though I chose to love you despite the way in which you were conceived.'

Her mother's hurtful reply had come as an admission that stunned Summer. She'd always known her mother had been young and no doubt foolish, but she had been taken against her will only to fall pregnant. It was the first time Summer had heard the painful truth from her only parent, even though she had suspected it her entire life.

How foolish she had been to pick a fight with a woman who had suffered as much as her own mother. Of course she would not have found sympathy on the edges of that roughly lived life. Summer loved her mother dearly and damned herself that she was so quick to disregard how anyone else felt in these matters. To make up for growing up as a single-parented child, Summer's mother had spoilt her at every opportunity. To such an extent that Summer had to remind herself now that she was not as special as she had been led to believe.

'I can't do what he is asking of me. It is not my place. It is not what I have been trained for. I knew one day that River would have to replace Volcan on the mountain but I cannot go there in her stead while she lies ill.'

'Child, you must stop rambling. Clear your head and get on with the task at hand.'

Summer shook her head and paced up and down her mother's small kitchen where she was cooking a sage and butter sauce. The aroma would usually turn Summer's head but it had made no impact on her on this occasion.

'She will recover soon, the argument is pointless. We can wait for her to get better.'

Summer said the words pleadingly, as if it was her mother that was forcing this on her.

'Summer, this task will never fall onto River. That is the truth that has been kept from you both all this time. You must listen to June and take heed of everything he has to say.'

That afternoon had been hard on Summer and it was not due to improve. June had waited for this tragic time to reveal to Summer how River had few signs of the soul-magic and she was too valuable an assassin to be wasted on the mountain. It contradicted everything River had been led to expect. Everything she had told Summer that would one day come between them. River had spent her adult life in fear of being sent to the mountain to take over from Volcan when he was no longer able to carry out his work. So why now, was Summer being told that there was no such plan in place for her to take over from Volcan's work? Summer was a simple student. She had always been looked down upon and yet now she was privy to the most key information about the future of Vermillion.

Then the shock came.

June told her it was for her, Summer, to take the reins of the volcano in her hands, not as a caretaker, but to become heir to the most difficult job on Vermillion. To have spent her life in the shadow of the mountain to now be cast into the full light of the sun caused Summer to shake uncontrollably and she ran straight back home to tell her mother what was intended for her. She broke down in the kitchen as if her life were over, sobbing into her mother's bosom, wishing she were still a child.

'You have much to learn, it was not meant to be this way for it is too soon. But there is little advice left that I can give you. I am just a simple woman. You are so much more than I am.'

Summer's mother embraced her and there were no more words between them. They enjoyed the moment together while they could for they both knew that Summer must return to the beach.

As the healers finished their rounds on the seventeenth morning, June took Summer to one side and spoke plainly for both their sakes. His subtle hints had by now worn thin.

'There is little sign of progress. Volcan is still talking in riddles and neither the captive nor River have stirred once. But they are stable. It is as if their fate is intertwined.'

If June was trying to comfort Summer with the news, he was failing.

'Volcan has offered no opinion on what you should do?' Summer asked pleadingly. She wanted so much for him to rise and talk sense into his brother instead of murmuring on about the wandering souls who were caught in purgatory at the base on the volcano.

June began a slow walk across the beach and signalled for Summer to follow. They began their saunter across the shore-line and away from the hordes of islanders.

'Volcan is experiencing the severing. The soul-magic is leaving him. It happens to us all when the body is no longer strong enough to survive the torment. Those who have been stronger in the magic will suffer the worst severing and it is as though you have lost part of your own existence. He is being laid to rest and I fear it will not be long before we will submit his body to the ocean.'

'I am sorry for Volcan, but I do not understand why you

intend to send me to the top of the mountain. I know you believe River has no touch of the soul-magic, but we all have a part of it inside us. You taught me that yourself. It is what allows us to reach all others.'

'The soul-magic is complex. It chooses its host indiscriminately and though you are right in saying that it exists in all of us, it lies dormant in so many. You should think of the quickening as an arousal of potential that lies there beneath the life force that makes us. The severing lays that potential to rest, and although it never vanishes completely, it makes us deaf to the call of the mountain.'

'There are others, much stronger than I, you must know that.'

'Summer,' he said, quivering. 'I still have much to explain. I first need to know if all I have taught you has taken hold. You spoke of the voices that have come to you in the night, what do they tell you?' He asked her as if for the first time, but she had told him before.

'They are just dreams, there is no sense to them and I do not understand why I must continue to repeat them. Obviously, with our loved ones in the dire state they are in, I would suffer nightmares.'

'They are not dreams, nor nightmares, Summer.'

He was moving closer and closer to the waves with each step as if he wanted the sound of the sea to drown out their words from any distant ears that may hear them.

He continued. 'When one of the blood of the soul-magic experiences the severing it is likely that the quickening will complete in another. We do not get to choose why or when, but we must respond to the signs.'

The waves were all she wanted to listen to. Not the discourse of this old man. Every syllable he uttered sent shockwaves of dread throughout her body. She wanted him to stop.

'You have learnt so much in your schooling, even though you took it up later in life than ordinarily would have been permitted. You may argue that I have been harder on you than the other students but that is only because your potential is so great. I feared this day but I hoped it would come under easier circumstances. You must understand that you will be needed more than you have ever been led to believe.'

Summer raised a single inquisitive eyebrow at her teacher. He had never supported her enrolment not complimented her abilities before. Her mother had fought and pleaded with June for weeks before he finally allowed Summer to participate in the school. Even then it was as an observer, withheld from practical sessions at first. She had been compelled to prove herself over time and relied upon private training from River to get to a point where June had accepted her.

'I recall a different engagement of my attendance. My mother, for all her troubles, made it clear how much it meant to have me find some purpose. Do you not recall how I was made to clear out all the latrines of the pupils' dorms whilst the advanced classes were taking place? Do you not recall how I was suppressed for as long as possible? Do you not recall the way my mother got on her knees and begged you to make me an equal at the school?'

June stopped then and turned to face Summer. He was building himself up slowly, as was his style. But the look he gave her, that Summer gripped with tearful eyes, was like looking into an hourglass with just a few drops of sand left to fall.

'Your mother has been a burden to our ways for decades. She made wild accusations when she herself was a student and was eventually expelled from the school. She became a social worker in Shadow Cove, caring for all the young girls who were orphaned. We are a culture of island hoppers and travellers, assassins and guardians of the soul-magic that keeps the world alive. Such a life of free folk burdens and adds complexity to our personal lives. It was natural for me to be cautious on that account.' He paused for a time, as though he waited to present some form of evidence to a council in session. 'You were never equal to the others at the school, Summer. You were so much more gifted than them and to put you against them in training, with so little prior schooling, would have endangered them all. Tell me, please, one last time of your dreams.'

Summer began to cry, as if being forced to admit to the horrible realisation that was rising inside her.

'I dreamed of my mother being ravished. Her body used and discarded like a whore. But she was no whore, just a young girl in love.'

'The quickening recalls to us many moments of our life, including the moment of our conception. It is rougher for some than others,' he said, sympathetically. 'Continue.'

Summer shook her head as tears streamed down her face. She hated him. She hated them all. 'My mother made a pilgrimage to the volcano, but not with her fellow students. Damn foolish woman, she wanted to go alone, to appeal her expulsion. She stayed in the cavern chamber for three nights. Each night she gave all of herself to him, both body and mind. But it was only her body he wanted.'

Summer broke down and fell to her knees. The wetness of the sea brushed against her as the tide closed in towards the sandy dunes where they had begun their stroll. Despite his age and the pain it caused him, June forced himself to join her on his knees and put an arm around her shoulder.

'I never believed a word of what she had told me,' June admitted. 'After all these years I never believed the quickening would reveal his darkest secret. He must have known this day would come and he never spoke a word of it. Instead we rallied behind him to protect his lie.'

'Oh, gods, damn you all to an eternal abyss!' Summer screamed a cry into the air and the waves carried the sound off with them into the depths of the ocean. 'You let me believe, all these years, that my mother had sold herself to one of any number of merchants that worked out of the bay. I spent years of my life, making enquiries to the folk of Shadow Cove if they might know anything. My mother never told me. Yes, she had admitted she was in love. Perhaps so I would believe she wanted me. Why didn't she tell me the truth?'

'She feared for your life. No one believed her and so you too would have been subjected to uphold a disbelieved truth. What easier way to kill the truth than to believe the lie herself?'

Summer found herself retching into the white sand, fine as powder. She took deep breaths as yellow saliva poured from her mouth with each torturous yell she exuded.

'If Volcan is my father, you know... You know what that means.'

'Yes, River is your first cousin.'

'Oh God, please! Please don't let it be true. My own blood. How can it be.'

June tried in his best solicitous voice to offer her some light at the end of the tunnel.

'The soul-magic is perhaps the greatest love that any of us will ever know. You have an opportunity to rise from the shadow of your past and seize the fire. Summer, the mountain is calling to you.'

The next moment was a swift and soft release. Release of blood into the water. Release of pain of her mind. Release of the blade she had plunged into June's heart as his life cascaded into the ocean and painted the white sands a red shade as fierce as the vermillion morning sky that surrounded them.

She whispered to him the final words he would ever hear, through the bile and the hurt.

'Summer is gone, there is only Winter left for me now.'

## 19

White heat forced the sweat. Blurred figures, intruding, swept across her vision. An opera of healers scurrying, their assistants cutting the dressings on her abdomen. She knew none of the distorted faces that worked her wounds.

Beside the stretcher, made of thin fabric and bamboo, was a large ceramic container that exuded a putrid smell of old pus and discarded blood, fish skin and soil.

They had set maggots to work on her shoulder. Eating away at the dying flesh and absorbing the infection inflicted by the fangs of the wild beast. River allowed herself to raise a weak hand to feel the wound. A large portion of her shoulder had wasted away but the outer layer had sealed.

She heard voices calling out to her and the obscured faces leaned into hers where she lay, blocking out the sun that poured through the slit in the tent opening. They called to her but the sound was a din of murkiness. River focused to regain her senses and forced herself upright.

'You must not move,' a concerned healer ordered her. 'Please lie back.'

River felt a cord tugging on the inside of her elbow. A tube filled with an orange substance was attached to a sack lined with stretched cow intestines. They had been feeding her whilst she had slept.

'How long?' she asked.

The healer gestured to his superior to take over. 'River, please remain calm. You've been in a coma for coming up on three weeks. You need to relax.'

Her first thought was the waste of life. All those days gone by without a conscious thought. How would she ever regain the time. Next she wondered if her shoulder would ever heal. Insects had eaten away a large portion of muscle with the rotten flesh they'd absorbed, leaving a cavern in their wake.

'I must stand,' she said, determined. 'Help me, you fools!'

The order was said with such vigour that the healers dared not refuse her. They helped her to sit up on the stretcher and then two of the medics grasped an armpit each to allow her to stand on the straw mat that was laid upon the floor of the infirmary.

Her vision sharpened and she looked at her fellow patient. Boscelito lay unattended but had a similar tube coming from his arm. His leg had been ravished in a similar way to her shoulder but the infection had passed. They had both been lucky.

'What the hell happened?' she asked the room. Any answer would do in her confused state.

'The beast you slew. The venom on its fangs was a sedentary poison. The dose could have killed you both but *he* managed to get you back to us,' the medic gestured to Boscelito. 'Most fortunate of all was that we were already prepared to receive you on account of Volcan's condition.'

Volcan. Of course. She had forgotten him.

'Where is my uncle?'

'We moved him to a separate tent. His condition is not good.'

River began to stagger out of the tent. She refused help from any who offered it but accepted a gown to cover her body.

The lead healer followed her across the beach towards a shaded spot that lay beneath the palm leaved branches of the tree-lined dunes. River entered the tent where Volcan lay. He was pale as the tent sheet that was his enclosure. His eyes were open and he had a fever.

'He hasn't spoken a word of sense for a week,' the healer pointed out starkly. 'He keeps on saying, *all is going quiet, they no longer speak to me.*'

River settled by his side and held his withering hand. A wreck of the strong palm of the uncle she had known as a girl who had picked her up and swung her around in circles. He had often thrown her into the sea and acted like a sea monster on his fleeting visits to the beach settlement, chasing her and oh how she used to scream and laugh. She had gotten used to visiting him at the summit of the volcano when he had become too old to make the journey; they never laughed on those occasions, instead he imparted his wisdom to her and treated her as his pupil.

'The severing is almost complete,' she said. 'The soul-magic is leaving him.'

River felt confused in that moment. She had been told to expect the quickening, unless perhaps it was skipping yet another generation. From her training, she knew that it was possible for one to act as a caretaker over the mountain but with the war on the mainland they could not afford such an absence of knowledge. She had not dreamed nor heard the voices she had been told to expect. Something felt very wrong.

Volcan rolled his head to face River; some semblance of

recognition was there as though his suffering would allow him a moment's respite.

'River.'

'I'm here, Uncle.'

He choked the strangled words that barely formed but a strength surged in him for he needed to force them out before he died. He had waited nearly three weeks to die.

'The mountain… is. It is not for you.' He wheezed and began to stutter as his breath was failing him. He gripped her hand tight, anger possessed him. 'You are the source. The source of the new line. There is a dark time on the horizon.'

Again he stopped. The words were a riddle and it was as though he spoke of a secret prophesy. The severing was worse than she had been taught to expect. No wonder, for Volcan had been strong in the soul-magic.

'Uncle, please just rest. Everything will be alright.'

River wasn't quite sure what she meant by that. He spoke of the future of their people and she threw him her childish hope. If he had been able, he would have rebuked her for the pointless sentiment. Instead he ignored it. Time was short.

'Summer will need your support, now more than ever. But not your love.' River felt the concern in his eyes. It was not aimed at her but it was as though he wept for a lost love. 'Promise me, River. You must.'

'I promise, Uncle.'

What else could she say? She didn't understand him, nor was she sure what she had promised or if she could keep it. But what else could she say to a man who had just said his last words.

Volcan loosened his hand and it fell to the side of his waist. He drew his last breath and his body went still. Every muscle relaxed and he appeared to have shrunk in size in that moment.

Only the stare of his eyes remained strong and they cut into River's guilt.

Volcan was dead. Even in death he charged her with his gaze, not to forget her promise. Whatever the promise was, she would have to wait for time to reveal it to her.

These were the moments where life should slow to a crawl. All the family and students would gather around to comfort each other and set their departed into the sea as tradition would demand. They would spend days of mourning, wondering how each of their own futures would have changed direction from this moment forth. For Volcan, those honours would not be bestowed. No period of rest would be afforded the islanders. His death was the mere opening act to an opus of tragedy.

The girl burst into the tent without hesitation. Jade, a young student of the school in Shadow Cove. She knew her place and under normal circumstances would never have been so brash. This could not wait.

'River, you must come immediately. We have found June. He has been murdered!'

Had it been a cruel joke, death would have been too kind a penance for the girl. But River knew her well; she had trained Jade in the art of short blade combat herself. She was a good student and not one for foolhardy commentary. River didn't wait around to understand the ridiculous implications of the statement or to question it with her own idiotic mind that was still preparing the arrangements for her uncle's departure. Instinct drove her to flee from the infirmary and out onto the sands.

She had forgotten the River who had just awoken, whose own condition was feeble and let the assassin, strong and elegant, take charge. River saw the gathering by the sea. Jade ran past her, gesturing for her to follow, and within seconds, River had broken out into a run and overtaken the girl, racing towards the crowd. She furiously fought her way through, to discover the body of her father that the onlookers surrounded.

River dropped to his side and saw the trail of blood that led across the sand and towards the sea. He had been dead for several hours. His body was freezing cold. She felt the incision that was just below the ribcage that had led to the puncturing of his heart. It was a clean kill, efficient. As though she had done this herself with her own skill. Or someone she had trained. As River looked around at the dumb expressionless faces of the students, she suddenly realised that someone was missing. Someone that should have been there to see her rise from her slumber.

'Where is Summer?'


A COLD EVENING fell upon the beach and creatures scurried up through the dunes to bask in the freshness gifted by the coastal breeze. Their peace was met with chaos, stretching from the northern cliffs to the peninsula at the opposite end of the beach where preparations were underway. River had charged Jade to ensure that the bodies were cleaned, wrapped and loaded onto their finest vessel. It had been years since the Audacia had left Shadow Cove and sailed the ocean as no attack had required its service since before the war.

River had never captained a ship as large. She always rode as a passenger, an assassin, hiding in the wings, but today she had decided to take control of the warship and commit her family to the ocean. They deserved to have the proper ocean burial that had been the custom for so long. But first she had to find Summer.

As fear and confusion spread, the islanders became increasingly tense. River's own suspicion grew as each moment passed but she simply could not believe that her lover would have wronged her so.

A loud rumbling sound began to fill the air and the earth shook. Cracks appeared in the sand on the beach and swallowed anything that lay upon it.

Everyone screamed.

The schooner prepared for the burials had disappeared beneath quicksand in the beach and taken a dozen people down with it. River cast her gaze towards the mountain and smoke poured from the summit.

The volcano had been angered. Suddenly there was so much to do. So many things to fix and too many people to save.

River ran to the soldiers who had survived the sinking ship where they gathered with Jade. They were suffering from shock at how quickly the earth had opened to claim the lives of their kin.

'It is the volcano. Something is seriously wrong. Get everyone off this island now.'

The soldier nearest to her was lost in despair. He forgot his place for a moment. 'We are tens of thousands of settlers, the townsfolk are an hour's ride away. Half our ships docked. What would you have us do?'

'Soldier, do whatever it takes. Get the students onto their training vessels. The schooners will ready in half the time of the warships.'

The gathering of soldiers looked despondently towards one another, but knew they must act immediately. Time was no ally.

The farmers and townsfolk nearby had come to pay their respects to Volcan and now had been plunged into desperation, a diaspora of confusion. Who would lead them now? They had lost both their fathers in one fell swoop and the ground itself had opened up to suck them beneath the earth.

River couldn't handle them now; she would have to further burden her fellow soldiers.

'Form groups of a dozen or so and make sure we are well supplied. The ships may be home for some time. Assign a soldier to each group and instruct them to act quickly.'

*Where are you, Summer? Damn you.*

A man broke through the forest boundary on horseback. He had been riding furiously.

'River,' the hasty soldier shouted breathlessly. 'June's private guard are missing.'

'What? How can that be? I was told they were stationed at Shadow Cove on my father's orders! Why else would they have not been with him when he was murdered?'

'I do not know. I would ask them the same if they were here. I sent a rider to track them down and none were in their homes, and all their weapons had been taken.'

'What is she doing?' River said, louder than she intended. It had to be Summer.

'Their families were scared,' the soldier continued. 'One of the wives claimed her husband acted as though he were possessed.'

'Come with me, soldier, and tell me all you heard.' River requested the man follow her to her abode as she turned and rushed to the room where her weapons were stored. She began to rummage through her drawers.

'Are they all gone. All twenty?' she asked.

The soldier nodded his head.

River put on her battle dress. As she pulled the jerkin over her head the pain in her shoulder caused her to yell out. What the hell was happening? This was madness. Surely River was still bed bound, suffering a coma and this was a wild dream. Her life was splintering apart like a straw house being blasted to pieces in a hurricane. Perhaps this was the quickening and none of it was real.

The sky darkened as the smoke from the volcano blocked out the light of the sun. Hours had passed since River had learnt of her father's death and the island had fallen into despair. It was almost time for the sun to set and the shuddering earth would not relent.

'Dammit, it will kill us all,' River said hastily.

'The volcano has not erupted for a thousand years. Surely it is just stirring?'

River shook her head at the man as she slipped on her boots.

'No, today is not the day for hopeful assumptions. Set up a perimeter on the beach. Guard the students while we arrange their departure. Ensure the armada is ready to sail. We will have the funeral rites and take every one of our people from this beach.'

'What of the prisoner? He remains in the infirmary, unattended.'

Damn him. Another burden she had cast from her mind and now the cursed mainlander returned like an anchor, strapped to her ankles.

'Leave him, we cannot waste our time on him anymore. Just do your best to see that everyone else is safe. The Audacia is yours to command until I return.'

River pulled open the hidden compartment to her cabinet and poured all the pre-loaded vials of poison and healing remedies into her jacket pockets. She placed both her killing blades in the sleeves of her long shirt and stopped a moment, hit by a wall of anguish.

'Leave now, soldier. Do not delay.'

'Ma'am.' With that he was gone. River was alone, and all of a sudden the burden of the whole world crushed her.

Thoughts cascaded into her mind and reminded her of the terrible condition she was in. She was ravished body and soul. No wonder she cried then, but for only a brief time as anger found her again and wondering how her injured form could cope with what must be done, she thought about what Summer had done. Had she mind-washed her father's men somehow? They were handpicked, specially, as those who were not of the Primavemani in order that their minds could be claimed. River knew now what she had always known, that she had very little grasp of the soul-magic and the quickening had not come to her. Had it come to Summer instead? She was not of the bloodline. River scorned herself for the myriad questions that fluttered around her mind like a starling murmuration in spring. But they were just thoughts. She needed proof.

River then did the thing she had vowed never to do again. To take the lava. She swallowed a whole vial of the potent remedy and carried with her a second for when she would arrive at the summit of the mountain. She had never known anyone to take such a dose and if it killed her, so be it. She would die with the truth.

She left the beach, running as fast as she'd ever run. Her body was overwhelmed but the lava made her feel twice the assassin she was on a good day. She knew the effect it would have on her when the come-down hit. She had to act fast and pray that the second dose delayed the onset of fatigue that would claim her.

River sprinted along the forest pathway and overtook several of the fleeing students and teachers, farmers and sailors. Her mind was focused on one thing as her feet brushed the floor for the brief moments that contact was made. Any who saw her would be forgiven for thinking she flew.

Her heart screamed and ached as she approached the thousand steps. No time to think about the climb. Simply that it had to be done.

A series of broken rock shards fell to the side of the stairwell as the ground shook and cracked and she launched herself up to a small outcrop to escape the debris that dropped from the heavens.

Each stride she took almost matched her in height. It reminded her of her training. The pilgrimage up the stairs had been a daily exercise and only when she had arrived at a point where the hike no longer caused her loss of breath was her teacher satisfied. But she had never run up them quite so furiously as now, diving aside to avoid the rock tears of the mountain.

The pattering of stone beneath her feet was like a rain shower hitting the roof of her cabin. Would she have anything left to offer when she reached the summit? she wondered.

The answer came with the final step that led to the plateau where the molten rock flowed like an estuary stream in a flood plain. River navigated the path carefully, winding her way through the tremendous heat towards the cavern. The hot air added to the natural heat of her body from the run and she felt sweat dripping from her brow. Salt stung her eyes and she wiped it away blinking. She squinted to sharpen her focus and protect her lashes from further intrusion. She had to be sharp. A deep breath of the sulphuric chamber awoke a caution in her.

River slid her knives out from her sleeves and walked into the cavern where Volcan had lived for so long. Standing at the far side of the chamber, facing the wall, was Summer. She was looking up at the engravings on the cave wall. The chamber shook. Part of the wall to one side split open and the sweating rock hissed as water evaporated.

'It is curious to me that so much of our history revolves around a certain degree of suffering,' Summer answered the cries of the cavern. River slowly approached. 'It seems as though we are captives of this island. Did you know that it was all water once? Until the day that the earth broke open beneath the sea and the liquid rock erupted into the air and The Vermillion Isles were born. A scattering of bastard children, born to plague the lives of those on its mainland parent.'

Summer spun to face River. The two were barely a few strides apart. They froze and their gazes met. Fuelled by hatred and undying love. There was no way to put into words the way they each felt. Summer had known it would be impossible to fight her lover. She was thankful she wouldn't have to.

The twenty guards, loyal to June, appeared from behind River and formed a semi-circle. She was surrounded on all sides. The exit blocked. This was the last place any assassin should allow themselves to be. She had chosen to stand in the very spot of a pig ready for slaughter.

'Summer, tell me it wasn't you. I do not understand how you could have done these terrible things. Will you allow me an explanation at least, to give me peace for when you are dead?'

Summer smiled at her. 'My love, peace is the reason I will tell you nothing of what I have been subjected to these past weeks. My gift to you before *you* die, is the ignorance of a hell that I could never have imagined existed.

River hadn't expected to be refused such a simple request. She wanted somehow to know the whole truth, as she knew life without it would taunt her.

The familiar sound of a collection of blades and axes being unsheathed rang around her from all directions. She gritted her teeth and broke the vial she had stored at the back of her mouth to keep her small swords drawn. The lava flowed down the back of her throat and the broken glass cut the inside of her throat, allowing the potent substance to run straight into her bloodstream.

Then she became possessed. Souls of the eternal warriors and assassins of Vermillion flooded into her being and she knew not how she had become one with them, but they said to her. *Come, Sister, we will kill them all together.*

A long arching swing of her blade came from nothing, as if it were a lightning strike. Visible only for a moment until the thunder clap reminds you that yes, it really was there. Blood sprayed into the air as the throats of three guards opened and as strength left their necks, the scarlet fountains decorated the rocks and those beside them roared before meeting River's blades with their own. A dozen bodies crashed to the floor and the delicacy of any swordplay was lost. This was carnage and human rage at its pinnacle and before the guards had noticed they were stabbing each other's legs and backs amidst the formless pile of bodies. River emerged from behind them and cut at their backs and torsos. All of those suffered who lay helplessly scrabbling to their feet.

Now she had their full attention, it would be harder to kill the rest as they would not fall for that trick again. But twenty had become sixteen and she had barely spent a single breath.

She smiled at her fellow dancers as they threw knives towards her and each of the shiny things passed gleefully to her side as she struck them from the air.

Her heart skipped a beat. The second dose of lava flooded her bloodstream. She screamed from the pain. It was like flying through a cloud formed of needles. But she was now the air, the sea and the mountain. She was everything and her two blades were no longer tools but extensions of her arms.

Three of the honour guard rushed her. River sliced at the face of the first until he was blind and mute. This was no mere battle of survival but a lustful slaughter. She knew no shame in the way she fought. Efficiency didn't matter. She had a demon in her heart.

Then two others flanked her. A sword came down towards her shoulder and she snapped her head to the side, watching as the steel drove into the rock beside her foot. She claimed the arm of the man who had swung it. She could have finished him then and there but instead let him squirm on the floor whilst she plunged the tips of both her blades into the throat of a third man who jumped from a boulder to gain an aerial advantage. He achieved little other than to increase the force with which he would fall upon the two spikes that awaited him.

*Thirteen, almost halfway.* River felt time slow and watched the running charge of the remaining soldiers as they pursued her. It was like watching a wave crashing into the rocks beneath the cliff that overlooked the beach where she had first kissed Summer. It was their favourite place to watch the sun go down. The waves always appeared to move in slow motion and the winter was their favourite time as sunset seemed to last for hours.

The wave that now crashed towards her was far less beautiful but they were not men. For River they were already corpses in her mind and she had only to seal their fate.

The way their lives ended was not fanciful. No elegant dance or manoeuvres from years of training would they be honoured by. The swordplay was a slaughterhouse series of vivid strokes. It was the fastest she had moved in her life. One bead of her sweat fell towards the ground and before it hit the rocky floor she had slit the throats of the thirteen, severed hands from those who had managed to raise a sword to greet her own, and driven the final strike into the skull of the man whom she had left clutching his severed stump.

By the time she had wiped the blood from her eyes and checked the last victim of her efforts for signs of breath, Summer was gone.

River fell to her knees. Despair took hold of her and the remaining fury of the lava was wasted on her with no one left to kill. It was then she looked around the cavern and saw the dismembered bodies for who they were. Some of them had been kind to her when she was young. Her father's most trusted cohorts. Had they betrayed him? Or was it Summer who was to blame for everything?

No time to dwell on the detritus of her life as the room shook and a flaming hot fountain spurted its fiery essence across the wall. The volcano was no longer whispering, it was ready to scream.

River sprinted from the cave and danced her way across the streams of lava that now overflowed the path. She jumped across a newly formed river of molten rock feeling the searing heat grapple the base of her legs and she tucked herself into a somersault to avoid the spitting, burning substance.

The stairwell was a mess and littered with rubble from the mountain. Off in the distance, large pools of lava poured down the side of the volcano. It was going to consume the entire island.

River descended the steps, jumping four and five at a time. Her legs burned from the pressure they suffered with each landing blow. Her knees were aching but the lava still ran through her veins. Lava against lava. A form of harmony, she thought. She was the lava and she flowed down the side of the mountain as though she and the eruption were a whole being.

The beach was a battlefield of bodies and screaming mourners, trying to rouse their dead and pull the suffocated victims from the sand that had smothered them.

The volcano stood angrily flooding the sky with its inferno. A wave of magma was approaching the beach.

Jade ran to River with a haunted look of desperation.

'We must leave at once; the Audacia is ready to sail. We have sent a charge of schooners ahead and the rest sail out from Shadow Cove. We have given coordinates for our bearing where we will meet, but there is no more time.'

'Thank you, Jade. You have prepared my father and uncle for the voyage?'

'Yes, of course. But there is something else. Summer has fled the island alone on your private vessel.'

River had assumed no less. There was no sense worrying about that now. Her personal suffering could wait.

'Why are these people not boarding the ships? They will be smothered by the bile of the mountain retching.'

Jade shook her head. 'They won't leave their loved ones. This is their home and they refuse to leave.'

'Dammit, we don't have time for this. Round up as many of the students and soldiers, farmers or anyone else who still has some faith in life and get them to drag these people onto the ships.'

River didn't wait for a response as she began to head towards the Audacia. The vessel was waiting and June and Volcan needed her now in death as much as they had done so in life. She had to submit them to the sea, to put their souls to rest.

She stopped midway across the beach, facing the rowboat that would take her to the ship just a short stretch out to sea. The boat was full and ready to go. She felt her limbs shiver as the lava began to leave her.

River raised her arm to the sailor who was in charge of the last rowing boat and waved him away. It was perhaps a moment of madness or some divine intrusion. A voice infiltrated her mind. It was clearer than the voice she had heard in Port Melees. But it was unmistakable. The voice of the boy she had heard there begged her.

*You must save him! If you do not march across the sands and take him from the path of the lava then I will never live!*

She trembled. The voice so clear she looked around in case he was there.

*Who are you?*

*That is not important now. But you and I are closer than you know.*

She staggered backwards, away from the sea. River didn't know why she was obeying the boy in her thoughts, but she felt his urgency pressing against her and turned, breaking into a run towards the infirmary. River knew nothing of the insanity that possessed her but whatever drove her was her desire to know the truth and she felt guilt coursing through her for having thought of leaving Boscelito here to die. What was this guilt if not affection?

The guilt replaced the lava in her bloodstream and as she entered the infirmary she flung the prisoner across her shoulder. The weight made her dizzy and as she made for the sea once more she saw missiles of molten rock flying across the sky. Several made contact with the ships that were sailing away from the shore. But the volcanic rocks vanished from her sight and her head pounded. Instead she began to see stars on a canvas of darkness and she knew they would not make it back to the ships.

*You must live. You both must live for you are the future as each of us are. All of us together.*

## 20

All was tinted in a damp frost as the kinder seasons rolled away and made way for the cold. Silence fell upon the town as its inhabitants waited indoors for the early morning chill to be assuaged. It was the best time for a walk. Baurticeford held no resemblance to the rabid heat of the islands or soft footing of the sand where she had not walked for years but Winter had never felt more at home. She sometimes missed the heat but dearly loved to dress herself in large winter coats and soft silken undergarments.

The quaint, northern town had treated her well these past months. She loved her estate and it had been longer than she could remember since she had felt such a physical urge for another as she did towards Resonance Qualchaid. Her host was almost half her age but she was so beautiful. Winter felt old and foolish to think her lust would be met with anything but ridicule. The life of feeling the warmth of another's skin against her own was gone.

A barking dog broke the quiet of the air as it ran down to pounce upon Winter where she stood by the riverbank. The dog's damp paws muddied her coat but she laughed heartily and squatted down to pat the golden furry beast.

'*You* love me, do you not, Arthur?' she said. 'You know your mother does not tolerate you escaping the villa. Resonance will hold me accountable if I let you join me.' She paused and smiled at the dog. 'Still the damage is already done I suppose, you may accompany me on my morning walk.'

Winter set off down the path beside the river that was lined with bristly fern hedges and Arthur followed by her side, a loyal companion, his golden coat, dragging through the icy puddles and his tongue lolled out panting. Winter felt a sense of pride that she could please an animal in such a way. His happiness was a reminder to her of the woman she had once been.

As she plodded along the walkway, Winter thought of her past and her troubles returned. *Peace is a fleeting moment like a whisper in a gale*, she thought.


HER EFFORTS TO return Tritan to his former physical form had not been wasted. Even without full use of one arm, his program had been successful. So impressionable was his mind that he had carried out his orders without complaint and he had given everything to the training that was expected of him.

Winter had burnt into him the desire and need to become strong again. She had willed out the panic attacks that he had recently suffered and squashed his fear. She spoke to him as an equal and his mind was slowly becoming hers.

Pietrich, she could sense however, was growing stronger as each day passed and Winter was incapable of reaching his mind any longer. Her only hope was that once he had completed the quickening and her the severing, that her mind would be protected.

If her teachings had been accurate, a Primavemani's mind,

once severed, is deaf to the reach of the soul-magic. The trauma of the experience ruptures the connection so completely it cannot be re-formed. For Winter, it would be a unique gift to allow her peace and protection from those who may use it against her.

Her efforts with Tritan had begun to show promise that her wild ideas may not be foolish, but she needed him to be resilient to Pietrich too. What good was it to create her own private warrior who could so easily be bent out of shape. No, she needed another way. As Pietrich's grasp of the soul-magic increased, her control over Tritan would diminish.

She had but one chance and timing would be crucial. The time to cut Tritan's mind from the soul-magic for good was close.

Winter took a moment's pause and fiddled with her exotic bracelet. The only memory of her former self that she carried with her. The Maluabian jewellery had been a gift. She recalled her first and only true love, stolen from her, or had River eventually been pushed away by Summer, the girl she once was? Winter didn't know the difference any more. That day had been so fraught with desperation and confusion.

Better to forget.

As she stared across the river with Arthur panting at her side a horseback rider approached from the rear. It was Troy, her favourite soldier. She liked him for his inability to lie. It was painful to know the thoughts of so many and to hear the lies that passed from their lips. She looked forward to the day when she no longer heard their minds. At least for now, Troy was consistent in speaking exactly what he thought.

'Troy, it is still early. You have no need to do your rounds until after breakfast,' she reminded him. 'Time is precious in this place.'

'Yes, ma'am, it is only that we have caught word of a trading town that is refusing to pay its tax. They said they have given enough and they shan't be paying any more.'

Troy was nervous, he hated bringing bad news to Winter.

'Perfect. We have our first true opportunity for a test. Ride to inform Thomas that we will need all sixteen of my private guard today. Oh, and, Troy, what town is it you speak of?'

'It is the one about three hours ride along the northern river from the split towards the coast, ma'am, not far at all, Haaguru-fur, the old merchant town.'

Winter rolled her head in a comic form of disgust. 'Oh, Troy. You do bring such untidy news, I always liked that little town.'

Troy wasn't quite sure he understood her meaning but he nodded in approval before he rode away. 'Ma'am.'

'Well, the day began as peacefully as a still lake, dear Arthur. Now I must go to start a fire. I'd best leave you with Resonance for such dirty work. We will keep you an innocent yet.'

As the preparations were made, a squadron of sixteen riders made their way to the town exit where Winter awaited them in her carriage. Tritan and Fritz rode at the front, and Winter noticed that Tritan now clasped at the reins of his horse with both hands.

Thomas was trotting on his pony to the rear like a Tornjak herding sheep. He cantered to where Winter was sat inside her carriage to answer the eager look she had thrown him as she waved him closer.

'Is it some secret you keep from me, or is today the day of some miracle?' she asked him.

Thomas turned his head to look at Tritan, whose serious gaze and purpose barely showed emotion. The warrior held his back up proudly and appeared twice the size of the withered man that Thomas had received into his clinic the season past.

'We had a breakthrough these last two nights. The lava, though in itself a short-term solution; when mixed with some of the stimulants that I work with, seems to have a lasting impact.'

'That is very good news, Thomas. Tell me, how much lava have you used? There is not an infinite supply, as I have mentioned before, and it does not grow here. Nor is it any longer cultivated.'

'Yes, I recall and I have used it sparingly.' He rushed to clarify the point that followed. 'Of course, we would be better off to somehow gain more of this substance, but for now we do at least know the formula that is working.'

'Very well, keep at it and do advise with all due notice if the supplies are dwindling.'

Thomas bowed before re-joining the rear of the caravan that was to ride out to Haagurufur. Winter cast her gaze across the small legion that was growing. All the soldiers were free of charge. Winter had requested volunteers from her castle guard and the infamy of the one who would be their captain intrigued those who had enlisted. Tritan was to lead them so they had been told. His orders would come directly from Winter herself.

The three-hour ride to Haagurufur was elongated on account of the carriage having a faulty bolt on the wheel. Troy, the handy fellow with ever increasing value to Winter, set about fixing it whilst Winter decided to take a stroll to pass the time. She invited Tritan to join her. She had no fear whatsoever for her wellbeing, despite the fact the warrior now seemed to have recouped his unnatural force of strength. He had hauled timber and hammered stone, parried sword against sword with Fritz, and Winter, aware of the monster she was creating, wondered if her confidence had grown too vast. Then again, she had once bedded the most dangerous assassin who ever lived.

She tried her best to engage him in conversation but there seemed to be little that was recognisable behind those eyes. It was a pleasure to see him retreat within himself and somehow it was also disappointing as she had previously enjoyed her conversations with the man. He had, somehow, piqued her interest. His former quips had not been thoughtless and at times were laced with potent ideology, not unlike her own. But if losing those insights down a dark tunnel, where his soul was trapped beneath her spell, was the price to pay for her creation to function as she required, Winter would sacrifice the ageing goat with infinite collectedness. No doubt there were plenty of thoughtful conversations to be had back at the villa with Resonance when the day was done.

Troy signalled that the wheel bolt was mended and so they continued to Haagurufur. Winter's guard rode off ahead to make sure the path was not overgrown, allowing the carriage to pass through.

The town came upon them as a flat plain, hidden beneath a mist that rolled over the central market square. The purpose-built trade town was bustling with the life of an evening market. Sellswords manned the four compass point entrance roads and stood to block Tritan and Fritz who rode up front as they approached.

The man who stepped forward to greet them was overweight and judging by the silver threaded jerkin he wore beneath his engraved breastplate, overpaid.

'What business do you have here? That's a lot of horses carrying a lot of fighters you've brought with you.'

'Step aside.'

Tritan offered the singular instruction in return, none of his former wit or self-loathing evident in the way he spoke.

'Well, I am afraid I can't be doing that. Not until you speak your purpose and lay your steel down in the crates yonder.'

Tritan looked at the point where the man gestured. There were several large wooden containers holding swords, axes, spears, bows and arrows. It was well organised and three watchmen stood charge over it.

Tritan nodded to his squadron and they rode to the crates and lay their weaponry down. The watchmen handed them each a cloth, indicating each item that would be returned on their departure.

'The Winter Queen wishes to have an audience with the town general,' Tritan said to the guard.

'She is no queen here but you may wait and hope that he will speak to you. My men will escort you to his offices. Only you four though,' the man said, gesturing to Tritan, Fritz, Winter and the man who drove her horses. 'The rest of your rabble can wait out here.'

Tritan glanced at Winter who nodded in approval, seemingly unfazed, and dropped to the rear of the caravan to keep a closer eye on her as the carriage rolled through the town gates. Fritz took the front patrol alongside their escorts.

The town centre was bustling with traders and the night market sent worldly aromas into the lungs of all who walked the streets. There were spice traders, herb and incense stalls, and meat grills with sizzling cuts of tender loins cooking on hot coals. Fruits and vegetables from the local farms boasted the largest portion of stands in the plaza and tucked to the side, almost hidden from view, were several members of a long-necked tribe from Maluabaw, with multiple rose gold hoops around their necks to signify their age, who had set up a stall with their jewellery and fine silks. Winter halted her carriage momentarily to peer from the window at the fine produce. These were not cheap items but indeed some of the finest.

Eventually they pulled up in front of a large stone hall that was lined with marble pillars at its entrance, as extravagant as the luxury market they had just passed through.

The guards who led them instructed the group to dismount

their horses and Fritz helped Winter dismount from her carriage.

'Fritz, you wait with the horses,' Tritan instructed. 'I will see to it that Winter gets her audience.'

The order was clear. Tritan walked with Winter towards the hall and four of the Haagurufur guards from the open courtyard that sat beneath the hall moved in to flank them.

Impoverished folk and gaudy traders lined the dozen marble steps that led to the hall. They were shouting amongst themselves and waving contracts in the air as they awaited judgement on their disputes. Tritan pushed past the fuss and allowed Winter to step through towards a desk by the high-doored entrance. The woman at the desk was swimming in documents and looked strained by the noise that surrounded her on all sides. She glanced up at Winter with judgemental eyes.

'What is it?'

Winter composed herself, remaining polite and calm.

'I wish to see General Magni.'

'That is quite impossible I am afraid. He does not hold audience at this hour. You'll have to see the night council or wait until the morning.'

'You may take us to the night council, but warn them that Magni will wish he were present.'

The woman gave Winter a mocking smile and wrote up a slip of parchment that she then handed her.

'Go in and wait for this number to be called.'

Winter tilted her head with respect and walked with Tritan into the great hall. It was crammed full of people shouting at the row of spear-wielding guards who blocked them from the chamber of councillors they awaited to advise or condemn them.

'We will be here all bloody night at this rate,' Winter complained.

'Perhaps we should skip the discussion and move forward with enforcement?' Tritan suggested.

'Well, perhaps,' Winter lowered her voice to a whisper. 'But let's give the benefit of the doubt for just a little while longer. Besides, I don't want word to get out that you're doing my dirty work before I have had a chance to meet this general or he will likely run to the hills.'

The pair shot glances around the hall. A skinny man with his daughter was called for by the administrators and they were allowed through the guard wall. Winter approached the man who'd let them pass.

'I beg pardon, sir, what number was that dear fellow who just entered the hall?'

'Seven hundred and eighty-three. It is a busy time.'

'Goodness, isn't it just. That is the age I shall be by the time I get my audience. Can you not see my age by the cracks beside my eyes and silver streak of hair, sir? I am likely to fall foul of the wait and I don't doubt I would be more of a hindrance to you as a medical patient than a simple petitioner.'

'Everyone knows the Winter Queen here, my lady. Young for her years it is said. You'll wait your turn as do them all, or go and lay your head down for the evening and return at sunrise before the crowds. We have plenty of fine residences here that wouldn't dent your assets I'm sure.'

Winter turned away from him. There was no negotiating with this cruel bunch and it was not yet time to spoil the broth. Tritan had waited by her side patiently and shuffling awkwardly behind him were their minders keenly observing their actions. Winter went to look just outside the entrance hall as patters of rain began to strike the stones of the square outside.

'Well, at least we have shelter. I guess we shall wait.'

They waited and waited and a storm came, washing away the filth of the courtyard that had accumulated and driving away the poor settlers who'd hung around in anticipation of donations from the business folk as they emerged from the halls all the richer for the outcome of their proceedings.

The functionality of Haagurufur pleased Winter. It was exactly the kind of place that would go nicely in her collection once she pocketed their general.

Thin pellets of hail began to rattle against the stairs beneath the overhanging fixture where Winter and Tritan waited. A dredge of ice stones sprinkled the square beyond them until the smoothness of the plain stone was hidden. All that remained at the back of the courtyard now was the carriage Winter and her companions had come through town in and the guards who kept watch over Fritz.

The administrator called out their number at last and the guards stepped aside to allow their entrance into the hall. It was a short walk to the second large door that protected the main chamber but so large was the inner court that the stroll towards the council bench took an age, with no company to guide them save for the echoes of their own footsteps. The guards who minded them remained outside the hall but along each side of the court room were a dozen spear-wielding soldiers.

Winter stepped to the edge of a large wooden table where she met the gaze of four council heads. Behind them sat an empty throne, not unlike those that had been used by emperors or kings.

'Mistress of Fort Vecchia, please state your name,' ordered the council scribe who stared blankly into a ledger she was writing in.

'My name is Winter, daughter of Volcan, former protector of The Vermillion Isles.'

Shock struck the hearts of all the councillors sat before her. The scribe looked up from her papers and set her pen upon the table.

'You would have us document your former residence as Vermillion? The isles have played no function in our society since the trading ceased towards the start of the forty-year war. The meddling that was undertaken at the behest of your leaders has been duly noted in our surviving archives.'

'The meddling, my sweet, innocent, council whore, has never ended. You were just not privy to its existence. And yes, I would have it documented officially here today that you turned over the governance of this trade town to the Winter Queen of Vermillion. Let all know henceforth from which fire this phoenix did rise to guide them to a better life.'

A procession of wooden drumming filled the chamber as the guards hammered their spear bases into the floor. It was as though they intended to intimidate and recall to Winter, just how vulnerable she was in this moment.

'Magni, were he here to dispute your claims, would have you punished and sent forth without delay. If the panel agrees, I will grant you a boon of exile with immediate effect and no repercussions, provided you never return to Haagurufur. We do not provoke violence here, but do not push your luck.'

The scribe sat back in her chair and shot an icy stare at Winter. It was unfortunate for the seated woman that her combatant held the coldest gaze of all. The scribe went to speak again but an elderly man to her side signalled for her to hold her tongue.

'It is all well here I say, we have a singular purpose. To see the people of our great town flourish peacefully. The destruction of the war brought us bleakness and it is this town that is the phoenix that rose from the ashes. You are a burden who puts strain on us all. The settlements in the southern lands are suffering by your misguided wisdom and I will not allow the same fate to befall my people.'

Winter smiled. Such a predictable man. To feign his absence and then reveal himself with the first words he spoke.

'Well, Magni, I would say it must be well past your bedtime. But I thank you for joining us. A fun little mystery from which your guest stands heavily amused. The sentence for such offence I think will be death.'

It was the last word spoken before several guards broke ranks and surrounded Winter and her unarmed warrior, Tritan. He glared down the face of the half dozen spears and slowly edged to a point where he could lure them from Winter. Each step was carefully plotted and eventually he shouldered the entire threat alone. The council heads and Magni stood to observe the rising tension. No longer interested in diplomacy.

'You should have left well enough alone, Winter Queen. We will kill your dog and then lock you in the jail until a fair trial is held. As for your men and resources, we will of course disperse them amidst our settlements and the supplies will be a tax upon you for the cost we have incurred. Let it be documented that the council of Haagurufur was where the southern invasion ended and all lands reclaimed by the natives.'

Tritan had heard enough words. He grabbed the tip of one of the spears, cutting open the palm of his hand and yanked it hard towards him, bringing the soldier who held it within reach of his other arm. He shot his palm up into the man's nose and sent a fragment of bone into the back of his skull. Before the soldier fell, Tritan had grasped the spear in both arms and parried the circle of spikes that lunged towards him. He deflected the worst of it, though took a large gash to his midriff where a tip grazed him. But he was quick, quicker than he'd been for half his life, and he slipped out of reach of the deadly blows and paid no mind to the specks of blood that were drawn with the insignificant cuts.

He whipped the spear like a lasso and struck another guard

through the eye, dropping him to the floor. But there was no time to retract the spear. Instead he rushed the man who stood behind the second victim and kneed him in his genitals. The fresh spear dropped into Tritan's grasp and he plunged the sharp point through the chest of one who attacked from behind him.

The last two of the first retinue pulled out short blades for a brawl; the advantage of space was no longer there. Tritan met their strikes with his wrists and the metal guards he bore deflected the steel across his skin, slicing the outer layers of flesh. But these were the cuts a child endures when play fighting in a field. He smiled at the two who raged at him with their daggers as he brought his fists upon the abdomen and up into the diaphragm of the first, causing him to vomit, and the chest of the other, whose lung collapsed. He failingly gasped for air.

Tritan continued to beat them until they died without grace or clemency.

The room went still.

Breath, hot and merciless, filled the chamber as the remaining lines of guards readied themselves to attack. There were a hundred more where they came from and red salty blood and a river of sweat poured from Tritan's arms. He ignored his injuries. He was ready for the fight but Winter surprised them all when she stepped in front of him and raised her arms. Was this a submission? Surely it was too late for that as the deaths would be paid for in kind.

This was no submission. She reached towards the high dome ceiling of the chamber, closed her eyes, and focused all her strength and energy on the men and, in the next moment they turned their spears to one another and each soldier, with a look of confusion and despair on their faces, ended the life of their neighbour with a short sharp jab of their killing instruments.

Tritan didn't wait for an invitation as he strode towards the council heads and took each of their lives with his bare hands effortlessly and without remorse. His heaving chest rose and fell as he stared at the massacre of their broken necks and twisted corpses.

Winter fell to the floor behind him, her body cracking against the stone and she moaned and held her head with her hands.

'Tritan, it is time. The severance! You must come to me.'

He obeyed her and knelt at her side, not understanding what she would do next or why. But she took her hand and placed it on his head and before he knew it she was in his mind. An eruption of molten rock, laced with love and despair filled his entire being and he saw a woman laying down to rest with Winter in her arms. She reminded him of his mother. But her face was a haze, as though the memory would not allow itself to be presented to him clearly. Winter was so much younger in that time. The passionate embrace between the two lovers that he observed lasted just a moment, for then Winter's grey hairs grew from her scalp like a lapsing of time and the shadow of a man flickered against the walls but then the fires were gone and the wind and cold of the night sea blew against them and Winter rose alone upon a ship deck. But he was with her. He, Tritan was by her side and she had been wronged and now it was for him to protect her before the storms and the crusades of all who would oppose her and it was no longer her voice that sang the song in his mind but it was his own. He had decided it. Tritan was hers and he had given himself to her of his own free will. That was the last lie he would tell himself before darkness took them both into the cradle of its arms and then he slept a dreamless sleep.

## 21

Tormented was his spirit by the awakening of such fierce consequence and power, merged with the flow of quicksand emotions of all those who lived now and had lived before. Memories were no longer a page from which he read but a stream in which he swam. The web was cast and he was the only spider left alive.

Seeking guidance and driven to comprehend the power, Pietrich begged the voices, now so clear as crystal stones, to provide for his need. One response came amidst the din. It was fire and life, death and water, all as one. Vermillion was calling to him and somewhere at the base of the lava flow of the volcano were the answers he sought. It was a promise made by a ghost with an eerie voice, though the voice was not of his current time where his body existed on the verge of manhood. Rather it was a voice speaking in unison across all time. The beckoning rang in his thoughts, an ancient whisper from the birth of the islands when hidden fires had split the earth and erupted through the waters of the world. Identical voices and echoes were calling to him. An infinite murky pledge that transcended the concept of a linear life. A pledge to give the greatest gift of all time.

Pietrich struggled with the bombardment in his mind. Something was happening unlike any sensation he had felt previously. A greater clarity distinguished itself in his mind's eye but it came at a price. A constant pain grappled his brain like it were trapped in a vice.

Pietrich squirmed on the floor of his camp and screamed out in pain, begging for it to stop. But it wouldn't cease.

'What is this? What is happening to me?'

He shouted the words aloud. Only his wolf and a distant crow replied with their howl and caw.

Pietrich had dreaded this moment, for it was planted in his mind by the nameless woman who had haunted his dreams. She called it the quickening, but he didn't know what any of it meant. Nor did he understand how she could have foreseen this change in him. But it had not been a lesson freely given, more that she feared the quickening. Feared it would grant him strength.

Anger. It was at the peak of all the throbbing and confusion. Pietrich used the anger to channel his suffering and found his way to his feet. He packed his things hastily and stomped his way to the cliffs above the gorge he had rested in.

Sparkling water glistened in the ripples of the estuary as Pietrich approached an overlook where sound travelled freely upwards. He heard the tingling sound of rippling water and felt the rare morning sun upon his cheek.

Beneath where he stood was a common dwelling for black market traders and slaver ships. The smuggler's harbour remained active with those who had removed themselves from the reach and interest of seekers of power. It was a place for no one.

Pietrich waited patiently atop the cliff edge, as a ship

pulled into the shabby port. It was anchored just shy of the brick wall that lined the edge of the street to the abandoned village. He shook off the pangs of aching, listening to the crew beneath dropping their cargo into the sea's waters where the estuary met a high bridge. They had cast a net to stop the crates from floating out to sea and members of the smuggler gang dived into the water to pull the crates towards a winch hook that dangled from the bridge. The sound of the crates crashing into the horseshoe shaped stone concourse, signalled Pietrich to move towards the street below where a gathering had formed. He had no real plan. He just knew he needed a ship.

The pulley squeaked and whined as a smuggler began to raise the last crate of the freshly stolen shipment to land. The smuggler gang was a band of more than twenty men and women. Young and old. Travellers and gypsies living outside the clutches of whatever society had been born throughout the war-torn remains. Some had been slavers in their past and others had been slaves. Now they were just a mismatch of people with a common interest: coin.

Their discussion began with the negotiations of divvying up the spoils.

This south-eastern tip of land was a peninsula with a bay that became an island at high tide. The bay had no beach, just a cliff edge and brick wall that had been built into it. The old stone building atop the cliff from where Pietrich had descended had been a prison at one time. Now it was a derelict hovel.

Pietrich knelt beside Jack and rubbed the wolf's thick coat; anything to bring him a moment of calm before he thrust himself into the fray. He walked towards the group, exuding a confidence he did not have. Jack, teeth bared, was at his heels.

None of the smugglers noticed him as he approached. He didn't allow them to. Instead he grabbed a handful of jewellery that had spilled to the floor and sat upon the wall that separated the sea mouth and bridge where they stood.

Water cascading beneath was a constant drone. A couple of small rowing boats battled with the current and Pietrich decided then to make his entrance. He lifted the fog from the minds of the smugglers. They were taken aback to suddenly see sat before them, a boy and his wolf.

'Fuck yer doing, son! Sneaking up on us. You lookin' to get yourself hurt?'

Pietrich took a small apple out of his pocket that he had lifted from their findings and took a bite, letting the juices flow down his chin.

'This is good fruit. My father's horse would devour these. I thank you for your generosity.'

A curved foot-long blade was pulled from a sheath and the man who held it stepped towards Pietrich who remained stationary on his perch.

'Think you're bloody funny, dontcha? I'll cut that apple right out of your belly, boy.'

'Now that would be a sight, would it not?' Pietrich mocked. He'd heard his father speak arrogantly countless times and prayed the smugglers would not see through his act.

Jack bared his teeth at the man and growled a chilling snarl.

'Easy, Shakes, look, the boy is blind. Reckon the wolf is his guide or something,' said one of the other pirates.

Shakes didn't back down but instead pointed his knife closer to Pietrich who twisted his head to either side as though he was unsure where the man was pointing the blade.

'I like your knife,' Pietrich said, his voice trembling. 'It sings beautifully.'

'You like it so much, I'll let you taste it!'

Shakes went to press the knife against Pietrich's mouth but as he began to press the blade against the boy's cheek it passed straight through him and Shakes stumbled towards the edge of the bridge. Suddenly Pietrich was not there. It was as though he were a spirit made of mist that had dispersed into the air.

Jack pounced on the man's back, pushing him over the bridge and into the water below. The splash caused the smugglers to run towards the brick ledge of the wall to spot their foolhardy brother in arms as he fought to swim to the muddy bank and pull himself out of the sea. By the time Shakes had realised what had happened, he was looking back up to the point from which he fell, but Pietrich was now standing at the other end of the wall, behind the group of smugglers who could not understand how he had moved so fast.

'I have a proposition, if you'd be so kind as to listen for a moment,' Pietrich began his address. 'Firstly, you allow me to explain what it is I expect of each of you and then we board your ship and sail towards my proposed destination.'

The smugglers burst into fits of laughter, their memories short as they had already forgotten the mysterious display that Pietrich had unveiled.

'What's the fee, lad?' one of them asked, jokingly.

'Oh, there is no fee. I cannot see nor sail, nor do I have a ship, but I need your help.'

A howling voice broke through the ranks but it was not the wolf, instead it was a woman mocking a wolf and as she stepped through the gathered crowd, Jack snarled at her feet and she snarled back, leaning her face straight into the beast's glare. The long flowing patchwork material of her dress lashed around her ankles and her torn leather shirt revealed parts of her scar-ridden skin. She had cracked white lines by the sides of her eyes that were grooves in her thick tanned face. She laughed and turned to face Pietrich with her hands held high. A taciturn peace offering.

'You're either a rich boy, or a stupid one. We're pirates, each of us. We work for pay. So we'll ask again, how much are you offering?'

Pietrich walked precariously along the wall and felt the rim of the ledge on the inside of his feet. The smugglers were somehow amused by watching a blind boy traversing a circular ledge that held a thirty foot drop beneath it, a tightrope walker, teasing them with self-inflicted risk.

'You can see with your own eyes I have no coin to speak of and my possessions are few. As you have said yourself, I am a blind boy with nothing but a wolf to guide me. It is crucial I depart immediately and if you are pirates as you say, I don't doubt there will be plenty of spoils at the end of the voyage.'

Pietrich was cut short as Shakes, now soaked head to toe, returned to join his pirate horde. He had retrieved his blade and the smile on his face was now a salt soaked snarl. His brow scrunched like dried fruit, he marched straight towards Pietrich and as he went to swing his short sword, fear filled his eyes for he lost all control of his body and tripped on a loose paving. He crashed to the floor and screamed out in pain as his sword cut into his leg. The cry was deafening and the howling woman yelled out in disgust as the pirate's blood sprayed up her arm from his spurting thigh.

'Fuck! What the hell, Shakes, you've cut an artery.'

'That little bastard! He tripped me.'

The woman wiped the gore from her dress and looked at Pietrich. His head tilted side to side, his glance floating freely towards nothing and he simply frowned and said. 'I am afraid of the things I might have to do if you do not agree; do not force me down that path.'

Shakes stood on his uninjured leg and pulled the short sword out of the wound. His companions winced at the squelching sound it made. He gripped the sword tight and hobbled towards Pietrich, ready to strike the boy down. Pietrich shook his head, dejected, and the man stopped. His expression changed to dread and his skin went pale. Despite the warmth of the air his breath was icy cold.

Shakes slowly moved the arm clutching the sword. He held the blade against his own throat. The pirates watched incredulously as the sharp point pressed against his windpipe.

'Please, stop. Please.'

Shakes mustered the words through gritted teeth and the next moment he cast the sword into the water.

'This is the point where *you* leave,' Pietrich said.

THE SHIP CRACKED against the side of the rocks as the anchor was hauled into the bosom of the timber. It was a strong vessel and Pietrich enjoyed listening to the scurrying of the crew. He had no real idea what they did but he intended to learn. Mutt had convinced most of the smugglers to join them after washing Shakes' blood from her clothes. Those who didn't were paid their dues and sent away. No hard feelings among pirates. Freedom was part of the deal. Even Shakes had been granted clemency and his wound bandaged at Pietrich's behest.

Pietrich was content with the eleven who had joined their captain. She howled like a wolf but wore the name *Mutt* with pride.

'It reminds me where I'm from is all,' she explained. 'Raised by my mother thanks to my bastard father running off with a piece of skirt from the local tavern. She used to call me a dog, said I was what drove him away, my father that is. Course, she would say that. Wouldn't want no blame in any of it, would she? Most of these scars you see were his parting gift to me as I refused to kiss him goodbye. Oh. I suppose you can't see them, can you? Well there are plenty enough. Each one a lesson in manners I was told.'

Her incessant retelling of her entire life so far was hardly endearing. But she held their course and stood by the wheel for a fair shift. Mutt didn't shy from her own duties.

Pietrich found the whole gang somewhat refreshing. He'd never associated with those who lived outside of communities like Knighton. The pirates hardly stayed still for more than a day at a time from the stories Mutt was telling him. A life Pietrich had lived himself for nearly two years in the sparse woodland mountains, and he wondered how much of the world these smugglers must have seen with their eyes. Pietrich had seen little of the world in his formative years but painted an image in his mind from the sounds he heard. Each new place he visited held a different song and the open sea was no exception. The roaring waves, deafening wind and flapping sails were the basis of this new tune. There was something rich about hearing his landscape but he could only guess what the splashing waves looked like as they tickled the side of the timber ship.

Of the things he had seen before his vision had left him, Pietrich missed the colours the most. Everything was now monochrome and he had forgotten what a yellow sunflower looked like. He could no longer distinguish between the shades of green that filled the lands of his home. He had heard of the richness of the blue sea that rested over silver sands but it would remain forever a mystery to him. The red of blood however, grew more vivid in his mind. The trail of thick viscous fluid was growing longer all the time.

Pietrich listened to the ocean caressing their vessel and felt the rise and fall as they drew further south from the coastal plains of Harmion.

'Today is my sixteenth birthday,' Pietrich said. Mutt shot a look at Pietrich and he felt her judgement. 'I would have been about ready to begin my schooling on history and governance. I would have learnt all about the kingdoms and lineages that make up the fabric of our land. I suppose I would have learnt to write and maybe, if I'd been able, I could have been a scholar of some description.'

'Bollocks, farming is the most useful thing you can do. None of that learning's gonna feed your kin, is it?'

'Kind of you to speak so honestly with me, Mutt. I was simply suggesting that the course of things has changed rather dramatically.'

Mutt shook her head and her furrowed brow creased intensely. 'If you expect to follow the path you were given at birth then you're a fool. Just sixteen, plenty of time to learn about the surprises you've got coming. You're blessed to become a man at sea. Not much better than being out on the open waters. You should consider yourself lucky. What are you anyway, some kind of runaway?'

'I'm not really sure. I used to think so. I was forced to leave my home. Though now it is as though I've never been home. Perhaps that is where we're heading to.'

'If what I know of Vermillion is accurate then we are heading to nothing and no one.'

Pietrich deliberated asking his next question. It was a simple one, but he knew it could open a can of worms.

'Spit it out, lad, your tension is making me nervous.'

'Have you killed many people? Sorry, stupid question to ask a pirate.'

'I never killed no one didn't deserve it. That I maintain as truth. Numbers don't mean nought once the first is dead. Just so long as it was a just death. Like if you had killed Shakes. He would have had it comin' to him.'

Pietrich paused for a moment. His conscience was stirring out of control.

'It doesn't seem right to take a life so easily. He will never walk the same again the way the blade cut him. That is enough.

My mother once told me that a killer isn't born. You don't become a killer until you take a life. The first life I took is a faceless blur as nearly one hundred lives were extinguished within a fleeting moment. I could never see their faces but I heard their last thoughts as they faded from consciousness. Men wondering if they would make it home to see the birth of their child. A sister, intent on making amends with her siblings over the estate of their family. So many regrets.'

Pietrich reached out to Mutt and showed her the beach. The beach where all those he had slain were sprawled out like a crow's feast. He showed her all the death which he now carried like an iron scar.

'It's not right, to have that much power over another human. I heard tales of your kind. The Primavemani were meant to have died out a long while back but reckon that must be what you are. Still, I guess it's not right that I can see and you can't. Not much is right with the world. You'll learn that more with each year that passes.'

Pietrich fidgeted uncomfortably. Mutt cracked a smile. It was a smile for herself that widened as the oncoming breeze stretched her lips and she chuckled out loud.

'You can beat a dog and make it cower but you'll never own its soul,' she said. 'I've seen plenty enough and stolen more than my fair share. But the only thing I've ever had worth having was my freedom. I'm working for you and I agreed to it without a fight. Doesn't mean you have the right to force me. Guess we'll see how that plays out. Don't expect us to be nice to you the whole time neither. It's not our way, we don't know how.'

Somewhere at the front of the ship a wolf howled and Mutt howled back. Another smile broke upon her face and Pietrich wondered if he would ever understand those he sailed with. Each of them held such a tight bond for freedom's sake and yet acted as though they were ready to gut each other as readily as a strand of hair moves in a sea breeze.

'You say you have seen it all and more. Have you ever seen The Vermillion Isles?'

'We never sailed that far from the mainland before coz the trade ships ceased their supply runs. Even so, when they was active, the Vermillion trade ships always carried assassins on board and you'd want to make sure you were well clear of their course if you spotted one. Impossible to invade and impossible to negotiate with. Unless they traded with you in secret under the guise of a mainland faction, you never got close. Smart they was. They had the most powerful navy ever seen. Now you can find their ships distributed amongst all the ports. Must have been sold off eventually or something. I heard nothing grows on the islands now. Heard nothing lives there now either. You'll see for yourself when we get there I suppose.' She looked the blind boy in the eye, he didn't look back. 'Oh, sorry. I keep forgetting, you won't see nothing.'

Mutt chuckled, the slight had been deliberate and so transparently delivered was her quip that Pietrich decided it was time to leave her to the wheel and wander on.

*There must be something on the island?* He hoped he'd find a settlement of people to tell him all the answers. Such a strange existence, to have the voices of so many in your mind and yet so many unanswered questions. He reached out to the island and he felt a searing heat. There was so much anger but he couldn't sense any life.

He strolled around the ship, trying to find his sea legs. Pietrich listened to the swaying air and felt his feet upon the deck as his body moved in time with the ocean's dance. The crew had easily succumbed to his demands, as easily as he had taken those lives. Mutt was right, it wasn't fair for someone to hold such power. His father had been powerful too, but in different ways. How many swings of his sword would it have taken to cut down all of those lives that Pietrich crushed with his tsunami in an instant. Was it the threat of the unknown that had convinced the pirates so easily.

*Perhaps the finality of their efforts makes them look to the future. What is a fortnight's voyage after all, in a lifetime of smuggling?*

'I am but a fleeting moment in their lives and they are a fleeting moment in mine.' Pietrich spoke to his wolf who always understood more than he should.

The mainland became a thin curtain hanging beneath the misty horizon. Pietrich returned to the wheel where the first mate had taken over steering. Mutt had gone to check on the cook and see that the evening meal was well underway.

'Before long we will have nothing but sea on all sides,' said the first mate.

Sums as he was known, was Mutt's main man. He got his name on account of the fact he knew how to divvy up a score and keep all the crew happy and so she had appointed him first mate ever since she had killed the previous captain of the ship. It was the only way to get promoted in a pirate crew. Being a gracious leader and unbeatable in combat were the two sure ways to avoid mutiny. Mutt had killed the last pirate captain on the decks amidst a disagreement of proportional takings. She had howled like a demon hound to ensure the whole crew had seen their fight. To emphasise her point, she had made the death as bloody as possible. She saw to it that the decks were not cleaned for days so the previous captain's blood now stained the wood.

'I'm sure it must be quite a sight. To be lost with nothing at your back, front or sides. Something I will never be able to appreciate,' Pietrich said.

'Ah don't think it matters what we see does it? It's what we know and what we feel that counts. This ship is your home now, lad. Mutt will see you safely across the void and no finer carriage than the *Defiance.'*

Defiance. It was a good name for a smugglers' ship. Especially one that Pietrich had commandeered for his own usage in the face of all the hurt and confusion and things that for certain, he could not comprehend. What was his life now if not some rebellion against all that he was before? The loss of love and tenderness was opening a chasm inside his very being and he felt burdened by his physical self. Were he simply able to fly or appear at the foot of the volcano to ask why he had been chosen to haul the hate of the world in his soul, it would have saved him time.

'I think I will head to my cabin. Call for me when it is time to eat,' Pietrich instructed.

'As you will, lad. Watch your back down there. You've not won them all over just yet.'

'I don't need to watch my back, my wolf does that for me.'

Pietrich and Jack headed beneath the decks and entered the small cabin that was beside the captain's chambers. He had no interest in making claim to the space that the captain usually occupied and Sums had offered up his first mate's quarters. It was a small space with a hammock in the corner by a small porthole that let a light breeze pass through the chamber. Pietrich climbed into the hammock and rested for the first time since they had left the smugglers' cove. Jack stood guard by the door as his master began to slip into a slumber.

Pietrich thought about Castellar and how they had flown together. The old pacifist had spoken with his wife as she was all those years ago, when she had lived.

Pietrich tried to reach out across the expanses of time once more. It hurt him when he did it but he had to learn and with no teacher to guide him he would be master of his own fate. He had not sensed the Winter Queen these past days; the voice that had haunted him for years was now the only one that remained silent. He had not been able to reach his father either, somehow he remained a weak image in his reach, but Tritan was now less present than he had ever been, and there was no shadow lingering in the distance as there had once been.

His torment over the responsibility of killing had distracted him so much that his focus had slipped. Somehow he felt in his soul that his very existence depended on the assassin he had spoken to that day in the market square of Port Melees. They had spoken years before his birth was even a possibility, when the war was in its infancy and as he reached for her he felt himself brush up against a cold, feverish body that lay beneath the decks of a ship that sailed away from a gushing island with streams of fire rushing through the sky like red waterfalls. River was dreaming and Pietrich joined with her in the dream. It held no reason or deliverance for she simply burned in the shadow of a mountain, though she was water and flowed through it for she was a river. River's body trembled and within her dream she felt sweat pouring from her.

*You are unwell. Fever.*

Pietrich offered warmth and comfort.

*Who am I to you?* River asked.

*I do not know, but I feel we will know more in time. For we are passengers of time you and I.*

River felt a shiver of familiarity in the intrusion. As though an old piece of her broken soul had reformed. How could she trust this strange child? Was it her own mind, playing tricks in her dreams? He acted as her guide and yet appeared as a demon all at once and she felt a bond with him that she was inclined to trust and somehow she believed that like a scolding parent, this boy was the answer to her purpose. So strange to feel compelled to follow a voice in her mind that was so young and so sweet and so dangerous that it made her afraid. She was very afraid.

## 22

The fever dream caused beads of hot sweat to pour upon the oak deck of the lower quarters. With placid oceanic breaths, the hammock swung and sodden through as it was, held its dormant guest in its embrace. River groaned and cast her head to the side in a futile attempt to wake from the deep slumber that held her captive. She failed.

The blind boy had slipped away for a moment as her fear shot into him, but then he appeared before her, no longer just a voice in her head but a vision of a ghost long since dead or not yet alive, she knew not which. His billowing brown cloak flapped in the stormy wind as rain lashed upon his brow and a wolf stood at his side. The rain was not from the sky but splashes from the sea, cascading over the side of the ship that battled the moonlit storm.

Empty decks surrounded the boy. No crew. Just the wolf. His mouth didn't open but she heard him clearly.

*I see you more vividly than a lightning storm against a backdrop of night. I know your nature and the things you have done. You are fleeing. Where do you flee from? I cannot see it.*

*I flee my home. Vermillion is pushing me away for the first time in my life.*

He frowned.

*So you sail away from the place I am searching for. Tell me. What happened?*

River held tightly onto the rail of the ship where she now stood before the boy and his wolf. The bolts of light cracked all around them and illuminated the pin-sharp blue of Jack's eyes. Pietrich remained obscured by the hood of his cloak but the profile of his silhouetted expression was plain and serious.

*Everything is on fire. I fear I am dead and not actually sailing at all. I fell as we evacuated the beach. From where do you speak to me? This ship is just a dream, am I right?*

*No. It is not a dream but neither is this the physical world. Here is just the place that exists for us in this moment. It is your projection and I am your guest. You do not have to fear me. I have so much to learn from you. But I am already so tired.*

*Who are you, and what do you expect from me?*

*Forces are moving in the physical world to wrap a claw of tyranny around all people. Those very forces have been at work your entire life and also mine. I am just a boy but I fear I will have to become the thing I despise to protect us from it.*

River felt a pang around her midriff that made no sense.

*I feel you crushing me on the inside; it hurts so much but it feels like the comfort of home. You are afraid I will let you down, but I don't understand what I am to do.*

*So many possibilities exist but they are laden with thorny brambles and I cannot say for sure I know which we must steer a path through. We must be patient, as I once was when I was sick as a young boy.*

River felt her legs tremble beneath her, as if she had slipped upon a rock and stumbled at a cliff edge. Adrenaline subsided, leaving her weak and it was all she could do to stand up straight but looking ahead of her, she saw the boy was gone.

*Where have you gone?* River reached with her thoughts.

*I am tired, the years between our existence are many. I will find the mountain on Vermillion that haunts me and then I will speak to you again.*

*No wait! It is too dangerous. The mountain is erupting.*

*No, it hasn't erupted for over forty years.*

As quickly as a candle extinguishes in a gale, the boy was gone. The ship and the sea were calm again and River felt herself swaying side to side in the sweat-soaked hammock where she lay. Her eyes were closed and lights danced around inside her mind. Little black insects and inky blurs dizzied her.

'River.' The sweet voice stirred her from discomfort. It was Jade. 'Are you alright? You have slept a very deep sleep.'

River forced herself to roll her legs out of the hammock and dangled them over the side. Her shaking, tired hands were covered in dirt and sand, so she wiped her brow with her forearm before looking up to the student.

'How long have we been at sea? What of my father?'

Jade handed River a cloth to wipe herself down with.

'We have been sailing east for three days. Your father and uncle have been lain to rest. We could not wait, for their bodies would have begun to decay. I am so sorry, River. But the funeral was done the old way and the mainlander offered a few words to honour them.'

'You mean the prisoner? He is awake? How dare he be allowed to speak at their sea funeral when I was compelled to sleep!'

Jade stepped back as River wrestled herself free of the hammock and bore down upon her.

'But, he saved you. He wanted to offer up some words of respect on your behalf. It didn't seem right to reject him after he pulled you from the flaming beaches and dragged you to the small boat.'

River turned her head away in disbelief. How could the man have come so far from death in time to save her? Not once but now for a second time. She didn't want to owe the man such a debt, not when she was filled with such anger.

'Take me to him. I need a full report of everything that has happened these past days.'

River stumbled across the top deck and the relief of feeling the sea air upon her face invigorated her. It was the kindest elixir she could have hoped for. Boscelito stood at the front balcony of the ship, overlooking the sea that was their horizon.

'You are full of surprises, mainlander,' River said. 'You have been awake this whole time?'

'The heat woke me. I never saw such ferocious fire. Not by the hand of man nor nature. The rower who had refused to leave you behind barely escaped the flooding waves of lava that spilled upon the beaches. We were lucky.'

Boscelito shuffled awkwardly and rubbed his arm where peeling skin had begun to itch.

'It seems a recurring feat for us. Perhaps you are a lucky charm, brought to me in a storm.'

River didn't know why she had said such a thing. But Boscelito turned to throw her a look, making sure she knew that he had heard it well.

'I am sorry we had to bury your family while you slept. I promise you we did you proud. Jade saw to the arrangements and traditions were honoured. They now protect in the next life what remains of the islands.'

River felt a tear forming in her eye. She wiped it away with the cloth Jade had given her and tucked it in her trouser pocket.

'I was angry to hear you spoke for them. I was wrong to be angry. For that I apologise.'

Boscelito nodded his head, accepting her remorse.

'A lot has happened these past days. The fleet we sail with

is plenty strong. Many escaped before the volcano stole the homes and lives of your people. As the ash settled, more ships came together and you now lead an armada of incomparable scale.' Boscelito ran his fingers through his matted hair, pausing to think. 'However, we have a problem as there was little time to load the ships with supplies to feed the thousands that you now command. The winds have eased and so our pace is slow. I have seen what comes next before. It is unpleasant.'

River turned away from him at the sour news. She should have suspected it, three days wasted already lying helplessly in her hammock. She took a deep breath through her nose and exhaled slowly, wishing to still time.

'I do not need to be forewarned of something as apparent as starvation at sea. You act as though you are my lieutenant or counsel. Yet last I was aware you were still my prisoner,' River rebuked. The bloody-minded assassin was clear in the tone of her voice but she kept her back held towards the mainlander. 'Why are you privy to such information? Who has been informing you as to our position?'

'I report what I have seen with my own eyes and overheard as I walked the decks. I am not under lock and key because I have worked the ship neither as enemy nor friend. It is for you to decide what will become of me, of course. I am a sailor first and foremost; if your crew finds me to be useful it is better that I earn my meal.'

'Perhaps I should have you thrown overboard as waste. After decades, my father's cohorts turned against him and I killed every last one of them, so I would not test the limits of my mercy.'

'More honourless deaths to add to your tally and you use their fate to score points against me.'

River spun on her heels to face Boscelito, anger rising in her.

'I did what was necessary, they were traitors and I would grant none of them any honour.'

'You now lead a fleet of ships with incomparable scale, but with no home to return to, your focus should be elsewhere. You can return to the vengeance in your heart once your people are safe.'

'I would trust Jade as my hand more now than any one of the cremated fools on the mountain, or you for that matter, who lectures me so freely. Do not forget every breath you draw is a gift from me.'

The outburst was swiftly delivered and she calmed herself as best she could. Boscelito recognised the false threat. He had heard many from new leaders, asserting their authority in the absence of confidence.

'My advice is given as freely as you may discard it,' he replied calmly.

River took a deep breath and allowed her rage to subside. It was not the time to joust with words.

'You will remain free for as long as you earn the right. Do you concede to oblige me and follow my instruction to protect yourself?'

'My life in exchange for service aboard your ship? As you wish, what would you have me do?'

'Fetch Jade, instruct her to gather the three she trusts most, even if they are not aboard this ship, they will be sent for and brought here immediately. Time is not our ally and our actions must be swift.'

Boscelito bowed his head and made to find the girl Jade, who would be first mate and hand to River. A student not yet done with her schooling. The fragility of the Vermillion people suddenly seemed like the weight of the world upon her shoulders and River couldn't think straight.

*How can I lead them?*

Their lives would be short if they remained ship-bound for too long and without a westerly wind to take them to the mainland at speed, their supplies would not last. River walked up and down the decks, pondering her options. They were few. She looked to the south and saw an endless horizon but squinted as though she sensed something beyond the clear blanket of the ocean.

River ran to the second mate who was at the wheel of the ship.

'Set a course for Maluabaw at once. Due south.'

'Ma'am?'

'We're not heading to the mainland just yet. We'll seek supplies from the artisan islands, should they receive us.'

'With respect, the tribes upon those islands are a small populous, they will not cope with our armada.'

'They have as little choice as we do. Set the course, sailor. No more questions.'

River walked away from the second mate and headed to the front of the ship. She stood holding onto the rail as the vessel swung its bow to their new heading. She prayed it was the right course.

So many thoughts clouded her mind. The war. The blind boy in her dreams. Her lover who had betrayed her. Boscelito was right, she should think only of the survival of her people, though it could mean breaking an age-old allegiance with the artisan tribes whom she held so dearly in her heart, Vermillion must live on. She vowed to her father and whispered her promise to him into the sea wind and knew that it carried off into the waves where he heard her pledge and she felt ready, finally, to lead her people.

.  .  .

THE EVENING BREEZE was warm and there was no respite from the heat of the day. As if they should cope with worsening conditions, a heatwave had blown north to meet their ships. *A warning from the Maluabian islands?* River wasn't sure she should be fearing bad omens. Death was chasing at their heels and meeting the wrath of an angered tribe was a lesser evil than a sea death. Rations had diminished to a single portion around mid-afternoon and they now shared less than a day's water among four.

Their saving grace was the meditation they had trained in. Calming the nerves and slow breathing enabled them to expunge their use of energy as they took shift breaks from the work above deck.

The crew looked thin. Just a week at sea and they were already diminishing. River had selected a few of her strongest fighters and given them an extra half portion per meal in case they were met with a fight. She had not taken the extra portion herself and feared she would soon lose the muscle and strength she had spent years building. Her shoulder still ached and had wasted away. She couldn't bear the thought that her entire being would suffer the same.

River took her evening walk along the top deck and saw that each of her crew were well and some were even in good spirits. But the overall atmosphere was dour and it came as no surprise. She wondered if she may have made the wrong decision. This northerly wind five days ago could have slingshot them towards the north-west shores of the mainland. Far from where they wanted to go but they would be close to beaching by now.

Doubt was the fear that time gifts to a leader and seeks to bend the spirit. River knew to expect the empty feeling in her stomach that was not hunger alone. Her skills told her it was too late to turn back now and use the wind to their advantage. She had made the right decision at the time based on the circumstances and she would see them through this turmoil somehow.

She had avoided Boscelito these past days. That was an aggravation she could do without. But he had barely left her thoughts since the last conversation. River had seen to it that he had the same work as any one of the lowly crew. Despite his abilities, he was not one of her trusted companions. He was already weak from the furore on the island and had not been one chosen to take an extra half portion, but he worked on silently and without complaint.

The shipping channels that River knew well had been against her since she awoke. The winds she had trusted so many times before had switched direction with each decision she made. She had kept their heading direct to Maluabaw for two days, like a spearhead pointed to its prey. The artisan isles still had not made their presence known on the horizon.

'Ma'am, begging your pardon.' It was Jade who spoke and severed River's line of thought. 'There is a request for an audience with you.'

'Jade, you hardly need to make requests to speak to me. Tell me straight what ails you.'

'The request isn't mine, it's the mainlander. He wants to discuss our course with you. I told him he should mind his manners but he insisted I at least give you the choice to cast him aside or no. What would you like me to say to him.'

River was taken aback, tired and hungry, and wasn't sure she had the stomach to see the man's face, let alone hear his accusations on her nautical choices.

'The things I would *like* you to tell him are not words befitting ears in this diminished condition we find ourselves, so I will concede to simply making him aware he may come and say to me whatever is on his mind.'

'Very well, ma'am.'

Jade turned about and went to fetch Boscelito as River took a deep breath and found her resilience. It was a moment over too soon as he approached her at the front of the ship.

'How are you faring?' he asked.

'Well enough, under the circumstances.'

'I'll just come out and say this plainly because you already know the truth yourself. We are out of supplies; tomorrow will be the last meal any of us has and the little water we have will be depleted not long after that. One of the crews on a smaller vessel has already run out and are refusing to take the share of the larger crew ships that have tried sending a supply run to them. If we continue this heading, directly into the heatwave… I dread to think what will become of your people.'

River hated him for the truth. She had learnt nothing new but to hear it out loud from him, as if he somehow cared, made her sick to the stomach.

'I cannot tell if you are worried for your own sake or if you have somehow come to care for the people under my command. Many a romance is born at sea under strenuous conditions.'

The rebuke angered him and he strode right up into her face. River didn't recoil. 'These are not strenuous conditions, they are deadly. And you suggest I would be frolicking about while you are left to ponder the demise of these thousand people we sail with? I am a captain, as you know. I have lost my entire crew, as you know. I am simply here to try and support you in not suffering the losses I have.'

'What would you have me do? Our last calculations have us just half a day sailing from Maluabaw.'

'Provided this heatwave stops imminently. But these winds may continue to blow for weeks. In which case, several dozen ships carrying corpses will arrive as an interesting gift to the artisans in a week from now.'

'And you're about to tell me how we avoid this unfortunate outcome?'

'Make a heading north east, for two hours, no more.' Boscelito took out a small parchment map that was recently drawn. It depicted a simplified version of the southern ocean. 'See here. This is us,' he said, pointing to a space in the middle of nothing. 'But we are close to the spiral, if we make it far enough east we will slip into the backdraught that leads directly to the eastern side of Maluabaw. Safe from the stillness and unbearable heat.'

River looked up from the map and shot two green daggers at Boscelito.

'You are suggesting we swing our navy around almost one hundred and eighty, to discover the possibility that we may or may not slip into a favourable wind?'

'Yes.'

'If you are wrong we will all be dead and only the skies will know when our corpses will wash upon a shore.'

'If I am right and we do nothing, we are dead anyway. It is a risk, of course. But the alternative is to sail as we are, praying for the winds to change, when you know as well as I, these obscure heatwaves can last for weeks.'

River walked away from Boscelito without saying a word. She didn't know what riled her more, that he was right, or that she hadn't thought of the idea herself. She went straight to the sailor at the helm and whispered her instructions. Within seconds their ship was turning and River shot a look at Boscelito that at first would have been mistaken for disdain. But she then looked him up and down and nodded, a silent admission from her to him that no one else would ever be aware of.

Two hours passed by as if they were weeks, with no sign of the backdraught at first. But then after another hour of dread they found themselves juddering in the twirling gusts where two winds met and their ships slipped into a coil of air. They braced their sails and pushed through the vortex until slipping onto a straight path of northerly winds.

As night fell, the whole armada were sailing in a line and speeding south at a sprint pace. Celebrations broke out amongst all the ships as crews danced and drank. It was the first time their wine and spirit stocks had been broken open. River allowed it, though she knew they were not out of danger yet; they had nothing left to eat and no drinking water. So either this would be a wake to end all wakes, or they would arrive at Malu-abaw drunk or hungover. Either state would be a success given the weeks that had passed.

River passed amongst her crew and smiled at those who were twirling to the sound of two young boys who drummed a lively beat. She laughed and felt at peace. She was not one for participating but loved dearly to watch others in their enrap-tured state. She could kiss the mainlander for his interference. If she could find him, she would.

Something happened then that took her by great surprise. A feeling she had never had dealings with at any point in her life before suddenly hit her in the heart like a falling tree in a storm. She looked across the deck and saw Boscelito dancing with Jade. They twirled and spun. Smiled and giggled and their arms were locked into one another's like a laced rope.

Jealousy.

River knew in that moment that she was jealous and she despised herself for it but on the verges of life and death at the edge of the world she looked upon her prisoner and she wanted nothing more than to be held in his arms. To kiss his grubby lips and smell the sweat of his laboured body. How could she not have foreseen this? Were her desires buried so deep within her clouded heart? It was confusion, nothing more.

It had to be confusion, exhaustion. Any of the ailments that starvation and delirium can create. She told herself the lie over and over.

River ran from sight, tears streaming down her face like a foolish child and the whole world was unaware of the pain she felt. The whole world save for one blind boy who comforted her as she hid in the shadows and for a second she felt as though she could feel his arm around her shoulder and a wolf laying its head upon her lap, howling a loving howl.

## 23

W hite blinding sands reflected the sunlight into her dry, dehydrated eyes. They stung and everything before her was a blur. Her vision, compromised though it was, presented a full circle of Maluabians surrounding her. Not the kind that wielded brushes or sculpted pots, these were hunters and they held tightly their long staffs with curved blade tips, fierce expressions on their faces.

River had made her way to the beach with the first row boat and sent out orders for the others to wait until a signal could be sent that all was okay. She stood proudly at the forefront of the gathering of Maluabian hunters, having left the rest of her crew aboard the anchored Audacia. She had spoken her piece clearly through a dry throat and with a weakened voice. There was suspicion amongst the tribe. She claimed they were not invaders but instead destitute and in need of aid. As she had made her plea, she recalled how Boscelito had sailed to Vermillion, looking for an alliance and was instead met with aggression. No sense looking back now. If fate would deem the irony of her position be handled with as foul an outcome as she had bestowed on Boscelito's crew, then so be it. She was not ashamed to dare to protect her people.

The Maluabians prided themselves on their patience. The artistry of their culture determined that each artefact be created over time with painstaking scrutiny. That same patience flowed through the blood of the hunters who made no sign of breaking their formation as they awaited Mamasufie, their guardian and most decorated sculptor. Mamasufie was also their chief nego-tiator and her word often stood as final.

As the Maluabian leader approached, her dress dragged along the white sands and the dangling metallic bracelets she wore jingled like chimes and sparkled in the light. Her neck appeared twice as long as any of those around her where she had closed hoops of silver locked around her throat from the base of her neck right up to her chin. A distinguishing mark of wisdom amongst the tribe was the length of their necks and therefore how many hoops they bore. Mamasufie had earned more hoops than any other and it was she who had crafted the bracelet that River had gifted to Summer. That simple truth, River hoped, would be the one thing that would save her. She had always been a friend of the artisan people.

Mamasufie stopped dead centre of her tribe's manned enclo-sure and smiled a wicked smile at River. She spoke with a thick, musical tone.

'What kind of silent assassin, invisible to the eye and provider of all that is fatal to those who never know it, would sail her entire fleet of ships to our humble land? Our neutrality does not suffer invasive fiends or friends.'

'I do not stand before you as an invading assassin, but as a woman in need of aid for her people.'

River felt the recognition pouring from the stare of Mamasu-fie, but she could not be sure that in spite of their friendly past, this intrusion would be forgiven so easily. After a pause, she continued to make her case under the watchful suspicion of her host.

'Our island has been forsaken by our own mountain. It is a graveyard of ash and I fear we will never be able to return. We are refugees, our supplies were extinguished on our journey here. My people starve this very moment in the ships you see before you. Will you help us?'

Mamasufie clasped her hands together and walked the full circle of her hunter guard as River awaited her reproach.

'The girl who paid the highest price for such a gift for her beloved, that she could have bought an island of her own, comes to me for help. I recall the bracelet I forged that day. One of the finest I ever made. Tell me, where is it now?'

'It has ventured down the path of deceit and betrayal along with its bearer. I know nothing more.'

'Then it has become a burden to you of economics and of the spirit. Have you ever been told the story of *my* people? Did you ever consider the burden you bring to the doorstep of those who have known more deception than any race that lives amongst this world?'

River shook her head, ashamed that she indeed knew nothing other than their artistry. Mamasufie recognised the guilt in River's face.

'I see. Well. You will not be aware then, that we once farmed the greater part of the southern territories of Harmion. Hundreds of years ago when we were not artists, just simple folk trying to find our way amidst all the betrayal that passed through the royal castle. Each king and queen that came to power, another twisted version of the one that came before. We welcomed the settlers who came in search of a simpler life. They joined us for a while but eventually their greed and desire to build and expand created a rift and the Maluabians were no longer welcome in our own homes. My people fled the southern land aboard ships, paid for by trading all that was left remaining to them and empty-handed, they sailed in search of a welcome that was befitting their ideals. When they found a series of islands they hoped could be home, they were met with force and many were taken as slaves and tortured and eventually killed. Of thousands, only a few dozen survived and fled on a single ship to the white beaches where you now stand. The islands that rejected my people were Vermillion.'

River knew it before Mamasufie even spoke the word. But shame hit her in the chest the moment it was said aloud. The shame was a torture. She had lost her home but now she had lost all sense that Vermillion was a place to be proud of. Could her ancestors truly have acted so horrendously?

'The Primavemani are always credited with their dark hair and striking green eyes. You were gifted these traits from my people, after they were raped and savaged. You come from us, girl. Now you have come back to your true mother, asking for forgiveness.'

River felt a cavernous space in the pit of her stomach. It was the physical manifestation of all the dark actions of her people's past. She not only carried with her the future burden of the thousand lives she had sailed away from Vermillion with. But now she carried the burden of the thousands of lives lost at the hands of her ancestors. It was a cruel day to be a leader.

River scrambled for some recollection of her own teachings. It came out as an offering and a plea. 'Our schooling teaches us of a race who came from the sea and flourished on the islands of Vermillion, given birth to by the volcano that has now sent us away. I do not doubt what you say, but none of those lives who are seeking your aid today played a role in the genocide you speak of.'

'That is true,' Mamasufie responded flatly. 'I will not condemn your people to suffer the same fate as my own. That history has been taught to them and you as a lie, is not their fault nor yours. Ignorance is pitiful but it is not sinful.'

'I understand the burden that feeding so many mouths presents. It is a new dilemma for me as we have lost our elders. It is not my intention to burden you for any longer than required before we set sail again for Harmion.'

'A considerate thought, and I will allow your rejuvenation to take place on these white sands, for we are now one people. Whether forced by nature or the hatred of man, we have arrived at this moment. Answer me this; what has become of Quicksand? Or does he insist on continuing to use the name June? I was expecting your father to step off his ship to make either plea or demand, not his daughter.'

'The grievance I have suffered was his murder. I believe he died by the hand of Summer. Though I do not understand it.'

'Mmm. I am sorry for your loss and your burden. You must confront this girl and seek answers, yes?'

'I… I do not know what course I should take. For now, I am only concerned with preserving the lives of a thousand souls.'

'You will rewrite the history of your ancestors, River. The Maluabians will know the tide turned the day you led Vermillion into the light. There will be no price for our aid. No price beyond a simple offering, that you return the gift you once purchased from me. A sign of a betrayal repaid. Let it be the symbol of a new beginning between Vermillion and Maluabaw.'

'I… simple?' River stuttered. 'But, how am I to find it? I do not know where Summer has gone. Nor if I will see her again.'

'You have as much time as you wish to complete this task. I ask now only for a promise that you will teach your young the history that deserves to be taught and when the bracelet is back on our haven, it will be a binding tool that will teach our children for centuries to come of our friendship.'

It was a wicked game, River thought. The bracelet was

hardly worth all the effort. But it wasn't really about that. Facing Summer was an inevitability she didn't want to accept. It was being forced on her as a means of penitence. An acceptance of the betrayal was all Mamasufie actually wanted. The bracelet bound her to that acceptance.

'I accept your terms and thank you for your kindness.'

'Then we had better help you find your strength. I fear you will need it greatly soon enough.'

That last statement lingered with River for the rest of the day as the ships unloaded onto the island. She was given space to make arrangements with Jade and two of the leaders of the Maluabian tribe in order to see that those who were in the weakest condition were treated first. It would be a long process to undo the damage of these past weeks. It pained her to consider that the strength that took years to build could be lost in such a short time.

After they had settled, River was shown to a private enclosure where she would stay. Mamasufie invited her for an evening meal and it was here where they would discuss much about the past of the Maluabaw people and the ties to Vermillion that had been unwritten until now. It was a deep sadness to hear of such things and made River's gratitude for their aid so much greater.

It took several days for the effects of starvation and thirst to be abated. A large camp was erected in the shade of a palm forest that housed those who were strongest. Private quarters were gifted to anyone who was feverish and, each night without fail, River would visit all of them. One face that haunted her dreams that she had not seen since they landed was Boscelito. She heard talk of his presence but somehow he was never close by when she took her evening stroll through the encampment. She recalled how he'd danced and swung Jade around in circles as they laughed but, as the vision of Jade's face became clearer, it was Summer that she saw. River felt a pang in her stomach and cursed her mind for pairing her lover and the mainlander together to torment her.

On the fifth night, there was a disagreement between a Maluabian hunter and one of the students who had no interest in his advances. The hunter seemed to believe he had earned the right to take her as his own for providing the food that she had eaten and he was brought before Mamasufie and stripped of his position. River felt the tension rising between the two cultures. Though they may be allies officially, it would take time for the people to understand each other's ways.

*Time to go.* River knew this was just the beginning of what would become a difficult situation and she made Mamasufie aware that the following day they would prepare to depart. As if fate had heard her decision, outcry came from the encampment by their side.

'What is all that fussing?' Mamasufie asked the guard who stood by the entrance to her private bivouac. He popped his head outside and returned a moment later.

'I think there has been murder, Mamasufie!'

'What? Don't let it be so.'

Mamasufie rose to her feet and River, who was sat beside her, rose too and then marched into the encampment to address the outcry.

It was a short walk across the dark sands of night and with torchlight only to guide them they saw red smears across the ground. Fearing the worst they stepped into the large holding area and discovered a Maluabian hunter cut from the chest to his abdomen. He was alive but bleeding profusely. River recognised the wound. He had been struck by a Vermillion assassin.

To confirm her thought, before her stood a man she had not seen for many years. He was covered in Maluabian blood and took a sorrowful stance.

'What are you doing here?' River asked. 'Why have you come here, Sol? Now is not the moment to hold your tongue.'

There was a new silence around the room as all the fussing died down and hundreds of Vermillion and Maluabians alike bent their ears to listen.

'King Elik is dead.'

A drone of moaning and surprised gasps filled the air. Sol looked around him, clearly he had not expected to deliver this news so publicly.

'I returned to Vermillion as quickly as I could, but I found a wasteland. I suspected many of you had fled as I saw abandoned storage crates floating offshore. My first thought was to sail for Port Melees but I knew the winds would have been against you and a slow armada could never have made that journey so ill-prepared. When I arrived here I regret I was not received kindly.'

Mamasufie went to check on the hunter who was bleeding profusely. His panicked breaths were a discomfort to hear. It was the hunter who had made his advances on the student girl just days past.

'Oh, Bao. Why did you do it? You make such trouble for yourself.'

'I... I am sorry, Mamasufie... I... only wanted to impress you. I thought it was an assassin come to kill you.'

'You are as foolish as you are proud, Bao.'

The hunter coughed up blood that smeared across his face. The blade Sol had wielded against him had severed the lower part of his lung. Bao would not live long.

Mamasufie instructed that Bao be taken somewhere peaceful and given what comfort was available. The rest of the report from Sol would not be given so publicly and so River and Mamasufie returned to the canopy where Sol was given time and space to recount all that had befallen him and the young king.

He recounted his steps for hours, as far back as how he had been appointed personal guard to one of the youngest advisors to the king by the name of Lynden. He spoke fondly of her and feared greatly for her safety. There was still confusion around how King Elik had died. His fortress was impenetrable, the opposing armies led by Augustus would never have breached his walls and Sol himself had kept watch for any likely infiltration other than his own.

'I became their man. I watched keenly and inspected the kitchens myself daily and used some of our finest telltale powders to determine the condition of the food. I even hired tasters to eat from the very dishes that were served to the king and there was never once an attempt on his life. He was simply dead one morning. The worst part is, there is no suspicion surrounding the death. He was planning his attack on Augustus. The accusations of having remained so docile for so long wore him down and he knew it was time to cut the head off the snake. He planned to run a lightning rod right through the heart of the warlord's army and then enlist Castellar as an ally in the efforts to form a peace treaty. Only us few closest to him knew the plan.'

River mulled over all she was hearing. The implications were huge. The war was now on the verge of reaching a catastrophic scale; if word spread, all the landowners' alliances would falter.

'Who else knows this?' River asked. 'Those closest to the king, the court and his advisors, all the bloody common folk in Harmion?'

River's distress was evident and she regretted not controlling it. Her mind swirled and multiple pathways opened before her that she did not know how to determine. Why did she feel so responsible for this king. Was it because her father had vouched for him and dedicated his finest assassins to keeping him safe?

'I believe word has not spread yet, but the king's court is making arrangements in anticipation of panic breaking out. I fear it may have done so already. They will keep him alive in the minds of the people for as long as they can but you must understand that the army had been assembled already. The attack was imminent and Elik was to lead them. The truth of his death will be public knowledge soon if it is not already so.'

Sol began to shiver. He looked down, horrified at the red stains on his hands.

'I am so sorry for what happened. I was so desperate that I fear he mistook me for an aggressor. Before I had the chance to speak he was on me.'

Sol showed a cut on his side, it was slight as he wore a lace of thin chain under his shirt that had taken most of the blade's point when it had been swung at him.

'That's enough talk,' said Mamasufie. We need to get you medical attention. Do not concern yourself about Bao. That is now our burden. You did right to bring this news as hastily as you could.'

Sol nodded and then looked over at River, a pleading expression in his eyes.

'River, tell me. Does my daughter live? Is she well.'

'Jade is well and more. She is now my main advisor. Much has happened since you last saw her and you will have much to discuss. We leave at the break of day so you will wash and have your wounds attended to and then I will send for Jade to visit you.'

Sol nodded, relieved. A glazed expression came over his face. The concern about his daughter's wellbeing had been a private weight he carried all this time. Despite the gravity of the news he brought, Jade always took precedence in his mind.

'I will need you by my side when we sail for the mainland, Sol. Rest and take care of yourself this evening. Tomorrow will see an end to our sly ways. It is time for us to step out of the shadows and to meet the warlord Augustus and his army face to face. Sharpen your blade and harden your soul. Very soon we shall end many lives.'

'I HAVE TO GO, I have been sent for.'

'Will you return? We sail tomorrow and I do not know if we will be able to continue as we have these past days.'

Jade sat up and wrapped her shawl around her shoulders. She wasn't sure if it was some form of rejection or if Boscelito had spoken a truth they both had yet to accept.

'Is it really so bad, to have found comfort in one another's arms?'

Boscelito took Jade's hands and kissed them. 'We do not know yet if this is circumstance or something more that brought us together. Above all else we must be cautious. You're hand to the leader of Vermillion now and she has suffered a great loss. Many losses in fact. It would not be wise to parade ourselves around her.'

'I know you care for her. Perhaps more than you do for me.'

Jade shot a deep and sorrowful look at Boscelito and he stared into the flickering amber of the candles that danced around the greens of her eyes. He knew deep down that those eyes did not cause his heart to misstep its beating the way that River's had but he cared deeply for the girl.

'I am unsettled and unreliable. I have been a prisoner of your people for long enough that I have forgotten my former life. But I do care dearly for you, Jade. I want no harm to befall you and my caution is the only thing I can offer you at this time that might protect you.'

Jade leant forward and kissed his honourable and reasoned lips. The two lovers drifted away in each other's arms and prayed for the moment to last and to never be broken. It ended all too quickly.

'Do not be a stranger to me, Bosc. That is all I ask.'

'That would be impossible. You will sense my longing eyes, stalking you from afar and often.'

Jade breathed out a heavy sigh, slipped her feet into her sandals and swept out of the tent. Boscelito found himself pining after her immediately but searched for the soldier inside him, knowing he was about to finally return to the war he had evaded for so long. Though he didn't know any more which side he was fighting for.

The night was coming to an end and Boscelito had hardly slept. Instead he listened to the enchanting songs and cries of the Maluabians who had hosted them as they said goodbye to one of their own and farewell to the Vermillion people. It was a sad way to part, by burying one who had died at the hands of a Vermillion assassin. Mamasufie made sure to compel people on both sides to accept the incident as a severe tragedy and that Bao's death was proof that now more than ever, their peoples had to join in unison. The funeral would be a procession to honour the lost life of the hunter and other lives before. Sol made his feelings clear and he was accepted as a brother by the family of the bereaved. Jade stood at his side throughout the ceremony and Boscelito lingered in the shadows to observe from afar. He could have sworn for a fleeting moment that River caught him amid a daydream as he stared at Jade and remembered the warmth of her embrace. Was it a furrowed brow that she cast towards him as he looked to the ground, both ashamed and confused.

Boscelito no longer knew who he was anymore and his name seemed alien to him for the first time. It had been given to him when he was a baby by the virgin mothers of the sanctuary that housed him, buried deep within a small forest. They had collected him from a step of the garden fountain but by the time he had been found, there was no sign of either parent.

*Befitting for an orphan who knew no home to feel detached from his name*, he thought. Boscelito, as many times before, would adapt to the world he was offered, knowing that he would never get to choose his own.

## 24

Diccon had not been disappointed. His desire for an exciting life on the high seas had been satiated just two weeks into their voyage, much to the distress of Castellar and Lynden. The main mast had caught a high wind and cracked at the base where the patchwork timber had buckled, sending the mast crashing into the decks and crushing half of the fruit crates they had loaded up for the journey. Thankfully, no crew were injured. An upside to sailing with diminished numbers was the lesser chance of injury during those sorts of incidents.

They were left in a bind, several days sailing from any land, The Vermillion Isles were still likely a week away and that would have been with a working ship. The carpenter advised they sail back to a construction yard as there was no way of them fixing and hoisting up the mast whilst at sea. So, painstakingly, the crew fumbled with the smaller sails until a small fishing vessel crossed their path and the Audacia was towed back towards a small shipping yard on the south-western coastline. The town they came across was sat at the base of a peninsula just beneath a disused border crossing.

Smithytown was named after the blacksmith's trade that had once existed there when the region had not been part of the Harmion mainland. A mountain range separated it from the flatlands to the east but the isolation of the town had made it advantageous for vessels to resupply during the war. The inhabitants had profited so well dealing arms and armour that most of the old trader families had moved away to seek a more luxurious life. Those that remained had set up trade in league with idle chippies who became out of work once the war ended. They worked together to forge the shipping yard as a means of riding the coat-tails of the inevitable boom in trade that would be needed after the war. Things hadn't quite gone that way, but for Diccon it was a better place than most to be docked for a month as there was good beer to be had in town and the chippies and steel workers were fair so a sailing crew never usually had to stay sober and keep watch over them.

'Damn lucky is what we are. Should ne'er have sailed out in that condition. Less haste is more speed and ain't that the truth.'

Diccon recounted their escapades to anyone who would listen at the tavern bar. He was more than a few jars into his evening's drinking by now and even the crew from his own ship had staggered off to get their rest.

'I seen some things you wouldn't believe. Once when I sailed with a legion of sellswords. We was crossing the waters off the west coast where pirates were hunting trade ships, and we was huntin' them. From almost nowhere, the peak of a mountain, buried for an age under water, cut at the base of our ship as we sailed past. Razor sharp coral it was. We crumbled it but it tore a hole so fierce in us we had barely an hour to abandon the vessel. Two days we trod water whilst we was breakfast and dinner. The sight of blood in the water as the sun drops below the horizon, knowing you might be the next to be dragged beneath and dismembered. Something else. Makes a man think. Makes you question your place in all this.'

Diccon downed the last drops of his ale and signalled for another. The serving girl behind the counter obliged as he dropped more coin onto the counter.

'You looking to save my job, Diccon? The way you keep going I'll be retiring before I turn twenty.'

'When life gives you hops, make ale. And I'll drink it.'

Diccon held up his jug and took a large swig.

'Well, you best make the most of it. We'll be shutting the hatches for good in the coming weeks. Just not enough ships passing through here anymore. Trade has all dried up and Father reckons we need to relocate the business. Bloody tons of barrels to move mind and God knows we'll never find caves as fine as the like in them mountains to store and brew.'

Diccon stared with glazed eyes at the girl. He was processing her admission but didn't seem to have the solution. Then eventually he slammed down his fist on the table.

'That's it, I got it. I'll invest in it. Give me time to get this nonsense endeavour out the way and I'll bring you enough coin to live off and you can stay here. I need a good tavern for when I retire. This'll do good as any other.'

'A kind proposition, sire. I shall pass on your generous offer to the manager and we'll give you our decision promptly,' she said, laughing. 'Well, best call it a night, Diccon. I'm knackered and someone has to be back here in the morning to serve you breakfast and more ale.'

'Very well, in that case. I permit you to close these premises.'

'Gracious of you, kind sire.'

As the girl picked up the empty glass, the door to the tavern burst open and Castellar came pounding through the room.

'Diccon! Come at once. We have trouble on the ship.'

'Trouble? What you howling 'bout, man. We're docked. Ain't no trouble aboard a ship when it's docked.'

'They are taking her apart! Apparently the agreed payment wasn't honoured and so they are stripping her as compensation.'

'Fuck, those tight bloody bastards!'

Diccon rose instantly and before he'd made it to the door a short wooden club handle with a steal ball hinged at the end had been pulled from the inside of his jacket sleeve.

They raced back down to where the Audacia was anchored and there Diccon found a dozen men, scrambling across her like parasites. The main mast had been fixed and a brand new sail fitted but the locusts were untying the fresh material and dumping it on the dockside.

'Stop this bollocks immediately, you cretins, or I'll crush every last one of your skulls,' Diccon shouted as he boarded the ship and met the first man who wouldn't tolerate him.

Drunken as he was, Diccon swaggered and nearly fell and the man laughed at him but then a steel ball swung upwards into the base of his chin and smashed his smiling jaw into pieces.

That got the attention of the others who ran to confront the drunken mate.

'Stop! Diccon, we're not here for a brawl,' one of the carpenters shouted out and stepped forwards. 'You promised us fair payment for these repairs and we slaved away in good faith. When it came time to collect this afternoon there was less than half the coin quoted.'

Diccon furrowed his brow at the carpenter and shot a look at the rest of the shipyard's crew who were ready with clenched fists.

'I said half payment now, and half when we're back. I know you heard me, you bastard, I speak as clearly as a full moon shines on your fat ass!'

'That was before your captain told us you were sailing to The Vermillion Isles. I don't expect we'll ever see you again. It's full payment now or we take the ship.'

Silence fell. Castellar walked forwards to make his own plea but Diccon held out his hand to stop him.

'No, Caste. This is not a place where your slippery, philosophical tongue can help us.'

Castellar leant in close to Diccon and whispered in a concerned tone.

'We do not have the luxury to get this wrong. The boy needs us and we've lost months already.'

'Yes, and I seem to recall that being coz of your belligerence to sail with a wrecked ship. Shut it for once and let sea folk deal with sea folk.'

Castellar held his gaze. He knew he was out of his station and Diccon, the skies help him, was their best hope now of exiting this sea-town purgatory. He nodded, unconvinced though he was at what good was to come next.

'Very well, you leave me no choice,' Diccon said as he pulled a ledger from his breast pocket. It was wrapped in a thin skin and the edges were dogged but he passed the ledger to the carpenter before him.

'If we're not back here before the year is through. You can keep these accounts for your own. Just under one condition. You do right by that family up town. Brewery and all. That's my price.'

The carpenter looked upon the ledger and as he flipped the

pages he almost staggered backwards. There were pages of claims and holdings. Property documents and trade debts.

'This can't be real. There's a fortune here of the likes I've never seen before.'

'It's difficult to spend money at sea. But don't get too excited, you'll drink most of it away I guarantee it. Life credit in Smithytown, reparations, accommodation and drink. Give me that and stick my name on the deeds of the tavern and when I'm back you can have it all.'

'What is this? Some kind of trick. This money has blood attached to it, doesn't it? I'll not take your riches and watch over my shoulder the rest of my life. No wonder you're always drunk. I'll take enough to cover the costs and wages and compensation for that poor bastard you've ruined. But you can keep your curse, *first mate*. Men, back to work. Let's get this ship ready to sail by sun up. The sooner we send this goon on his way the sooner we can sleep soundly.'

'Too bloody right.' Diccon kicked the backside of the man whose jaw he had smashed. 'Now get this fucking bleeding twat off my ship and do your fucking jobs.'

Diccon skulked away and Castellar didn't dawdle behind him. The first mate had been a mystery to him from the time he'd been under his employ. How could he have suspected him of such wealth? Diccon had worked harder than any other who sailed with him and none of it had been needed. Castellar finally felt as though he was beginning to make sense.

'I'm going to sleep. Wake me when the birds start singing.'

'Diccon, wait. I don't pretend to know the answer to all riddles but yours is beyond comprehension and I don't know where to start. Am I now a debtor also? Have I signed up for something that can't be paid for?'

'Don't bend out of shape for me, Caste. Just eager to get

back to the sea for a time is all. My legs start shaking if they spend too much time on land.'

'That'll be the beer I expect.'

'Hah, funny bastard. I knew you was a witty one. Don't fret, the beer ain't goin' nowhere. I'll have a barrel or two sent down from the cellar for when we set sail.'

Diccon headed up into the small cottage where he was staying and shut the wooden door behind him. Castellar liked the man more than he could understand. There was something very real about him and despite his frivolous tone, he was a caring kind.

*There is no way to corrupt a soul when it cares little for coin,* Castellar had said as a young man. He felt as though he perhaps understood his own words for the first time.

A clear sky rewarded them for their patience as the Audacia was loaded up ready for departure. The anchor rose swiftly. Well-oiled gears had been fitted and with a strong mast and fresh sails the ship in all her glory pulled away from the docks. Lynden thanked Diccon for everything he had done, though she feared for the man greatly as he had not stopped drinking since she had met him. She had known such destructive behaviour before but she could not allow her focus to shift from Pietrich. They had lost too much time already. One day, when all was said and done, she would try to get through to the man, if she could convince him to permit it.

Lynden did her best to provide well for the crew when it came time to eat and the evening meal had become a time of bonding between her and the sailors. She recounted tales of her time with Elik and the years of hiding that came after his death, always expecting a knife in the back at any moment.

There had been some relief in those years when rumours of Augustus' disappearance had spread but she still never felt at ease without sitting with her back to a wall. In turn the sailors recounted their tales of a life at sea and how they had become disciples of sorts to Castellar. He had instilled a deep-rooted faith in them but as sea folk, where no roots can easily take hold, they remained witty and Castellar was considered an equal, not a leader. Though he would have it no other way.

They made good time as they sailed away from the mainland. Finally, back on course to their destination with no idea what they were likely to find. Lynden thought about Pietrich and the last time she had seen him as their ship had been attacked at Port Melees. She feared what had befallen him these past months since that day. Though she did not fear that he was alive, but more she feared what he had become. It didn't do well to dwell on such things. She recalled what Elik had said to her the day he died. Just hours before his body was found mysteriously cold and still dressed head to toe in his armour. *When the body of a child becomes a man so must the soul.* The words stuck with her and she knew he'd meant to fight with his army though she still knew not what ailment had denied him the chance. He was little older then than Pietrich was now. Lynden wondered if she hadn't placed an unfair burden on Pietrich, for history to be repeated as though he were Elik reborn and this time she wouldn't let her king die.

Tumultuous surges accompanied them through the nights as though the sea was angered. It made for difficult conditions to rest and Castellar was not well equipped to deal with the nausea below decks. Lynden, suffering a sleepless night, went for a stroll to the bow for some fresh air and found Castellar shivering in a ball on the ground, wrapped in several woven cloaks.

'I can't get used to the ebb and flow either. Less than thirty seconds in my cabin and I feel as though my guts are going to come out of my nostrils.'

Castellar laughed to himself, though he were freezing cold.

'It always takes me a few days to adjust to the ocean again, I just can't get bloody warm.'

Lynden took her skin cloak off and wrapped it around Castellar. He nodded gratefully and she gave him *the look* as though she were his nanny schooling him.

'Those blankets are wool and the wind cuts right through them. You need to block out the gusts or your body will never cope.'

'Thank you. I'm not sure how I feel about wearing an animal to keep myself warm, but I am freezing. If I step foot below I'll be throwing up bile. The ocean already claimed my dinner.'

'You don't have to wear the skin for fashion. But the bison around your shoulders died to feed dozens and better for the skin not to go to waste while a man freezes himself to death above deck.'

'Do you ever sense it, Lynden. That we are the takers of the world. Intelligent, yes. Productive and creative, certainly. But we live on the bones of all the species in existence.'

'Wild animals kill and eat each other all the time; we are just animals, Castellar.'

'But do they not act on instinct? The basis of survival forms the food chain. If we are the only truly conscious beings, do we not have a choice to ignore our instincts and find a truer path. As I wear this skin I wonder do we walk the line of evolution or have we shattered the path with our ability to create and to invent. Every human invention eventually becomes weaponised and used for destruction.'

'That is not true. We also build. Some of the most marvellous buildings I have seen were designed by well-meaning artists, and great feats of engineering were employed to allow for their construction. Wooden towers with pulley systems that allowed them to create a home for thousands of poor folk.'

'Yes, I am aware of the towers. Did you know that for each

castle to be built, two hundred lives were lost as the work towers buckled under the weight of the rocks? The towers themselves were adapted by a general during the war to create a slingshot that could throw rocks as big as houses for thousands of feet, crushing those who stood in its path. Find me something built for good and I will show you a machine of war.'

'The cold has made you despise your own kind. Do you not see any good in people anymore?'

'I do not know. I have been cold for so long now, I do not remember the sun, even as it shines down upon me. I just feel in the depths of my being, in the places where physicality no longer has meaning, that Pietrich is the key to the light. His warmth will shine down on all things and perhaps we will once again walk nature's line, as we were meant to.'

'I feel that about him too. I know he will see us to a brighter future. I only fear the cost will be his own life. I do not know why, but I sense he is changing and will never be the same.'

'His father was corrupted from the day he was born. More than thirty years passed by and yet Tritan found his way from within the dark chamber he had been trapped in, may the waters of this world protect him wherever he is now, and whatever Pietrich may suffer in the years to come, he will not be left to season in a vat of hatred or despair. He will emerge once again as the boy you love.'

'I hope you are right.'

Lynden sat down beside Castellar and took part of the cloak to wrap herself in.

'Forgive an old maid, for needing warmth and comfort.'

'Who would I be to deny warmth to the one who gifted it to me?'

Lynden rested her head on his shoulder. It felt so good to have the breeze of the ocean whipping all around them as they created their own heat and comfort beneath the skin they shared. It was like two misshapen stones forged over the ages, deformed, had finally been washed together and the fit was exact. So exact that they become one whole and the cracks between the places where they were bound disappeared as if they were one stone and would always be.

## 25

F ear is but a grain upon a beach of infinite sand. As the winds of life blow and the grains reform into shapes anew their nature is warped but the trepidation remains. Buried for a time, the fear lies dormant until nature's breath blows once more and the grains reform and fear rises to the surface, sitting proudly atop all other emotions. Could one but predict the wind and bury fear indefinitely they would find themselves complacent. There is depression awaiting those who lose fear for with that loss comes the loss of hope.

The wall was dense. Several feet of brick separated Tritan from the dining hall that he had been instructed to attend for the evening meal. He stood with his head leaning against the stone partition beside the oak door that he could not bring himself to walk through. Conversation had become so great a chore that he felt the insecurity of dining and discussion. Were he merely able to attend and eat and not be spoken to, it would go all the smoother. But he had a sense that he was to be interrogated. As he had been for several nights past. Something to do with a boy who he was told he once knew. But hard as he tried to recall his past, he knew no child. He had never fathered a child; of that fact he was certain. Why he was quizzed about it incessantly he could not say. Abstraction from love and responsibility. That was his life.

Tritan's training had become more severe since he had returned from Haagurufur with Winter. Four hours daily he wielded his sword and ran the forest paths to the peak of the hills of the valley. It made his appetite fierce and he could smell the steaming ox through the hinges of the door. His hand rose to the handle. *Time to do battle.*

The dining hall was akin to a grand palace ballroom. Chandeliers hung from the ceiling above the long table where Winter sat with Resonance. Candles lined the length of the table, illuminating the twenty or so places that were laid out. But all those seats remained empty as though his hosts dined with ghosts.

The two women were deep in discussion and paid no notice to Tritan as he entered the room and walked the long stretch alongside the empty table to sit by their side. Resonance was at the head of the table and Winter had sat at the corner closest to her. The younger woman was laughing and taking occasional small bites of a fresh stick of celery. The crunching sound it made as she bit into it was, to Tritan, like nails scraping against a metal plate.

He sat down quietly and was promptly visited by a serving boy who first poured his wine and then refilled the glasses of Winter and Resonance. Finally, Winter looked towards Tritan and shot him a steely glare.

'Well, finally we can eat an actual meal. So very good of you to join us promptly.'

Resonance laughed and looked at Tritan pitifully as though he were some sort of disobedient dog. She rang a small bell that was placed neatly beside her placemat and within seconds a retinue of serving staff emerged, holding steaming hot plates.

'Oh, delightful, it appears to still be hot. Thank goodness,' Resonance chided.

All the bloodied wounds and beatings of a lifetime couldn't rattle Tritan the way this patronising woman did. He had remained indifferent to her when they had first arrived in Baurticeford but she seemed to increasingly believe that she shared in Winter's right to chastise him. He didn't understand why Winter had the right either, but it was a simple fact that he was bound to her. He could not remember the reason why but it was not the way a slave is bound to a master or a lover to their betrothed. It was something else entirely as though his soul was linked to hers.

'Eat up, Tritan,' Winter instructed. 'We have much to discuss but we should not do so on an empty stomach.'

Tritan nodded and followed suit as the two women began to cut away at the ox meat laid out before them.

'These cuts have travelled well. I'll remember to put in a repeat order to the butcher's boy when he passes through town again. There is no such meat in these parts, it pains me to say.'

Resonance was talking with a mouth full of the fatty steak. It was enough to put one off one's meal. Winter pointed her fork down at the steak and nodded as though in agreement.

'It's damn good. The seasoning is perfect. Perhaps we can repeat this meal upon our return. It will give me something to look forward to after weeks at sea.'

'You're leaving soon then?'

'Yes, we leave the day after tomorrow. Preparations are underway.'

Suddenly a shift in the landscape made Tritan quiver. He was sick of this purgatory but at hearing the news they were to depart soon, he felt a sense of dread for the journey ahead.

'Well, your place at this table and your sleeping quarters will be reserved, awaiting your return.' Resonance placed her hand over the top of Winter's. It was a gesture Winter appreciated, though even Tritan could see through to the true intent behind it. Money was Resonance Qualchaid's first language.

'This wine is foul,' Tritan said plainly.

Both women were taken aback at the rude comment. Tritan hadn't offered so much as a huff since Thomas had finished with him. Any unprompted contribution was unexpected but this was particularly offensive and out of character. Tritan didn't miss the administrations of the burning concoction that was injected into his arm. But he wondered if it had been worthwhile as he raised his glass with the hand that had been useless. Its grip had returned. 'I think it has been soured by breathing in the foul air in this manor.'

Winter began to burst out laughing as though it were the funniest joke she had ever heard.

'Oh, my dear boy. If you are trying to regrow your abhorrent personality and joy of passing negative quips, you'll simply have to do better than that.'

Resonance joined in the laughter but her pride had been stung; it was enough for Tritan. So many words formed in his mind and in recent weeks he had lost the will to speak, but he found himself regaining his joy for the discomfort of others.

'Gluttony leads to all ends. For of itself it cannot sustain life. If you suck the well dry, those who drink from it will move on as survival demands.'

'Tritan, do not pretend to understand the purpose of my intent.' Winter became vicious with her words as she retorted, 'You are muscle, as you have always been and things do not go well when a brute pretends to have valid thoughts. Look what state your father left us in when he defected from his leaders and led his own army. Do not think that we are not living in his world still. All the famine, disruption, and state of the land is down to him and I am here to undo that damage. It is true that having you here with me is a personal boon. Call it revenge, or greed if you like. It is simply what it is.'

Tritan listened to the scolding and it settled deep within him. Guilt rose from his bones and flowed into his blood. Suddenly his head was pounding; he had stepped over a line that he had not seen. His negative thoughts escaped him and he could only think of simple facts. Like the fact he would die for this woman. He didn't know when or how he had decided it. It was simply truth.

'If you talk of Augustus, then you are wrong. He is not my father.'

'Oh, come off it. He raised you and made you what you are. Do you even know your blood father? No. Of course not. Let me be the one to tell you, if you did, you would be the worse for it.'

'I knew him for a time.'

'Not like I did.'

'Tell me.'

Tritan asked the question like a small boy. The revelation struck him that Winter knew all his secrets. Maybe his servitude would be repaid with answers to past questions.

'One day, far from now, I will tell you a long story. But before we deal with the past, we will address the present and future.' Winter took a pause and placed her cutlery on the table, leaning forwards to address the true purpose of this dinner meeting. 'Tritan, tomorrow is an important moment for you, as you must select sixty of the best men to accompany you. Fritz of course will be at your side but the rest, I leave up to you.'

*Back to business then.* Tritan cast aside the child that wailed inside him. 'We have hundreds of soldiers in the camps. It will take time to assess them all…'

'Yes, yes of course, but you'll have the full day. No training tomorrow, just be sure to confer with Thomas that they are suitable.'

'You mean to take the strongest soldiers?'

'No, not at all. It is required that these soldiers are true to the fight. You recall how I saved you from the destruction of the soul-magic. We must be sure that those who join us are safe from it as well. That is our only chance for survival.'

'How will I know?'

Winter wiped her mouth with her serviette and placed it down gently in front of her.

'My final act as one who bore the burden of the evil magic, was to sever you from it. Fortune saw that you were quite resistant to its pull before so it made the severing all the easier. I reached out to as many of the others as I could and planted a dream in all their minds. You recall the dream, do you not?'

'I recall only one dream.'

'Tell it to me.'

'I am a child running through a sunny field. The wheat is higher than my head. It's so yellow in the light of the setting sun, but it is also covered in blood. There is a rumbling sound. Hundreds of horses are approaching the fields to begin searching for a man with blood on his hands. I look down and mine are clean, but I am afraid they will kill me anyway.'

'Yes, yes. That is it. And the end? Tell me how it ends.'

'I'm in a cage, being shouted out by a crowd of villagers. They point their spears at me and I ask them to kill me. But instead they take me to a woman. She sentences me to death, or a life repaying my debt in servitude. I tell her I am ready to die, though inside I know it is a lie. She tells me I must climb a mountain and speak to a ghost who wanders aimlessly at the summit. So I climb and when I arrive there I see a child. He is young and he turns to face me but he cannot see. He calls me father and before I know how to respond, he begs me to kill him.'

A smile formed on Winter's face and the cracks beside her eyes wrinkled. She held it for a time and nodded, content. Something about the dream bothered her but it was her secret and she shared it with no one. She took a deep breath. Hearing the dream spoken through Tritan's words shook her.

'It is almost as though it happened. The way you tell it makes it real.'

Tritan felt dejected, as though the dream were a memory and not a stolen story. He did not dwell on feeling sad for not owning this dream that had been planted inside him. He picked up his knife and fork and cut himself another slice of tender ox.

'The story truly is beautifully constructed, I must say. Perhaps we have a storyteller amidst us. A warrior and an artist. Don't you think, Winter?' said Resonance.

'Yes, it is quite beautifully constructed indeed.'

Both pairs of eyes clung to him like rain. Tritan chewed until his mouth was empty. His mind racing. Thoughts cascaded like waterfalls through empty caverns of space and time. One moment he had so much to offer, truly believing he could change the course of things with his words, instead of his sword. But in the next moment he could not recall his own past and his mind became blank. Tritan's focus returned to the mission, as it always did.

'You require me to insist that each soldier recalls the dream to me in full,' said Tritan.

'Correct.'

Tritan nodded at Winter and then drank a large gulp of his wine. It tasted sweeter now and as he placed the glass down it knocked against his plate and a chiming sound like the servants' bell rang out. The servants came running in to address the call and Resonance giggled and immediately sent them away again.

The three of them shared the humour of the moment and it made Tritan feel a sense of belonging. Should he fear belonging to such a grouping, or did he truly desire it? He was not sure.

'Any who do not know the dream in its entirety are likely still tainted,' Winter began. 'I may not have reached them fully. It is a dangerous place where we are going. And most dangerous of all is the boy.'

'The boy from the dream?'

'Yes, you will meet him soon. His name is Pietrich. He is a danger to any within reach of his mind if they carry but a pinch of the soul-magic.'

'This boy, what is he to you?'

Winter smiled at her warrior pet and leant forwards. 'The question is, Tritan, what is he to you? Do you feel somehow doubtful of our intentions?'

'I don't know anything of this child or any other for that matter. He is nothing to me.'

'Good, because he will be more than just a child when you come face to face with him. You must be focused and swift, or I do not know what fate will befall us.'

'When we find him, what must I do?' Tritan asked.

There was a long silence. Suddenly the air seemed so still and the sound of Resonance shuffling in her chair echoed throughout the hall. Winter hesitated, as though she awaited a deadly silence before giving the answer that Tritan already knew.

'You must kill him, of course.'

## 26

Could it be the swaying monotony that angers a pirate's heart? Destined to spend so few moments of their life treading on dry land. Vast expanses of time at their fingertips to contemplate all that ails them. The deep places within a mind that there is never time to dwell on during the pace of a town life. Thoughts of the places one misses when there is nothing to see but water all around you. The open air of a market square and the smell of hot fresh food. Walking trails through woodland areas to summits of beautiful mountain ranges that gift them with views that inspire their love of the world. Time with family and friends, spent laughing and in comfort.

Pietrich felt trapped between a pirate's life and one of a boy who knew the joy of such places. But he didn't even have the comfort of a view. He simply sat listening to the wind rattling the sail ties as he sat out on deck contemplating his own short history. He began to feel a chill in the air and knew the light of day was dwindling, reassuring as it was, for Pietrich had grown more accustomed to night. Not because his vision differed in the darkness but because it was his new home, the eternal black void. Better to be amongst others when they shared in his burden. Of course, his shipmates all used oil lanterns and candles to guide themselves but it was comforting to know he was not alone in the cradle of dark.

Pietrich wondered how the fading light might appear to others. What variation the clouds would hold and the colours they would display as the lingering sun tickled their edges. The view would always be the same this far out into the expanse of the ocean, but to him it was no infinite landscape of water, just a chorus of splashing and creaking wood as the ship stressed and buckled under its own weight against the waves. It still surprised him that none of the pirates had attempted to attack him whilst he slept. Jack had been a good companion and no doubt kept them at a distance but he also sensed in the crew's thoughts that there was a certain curiosity about their destination and the role that Pietrich played in their present voyage. Thoughts of encouragement, slipped to them as subtly as he dared, had not fallen on deaf ears.

All the intentions and feelings of the crew were made plain to him. With so few people around to disturb his thoughts he could hear them clearly. The rest of the voices in his mind were barely whispers.

The overriding sensation was that for the crew, an itch needed to be scratched. Pietrich was that itch. He had no idea himself what awaited them. The future was a dense fog in his mind, less clear to him even than his sight.

As much as Pietrich loved the sea it had become a prison. A reminder of all the things that were no longer a part of his life. So much time spent listening to the lake of the world with no more than a few hundred square feet of ship to wander around.

Mutt had told him he wasn't built for a pirate's life. She maintained that one of the things that made a good pirate or sailor was someone who had known the inside of a prison cell. For being at sea was like a prison sentence and to be content within your own mind was essential to retaining sanity.

Pietrich wasn't sure if the sea air had stolen a bit of his sanity already or whether that had happened well before they set sail. He knew he wasn't the same anymore. But despite the regretful path he was treading, he managed to cling onto one memory that made him smile. The knowledge that he had visited his mother one last time before too much of his spirit had rotted.

A crashing sound came from below that startled Pietrich onto his feet. He focused his listening to determine what had caused the disturbance. It sounded as though the kitchen had been turned upside down.

There was shouting coming from all directions and the crew above decks ran into the belly of the ship. Three men had been trapped under a fallen timber joist and there was a fire burning beside them. The cook was screaming and jammed a skillet beneath the wood, leveraging it with all his weight. The timber hardly budged. Pietrich hovered above the stairwell that led below and he could hear screaming. The heat of the fire was growing and he felt it on his face.

'Sums, cut the rear sail. Do it now, man!' Mutt shouted the order at her first mate and he ran up the stairs, nearly knocking Pietrich over as he scrambled for the pulley. Sums cut the rope and the bottom of the sail flapped about helplessly. By the time he had returned to the stairwell someone had appeared with a different rope and Sums, already knowing what was required of him, tied the rope into the pulley system and began cranking it.

'Faster, Sums, damn you. Pirates are burning alive here, man!'

Sums didn't waste his breath replying. This was no time to throw concern to lost pride. He jacked the crank until a point where he could wind it no further and cried out for help. But the rest of the crew were downstairs, so Pietrich ran to him instead.

'What can I do to help?' he said.

'Just hold the crank steady while I try and jimmy it.'

The shouting below turned to incessant desperation and cursing. The flames had reached flesh.

'Pull harder!' Sums screamed with all his being.

Pietrich kicked his foot against the mast behind him and used himself as a lever against the pulley. It moved and creaked forward piece by piece until finally the whole thing buckled, tearing the base from the oak decking and the whole system whipped right across the top of the ship, crashing into the front rail.

'Holy seas of fuck. That could have taken your head off, lad.' Sums didn't hang around long enough for a response but planted a reassuring palm on Pietrich's shoulder before jumping below deck.

The pirates who had been caught beneath the timber had been freed by the force of the winch dislodging the joist. They lay rolling on the ground as others tried to cool them by throwing the water reserves across their steaming bodies. Mutt was fighting the kitchen fire by pouring a huge sack of lentils at its base. To her own surprise it was effective and as the sack finally ran empty, like an hourglass dropping its last grain of sand, the fire was quashed. She leant back and caught her breath, as did the rest of her crew. The kitchen was a mess and before Sums had a chance to expose to her the extent of the damage she flicked a palm towards his face. She already knew.

'I'm sorry, captain, I—'

'No excuses, please, I can't stand excuses.' Mutt cut off the cook who was about to confess.

She looked around and saw gambling chips and singed

playing cards scattered across the floor. *All this mess for a bloody game of cards.*

Mutt leant her head back where she sat. The game had nearly cost her the Defiance.

Pietrich stepped down into the wreckage and smelt the burning. The space was filled with ash and fear.

'I know you blame me for this. I'm sorry, I am useless in such instances. I can ride a storm but I can't abate it.' Pietrich addressed all the pirates in unison. 'You have me at a disadvantage, I cannot sail this ship alone. But now you're thinking you barely have supplies enough to turn about and head home, let alone finish the voyage and then sail back.' He shot a glance through sightless eyes towards Mutt with the statement. 'That would be dependent on fixing the rear sail at any rate and I doubt there will be a shipyard where we are heading.'

The crew stood gawping at him as he made his lecture. Jack, as ever, was present at his side whilst emotions were running high.

'I don't blame you, lad. These poor bastards shoulda been paying attention instead of drinking and gambling. But you are the cause, and there ain't no hidin' from that fact.' Mutt stayed seated as she spoke, a despondent tone in her voice. She looked about at the wreckage of their kitchen and wasted food supplies. 'But you must admit, our options are somewhat diminished.'

There was shuffling amongst the pirates, but none other than Mutt offered so much as a nasal whistle. Pietrich continued his address.

'You've spent your lives trading in stolen goods, acquired by force. Killing at times, when the situation required it. But when the fighting stops and the blood has dried and you sit to dine with your family, with food paid for by pillaged coin. You do not feel content. Because I know the adventure is the thing you treasure the most. Your responsibilities, few though they may be, are a canvas on which to paint your excuses.'

Mutt stood on her feet, towering above Pietrich. Jack bared his teeth at her and she didn't flinch.

'Going somewhere with this diatribe, are you, lad?'

'No one has attempted to take my life. There have been no creeping shadows in the night to my sleeping quarters. I must ask myself why? What is it that a ship of pirates could want from this ordeal. But none of you are here for riches this time, or because you consider it a means of survival. I have heard the chatter and felt your desire. You need to know the same as me. What is waiting for us at the end of this ocean.'

Mutt began to laugh and tried her best to speak through her uncontrollable outburst. 'You think this bunch care one squat what is there? We're goddamned pirates, lad. Not a soul left between us.'

She turned to see her crew join in the joke with her but none of them were laughing. Instead she saw something else in their eyes that didn't make sense. A look she had never seen. The boy had swayed them, somewhere deep inside them he had found their humanity and she saw it now staring back at her through a dozen gazes.


'VERY WELL,' she continued. 'As long as we're all clear this is a one-way journey. I know what awaits us. There may be ancient magic, yes. But we can't eat that shit. If we find nowt else but dust we will die there. Is the price worth it, for the prize this time will be nothing more than air. There will be no trinkets to trade or produce to consume.'

'There will be a prize, I promise you that. You who have seen the entire world will know the true beginnings of when the world was changed.'

Pietrich walked forwards and slowly lifted his hand to find Mutt's forehead. She flinched at first but after a moment's hesitation she allowed him to place his palm on her brow. He was right, her curiosity was stronger than her greed.

The sensation was like being blown into a thousand pieces. She was torn apart and her mind thrust through every possible moment that she could have ever lived. The energy it took to see every second of her life presented to her at once was like lifting a thousand ships. All the sadness and hatred, ambition and disappointment. They flooded her heart and though she had no concept of her physical being anymore she knew she cried rivers. But somewhere in that expanse of hurt was a flickering light of joy. It was buried deep beneath abuse and abandonment but still it burned in isolation. The memory had been long lost to her and Pietrich had guided her to it.

Suddenly they were broken apart as one of the crew charged Pietrich with his shoulder to get him off their captain. The three fell to the floor in a bundle of fatigue and confusion.

Jack gnawed at the ankle of the one who had charged and dragged him away from Pietrich, drawing blood as he pulled and snagged at him.

'Stop, Jack. It's okay!' Pietrich commanded.

Pietrich felt for a sign of Mutt, she was breathlessly panting on the ground beside him and he placed a comforting hand upon her back. She coughed and wailed like a young child.

'What did you do to me? Is this death?'

'No, that was merely the beginning of your understanding of what is to come.'

Mutt shook her head in disbelief. 'I remembered her. I saw her eyes.'

Pietrich placed his fingers over her lips.

'That memory is for you alone. Keep it.'

'Thank you, Pietrich. You are a bleedin' wonder, lad.'

Mutt did something then that she couldn't believe. Nor could her crew, but Pietrich allowed it. She wrapped her arms around him and sobbed. She clutched him so tight that his breaths were thin drawn wisps. None of them felt like pirates in that moment. They were a family.

DAYS PASSED by in silence amidst the new dynamic aboard the Defiance. None of the crew truly understood what they were to each other anymore. It had been so simple once. They were all equals. Pirates with private lives that none of them ever discussed. It was part of the former captain's code. To keep home on land and not bring it to the sea. It made it all the easier to suffer losses and cut loose any stray members.

The initial fears of the damage caused in the fire had caused no panic. The rear sail had been tied off to the outer railing and it was shifted regularly to determine their direction. Disregarding a return journey, there was plenty of food and water to get them to The Vermillion Isles. As it turned out, the entire retinue had decided not to concern themselves with ideas of sailing back. The consensus was to figure out that problem later. So, they feasted nightly in high spirits.

Mutt had become a recluse and awkward around Pietrich. Old wounds and lost childhood joy that had been recovered were a burden to a pirate and made it all the harder to captain the ship. But she was afforded her space and appeared only when required.

Pietrich loitered around the decks as before. But he had become a ghost. No one paid him any mind save for meal time when he ate beside them. He too had retreated inside his mind. He felt the distant calling of the mountain increase and he knew they must be close. The echoes in his head never stopped and the pleading cries of voices, lost in the waters of the islands, were a constant song looping around his skull and he could only hum to sedate the tirade.

'Land. There be land ahead!' Sums cried out for all to hear and he ran to the front of the ship, passing the wheel to the second mate.

'Nowt but grey rocks, reckon that's our destination.'

'Yes,' Pietrich said. The mountain was screaming in his ears and he knew he was where he needed to be. 'We are here.'

Pietrich had a look of distress on his face that sent a shiver down Sums' spine. He pulled up his hood to hide his face and walked away.

'Wait, are we expecting company?'

Sums pointed at a clutch of vessels just beneath the rocky beaches. Pietrich turned back, concerned.

'What do you see?'

'There are three ships just offshore. Look like attack ships to me.'

Pietrich concentrated and tried to sense life aboard any of the vessels but there was nothing, just emptiness.

'They are abandoned,' he said, his face a deep glaze of concentration as he reached his feelings out towards the rest of the islands in case the crews had disembarked, but he could hear no voices.

Sums smiled at that. 'Well all the better for us. We may just have a way home after all.'

Pietrich nodded but turned away and went to stand by an empty part of the top deck. The discomfort he felt was fierce. Not quite pain but it was almost as if he was not the sole occupant of his body. He clasped his hands together and squeezed them tight, trying to recall the sensation of touch as he became more and more aware of everything outside his body.

Pietrich dropped to his knees and tried with all his might to remain aware of his own self. Too many others were a part of him. They had entered his being and he began to struggle to recall which life was truly his and which he had inherited through the swell that reverberated from the depths of the volcanic mass they approached.

Sums ordered the anchorage of the ship and called for the small row boat to be prepared.

'What does it look like? Tell me,' Pietrich shouted desperately and Sums took one glance at the island and told him the simple truth.

'It's a grey rock, lad. Far as I can tell from here. There's not a single living soul on this island.'

'We must get to the beach at once.'

'There ain't no beach. Just old rock from lava flow. We'll have to approach with caution if the winds pick up.

'Whatever it takes. We must set foot upon that island at once.' Pietrich was determined.

It was a bumpy journey in the row boat. The unsettled waves were a warning to their intrusion. Pietrich buried his head in his hands and tried to calm the voices. Mutt saw his distress and her expression betrayed her previous claims that she cared nothing for his discomfort. He knew she felt a sense of protectiveness over him but she never voiced it and Pietrich would never reveal his awareness of her feelings. That secret he would leave to her.

When the row boat finally reached the shores, it scraped across the island's jagged volcanic formation and the pirates had to disembark carefully, lest a fierce wave would crush them into the rock.

Mutt helped Pietrich across the waterlogged stone and eventually they made their way to a dry plain. All around them was grey dust. No sign of vegetation or wildlife. It was like some sort of parallel world. A graveyard for all things and specks of deathly ash floated all around them, invading the passages of their lungs.

'We'll last five minutes breathing in all this shit.' One of the pirates complained, bitterly.

'The rate you smoke, this ought to be like fresh mountain air,' Mutt retorted as she began to lead the march across the island.

They scoured the landscape for near an hour and headed towards the base of the mountain peak. It was all the same wherever they headed. Nothing and no one.

The atmosphere amongst the pirate crew was tense. Pietrich, even in his distressed state, could feel they were about to snap.

'Wait, we are not alone!' Pietrich stopped suddenly and Mutt signalled for the rest to hold their position.

'What is it?'

'I hear voices, there is a camp nearby. Only two or three men, they haven't been here long.'

'Camp, you say?' Sums asked, relieved. 'Best we get on with it and have ourselves a bit of nourishment then. Are you sure there are only a few of them.'

'Yes, I'm sure.'

Mutt and Sums shared a look and she nodded her head to the first mate and began to follow behind Pietrich who was stumbling across the uneven ground. The group stepped carefully towards a ridge and there beneath them was an encampment with a healthy array of supplies. Sat by a small fire were three men. They were chatting wistfully. Regret and concern in their thoughts.

Mutt hadn't lingered and several of her pirates charged the three by the fireside but before they had a chance to attack, one of the men in the middle blew a loud horn that echoed around the camp and reverberated against the volcanic rocks that towered above them.

In the next moment sixty or so swordsmen, axe wielders, and club bearers emerged from their hiding spots to surround the pirates.

'Fuck.'

It was the only word Mutt had time to muster before they were charged. For every pirate, there were four trained warriors. It would be a massacre.

Pietrich, for the first time since he had fled the ship with Castellar and Lynden, was afraid. He didn't understand why he hadn't sensed the battalion of soldiers. But he had no time to condemn himself to fear. He focused his thoughts and reached out to extinguish the lives of their attackers. He just needed a moment to be the bearer of a wave akin to the one he had formed on Port Melees.

With a fierce yell, he delved into their hearts and encased a protective barrier against himself for each of the pirates. *No collateral damage,* he promised.

There was a short moment of confusion as the three who had been at the campfire keeled over, dead. But the enraged warriors who had started their charge against their prey didn't even flinch. Pietrich realised then those men at the centre had been bait.

It was a trap.

Someone knew he was coming and he had fallen for it. He tried again to reach out to those who were about to slay his companions but there was nothing there. It was as though they were soulless beings. He suddenly felt totally useless and collapsed into a ball on the floor. He was a weak boy again, cowering in the dirt. What had happened to his strength?

There was no time for further contemplation. The swords came down hard and fast and the pirates met them with their own.

Flesh was torn from bone, and blood spattered the volcanic

rocks, painting the grey stone a shade of vermillion, restoring the island's hue to its namesake.

The warriors were well trained and their strength was brutally unbalanced against the rabble of pirates, though the pirates were vicious men and women and they gave back as good as they received.

Sums had been cracked across the skull with a stone cudgel but this only enraged him as blood flooded across his face. He drew two daggers and slashed furiously at the three who stood before him. He caught one in the neck and tore out their windpipe. His own heartbeat pulsated on the side of his head where blood was pouring out profusely. He didn't have long before he would pass out. He had to make the most of the short burst of adrenaline. A woman in front of him brought her axe down towards his legs, trying to take his footing out from beneath him. But he jumped high enough to avoid the swing and plunged two daggers into her belly.

He spat on her as she fell to the ground. No need to finish her, she would bleed out slowly like the stuck pig she was.

There was no final thought or regret for Sums as his head came clear from the nape of his neck. His eyes saw the world spiral around him as his head toppled to the ground. The last thing he saw was his decapitated body collapsing to the floor in front of a terrifying beast of a man, wielding the most magnificent sword he had ever seen.

Tritan flicked the blood free from his sword and continued his barrage of attacks. There were just a handful of pirates left and it was almost time for his afternoon meal. It was tiresome and hungry work, killing pirates.

Then through the carnage of the slaughter, Tritan saw the boy. Curled up helplessly and blind as a bat. It was as though the boy was trying to make himself invisible by cowering in a corner. Tritan clasped his sword with all his strength and walked slowly towards Pietrich, the rest of the fighting had become a dream to him.

He stood above the weak and helpless boy. How he could be deemed a threat, Tritan had no idea. It didn't matter; he was here for one reason only and he raised his sword above his head ready to make a killing blow.

With his heavy breaths, Tritan saw the boy's expression contort and his ears pricked. There was recognition strewn across his face.

'Father?'

The boy's frail voice was pathetic and Tritan pitied him as he called for his parent in his last moments.

A cry came from beside him and Mutt dived in front of Pietrich as Tritan brought down his sword. She caught the blow on her shoulder and it cut right through to her lung. She spat blood into the air as she held Tritan's sword like a lodged spear in her body.

She pulled a dagger from her jerkin and plunged it into Tritan's chest. He didn't flinch for it was like being pricked by a small pin in the hands of a child. He drew out the sword from her body and readied himself to finish off the aggravating bitch as she slumped to her knees.

'Father, don't please!' Pietrich compelled him. But his pleading fell on deaf ears.

Mutt looked at Pietrich through bloodshot eyes. There was little of her left beneath the gaze but what still existed smiled at him. He sensed her gratitude and damned himself that he could not look upon her face.

'Thank you, lad. Thank you for your gift.'

Her words were cut short as Tritan's sword slashed at her chest, hacking off the half of her body that had been left flailing in the air.

Pietrich sobbed and his blind eyes flickered around hopelessly. All had fallen silent. He knew then that the rest of the pirates were dead. Mutt had bought him seconds but now it was just him, all alone again, and he sensed the fear of his wolf. Jack howled at his side, appealing to his old master. But Tritan booted the wolf hard in the side of its skull, sending it reeling and it fled.

Pietrich raised his head and shouted the only words he could think of.

'I love you.'

The desperation of the scream would have stunned a hardened brute. But as Pietrich's yell turned into a breathless pant, Tritan stuck every inch of his sword through the boy's chest.

Something happened then that Pietrich could not have expected. He didn't feel pain. He did not pass out or see images of his life flicker before him like a dream. But for the first time in years he saw with his own eyes.

The blurry face of his father came into view and he saw stillness and no remorse. Over Tritan's shoulder, approaching through the scattered corpses was an elderly woman. She looked down at Pietrich and before darkness enshrouded him she spoke.

'Winter has come for you, my boy. This is where your journey ends.'

It was the last sound he heard.

## 27

Time seemed to slow to a crawl. His stomach lurched up inside his body, pushing against his lungs and stealing his breath. The fall felt like floating at first, before his weight dragged him down into the dirt. His shoulder smashed into the boggy, shit-infested field and he gasped for air. A stirrup was caught around his right ankle. The respite he enjoyed as he lay still on the floor was short lived, for as the horse who had thrown him bolted across the field, Boscelito whipped behind like a rag doll, bouncing on the dirt and spinning in the air as he desperately scrabbled at his boot to unbuckle the strap.

When the horse reached a fence towards the far side of the enclosed field it stopped and stood up tall on its hind legs. Boscelito rolled out of the way to prevent the hoofs from crashing down into his chest. His boot slipped off and he ran to the fence and hopped through an opening between the timber struts towards the crowd of onlookers who had watched the fruitless performance.

He pulled himself up and wiped the sloppy mud from his shirt then reached through the fence to grab his boot.

'This one we leave behind.'

Boscelito spoke to no one in particular as he made the statement, passing beside River as she stood with the crowd. He lifted his elbow to his face and nestled his head against his top to wipe away the blood from his temple. Mud streaks remained where the red trickles had been.

'Let it run wild,' River said to the stable master. 'This horse cannot be broken.'

'If we had more time we could calm its fiery spirit.'

'We have no time, and we could not. Set it loose.'

The stable master nodded his head and signalled to his boy to clear the crowds and let the horse go.

River didn't linger at the field. She ran to catch up to Boscelito who had headed through a woodland path. He was marching swiftly to their army's camp.

Of those thousand Vermillions who had set sail for the mainland in the wake of the hospitality they had enjoyed on Maluabaw, only six hundred had been deemed fit for service. The rest lingered within the castle walls where Sol had negotiated their rest with the council who still pondered the next move.

It had been no easy task to come to the aid of the king's army without revealing the origin of the naval battalion. Sol was the inside man and he invented a story of the hardship that the islanders had suffered at Augustus' hand. Their Vermillion identity would remain elusive but their fighters and ships would be a worthy resource.

The mystery surrounding Elik's death remained and rumours had begun to spread throughout the royal army. Ten thousand soldiers had been assembled and, on the verge of battle, were stood down with no explanation. For three months, they had waited in the camps, growing restless and gossiping. Some of the guerrilla fighters and skirmish squads formed of farmers and simple folk had left to return home to their families.

The Vermillion legion had been formed with the help of Sol, and Boscelito had been made responsible for readying the horses. This slow process had led the council leaders to inform the royal army of the delay and tell them the lie that Elik would address them as soon as their new allies were ready for the fight.

The journey to Fort Vecchia by sea had been long and awkward. Boscelito found himself caught in a web of feelings that made it harder to think straight. River had been dismissive throughout the voyage and had dished out more than his fair share of gruelling tasks. There was something about her growing resentment that made him desire her all the more; their relationship so far had been formed out of anger and spite after all.

There had been whispers amongst the camp that Augustus had a new adviser, a young woman that none, other than the warlord himself, had seen in the flesh. Boscelito wondered if it was love driving River on her crusade.

Despite all he mused over, he found his feelings for Jade growing too. He had never been lucky in love before. Usually he would remain introverted as the rest of the army mingled and formed romantic unions. He had watched from afar as many hearts and minds were unified. Now his own heart was torn in two. *Can it be possible to truly love two people?* he wondered.

'Slow down, Boscelito. I need to talk with you.'

The captain huffed at her and barely slowed his pace.

'I'm in need of a bath, I have wounds to clean and dirt in my fucking eyes.'

'I'm sorry about the horse, he was the strongest and came at a fair price in the trade.'

'They should have paid you to take it off their hands. It was raised wild and captured too late in life. I'm lucky it didn't kill me.'

River ran in front of him and stood firm to halt his march.

'We must be ready to lead the army soon. If there are further delays then Augustus will bring the fight to us and without Elik to lead his king's guard, morale will be non-existent.'

'This war is about to explode. I don't know how we will fare hitting Augustus head on. It is true his numbers are few but we still don't know how they got to Elik and the cause of death has yet to be determined. Rumours of traitors are flooding the encampments and the healer closest to the dead king spoke as if his life simply left him with no cause. No sign of poison nor wounds.'

River stepped closer to Boscelito and gazed deeper into his eyes.

'You and I know that Augustus has started a blaze. If we don't stop him, it will spread out of control and Harmion will enter a state of turmoil for generations.' She looked away from his judgemental frown. 'You act as though I am punishing you, like a scorned child. You avoid me where once you couldn't take your eyes off me. What would you have me do?'

'I only wonder that you are here, hiding behind a sense of false duty, to avoid what truly ails you. For as long as she is out there, you will never rest and your actions have become misguided. You believe she could be with Augustus' army? Just tell me that is not why we are here.'

'How dare you speak to me of her. What business is it of yours?'

'Why do you avoid the truth? Is your need for vengeance to allow your father's soul some peace so fractured that you would join a war you have only observed from behind an invisible veil?'

River turned away from him. His cruelty was immeasurable.

'She has been wronged, I know it. She never could have done those things without motive.'

'You give her too much credit.'

'I love her still.'

'Then you are a fool.'

Boscelito continued his walk and knocked her shoulder, he hadn't meant to but his footing was still unstable from attempting to break the horse. But River took it as a sign of aggression and kicked his legs out from under him, her wildness getting the better of her. Boscelito rolled over to face her as she grabbed his shirt and began to scream in his face but he lifted his knee in time to gain purchase of her weight and flung her to the ground beside him. He rolled on top of her and pinned her shoulders to the floor.

They shared a disgust for each other and their hatred made them feral. But the green daggers of her eyes stabbed his heart once more and Boscelito fell into a loving despair. Both set their gaze upon the other. The unmistakeable bond between them did not require words to articulate. A fire burned between them but neither was capable to feed it fuel and it died out. The awkwardness that they had become so used to resumed.

'Get off me, soldier, we both have work to do.'

River took short panicked breaths as Boscelito rolled to his side. 'You are a curse upon me. But I cannot set my heart free of you.' He hesitated for a moment, waiting for her reply. None came and so he left her lying on the ground where she stayed.

Night fell and Boscelito stretched his limbs for they ached and stiffened from the horse fight earlier that day. He kept to himself while the army dined together and awaited their orders. There was a part of him that wanted to sneak away and travel

north from the eastern territory they had settled in to warn
Augustus. A series of Vermillion ships were awaiting orders to
set sail around the coast and flank his army from the estuaries
north of his supposed position. It would be the signal for the
army to mobilise for the attack and it was also a window to
return to his former position amongst the warlord's army. He
could escape when they made land, wiping away everything that
had befallen him in the time he had been missing. There would
be forgiveness or he would forever be seen as a turn-cloak. It
was a strange pang of loyalty, though he knew he owed the man
nothing now. Too much time had passed and his conscience
would not allow him to dwell on his misplaced steadfastness.
No matter what, he would stay and fight for River and die for
her if it was his fate.

Boscelito took a pot from a small fire he had made and
poured a cup of broth to sip. It was a hearty soup and it warmed
him. His mind wandered and he felt guilt overcome him. He
missed Jade despite knowing his heart truly belonged to
another. They had kept apart for appearances' sake and only
once had Boscelito found a flower, laying on his palliasse, that
carried her scent.

*Perhaps the war will set me free.* He wondered if the convenience
of death would be worth the fight alone.

The broth made him sleepy and he finished the cup and lay
his head down to rest. Morning would bring news and he would
wake refreshed and ready for it.

He didn't dream that night, for as he slept a figure snuck
into his bivouac and lay down beside him. She undressed him
and he felt the chill of her naked body against his own. He
recognised her sweet smell and though it felt like a dream he
knew it was real. He allowed himself to become aroused and
grabbed Jade tight in his arms.

'I love you,' she told him as he entered inside her and they made love in silence. Just the soft sounds of flesh moving against the floor and blankets.

For hours afterwards they remained enclosed in each other's embrace. It was a moment of lust and tenderness before a rising squall. Boscelito drifted off to sleep and when he awoke he was alone. He knew then that Jade had carried with her a secret. That today was the day they would ride to confront Augustus' army.

Morning birds sang and a soft amber light drew through his bivouac along with a chilling breeze. He rose and dressed himself and before he had a chance to adjust his eyes to the bright morning light, he could hear the soldiers readying themselves for the fight.

'The king has marched ahead!' shouted a frantic soldier who ran past Boscelito, attaching his sword belt as he ran.

'What? Speak sense, man.'

'He rode in the dead of night with a small legion of his most loyal soldiers. He has gone mad. We must ride at once or he is done for.'

The soldier left Boscelito in his wake. He stood intrigued and he knew the council had faked the fuss. Elik's loyalist guard must have been privy to his death all along, Boscelito realised. Now they were riding to certain death to bait and inspire the rest of the army. It was a good plan but it required sacrifice.

Boscelito put his war garments together and headed for the stables where his own legion were making preparations. Two hundred horseback riders and two hundred on foot. The rest would lead the armada and the two thousand royal troops on the ships would squash Augustus from above. Any other day it would seem like a solid campaign, but something made Boscelito feel uneasy. He had been sent to find a navy and failed. If Augustus had his wits about him he would know that the battleground placed him too close to the estuaries where a navy could alight. There were too many variables for such a battle to have a certain outcome. The question in his mind was whether Augustus would assume Boscelito dead or a traitor.

The foot soldiers were already marching to make ground as the last report from the scouts had determined that the major part of Augustus' army were a three-day journey north.

Provisions for the march and thin skins to sleep beneath were handed out to each man and woman along with their steel. The atmosphere was uneasy, not for the wellbeing of each individual but for the wellbeing of their king. The ploy had worked.

Three long days passed by and it was all those in charge could do to instil caution to their regiments lest they burn themselves out before being required to kill.

A small scout pack had gone ahead with two fresh horses for each rider to confirm the location and numbers they were up against. Augustus had diverted from the salt flats where he had previously been spotted and now remained patiently in the foothills of the Infantus peaks. It was a slaughter house for so large a battle. No open fields. Overgrown forests would host their battle instead of open land and the confusion would be an advantage to Augustus' fewer numbers.

Boscelito's fears had been confirmed for Infantus was too far from the waterways for the navy to reach them in time. The cannons would be useless and their soldiers would be exhausted by the time they made it to the fight. The count had spotted at least four separate camps and each one held close to one thousand soldiers. The silver lining at least was that the numbers were on the side of the royal army.

Boscelito had been charged with the oversight of a hundred Vermillions. A strange order for a former enemy and captive, but he accepted his duty, knowing that the demand had come from River via one of her consorts. He wanted to see her one last time should either of them fall, the regret of his last words to her tearing him up and he instructed his captain's mate to lead the approach.

Boscelito declared that he would return before the battle charge and he knew his time was short as he rode on horseback across the lines of the legion. It was an impressive sight to see so many finally come together to take on the warlord that had haunted them for so long. If it had been decided sooner that the royal army would take a role in the war, the king may yet have lived, though Boscelito would have been on the wrong side of the fight.

It didn't do to dwell on such things now and as he approached the front line, he cast his keen eyes around for signs of River in her war dress but she was nowhere to be seen.

'Boscelito, what are you doing out of line? Get back to your regiment at once, the war horn is about to sound.'

It was Sol who had spotted him. Jade would be close by as her father had asked to take her within his own wave. Boscelito felt eyes on him but he didn't care. Bloodlust was boiling in his veins and sense and reason, as it always did before a fight, abandoned him.

'I have brought a message; you must get it to River for I cannot find her.'

'What is it?' Sol asked.

'Augustus has dragged us to this place on purpose for he will sacrifice every man and woman under his command if it gets him the advantage. Take care of the rear waves for our navy will not reach them before they make their crushing blow. There may also be soldiers hiding with the intent to blend with our own army. Do not trust any face you do not recognise. The tactic won him the last battle.'

'How can you be sure of his tactics?'

'Because I was there.'

'And you survived?'

'Of course.' Judgement descended upon Boscelito's shoulders. The heavy gazes around him crushed against his pride. 'I fought at his side. I saw no mechanics in his strategy, only greed and horror. He puts greater risk on the lives of his soldiers to confuse his opponents. But those are only things that can win in war when the other side fights honourably.'

'We will fight as the royal army has always been trained to fight, the system has never let them down.'

'Watch your backs, that is all I ask of you.'

'Very well, I appreciate your concern, soldier, now return to your post before you are lost in the madness of this day.'

'We will all soon be lost in the madness of this day, Sol. In fact I fear we are lost already.'

Boscelito turned about on his steed and rode back to his regiment, dissatisfied at his failed search. But he had made his point clear. It didn't matter, for when the fight began, each soldier would be their own determiner of fate.

*How had it all led to this?*

Boscelito thought about the day he had been sent away. He had felt scorned and unwanted. His orders were to bring allies from the islands and instead he now led Vermillion warriors against his childhood friend. Perhaps being sent away that day was the kindest thing that Augustus had ever done for him.

He cleared his thoughts; they were obstacles in the swell of a sword storm. The horn sounded from the front line and the echoes of pounding hoofs on soil and the thud of marching boots resonated throughout the dense overgrowth where they had waited. Trees and shrubbery broke the lines of soldiers apart as they set off into battle. It was exactly as Boscelito feared.

Screams and high-pitched clangs of metal pierced the air and volatile shouts of anger rose amongst the royal army. The killing had begun.

Boscelito rode fiercely with his one hundred soldiers and broke ranks to sweep away from the front lines. No one questioned his diversion for when they came about to the position he intended, they had flanked a battalion of foot soldiers who were charging forwards.

It was easy killing at first, using the warlord's tactics against his own soldiers. Those who rode with Boscelito were like a swarm of flies, moving from one patch to another, no structure or sense to their orders. Just unpredictable carnage.

Boscelito near blunted his sword as he hacked at his side, carving limb from limb and trails of dead were left in his path. He hadn't killed for so long. He had forgotten the sensation and he averted his eyes from those whose lives he ended. He would have known some of them once. A sense of shame overcame him but he fought no less viciously, for he knew they would give him no quarter.

When a quiet moment came, he looked about the forest and saw half his soldiers still on horseback. Some had fallen and others had been thrown from their steeds but fought on. The bushes and dense trees formed multiple hiding spots and in a moment's confusion, one of Augustus' warriors lurched from within a hedgerow and landed her club in Boscelito's side.

He fell to the floor and felt his cracked rib like a fire burning inside. No time to worry about the pain or the damage. He spun on his back as the woman came down on him again with the club. She was a brute. Over six foot tall and her swing was deadly.

Boscelito parried the club to the side and it shook the earth beside his skull. He bit her arm where her jerkin had rolled up, and tore away her flesh in his mouth. She screamed but the scream became a laugh and she placed her hands around his skull, pressing on his temples as though his head were a soft fruit.

He grappled at her wrists and felt his bones bending beneath her strength and will. His attempts were hopeless.

Then the club came down again. The one she had dropped. Only this time it was wielded by the captain's mate and it crushed the head of the woman. Boscelito felt her twitching hands tickle his face before she fell forwards on top of him.

'Get the bitch off me,' Boscelito cried.

The captain's mate pulled her away and Boscelito clambered free, his head pounding and senses dulled.

'Thank you, boy.'

'Here.'

The boy handed Boscelito his sword and ran off to re-join the fight. Boscelito followed him and the two men approached a band of soldiers who had formed a semi-circle. They were like a single sword blade ready to mow down whoever approached them head-on.

Better not to be overwhelmed by such a sight. *Just get on with it.* And Boscelito, with his sword held high above his head, his brains shaking inside his skull, brought down a rain of metal lightning onto their defences. Logic would have seen him killed in that moment. Fate had other plans for him.


THE WARNING from Sol had come as no surprise to River. She knew a kill trap when she saw one and she felt no concern for she was at home amidst such pandemonium. An open field on which to do battle was no friend to an assassin. But an overgrown forest with rolling hills was a playground to her and her game was death. She would make up for the naval crews ten times over if it was the last thing she did.

River had packed her strongest poison powders and coated the blades of her knives with them. Her gloves and gown were thin but resilient and the risk, although high, was worth it for the efficacy with which she was dispensing of her prey.

Simple quick cuts to the un-armoured body parts were enough to leave her victims dead in seconds. Hundreds had already fallen to the strikes of her blades.

River saw a long hanging branch before her and reached up to swing herself into a tree just moments before an axe was swung towards her midriff. The man who wielded the axe didn't divert his attention from her.

'Fucking coward, fight me fairly!'

River threw a small, thin dart towards him and it stuck in his neck. He convulsed and fell to his knees, his reddened eyes condemning her as the life ran out of him. There was nothing fair about the way she fought and she knew that fact had kept her alive this long.

*No reason to start playing fair now.*

River had ridden with her soldiers to the front lines and caught up with the king's guard. The truth had not yet broken out amongst the soldiers but even amongst the turmoil of battle, questions were being asked. The only way to dispel the verity of their situation and Elik's death, was to cut the head from the snake. Augustus had to die before their advantage would be lost. But he was nowhere to be seen.

If River had to kill her way to the very last soldier just to confront him, she would.

Wiping the congealed blood from her blades, River checked their sharpness. Her powders had been depleted. She would have to make fatal cuts now.

A series of archers emerged from an opening and a flight of arrows filled the forest air. Half of them stuck within the trunks of protective trees but enough got through and penetrated the armour of River's allies.

One arrow that had been meant for her passed by her face as

she lurched at the last second. These were heavy shafts, designed for bringing down charging horses and the speed with which they flew made them all the harder to evade.

River didn't wait for the next round of arrows and broke from her fellow fighters at a pace through the forest. She moved like a blue marlin in a rip tide, slipping between trees. She reached the centre of the archers' line so they would fire upon each other if they attempted to take her out. Instead they drew their swords and River danced between them, severing arteries and piercing hearts.

One of the archers caught her thigh with the tip of his sword and it brought her to a kneeling position. She didn't allow him the pleasure of bleeding to death after that and sawed the man's head clean off.

The cut on her leg wasn't deep but it unsteadied her and River tucked herself behind a tree to catch her breath.

'Shit.'

It was time to take the lava, the last of it. Sooner than she had hoped, but it was too risky to wait longer.

*No! You must not.*

The familiar voice intruded her mind.

*Please, this is not the time! Get out of my head.*

*There is a hidden legion, not yet in the fight. Augustus is not with the army.*

It couldn't be true. How could they be fighting so fiercely without their leader to inspire them? River didn't understand the people they were up against. They were monsters not men.

*I must find him. He must be stopped*, she said to the voice in her mind.

*You cannot take the substance, I know you fear it for it will fail you before the fight is done. If you die, I can never be.*

*I can feel your breath. And your smell. Why do you force such things on me? I know what you would have me do. But why do you pull me away from this fight. So that I can mother his child?*

*River, you must listen to me. I have sent you false feelings. Boscelito is my grandfather, and he must live. But you are wrong to think you do not a play a part.*

River squatted against the tree where she had stood, hiding her head from view.

*This is madness. You tell me one thing but your heart says another. I can sense your pain and your regret.*

*Yes. Regret because I believed something that is not true. You and I both believed it for a time. That you would bear Boscelito's child. But his child is already growing inside the true mother. I was wrong to think it was you. But it is the girl Jade. You must save them both for if you do not, they will both die today and the world will be lost.*

The truth that River had suspected hurt more than the wounds she carried. She'd never wanted the burden of this blind boy's desire. But now that the very thing she had not wanted had been taken from her. It left a hole inside her. Deep down, despite everything, she felt a bond with Boscelito and she thought somehow they would find a way to be together. But it was not her, she was no one special. Just a killer, and those who mattered most needed her blade.

*Why do you send me so much pain? Is it your pain or mine?*

River reached out to the blind boy, the agony of a sword in the gut was ripping through her.

*No. You are not hurt, River. I am sorry, I cannot help it. I am using everything that I am to reach to you. I am dying and my pain flows through me and to you. I don't have long left. There are so many pathways that lead from the moment where you are now and to where I lay. I wish I had time to tell you of all the steps you must take. But for now, you must pull Boscelito and Jade from battle and protect them. Until they are safe, nothing else matters.*

*Wait, please. I feel you slipping away from me. Don't go just yet!*

*Why have you come to me now? Why not reach back further to before this day began?*

*Time is a series of waves. I can only go to the places the waves take me. Perhaps one day, I could focus my skill. But I have been floating down a stream beside you all this time and the river now carries me to the banks on the shores of time where death awaits me with hands held open like a mother's welcome.*

*Don't give up! Fight please, I need your guidance.*

*If you succeed in all that I ask, then the day will come when I will speak to you again. I do not know when that will be but I will find a way.*

River waited for further explanation but there was nothing more than silence. The pain of the sword in her chest had gone and the sounds of the fighting all around her ensued. She wanted to break down and hide in her calm corner of the world. It was too much to take in and at such a terrible time. How could she fight now? Her life had become a vacuum and where hope and desire had once enveloped her, a destitute cavern had formed.

There was no time to wallow in the misery she had been left with. An axe swung towards her as a soldier stepped out from behind the tree where River had hidden. She ducked and stabbed her blade upwards into the armpit of the one who had wielded the axe and the man spat phlegm across her face before falling to the ground.

A wave of heat blew across River's face as she wiped away the spit. Ash landed on her cheek and attached itself to her. There was an orange glow coming from over the hill beyond the treeline where she stood. A man came running towards her. But he held no weapon.

'River! Are you alright?'

It was Sol, wounded but alive.

'Yes. No… I'm not sure.'

'We must regroup. All clarity is lost.'

'Sol, you're injured. We must get you to a healer.'

'No, it is not a deep cut. It will be far worse for us all soon. We have lost the central regiments. Three thousand were wiped out in less than an hour. Augustus had laid a trap and they were surrounded by a spear legion who penned them in.'

'The fire?'

'Yes, they are all gone. Burned alive, every last man and woman. It has split our forces in two.'

'Dammit, what of Jade and the horse battalions?'

'Jade is missing. My unit is reduced to a mere handful and I cannot find her.'

River felt a sense of panic rising. She'd thought they had been winning. Their numbers were greater after all. But half their army had already been lost.

'I will find her. Gather the others and make our withdrawal. Augustus is not with the army.'

'What? How can you be sure?' Sol knew better than to doubt her and regretted the questioning; there were forces beyond those he could understand at work.

'Just trust me, it's a trap. He was relying on us to march upon him.'

'I'll ride to the king's guard and tell them to fall back. We may be too late.'

'We have to try.' River raised a hand to Sol's shoulder and found her own strength. 'Good luck to you, brother.'

'And to you, sister. Find my girl. If you do not see me again, tell her that I love her.'

'I will.'

Sol ran back towards the flames and mounted a stray horse that had lost its rider in the mayhem. The ripples of heatwaves distorted his figure as he rode away and River looked around at the quiet sea of corpses that now scattered the earth where she stood. Somehow, amidst her joint dream with the blind boy, a thousand bodies had fallen beside her. She was the only one left.

River came to her senses and tore off a piece of shirt to wrap around her leg, wincing as she bound the wound, and headed off to find Jade. If what the boy had said were true and she were already with child, then she was all that mattered. But if fate would guide her hand and allow her to find Boscelito still breathing amongst the slain, then she would save him too.

## 28

B lood stained the soft mossy clearing where battered armour plates lay atop their slain bearers. An eerie still air carried the dank odour throughout the forest that had claimed thousands of lives. It was a massacre on both sides.

Augustus didn't care how many numbers he had lost for he was ready to finish what had started that day, even if it left him all alone, to fight one on one with the last man standing amidst spectators, watching from their new home in the afterlife.

He re-sharpened his blade and trod slowly across fallen oak and sodden shrubbery. The moans of his enemies pricked his ears as they suffered slow deaths, the life dwindling from them. He walked past and left them to their pain, for he would not blunt his sword to secure passage for one who was already traversing to the other side.

A swarm of flies descended on the corpses and began to suckle on the drips of gore. Augustus wrapped a thin cloth across his mouth so he could breathe freely. His heart was racing and despite the depletion of his own army's energy, he had joined the fight late and was ready for more.

Far up ahead, with keen eyes he saw subtle movements in the brush. He pursued the fleeing cowards, slowly and with caution.

Suddenly from beside him, a man who had been cut at the midriff, stood wielding a small dagger.

'You, bastard, I'll kill you for what you have done.'

The man screamed fury down upon Augustus, pointing his knife towards his heart, but with a single swing of the warlord's sword he severed the man's arm at the shoulder and a with a return swing lopped off his head.

'I like proud soldiers; they die so quickly.'

Augustus amused himself but he knew he was right to make his course with eyes and ears sharpened. He wouldn't let a dying soldier have the glory of his death.

Somewhere beyond the clearing ahead were flames that still burned strong, a sour stench of human flesh filled his nostrils and it made him hungry. There were few men who deemed cannibalism an honourable course to pursue, but his mind, though grazed with clarity, could not prevent him from wetting his lips.

His boots were soaked through to his skin and blisters had begun to form. Augustus didn't care. Let the throbbing pain of his heel enrage him all the more.

Then came night and echoes of life, high up in the branches that cut jagged shapes across the deep blue shade of the sky. The sound of horses, riding from behind Augustus, disturbed nature's nocturnal voice. They were his few remaining men and a gift had been brought to him in the guise of a fresh steed. His man passed over the stirrup and Augustus mounted the wild steed.

'Sire, do we push on? There's hardly anyone left but I heard a battle horn signal their retreat.'

'Yes, I heard it too.'

Augustus shifted his back against the saddle. Reins in hand, he resumed his pursuit. The soldiers followed his course. They were amongst his fiercest and they rode by his side like a flock of carrion crows, hunting for survivors.

Augustus had won the battle. Now he rode as executioner.

'THEY ARE ADVANCING ON US. Without horses we'll never escape in time.'

Boscelito staggered through the woods with Jade leaning against his shoulder. He had found her with an arrow through her thigh and their retreat had been slowed.

'We can't outrun them. We have to stand and fight,' she said with gritted teeth.

'We cannot stand and fight when you can barely stand at all. Here wrap your arm around my shoulder, you need to get the weight off that leg.'

Inch by inch they fled through the thick wood. They had passed beyond the point where bodies were strewn at their feet but any survivors of their own army were nowhere to be seen.

'At least the others have made it clear of the front. We can hold Augustus off long enough to assist their escape.' Jade hoped she spoke the truth.

'No, if he finds us we will not die slowly enough to gain them any ground. We can't give up.'

'I hear them, Bosc, the hoofs are nearing, we haven't long left. I have to tell you something.'

'You can tell me when we are out of this mess. I promise you we will make it out.'

Even as he made the promise he knew he lied. He felt so ashamed and greedy for silencing her final confession. And why? What could she tell him that would be worse than death. But moments before he would change his mind and sit her down and lend her his ear, his promise grew strands of truth like fresh rivulets released from a dam. River emerged from the undergrowth beside them to secure the promise. She had climbed a steep rocky incline and found them wandering above. She caught Jade under her arm and stroked her face with kindness and with love.

'River! You're alive.' Jade felt the relief exit her from the depths of her bones.

'Barely alive from the fight, but still ready for war. How are you, are you hurt?' River rubbed her hand across Jade's stomach and checked for signs of penetration or bleeding. 'Thank goodness you're still in one piece. Both of you.' River finally plucked up the courage to look Boscelito in the eyes.

'If I am right about what is coming, we have no more than minutes before Augustus rides upon us. What should we do?' Boscelito asked River as her captain, her servant and whatever else she needed him to be.

'Get Jade away to safety, I do not know how long I can hold them off, but you must live on to fight another fight. It will be harder than any mission either of you has carried out. It is a role I will never play myself and so I cannot advise you, but you must trust me, it is the most necessary thing that you will ever do.' River lifted her hand from Jade's stomach and the girl turned to face Boscelito who met her confused expression with his own. 'Go now, there is no time to explain. Run far from here and never look back.'

River stood and the horseback riders who were drawing near came into view. She pulled out both her blades with no time to take the lava. She would fight them as River, the assassin, with all her heart unhinged and without being roused by fire. She prayed it would be enough.

'Go now, damn you, do not stand there like scorned children. Run!'

Boscelito sensed a secret between the two women. A maternal instinct had passed between them. Deep down he knew the secret too.

Boscelito raised Jade to her feet and placed her arm over his shoulder. They hastened through the clearing, away from where River stood.

The assassin of Vermillion held her arms wide and the blades she wielded sang as droplets of night rain pattered against them. She was ready to die.

In the dying light, she counted eight horses. River liked her chances, eight horses meant eight soldiers. Augustus was nothing to her but another man, dressed in armour, with veins and arteries ripe for severing.

As every soldier who had met her blades had done before, he would bleed and his blood would quench the thirst of the dark soil.

Sixteen pairs of heavy hoofs drew to a close around where River stood, these were no usual breed of war horse. Something about the way they breathed made them wild and yet they bore their riders obediently. Only cruelty could break a horse in such a way.

The eight moved as one, a coterie of shadows, mimicking Augustus as he pointed his sword towards the assassin. He appeared like a giant upon his steed, with thick armour and intricate markings. The seven men who rode with him were similarly large and the weapons they each carried were brutal instruments of death.

The first two riders charged River, one with a lance directed towards her chest and the second, just feet behind, a mace clenched hard in his grip. She didn't flinch, best to hold firm and wait until the final moment.

*The charge is unclean,* she thought wryly. They meant to intimidate her. But she knew the fight on this uneven ground would be on foot once the charade was over.

River flicked the tip of the spear that thrust forwards with her blade and made it wail before she sidestepped the horse, its long mane brushing her arm as she raised her other blade to cut the warrior's thigh. It was no deep cut but enough to make her presence considered.

She doubled back to duck beneath the mace that was inches from her face. She could not believe the speed with which it was thrown towards her for such a heavy tool.

Panic struck her as she felt the air rush past whilst the mace tore a path through the air. She had thought her one advantage in this fight would be speed but it seemed less an advantage now after that close an encounter with the steel-studded mallet.

She took a short deep breath. *Patience, River, patience.* She knew she would have to play the long game, making each cut when the risks were low. If she overreached but once she would be done for.

River focused her mind, she was better than all of them and she knew it. The hours she had fought this afternoon had made her tired and these cowards had ridden from their secret hiding place, fresh-armed and senses heightened. They would die cowards, she had plenty left to give.

She swept her blades against each other and the zing cut through the forest and birds flocked into the sky from fear. It was a lightning bolt to the hearts of the first two riders as she charged them. Her feet pounding on the soil as she approached the spear-wielding soldier, he dropped it to favour a shorter weapon and pulled out a sword. He was swift with his movement but River sprang from a rock beneath the horse's head and leapt into the air to meet his height. He swung at her as though he were batting a thrust ball with a club. But before the short sword carried towards her she was on him, her knee in his groin where he was saddled and two blades primed, one for each of his eyes.

The man's sword clattered against River's back like a friend patting a drunk comrade. It was as though he had thanked her for his death.

River took a short sharp breath of relief as the horse ripped beneath her and the eyeless man fell backwards. She retracted her blades, placed a light foot on the rear of the horse and sprang towards a high tree branch just moments before another heavy mace flew through the air towards her.

She tucked into a ball to miss the well-flung weapon but it caught her shoulder, sending her spinning like a mill blade, crashing into the tree.

Her weak shoulder throbbed; the throw had been exact and her impaired muscle took the full force of the impact. It was as if they knew her handicap.

Rage filled her heart. She shook off the blow and let adrenaline distract her from the pain as the man approached and retrieved his mace.

'You, bitch, I'll fuck your corpse.'

Words were a waste of time in battle. It was always curious to River that men gloated before they had even won. She snapped her foot upwards and a short blade sprang from the sole of her boot. It was just a few inches long but enough to tuck under the mace bearer's armour and cut through his scrotum.

*Fuck me with what?* River asked herself, before she kicked him again and sent him screaming to the floor.

His hands cupped his genitals and the agony in his cries was almost pitiful. River picked up the heavy mace and with a ferocious swing she brought it down onto his skull and crushed his face into the mud.

She flung the mace to the side; satisfying as the kill had been, it was no replacement for her blades.

The six remaining men had dropped from their horses as River had anticipated. They formed a circle to surround her.

The time for taking it in turns to wear her down was done. They would fight as a single unit and she would be a hare, snared in a trap of bloodied metal.

River readied herself.

*Kill Augustus. He is all that matters,* she thought. With that, River rushed towards the warlord but two long swords swept down in front of where he stood and River had no choice but to deal with those first. She placed a foot atop one of the blades that had struck the ground and buried itself into the mud. The other raised upwards and skimmed the metal plate on her shin. Her left blade slashed out like a whip and cut at one of their throats. But the thick armour deflected the blade away from causing any severe damage.

The next attack would come from behind and those affront her position swung back to take the next blow. Too many heavy swords were falling upon her spot, she couldn't deflect them all. Instead River rolled backwards into the path of the one behind her. It was a risky move but she grabbed his leg and bit into his calf like a wild dog and, as the long swords tumbled down, he fell into their path, blocking River who tucked underneath him.

River snapped her leg and rolled out from under him. She flicked herself back onto her feet just in time to assess what burden she would bear next. She had broken the circle. The man who had fallen into the middle had taken a sword to the head and it had cut through his skull.

She didn't wait for the aftermath, for she was the aftermath and she drove her blades between two plates of metal into the shoulders of the nearest foe and felt as they cut downwards. She twisted them as though she was uncorking a bottle of wine and the scarlet red that spiralled upwards would have filled enough glasses for a banquet.

Four left.

Amongst the rabble where they fought, swords and elbows, flailing and crashing against thick brutal armour, blurred the vision of bloodthirsty eyes. River's legs, shaking, still moved fast and though she felt wounds appearing at her back and on her arms, she knew she dealt out a dozen cuts for each she suffered.

Through the abyss of death, a pair of eyes looked back at her. One man remained still, unmoving. It was Augustus and he glared at her and his eyes pierced hers. For a fleeting second he seemed possessed and River saw a look that reminded her of Summer. Those eyes were a dream and they told her all she needed to know. For Augustus stepped backwards and dropped his weapon. He appeared as though under a spell and the only regret in leaving the fight was his.

She broke her stare from him to return to the massacre of the three men who now wielded no weapons, for their wounds were too many. Instead they grabbed at her and their limbs became entangled with hers and a great weight fell upon River that she could not muster the strength to surface from. She slashed about frantically like a wolf protecting its cub. Blades tore through armour and scraped bone. Flesh was torn from limb and veins were severed and eventually when she stopped screaming, she realised they were all dead.

She simply lay there, buried beneath the weight of the corpses she had made and she could no longer move.

River cast her eyes amongst the forest and all was quiet and still. In the darkness she saw no shadow. Augustus was gone.

## 29

Damp ash fell heavy like a thick snowfall and as it touched the bloodied mess of the previous day's battle the deep red and grey turned to a black coagulated substance.

The fires set by Augustus had burned right through the dense treeline all night and only that the forest had been afforded a night of rainfall saved River where she lay.

Barely able to move beneath the stiffened detritus of dead soldiers, she slipped a hand free and removed her glove, wiping away a layer of ash from her eyes. She blinkered them open and awkward bits of the dusty glue had settled in the corners of her eyes. She desperately poked around the surface of her eye and scooped out what she could of the tarlike substance until eventually she could see clearly.

A dawn of crows was what she saw before her, feasting on the dead and carrying off the fatty cuttings that had been prepared for them. Their young would dine for days.

River tried to pull herself free from her prison. But the bodies were too heavy and she was too weak. She felt anew the cuts that throbbed and bled. She strained as hard as she dared and the black floaters she saw in her vision told her she was close to fainting.

The reality dawned that she would have to exert herself to break free of this fleshy cage but doing so could rupture her wounds and she would suffer further loss of blood.

She waited and waited, until the afternoon sun broke through the rows of trees that were now charcoal ghosts.

Rising heat warmed the bodies around her and a putrid smell rose with it. To River the stench was vomit inducing and she gagged. Little did she need to throw up stomach bile all across her face and chest. She swallowed hard and tried to imagine the smell was a fine meal, being prepared in the kitchens of the school where she had trained Vermillion students.

That seemed such a lifetime away. Her mind drifted fondly, back to the time when everything was as simple as teaching the arts of assassination and carrying out her father's bidding. Those beautiful beaches where she and Summer would run along the sand, splashing in the white wash of the rising waves that caressed their naked feet. They had lived well for a time, she thought. Perhaps dying with her mind rested on the Vermillion shores with Summer in her arms was no bad way to pass from this life. She could scarcely wish for a better death.

Scurrying sounds of the wildlife in the forest disturbed her daydream and she wondered what had startled them. Flocks of satiated crows fled their feeding ground and a coterie on horseback arrived moments later at the scene.

River strained her neck to see those who were approaching but her attempts were futile. Instead she looked ahead, the only way she could, because her body was pinned and in the space between her and the looming trees stepped a young girl. She was well-dressed, warmly wrapped in a thick fur layer and bore a royal emblem around her neck.

'River. Can you speak?' the girl asked.

*Yes,* River heard herself say in a waking dream.

She tried to make a sound but no words would form in her throat. She realised then that she carried a wound just below her chin that had partly sealed and her jaw would not move. She nodded her response in lieu of speech.

'You are severely wounded. We've come to see you and the other survivors to the castle infirmary. It is a wonder you are alive.'

The girl gestured to her side and a half dozen legionaries from the royal army, some wounded and others fresh, began prising away the bodies from where River lay.

Once the path was clear, they helped River to her feet, though she could hardly stand and so they lay her on a stretcher with two handles at each end. It would be a painfully long journey if they were to take her back to Elik's castle in this thing, she thought, ruefully.

'Our camp is a few hours' ride away. We'll get you there and have you fed and dress your wounds properly before we make our way home.'

River blinked at the girl. So many questions she wanted to ask but when she tried to speak again, a whistling sounded from her mouth.

'Don't try to speak. Not yet. We'll have plenty of time to talk once you are better. I expect you are concerned for your people. So I will tell you that some of them survived. Because of you, several battalions were able to retreat from the battle to the waterways to meet the fleet of ships. None could have predicted that Augustus would flee at the very moment he took the greatest advantage. You saved thousands of lives with your bravery, and won the day. Let that comfort you on the journey back.'

River didn't feel as though she had won anything. The stare Augustus had given her haunted her mind. There was something wrong about the way he had fled.

River, laid out on her back, was lifted upwards and the long walk to the nearby camp began. But as the young girl mounted her horse, River flicked her arm out towards her randomly. The girl smiled back at the delirious assassin beneath her.

'River, my name is Lynden. And I am pleased to meet you too.'

Lynden's smile was sweet and innocent but she already seemed wise beyond her years. The coterie carrying River walked slowly and carefully. The horses followed suit to allow for the pace of those who carried River in their arms. Each half an hour they would rotate the carriers who bore her weight. River felt like a baby being rocked and she breathed in deep nasal breaths and allowed herself to sleep, and asleep she remained; even throughout the journey across water aboard her ship, she did not stir.

Days passed by in a state of delirium. Infectious wounds caused a fever and her dreams were filled with fire. The castle had been prepared to house a tsunami of wounded but they had not counted on the morgue filling so overwhelmingly with the bodies of the fallen. River was sent to a bed in the corner of a crowded infirmary and watched as healers darted around, trying to stave off infection and rigors. She thought she might be treated for anything up to a week. She knew her wounds were severe and her muscles cramped every time she turned. But it had not been merely days she was held in the infirmary; several months had passed by and she was making slow progress. It was unlike her to heal so slowly. Back on Vermillion she would recover from minor wounds with long walks to see her uncle at the mountain summit. Something about the air at the mouth of the volcano roused an energy in her and she would awake the next day to find her cuts scabbing. Mainlanders had always been accused of healing slowly and she recalled the way the captain had possessed unusual strength when he had been captive on the island. Perhaps it was the island air after all.

The time she had spent recovering at Elik's castle was long and dull. She would simply stagger about the halls, attend the evening meals with the council and wake each day in hope that the scar under her chin would fade a little more.

Her speech had returned but the strength in her arms had not. Simple tasks such as dressing her had been appointed to a serving girl from the kitchen staff. Grub was a sweet, stout thing. She had told River that her name was given to her by the kitchen porter's son on account of her grubby nose, but River had heard all the stories throughout the castle by now and knew that it was more to do with her fondness of stealing rolls of bread to eat on shift. Only that Grub had volunteered to taste Elik's meals before he would dine kept her in employ after she had been caught stealing.

Lynden had been given the task of managing the castle staff since Elik's passing and deemed it prudent to promote Grub to the station of River's personal attendant, hoping perhaps that the girl would learn some propriety from the honourable assassin.

River was eventually moved to a private chamber and sat staring out towards the coast, contemplating the wasted time she suffered each day. She had requested that Grub bring her some drawing equipment the night before and had begun sketching the view from outside her window. It was a wonderful view of the Arn river, stretching out amongst the green pastures and eventually towards the eastern chalk cliffs of the Harmion coastline. On a clear day you could just about catch the glimmers of sunlight on the sea.

'I was pleased to hear you taking up your creative streak,' Lynden said, as she stepped into the room.

'I'm just biding my time. It seems I have no choice.'

Lynden walked to the easel beside River and looked at the sketch.

'Sometimes, it is okay for time to stand still. We learn more about ourselves when we are still than when we are moving forwards.'

'I've learnt plenty these past months. Enough to keep me going for years.'

Lynden laughed and stepped towards the window.

'I never grow tired of seeing this vista. Every day the formation of the clouds and the way the sun bounces off the water in the air changes. You can see the sight a thousand times and it will never be the same twice. It should keep you busy.'

'If I am to recover for long enough that I should be able to paint the view from this window a thousand times then I would rather jump out of it.'

Lynden pulled out the chair from under the dressing desk and took a seat, gesturing to River to sit with her.

'Elik used to draw the view from this very window. It brought him peace. I hope it can do the same for you.' Lynden paused. 'River, we have some news from the front. Augustus has withdrawn to the midlands where the remnants of his army are focusing their efforts on disbanding town defences. There is word that he has put out a bounty to all the sellswords who have keen enough ears to listen for news of a traitor. We think they refer to Boscelito.'

'That's impossible. How could he know? What of Jade in all this? She is the one who matters most, and the child she carries inside her.'

'Jade has not been mentioned; they think the traitor travels alone. Our scout infiltrated the camp of one of the surviving legions for a night as a passing meat porter. In the camp there was talk of a strange girl. So it seems as though the rumours were true. Augustus has taken on an advisor. Though I myself am suspicious that it is he doing the bidding of another. Someone who can see things that the rest of us cannot see.'

*Could it be true?* River wondered. Had Summer found her way into the arms of the warlord? Had she bent his will to hers? River couldn't imagine what good could possibly come from any of this. The look Augustus had given her as she fought against his men suddenly made sense to her. But why was she spared. Would Summer not wish her dead by now?

Lynden stood and walked circles around the room. She was disturbed and anxious.

'I have word that Sol is improving. His coma continues but his breathing has stabilised. Jade made me promise to ask you to look after him when they left. But I can sense your unease, I know you won't wait here longer than required.'

'You're right, I can't wait here any longer. I must regain my strength. If all I fear is to come to pass, then I have yet to fight my greatest battle. Sol needs you more than he does me, but I will check in on him when I am able.'

'Yes, I understand. I hoped that we were nearing an end to the war. It feels as though the past years have dragged by excruciatingly. The burden of youth is the slow passage of time. My gut tells me the war is only just beginning.'

Lynden held her chin in her hands, appearing far older and wiser than the child that she was. Her maturity was such that River hadn't even thought to question her station for one so young.

'Lynden, we will need more like you. The young must guide in the tide of our future, for as the world changes, we will need eyes that look forwards and not backwards. Boscelito and Jade must remain hidden. I am not sure if it is even safe for us to know of their whereabouts. If any who are privy to their position are caught and tortured, I don't doubt that secret would soon become common knowledge.'

'I sent a retinue out with them and they have gone into hiding. But I fear now it will not be enough.'

'Until I am strong enough to lead some sort of diversion, it has to be.'

River stood, went to her wardrobe and opened the door. From inside she took out a case which contained her two small blades and she brushed her hand across her shirts, checking the condition of the sewn-in thin metal plates. They had been well washed but the bloodstains had discoloured the leather lining.

'I'll let the training marshal know you will join them in the morning. I hear the students are doing well but with a few weeks by your side, we may just recover our army,' Lynden said as she left the room, giving one final look back to the broken assassin.

Broken or not, it was finally time for River to begin her rehabilitation within the army training grounds. She knew she had to head back out into the teeth of the war, waiting for the voice of the blind boy to once again speak to her.

She would play her part in the fighting. But until she was strong, she knew it would be futile to venture towards danger. She had suffered the loss of her skill and strength that day in the forest. Aside from the hundreds of Vermillion people and royal soldiers that had perished, her own muscles and ability had wasted away throughout her recovery. But now she would rebuild her strength and grow faster and fiercer than she had ever been before and let the skies save any who would stand in her way.

## 30

Forty years of waiting, doubting and wondering. So much turmoil and uncertainty had been exuded and the losses suffered, when they had seemed so wrong and abhorrent, culminated to place her at this precise point in time.

The war had been lost, but it was everyone who had lost. There was no victor, only suffering and birth of a wasteland. Lives had ended that River had vowed to protect, but it all somehow led to where she stood now. She had recalled every night as she slept, the voice of the blind boy when he had come to her at the moment of his death. Appealing to her to set a course in motion that could bend the shape of time and render fate a useless beast.

There had been times when she wanted to stray from her path, to reveal herself and prevent what she was there to prevent. Somehow, through the particles of coincidence and time, luck and determination, River had been pulled back into the stream that set a course for one singular destination.

Pietrich had promised he would come back to her one day. So she had waited, a passenger of life, observing from afar all the horrors that had unfolded. She fought herself not to intervene, as she had done so often in her youth. Now she was an old woman, waiting, waiting.

It was a cold, starry night at the shipyard where she worked as a cargo checker that the voice came to her. For years she had done humble work, isolated and with enough pay only to sustain a simple life. She had witnessed the disbursement of her people and the theft of her naval ships when the council had been broken from within.

The kill list of the royal council had brought about Tritan's infamy. And she had watched from afar, because no matter what she desired, she obeyed the task, awaiting the garbled words as they would be when they arrived, of the blind boy.

*The blind leading the blind,* she had thought many times. Was it cruel or true? After so much time, she didn't know.

The words had come to her as though an echo of a whisper. She scrutinised them and took her mind back to when she had been younger. Was it the same child who now compelled her to sail back to Vermillion? River didn't believe in coincidences, so when she had seen the Audacia pull into the port where she had stayed for years, she knew all the truth she needed to.

At first she wondered if it was a trick of old age, but as she squinted and focused her vision she saw before her a face she had not seen since she was a young woman.

It had been so long since she had laid eyes on Lynden that River thought they would barely recognise each other. She wanted nothing more than to run to her and throw her arms around her, so joyous she was that the girl lived.

She had aged too.

River knew she must keep her presence secret. Nothing good would come of revealing herself on the knife edge of her true purpose. A final warning to her from the blind boy had been to keep him a secret from everyone, even those she trusted. Especially those she trusted, for they would be the ones who would interfere and sever the tendrils of time and ruin all hope that River would be his tool in the darkness. Instead, she had waited and still she clung onto her faith that he would return.

River snuck aboard the cargo hold as the last container of grain was loaded, pulled up her dark hood and slipped through the belly of the ship towards the damp bilges beneath the decks.

It was an unpleasant place to hide, water filled and flooded the area in the storms and River would have to sneak behind the slimy support structure when crew were sent down to drain the area with buckets. But it was the only place she could stow-away and she began to tuck her rations within the rotten cracks in the timber joists, hidden from view.

As the ship set sail, the nauseous sensation set in. Nothing worse than being rocked back and forth in a chamber with no fresh air at sea. Even for River, after a lifetime of sailing, where dry land felt more surreal beneath her feet, it was trying work to contain the vomitous inclinations of her stomach.

The floor of the space she inhabited became wet and flooded before long. River took to stepping on the ridges of the girders that were almost submerged and hung a hammock on two hooks where the buckets were stored. Every time she heard the clanging of crew members making their way down through the welded hatch to remove some of the water, she packed up the hammock, replaced the buckets and moved to the back of the chamber, hidden in the darkest corner.

The gift of the close encounters was that it was the only time she saw daylight. As the hatch would open, beams of bright light would pour into the chamber and a wave of fresh air would brush against her face. The torture of such a teasing moment worsened each time she suffered it, for the hatch would be replaced and she would once again be plunged into darkness. Waiting, waiting.

DOCKING AT NIGHT upon the wastelands of Vermillion was a task even for the hardiest of sailors. Diccon took up the challenge and determined that the main beach was too treacherous, so he sailed the ship under the cove that he prayed led to a harbour of sorts. Only a speck of daylight convinced him they would find a place to set down the ship and as they sailed within the confines of the cove, the speck of daylight became a beacon. The inner walls of the cove were no more than the length of a tall man from the sides of the ship. It was as though the vessel was built to fit perfectly through the rocky embrace.

As the Audacia exited the cove, it arrived in a deep lagoon. Around them, lined along the curve of the ashy harbour, was the ruin of a town. They came across a natural dock of shallow rock and as the ship began to scrape against sand on the lagoon bed, they dropped the anchor to settle their position.

'Be damned lucky to get this hunk out to sea again,' Diccon cursed.

'Well, for now we think only of the task at hand.'

Castellar rebuked the sailor but seasoned it with a hand to the shoulder. It was as close as Diccon would come to hearing the words, *a job well done, sailor*.

The crew unloaded from the ship and set up a camp besides the rocky makeshift port. Lynden readied a crew and spoke with Castellar about their approach to searching the islands. With their reduced numbers it could take weeks to investigate the main island, let alone sail out to the smaller outlying islands should the search require them to. The terrain all around them was treacherous.

'Stowaway! There's a stowaway amongst us.'

It was the carpenter who shouted to the gathering crowd. He had a small metal tool in his hands and thick gloves.

Castellar and Lynden turned to face him as he came running up the rocky beach.

The man caught his breath before revealing his suspicions. 'I was checking the bilges for water damage. Sure enough they've seen better days though she'll sail fine for months yet, but when I was down there I found the remnants of a stash of salted fish and meats. They were wrapped in a greasy paper and tucked into the alcoves above the support structure. I don't know how we missed it, nor how anyone could have slipped past us when we docked. But sure as fire burns we've had a stowaway aboard.'

'We are all accounted for, our core crew?' Lynden asked.

The carpenter turned about and began counting heads, as did Castellar and the rest of them.

'Yes, all of us are here. There is no way whoever snuck on has got away from this harbour, there ain't no hiding places amongst us.'

'Search the ship, we need to know what we are dealing with. Caste, you should head out with the first search party and look for Pietrich. We cannot delay.'

'Very well, just watch your backs. I dare say it must be a desperate soul that would hole up in the bilges for the best part of a month.'

THE SWIM WAS as she had remembered it. Long swathes of tidal rips that could drag you under if you were swept into the wrong spot. But the crashing waves that River knew so well welcomed her and she rippled like a fish through the water and towards the beach that she had not seen for a lifetime.

When she had last laid eyes upon the island, everything was

on fire. But the sandy beaches had still been there. Now they were covered in rock and though the formation of the landscape was much the same, the colours that had once brought light into her eyes were dulled. It was a graveyard, and the furthest thing from the home it had once been.

River disrobed and wrung out her sodden clothes of seawater. She placed all her powders and two blades on the rock beside her with caution and re-dressed, hiding the items within her jacket and trouser pockets. Even with her provisions she had lost some weight and had to tie off her upper leggings to her thighs, for the baggy material caught as she raised her legs.

The ship's bilges had done her physique no favours. She stretched out and placed her heel upon a rock, contorting her muscles and feeling the tiny ripping sensation as they loosened. She then hung from an overhanging outcrop above. It was far out of reach but her reduced weight allowed her to jump high enough to clasp a hand around the rough stone. Her back clicked and cracked in various places as she dangled there and after a few minutes of allowing her spine to be extended, she dropped back to the ground and tied her boots.

*The base of the mountain.*

It was the last intelligible thing she had heard when the voice had come crashing into her mind. The voice in the night as she had waited those long years was fleeting and purposeful. She prayed it was from her future and not the past. River knew she was being guided, but time was a mysterious thing and it could be both friend and foe.

Blades in hand, River began her run across the rocky plain that was once a dense palm forest. Nothing looked the same but the mountain was her guide, for it towered above everything as it always had.

She eventually came to a wall that jutted outwards in a snakelike formation. She hugged the wall and crept forwards as she began to hear voices. Before her, in the distance, was a camp, but it was far away. The voices she heard were nearby.

River rolled her heel with each step, making no sound, and slipped forwards to where two armed soldiers stood. Their posting was peculiar, as though they were waiting to charge their own camp.

A boulder was lying at the base of the mountain wall, just feet between her and the two soldiers. River knelt down behind it. Her knees cracked and she cursed her aged body, but the sound did not betray her position.

She waited for a time, until eventually one of the men began to remove metal plates from his war garb.

'What are you doing?' one of the men asked the other.

'Winter told us it's one boy, and he may have magic coursing through his veins, but he's no fighter. I don't intend to slow myself down with this useless shit. You think that helmet will protect you against magic?'

'I suppose not. That won't matter anyway, not after what they've done to us. We're immune.'

The second soldier then began to take off his armour plates too, and he ditched his helmet on the floor. He looked at his fellow warrior and gave him a wry nod of his head.

The rocky wall in front of where they stood was sprayed with gushing blood. Both men opened their eyes in horror and looked at each other's throats as a blade protruded from each of their jugulars. River pulled the blades out swiftly and then brought them down again into their spasming shoulder tissue.

Two clean kills. It had been so long but she had not forgotten how to end lives swiftly. River suddenly felt a surge of confidence rush over her. She could do this, she knew it. But her timing would have to be perfect.

Several hours passed by and River made use of the soldiers'

provisions, eating an energising portion of food but little enough so as not to tire herself.

As she picked the dried meat from her teeth she caught sight of a horde of pirates approaching the camp in the distance.

*What are pirates doing here?* she wondered. But walking amongst them was a hooded figure, being led by a wolf.

The pirates charged at the three sat in the camp and a horn sounded, reverberating across the landscape. Pietrich raised his arm and flicked his wrist and the three men in the centre of the camp began to swipe away what appeared to be an invisible swarm of flies before dropping to the ground. A few of the pirates descended upon them and stuck them with half a dozen blades for good measure. But a wave of warriors emerged from all around. Pietrich and his pirate allies were heavily outnumbered. It would have been a slaughter that day, forty years ago. But it was no longer forty years ago she had felt the pain of Pietrich's death, it was now.

*Today, now.*

This instant was the one that everything had built towards and without further hesitation, River swallowed what was left of the lava that she had carried all these years and she sprinted towards the fight.

She avoided the dozen or so pirates, for amidst the confusion they would see her as one of their enemies, as would those who fought on the opposite side. She was a singular entity fighting for neither group, a thorn in the side to sway the outcome the way she determined suitable. Just like she always had.

The bloody carnival began as the lava took hold of her and she felt her blades cutting tendons and arteries apart at a rate that she could not comprehend. Neither could any of those who were victim to her brutal onslaught.

River ducked and weaved stealthily and floated in and

among the pirates to deflect as much attention from herself as possible. It worked for a time, but before long, fighters on both sides could not ignore the devastation that she unleashed.

A woman wielding a spear rushed towards River and though she jumped cleanly from its path, she landed in the way of an axe that was intended for a pirate. It dug deep into River's left arm, rendering it useless, but as she looked down at the wound in horror, she saw at least that the arm remained attached.

River quickly sliced the throat of the one who'd swung their axe and tore a slip of cloth from their shirt before they crashed in a heap on the floor. She frantically tied off the cloth to seal the wound of her arm and keep it in place. Now she would have to fight one-handed. Half the strength but twice the fury.

River clutched her dagger in her right hand and it became an extension of her, like a long claw. She focused on the anatomy of each of her victims, gutting them and tearing out their organs, a purposeful display to strike fear in all who trod near her.

It wasn't long before most of the pirates were dead. River had killed many of the sixty soldiers but plenty enough remained. Her arm throbbed but the lava still affected her deeply.

The next thing she saw was the blind boy, cowering on the floor, and the blade of the most terrifying man she had ever seen. It came swooping down towards Pietrich, but that was when the pirate captain jumped forwards to take the blow. She was the last of her horde. Her body was split in two but somehow, through the dying pain, she said her last words to Pietrich. River couldn't hear them but she looked at peace.

The next strike cut her in half.

The warrior who stood over Pietrich, readied himself for the next strike.

'Father.'

Pietrich cried out and River knew that she was about to

rewrite the course of time. She suddenly felt the weight of the responsibility. What could it mean if one as insignificant as she could change history? There wasn't time to contemplate the consequences.

River charged towards Tritan and she was terrified. Never had so much been asked of her as now.

Single-bladed and bleeding, River rolled into the trajectory of the sword that was heading towards Pietrich and she flicked it from the fatal path.

She came about on all fours and forgot her wound, her arm collapsed from under her and Tritan didn't wait for her to regain her balance.

He twisted backwards, lining the sword up behind his back as though he were about to sever a tree trunk with a single swing.

'Stop!'

Thunder rolled and cracked. The earth shook and the hearts of all who were present stopped for a moment, as if the binding life-force that connects all things halted its eternal cycle.

Winter stood staring at the old woman who was before her. This assassin whom she had loved so much in her youth. How could it be that she were here?

The two stared long and hard at each other, the shock of the sight of each other's wrinkled faces was momentary, for the next feeling was a buried desire unearthed. They shared a scintilla of pleasure that was just for them. Nothing or no one that surrounded them could take their love from them for as long as they wished. Time stopped for River and Winter and it would not begin again until they permitted it. They were young lovers once more, and it was as though Summer was still that playful, innocent girl. The unforgiveable things that she had done were a blur.

'Summer, I...'

But there were no words that could be spoken. Everything was said in the soulful gaze of their shared look. It felt as though everything else was so meaningless, all the death and fighting. The soul-magic, past offences and betrayal. Could it be possible to end it all and find a way back to the way things were?

It was Tritan who answered the question that wrestled in both their minds. For he had been trained for one purpose and even Winter couldn't tame the beast she had created now. His sword still poised ready to swing, was unleashed with an indeterminable fury.

Winter smiled at River, or was she Summer again? The Winter Queen herself did not know, though she prayed she could be as she once was.

As the sword was mere inches from River's neck, she flipped back and snapped her head from its trajectory. She was a lightning bolt and even Tritan didn't understand how she had fully evaded him.

River was on him next, slashing with her blade and cutting him deeply, slits to the thighs, shoulders and chest. None were killing blows. She wanted to disable him and she knew she had the skill to do so.

As his arms could no longer wield the sword he held, Tritan whipped his head forwards. It meant taking the blade River held firmly in the side of his ribs but it was worth it to bring his forehead down upon her cheek. Her bone cracked and her face bled. Her head was pounding and she knew the lava was leaving her.

She had seconds left.

River spun a dozen times with a single jump and slashed through Tritan's armour and before she landed again, his shirt front fell from his attire. His chest and abdomen were revealed. The scar he bore from when he had nearly died in the battle of the northern territories was red and ripe for reopening. Still he fought on, grabbing a loose rock from his side and preparing to make a final stand.

A cry came from behind them. It was a cry that River had never wanted to bear witness to. A sound that had haunted River since she had first fallen in love with Summer. The cry of her pain, the cry of her death.

River turned and saw Winter fall to her knees. Pietrich was stood behind her with a broken sword in his arms. He threw the blade down; they knew the deed was done.

River flicked her attention back to Tritan, but he was no longer holding the rock in his hand, instead he was caressing the scar on his stomach. He looked up at River and saw Pietrich over her shoulder.

'My son, my son.'

As if a spell had been broken, something changed in the fearless warrior before her. River's instincts told her to remain vigilant but the tears forming in his eyes, laced with self-loathing for the things he had done, told her otherwise.

Surrounding River and Pietrich were the sixteen-strong surviving squadron, standing firm. But as Fritz mimicked Tritan's actions and lay his arms down, the rest of them followed suit as if there was no use in fighting anymore; they were all Tritan's shadow. They moved as he moved and knelt down upon the rocks.

Pietrich ran towards Tritan and wrapped his arms around him. The wolf joined them and licked the salty wounds that River had given to the warrior. She had done her bidding, saved the blind boy from his fated death. But she herself felt empty and hollow. Winter was sobbing and crying out as pangs of pain rippled through her body.

River wiped back the hair from Winter's eyes and they held each other for a time.

River looked around her, yelling out for a healer. 'Bring a medic, anyone! We have to stop this.'

There came no reply from the crowd, only Winter's.

'Thomas, do not fret, if you are there.'

'Thomas? Your healer? Wait here, I'll find him.'

'It doesn't matter, it's too late.'

Winter coughed and blood dribbled down her chin. 'River, you must understand something. Everything I did, it was for us. To wash away the sins of the Vermillion people. Forgive me for never telling you the truth. I wanted to protect you from it.'

'Shh, don't speak now. There's no need to make confession.'

River placed her finger across Winter's mouth but even with the agony of raising her arm, Winter pulled her hand away.

'You do not understand, today was meant to be the ending to all the horrors of our world. Instead a treacherous dawn is upon us. I wish only that I could be there, to guide you through it.'

River checked her wound, it was bleeding profusely, a fatal cut, with or without a skilled medic. She looked down at Winter in disbelief and shook her head.

'I do not blame you anymore. Must we spend our final moments debating right and wrong?'

'We must spend our final moments, as we always did before I betrayed you, as lovers, truthful and forthcoming. Even if it means rebuking you, River. I will not die without warning you of what you have done.'

'I saved the boy from you, that was all that was asked of me. Our people survived, numbers, few as they were, despite your efforts to render all of Vermillion extinct.'

'I must tell you of how I killed the last king. I went to Augustus, what better ally as an exile to pick the most monstrous warlord of them all. I told him of my strength in the soul-magic but he did not bend easily to my will, he needed proof. Without thinking I reached out to Elik where he slept and decided that his life would end. It was that simple. I never knew such a thing were possible. But from that moment I realised that we do not deserve to carry the soul-magic. None of us do. It is a plague to end all life, in the wrong hands...'

River digested everything she heard. An impossible truth but it was so clear now.

'You saw me that day, in the forest. When Augustus was alone with me and could have killed me, you sent him away. You saved me.'

'No. I wish it were such. But the truth is that I knew you were better than him, you would have killed him and I needed him.'

A rebuke and a compliment all laced in hatred. River couldn't stand the concoction.

'Why did you need him? You abandoned everyone who ever loved you for that fiend. I don't understand the roots of your betrayal.'

'Volcan had to die,' Winter continued. 'I have no regret for those actions. I owe you my remorse for killing June however, though he was complicit.'

'What are you talking about? Please do not drag my father into this, do not die with me hating you.'

Winter could not hold herself up any longer and she lay down, resting her head on the soil of her homeland.

'River, Volcan was my father. He raped my mother and I am the result of that abhorrent act. I was plagued to be the downfall of our people from the moment he spread his seed inside her. I hope that truth does not cause you the harm it has caused me.'

'How can that be so? Our relationship was never secret, June, he...'

'Yes, he allowed it, to keep the truth buried deep.'

River suddenly felt sick. Her entire life had been a lie. She could never have imagined such depths of torture would be cast on her. This was supposed to be her moment of glory. Forty years to return to the island that shaped who she was. Now that same island revealed a dark truth that killed the remaining light in her soul.

'I see it in your eyes, the hatred I have carried all this time. Do not succumb to it as I did, River. You will need to be strong for I fear the worst is yet to come. You wonder why I needed Augustus. His greed is why. Who else would charge forth into the abyss in search of the power to grant life. I convinced him to go into the depths of Orldin where even his own men would not follow. His task, to bring back a canteen of water from the lake where the Maldus tree exists. But he failed me. Where he failed, his adopted son succeeded. Tritan brought the water to Pietrich. It has been the cause of all my fear. Do you see? The boy is stronger than I ever was.'

Winter coughed and her body shuddered but she was not done. Not yet. 'River, I know you were raised to believe the soul-magic would one day be yours to yield. But our kin were arrogant to believe we were chosen by some divine right or hereditary kinship. The magic does not work as falsely as does a royal kingdom. It finds us simply when it needs us and the burden is that when it does, we realise how futile our efforts are to truly control it. But the blind boy is something else, something we have not seen since a time long forgotten and so we do not know what mistakes we must learn from. He is of Vermillion blood, the Primavemani, but he also has the life force of Maldus flowing through his veins. The world will become something I cannot imagine. I hope you find goodness in it. All I have built, you must claim it. You will need everything in the fight I fear is to come. Good night, my sweet, my love. My life. It is still there, in the depths of your emerald eyes. The light of the rising sun. I have been Winter for so long but keep me in your heart always as Summer.'

Summer breathed her final breath as River pulled her upwards into her arms. Her body went cold and still. River convulsed as she cried, but it was a silent cry for the pain was too fierce and her voice was lost.

She didn't know for how long she dwelled upon all that she had lost, not only her immediate loss but her history had also been re-written in an instant. Each time she recalled a joyful moment with Summer, it was another blow to her heart and she cried once more.

The lava left her and she became so tired that she fell onto Summer's body and they lay together as the sun found its way to them through a crack in the cloud filled sky. A single ray of light shone upon them and nothing else. They were a golden vision amidst a grey world.

## 31

S tep by step we force ourselves to tread a path that seems righteous and each action is a tipping point for the weighing scales that define us. A boon upon a brother will be a slight to a sister and upholding loyalty to one friend will lose us another. Appeasing the crowd is the road to isolation. Many have tried to find the common good for all people but amidst all the love and honour is a sea of greed and jealousy that shapes the cultures and communities as much as an outcast.

Pietrich felt determined to condemn all people and would they be judged within a void as wide as the ocean, he would ultimately see them as the same being. How could he discriminate in his verdict of such meaningless creatures? The creators of poverty are wrong to pursue wealth and comfort and then as they repress and control those they have crushed in their path, they act as if the retaliation were an evil deed. No longer capable of seeing that they created the very thing they despise. Sometimes, those who are left to lurk in the swamps, rise upwards and fight their way to the heights of society, are perceived as icons to those they leave behind. But they do not only leave them behind in wealth but in mind. The cycle is perpetual. What hope could there be for such a race as this?

Pietrich asked himself the question over and over, as he dragged his father to the base of the unending stairwell at the foot of the mountain. He cocked his head up, already exhausted from moving the hulking warrior, and listened to the sounds coming from above. The high steps had remained protected from the eruption all those years ago, tucked away and hidden. Jack guided them, as amongst the thousands of voices of the Vermillion mountain, Pietrich could no longer sense the path he trod upon. His muscles shook and sweat poured down his cheeks. He absorbed more knowledge and clarity with each step but his physical form was nothing short of a teenage boy. He could not grow his strength the way he grew his understanding. What little life was left in Tritan, aided Pietrich on the long and drawn out slog up towards the volcano's peak.

FLOWING through Pietrich's head was the greed of mankind, a murky lake overshadowing hope and love, buried so deep beneath the narcissistic tar that it was as though they no longer existed. But of one love he was sure, his own for his father. That love was not in question, and should his act be a burden to others, he would care no longer.

Loss of blood made Tritan dizzy and his strength was leaving his body. He was a mental wreck of the father Pietrich had come to know in those happy days on the farm. Somewhere, beneath the spell that had been cast on Tritan, was the man who had found light in the darkness.

Hours passed by and night came and went. It took several rests and they even slept for a time, lying silently upon the stone steps. But eventually they reached the summit.

Pietrich felt the strong breeze of the mountain top pushing him like a warning. How desperately he wished he could see.

Tritan forced his eyes open and gazed out upon the islands and saw a landscape, so beautiful and serene. 'This was her home,' he said. 'This is where my mother was born.'

Pietrich felt his father's heart racing and he reached out to send him feelings of comfort. He was a stone wall against Pietrich's thoughts. But for a second, flickering amidst the distance between their souls and the barricade that Winter had created, Pietrich saw the sea and a golden rising sun through his father's eyes. The islands were beautiful, natural rocks. All sign of civilisation had been buried deep beneath the lava of the eruption and he knew that Vermillion had been returned to the way it had once existed.

The vision passed and he was blind again.

Tritan collapsed suddenly in an unconscious heap and Pietrich shook him violently.

'Father, Father! Wake up.'

He didn't. With all his might, Pietrich lay his father upon his shoulder and began a slow, difficult walk towards the mouth of the volcano.

The searing heat rose and he sweated, but still he carried them both inwards, through a chamber, and eventually he came to a small inner dome. It too had been preserved amongst the eruption and as Pietrich lay his father down to free his hands so that he could rub the inner walls of the chamber, he found etchings that were carved out over centuries. It told a story in the form of images and the images were created as if for someone who used their fingertips to see. A tree at the centre of a lake. A volcano's mouth at the summit of an island mountain.

The heart of the world.

And the soul.

And there was Pietrich. Caught between the mother and the father of all life.

He focused his thoughts and let the volcano take over his soul. The awareness of all things was a rapturous sensation but also torturous. No matter the strength of the soul-magic within him, however much it grew, it was still a child who bore the burden. He was aware of the greater deeds of humanity and the nestling wild creatures who fed their young. The movements of the wind and the tide of the ocean. It was all the same force and he alone absorbed it into his being. As it crushed against him, the threat to be overwhelmed was fierce but within his physical form, Pietrich felt roots taking hold like the roots of a tree and he knew the strength of Maldus would save him.

At the peak of the flow of existence, his father's cry for help lingered in a shadowy place, beyond those that Tritan's own mind could reach. Pietrich led him there. Guided him back to the man he had once become, in the wake of all the death and war he had seen.

Tritan's love for Marilia, his fondness for his blind horse who had been his brother, and his son who he had once saved, and now saved him.

Tritan opened his eyes. He felt feeble and afraid and yet he recalled everything that had been taken from him all at once as though a wave of memories had crashed against a cliff face that was his mind.

He stood and looked about the chamber. The walls were glowing from the lava flow that rippled at the edges and cracks of the rock. A clean path of energy that soared through him. He was alive. Too many times he had evaded death but once again his body had been forced to live on.

*How many second chances can a man hope for?*

But a second chance for what. To be a father again? If he believed that were the reason for his being restored, that belief would last no longer than a second for as he cast his eyes around the chamber. He saw no sign of Pietrich. His son was gone.

'I WONDER, should we live to over a hundred years of age, would we meet again as we do now?'

As River opened her eyes she saw a wrinkled hand extended out to her. The silhouette of a woman was standing before her, blocking the light of the sun from her face.

River reached out and took her hand and struggled to her feet. She saw the weathered face of a beloved friend. Lynden stepped forwards and hugged her. No words could match the meaning there was in that embrace.

'Where are the others, where is Pietrich?' River eventually asked.

'I was hoping you could tell me that.'

'I do not know. I know only that he lives.'

All about them was the billowing dust and the lives lost. The survivors from all sides, confused at whether or not they were still one another's foe, stared blankly all around them.

Fritz, not really understanding why, walked towards Lynden and apologised to her for all he had done wrong. But his mind was too broken to ever be repaired and remember who he was. Winter's remaining soldiers began to collect the bodies of their brothers and sisters. Tritan and Pietrich were nowhere to be seen.

Castellar wandered amongst the cadavers and it was Diccon who walked at his side.

'Well, it's a bloody fine mess you've all made but let it end. Let it end now and I'll help yer say yer goodbyes.'

The first mate knew there was tension in the wake of all this bloody mess. But as he and Castellar began to make arrangements for timber to be brought from the ship, soldiers and sailors on all sides began to create a pyre, ready for a cremation.

'I AM SO LOST, Lynden. We did everything we could, even when we would turn a blind eye to the sacrifices that were made by our allies. Now I am not sure what I have achieved.'

'If you saved the boy then we are safe. That was always the end of this path. It is why others were sacrificed along the way. We must find him, to know he is alive.'

'Lynden, there is only one place he could have gone. The summit of the mountain. He was searching for answers and it is there he would have found them. But it is a treacherous climb. I will go, you should wait for me here.'

'Do you think that wise. To go alone?'

'As I have always done, alone is what I know.'

'Very well. We will wait for you.'

River rubbed the dirt off her shirt and cried out as she felt a stab of agony in her arm. She had forgotten all about the severe blow.

Castellar doubled back after hearing the pain in her voice.

'Show me the wound, we must dress it before it infects. I am no healer but perhaps the best we have left.'

River nodded to him and Castellar undid the makeshift bandage River had made and revealed the congealing mess. The wound opened like fish gills and fresh blood poured out.

'Use this to clean the wound.'

A man to Castellar's side handed over a cork-stoppered bottle and Castellar thanked him. Thomas nodded in response, staring blankly as he watched Castellar pour it across the wound, washing away the rock dust that had merged with the blood. River winced and she knew what must be done. Thomas confirmed it for her.

'It is a deep wound, we must burn the flesh.'

Castellar agreed and Thomas gathered a blade, heating it in the base of the funeral pyre that had now been lit.

River screamed out as the blade was pushed against her arm, binding the open wound and burning all the flesh that surrounded it. She fell onto her back and held her arm just beneath the entry point and Castellar's man poured water over the arm. It sizzled and steamed as it cooled.

'Nothing says good morning like sealing a wound with iron, hot as the sun,' River joked, her voice trembling.

She rolled back onto her feet and Lynden helped her gather some supplies for her hike. Spare water and one blade. That was all she needed.

'Leave me with her for a moment,' River said, as she stared at the body of Summer. All those around her walked away and gave her peace. She knelt down beside the aged body of her former lover. Somehow she'd known it would come to his, but River had always believed it would be her that made the killing blow. Not the blind boy who had led her to this moment. Pietrich had led them all to this moment, and River felt the crushing hurt within her for everything she had lost. Summer's last words haunted her. What had Pietrich become? She hoped Lynden was right and that Summer was wrong.

'Do not place her on the pyre,' River instructed Lynden and the others. 'I will bury her at sea, as is the way of my people.'

River tucked her things into her jerkin and removed her outer jacket, laying it across Summer's face. She looked out across the camp at all the long faces, lifting dead soldiers and pirates onto the pyre. She watched for a moment as their bodies shrivelled in the heat and the flesh was burned to the raw bone. How easy it could be, to wipe away the history of a life.

She set off and left the towering inferno of the mass cremation in her wake. Castellar, Lynden, Diccon and the rest of the crew paid respects to the dead. No one cared anymore who they had been fighting or why.

Past memories flooded River's mind as she made the walk. Each step was a memory of the thousand times she had done it in her youth. She recalled the ease with which she had made the climb at the peak of her health. It was more trying at her age now and she felt a subtle sense of fragility as she looked over the edge of the rocks to the ground far below.

*Nothing lasts.*

The summit was much the same as it had always been. The cracks in the ground of lava flow were still alive and fiercely hot. The opening to the chamber where she had visited Volcan so many times still resided as before. She entered it, and though she knew he was dead she still expected to see her old uncle, the memory of her time with him now tainted. Summer had shone a light on truths she never knew could have existed.

As she walked into the chamber a man was sat at its centre. His bulky shoulders hunched over as though he were asleep.

'The boy has gone.'

The deep voice broke through the hissing of the volcano. Tritan didn't move, his head slumped.

'What happened?'

'He carried me here, he saved me. I do not know if he could save himself.'

'Then he has truly gone.' River felt relieved in a way. 'What now?'

'For a blinding second, I sensed a fraction of the burden that he has inherited. As he poured life into me and found my spirit buried deep beneath a mountain of rubble, I heard the immeasurable voices that cried out to him. Voices of the dead and of the living. They demand so much of him. What will become of the happy boy I knew once?'

'That boy will live on inside him. No matter what else. As he found you drifting deep, he will remain also. A thread of life that is his alone and no one else's. It will stay attached to him. An uncuttable rope. We must have faith.'

River knelt down beside Tritan and laid a hand on his shoulder. He sobbed as her fingers met the skin of his neck.

'I have done terrible things. I remember it all,' he began his confession. But River silenced him.

'You were forced to do those things. By Augustus once and then by Summer, though she was Winter then. Years ago, Pietrich told me of a time when you taught him to ride a horse and sow seeds, in spite of the fact he could not see. You encouraged him to be independent where it were possible. That is the man and father you are. Remember that.'

'I always hated the idea that those with whom I am unacquainted know personal things about me. But I thank you for your words. Tell me, what are you? Some sort of deity, come here to save us all.'

River laughed.

'I am just an old woman, but you are wrong to think of me as a stranger. I knew both of your parents. I knew them well.'

'You knew my mother?'

'Yes, the sweetest and most loyal girl I ever trained. I know she would have loved you fiercely.'

Tritan bashed his fist against the ground. Striking his rage and sadness into the stone. His knuckles bled but he was numb to the physical pain.

'He took her from me. Let me believe I killed her for almost all of my life. I never even knew her name.'

'Her name was Jade.'

Tritan looked up at River and stared deeply into the green glints of her eyes. River felt afraid of the affection in that stare.

'The only memory I have of her is the sign of her emerald

eyes. It must have been the moment of my birth and the moment of her death. Who were you to her?'

River pondered the question and all the strands of history awakened her to the belief she had once held, that she should have been Tritan's mother. But that was not for her to dwell on and she would not take anything from Jade of Tritan's affection. Not now or ever.

'My story is too long to tell. It is time to go home, Tritan.'


VERMILLION GREW SMALLER and smaller on the horizon and River knew she would never set foot upon its land again. It was a graveyard to her people. Their triumphs and their failures. It was not pride nor disgust she felt, just sorrow. The nostalgic sorrow of one who has so much to look back upon. She cast Summer's body into the water and watched as she sank into the depths of the ocean. In her hand, River held a promise. A final gesture she could make to right a wrong, once committed in the name of her ancestors.

It was a mournful farewell after a week of sailing to the Maluabian islands. Lynden and Castellar had agreed to give passage to River to the artesian shores and though Lynden begged River to come with them all, back to the mainland to rebuild, River was determined to stay and find peace, if peace could find her.

Mamasufie, frail and immobile as she had become, lit up with a glow and energy that her tribe had not seen for years. She rose to her feet and embraced River as an old friend and sister.

River took a bracelet off her wrist and handed it to Mamasufie. It was a silent gesture but powerful in all its meaning.

'Never doubt an assassin of Vermillion,' Mamasufie said, with a wry, cracked smile.

'I fear I have ended the reign of Winter only to enter us into a time of uncertainty. Where spring should come, a shadow lingers. I do not understand why I feel as though I have failed.'

'River, you have not failed. Life is too complex to believe in right and wrong, for sometimes right actions lead to wrong deeds and sometimes, something that feels wrong, can be for a greater purpose. You are strong in ways you cannot imagine.'

'I feel so ashamed. To have desired the soul-magic for myself. As I was raised to expect. But it was all a lie.'

'If you have believed for years that the soul-magic passed you up because you were not special, then you were wrong to do so. It chose to abandon you because you *are* special. How else could you have done the things you have done?'

River wondered if somehow she might be right. Was not the soul-magic a burden? Had it not allowed its bearers, stronger than those around them, to control their thoughts and actions and in doing so twisted their souls out of shape. But it was the same as everything, soul-magic or no. It seemed that people were destined to control each other for their own gain. Since the first time when two men stood upon a hill and the stronger man beat the weaker into submission, to take his meal, so determining that he was the leader of the two. That was the way people were. River decided she would never live like that again.

'My people have dispersed amongst all the lands of Harmion. Generations of integration. We are a lost people now. We have no home.'

'This is your home now, River. Vermillion lives on in you. I have someone I want you to meet. He too was lost, but my traders in the northern territories found him years ago and brought him here.'

River felt a tingle in her spine. A ripple of fear and then a sea of hope.

They walked together, River and Mamasufie, across the

beautiful white dunes to a small tent, nestled amidst the beautiful line of palm trees that reminded her of home and Mamasufie knocked on the outer post.

Moments later an old man appeared. He was lean and he looked into the green eyes of the woman before him. Those very green eyes, that despite the aged skin that surrounded them, burned brightly and stole his breath. He smiled at River and she saw the hole where a tongue had once been and she knew he could not speak. So she spoke not a word either and they simply sat together for a time, left alone as Mamasufie drifted away across the amber sands of the setting sun. River and Boscelito stared into each other's eyes and relived a lost hope that maybe one day things would be set right for those who, despite all else, felt as though they shared a soul.

# EPILOGUE

**B**raced shoulders, silent determination against a lingering fusion of threads. Treading water whilst drowning and longing for peace amidst a thousand burning fires. The fires of the worst deeds of men. They burn fierce and bring the forests of all that is good to their knees.

Only amidst the smoke, where the winds blow away the ash will the corpses of the trees be seen. A symbol of the light beneath the darkness. How long it will take for the seeds to fall and find a way for life to flourish; that was the worst uncertainty of all.

He no longer needed the island.

No longer needed the mountain and the power it emitted or the stories it told. For he was the mountain. He was the stories. All the stories that had ever been. It was so simple now, to look inward at all the truth. Pietrich realised why people must lie. For the lies were a sheet to cover up the repugnant reality from others, to mask the way they lived.

Each reprehensible act would lead to another and like a virus spreads, suffering would spread.

But did water not spread in such the same way? Seeking the lowest point in order that it could return to the earth. Causing rivulets and streams to form like flowing tentacles.

Pietrich had sailed away from Vermillion and months had passed in contemplation. Or had it been years? He had docked and replenished his stocks and set off again on many occasions. He hated civilisation and dry land now. Only the ocean brought him comfort.

The moment he realised that he no longer had a use for the volcano nor it for he, he had abandoned it. Left his father lying in the centre of the cavern the way his father had once left him. Pietrich knew he had played his part. He would be linked to Vermillion now for as long as he lived and no distance could separate them anymore.

His wolf had run about the decks of the tiny vessel Pietrich had claimed from the harbour, enlivened as though his master had finally found his true calling.

Jack was a reminder to Pietrich of the boy he had once been. It was hard to know the thoughts that were his own now, for so many flooded to him. He was lost in a myriad of false desire and drowned in the vengeance of so many hearts.

There must be one out there who would remember him as he always was. A girl he once knew perhaps might find a way to bring him back to his past self. He knew her name once.

Eira. It was Eira.

That was the name and Pietrich knew she had been his best friend. Perhaps she could tell him of all the things that they had done together as children, so that he may remember which of the memories that swam about his mind were his and not just those that infiltrated him from the million souls that had merged with his being.

The destination was aimless and Pietrich and his wolf simply drifted in the sea with nothing to guide their purpose. Wherever the ocean would take them they would make land and each moment would be lived without a greater meaning. Was that not the way to live without greed? To hope for nothing. To long for nothing. To do nothing.

Greed would not leave the boy however, for he so desired the girl. If there was one thing missing from his life it was her touch, her smile and her love.

He had never been able to reach her before when he had been a boy. But now he was Vermillion and Maldus both intertwined, more so than he was Pietrich, and he reached out for some sign that she was well.

In the darkness he saw a hint of her fair hair, it was longer now and she had grown to be a woman. He felt a hole form in his stomach as she ran about a small garden at the base of a quaint cottage. Spring seeds floated in the cool breeze. She laughed and ran her fingers through the falling pollen as it fell from the trees and landed in her hair.

A powerful embrace made her feel so secure and loved. Pietrich wished so dearly that it was his embrace, no matter how far from her he was. He wrapped his arms around her but she felt nothing from him. It was not his warmth she had felt. It was the warmth of another. Someone who stood beside her and gave her a home. His arms were not a promise from a thousand lifetimes away but they were real. Right there with Eira in the garden of their home.

He kissed her and smiled at her and she smiled back at him.

They had made a sweet life together, running freely and carelessly. It was a life that had eluded Pietrich. A small infant girl ran around the legs of her parents and tugged on the long floral dress that Eira wore. She was a little over one year old, Pietrich guessed. In the past years of his turmoil, Eira had created a life.

She was a mother to a child and Pietrich was a stranger, a shadow floating amongst their joy. They could not sense the darkness that surrounded them and he protected them from it, though it hurt him, and he made to leave but before he could, the feelings he despised of humankind weighted him down like an anchor.

Greed and vengeance.

Those were the things he was made of now.

Before he broke himself away to contemplate his despair, Pietrich brushed up against the man. He sensed he was a decent man with a strong heart.

A strong heart that was beating with love for Eira and his child.

Pietrich felt a cry coming from a place he had never known and words that sounded like pleading in a language he did not understand. A girl within a cave prayed, surrounded by her tribe, but she began to sob for she sensed Pietrich and what he had become.

In that instant, the man's heart would beat no more and Eira would scream as he fell to the floor. Pietrich fled, turning his back on their pain, confused and ashamed of what he had done.

END

# A WORD FROM RICHARD

Thank you for reading THE VERMILLION ISLES.

I would love to know your thoughts, so please consider leaving a review on Amazon or Goodreads. This also helps spread the word about the world of HARMION and will make this writer very happy indeed!

Building a relationship with readers is one of the very best things about writing. I occasionally send newsletters with details on new releases, special offers and other bits of news relating to the Harmion and Time Thief series.

Join the Harmion newsletter today and I'll send you a FREE Harmion prequel novella - THE KILL LIST. The Novella will charter one of Tritan's most challenging missions during The Forty Year War as he is given a very specific list of people to assassinate, the last members of the royal council.

You can sign up to receive your free prequel novella here: www.richardaswingle.com

# ABOUT THE AUTHOR

Richard A. Swingle is a British fantasy novelist from Brighton, in the UK. He comes from a background of working in the Film and Television industry and has been actively writing since the age of 14 when he discovered his passion for storytelling through making short films.

Since then he has developed his storytelling interests as both a musician and novelist and continues to work as a director of photography in the film industry.

Visit: www.richardaswingle.com to find out more.

facebook.com/raswingleauthor
twitter.com/raswingle
instagram.com/raswingle

# ACKNOWLEDGMENTS

The Author would like to acknowledge the following people for their contribution to The Vermillion Isles.

To Mhairi, for her scrutiny and encouragement that helped shape the final draft of the book and kept the characters in check.

To my father, Anthony, for continuing to support me and help improve my books through his valuable suggestions and critique.

To Melanie for her eagle eye and sweeping editorial skills.

To all my family and friends, each of whom helps shape my stories in their own unique way.

Printed in Great Britain
by Amazon